I0557468

The Wilds of Mars

Where understanding begins

Mark Hazell

The Wilds of Mars

First paperback edition May 2024

Cover art by Flintlock Covers

ISBN 978-1-7635484-1-1

(paperback edition)

The Wilds of Mars

Prologue

Three times a week after school, in fair weather or foul, Kalen Rance pulled on his shorts and hoody, slipped into his running shoes, and set off down the street. Under the old wooden railway bridge, he ran, along busy Studley Drive for a couple of blocks, then into the park with its broad, winding paths overhung by old trees.

Properly warmed up, he settled into his natural, cruising stride and quickly forgot everything except the piston-like pumping of his leg muscles, the rush of fresh air into his lungs, and the rhythmic thudding of his shoes on the footpath. He loved the animal physicality of the movement, the power, the independence. In those moments, he was a creature of the wild, roaming free, with ties to nothing and no one. He planned to go on running forever.

Until the day the stranger arrived.

Melbourne's weather that afternoon had turned grey and wintry. Savage gusts of wind battered trees on the nature strips. Sheets of cold rain soaked gardens and slicked the sweeping curves of Acacia Street as Kalen sprinted homeward.

Reaching his house at number twelve, he shoved open the squeaking gate and raced up the path towards the wisteria-wrapped veranda. With his head tucked down against the blinding downpour, he didn't notice the car parked on the other side of the street. Nor did he see the driver open the door and get out.

'Scuse me.'

Kalen heard the gravelly voice but mistook it for a loose branch being dragged about by the storm. He climbed the steps two at a time, jumped onto the veranda and waved his key pass over the lock. It clicked open.

'Pardon me,' the voice called again, more urgently. 'Can you spare a minute?'

Kalen threw a glance over his shoulder in time to see a man, huddled under a black umbrella, come to a stop at the front gate. He made no attempt to push it open. It was a boundary he seemed reluctant to cross.

Kalen stepped back to the edge of the veranda and looked more closely. Around thirty, the man was a little overweight with thinning hair and the pasty complexion of someone who needed more time in the sun. Angled against the beating rain, his umbrella sheltered the upper half of his smart, grey overcoat, while the sharply creased cuffs of his trousers hung soggy and shapeless over expensive shoes.

'Terrible day to be out,' he called good-naturedly. 'You must be keen.'

Kalen didn't respond. His natural distrust of strangers made him cautious. Where had the guy come from? He didn't look fit enough to have been following him on foot, nor was he loitering in the bushes near the house.

Then Kalen noticed the unfamiliar car parked opposite. An older model, pre-electric, dating from somewhere around 2020. Rare these days, and undoubtedly expensive.

'This the house of Doctor and Mrs Rance?'

Kalen baulked at the question. 'There's no Mrs,' he said curtly.

'Oh.' The man pursed his lips in self-admonition. 'Sorry, I didn't realise. What about Doctor Rance, then? He about?'

'Not at the moment.'

'I see. And you—' A strong gust of wind grabbed his umbrella, threatening to turn it inside out. He wrestled it back under control. 'And you are?'

'Wet.'

The man let the brusque reply pass, putting it down to youthful bravado or maybe an understandable eagerness to get inside. A kid in his mid-teens, he noted. Average height and unremarkable appearance; not one to stand out in a crowd. Finely built, but strong and wiry; the physique of a runner. Closer scrutiny hinted at intelligence in the bright, green eyes. A steely defiance, too. Probably someone who didn't mince words or suffer fools gladly.

'I need a few words with him,' the man continued. 'Know when he'll be in?'

'Later, after work.'

'Right. I'll pop back then.'

'You can try.'

'Sorry?'

'I mean you can come back but he probably won't wanna see you. He doesn't talk much.'

The man stood unmoving, apparently weighing up a course of action. Coming to a decision he said, 'Listen, I don't suppose you'd do me a favour?'

'What sort of favour?'

'Just tell him Alpha in Aquarius.'

'What?'

'He'll know what it means.'

'Alpha in Aquarius.'

'That's it.'

His message delivered, the man turned to go but Kalen called after him, 'Maybe you better give me your name. You know, in case he asks.'

The man paused on the kerb, half-turned and realigned his umbrella against the tumbling rain. 'I *could* do that. Trouble is, it won't mean anything to him. Better I just come back later. Say about seven-thirty? Don't forget: Alpha in Aquarius. It's important.'

Kalen watched him cross the road; saw him collapse the umbrella, spear it into the back of the car, then climb into the driver's seat.

The petrol engine coughed to life and propelled the car up the hill, trailing a haze of pungent fumes. Old-world, fossil-fuel technology, it seemed out of place now. An unwelcome visitor from the past.

♦

Later, showered and dressed warmly in jeans and a sloppy windcheater, Kalen sat working at the student's desk in his bedroom. On the wall above hung a small inlaid wooden crucifix which gave the rest of the sparsely furnished room an air of monastic austerity.

His homework tonight was a five-page essay on humanity's first crewed visit to an asteroid. While he wasn't remotely interested in history, he had to admit the more he read about the oldies from earlier in the century, the more he admired their courage. For the past few minutes, he had been learning how asteroid miner Roo Millan got his name. It was first coined by his older sister who, as a child, called him "Kangaroo" for his jumping prowess. "Kangaroo" was later shortened to "Roo" and followed him into adulthood. This wasn't crucial to the success of the mission, or the essay, but Kalen thought it would add some colour to the piece. And Miss Trudy, his tutor, was big on colour in history. 'It's not all about great achievements in science and politics and power,' she had explained that day. 'It's about the small things too. The ordinary people. The colour of everyday life. So, my dears, I want to see colour in your work; big, bold splashes of colour everywhere.'

Kalen splashed the newfound colour into his essay and, just as he finished, he heard the garage door open. The clock on his computer showed 6.15 p.m. His father was home right on time. Kalen turned off the computer and went out.

Through the lounge room window, he saw the familiar silver Model Q electric sports car roll silently down the steep driveway.

As was his habit, his father spent a few moments fumbling around with his briefcase and document holder, got out, set the car charging then walked in. He found Kalen waiting for him inside the back door as he stepped through.

'Hello,' he said in his quiet, formal way.

At fifty-eight, David Rance was much older than most men with a fifteen-year-old son, but he carried his age well. He was fit and lean, the result of a careful diet and a rigid regime of exercise. His brown hair, closely cropped, had lightened as he got older and was now streaked with grey. He had a thin-lipped mouth not given to smiling, and his small eyes squinted impassively as if uninterested in what sights the world had to offer.

'Hi.' Kalen looked at him expectantly; at the briefcase, at his document holder. 'D'you pick it up?' he asked hopefully.

His father stopped, bemused. 'Sorry?'

'The Chinese. You said you'd get it on the way home.'

David's lips twitched as he remembered his parting words that morning. 'I did say that, didn't I. Sorry, it completely slipped my mind.'

'Oh.'

David heard the disappointment in his son's voice and immediately went on the defensive. 'The system went down. I've been running around like a headless chook since half past one. But if you really want it, I can nick out and get some.' He placed his work stuff on the bench and began to fish around inside his suit coat for his wallet.

'No, don't worry,' Kalen said.

David regretted his forgetfulness but the damage was done. And it couldn't be helped anyway; his day had been brutal. 'You sure?'

'Yeah, yeah. It doesn't matter.'

'Okay, well, there's some frozen lasagne in the freezer. We'll have Chinese tomorrow night. I promise.'

'Huh.' Experience had taught Kalen that for every promise his father made there was an excuse for not keeping it.

'Kalen?'

'Tomorrow. Right.'

'Okay. Can you start zapping it while I get changed?'

Kalen let his father go without further protest and pulled two frosted packets of lasagne from the freezer along with some chips. He slid them out onto a plate and placed them in the microwave. While they were heating, he gathered up some cutlery from the drawer and set two places at the table.

'So how was your day?' asked his father, returning to the kitchen in a pair of loose jeans and a woollen pullover.

'Alright, I suppose.'

David took a drinking glass from beneath the sink. 'Been for your run?'

'Yep.'

'You would've got wet.'

'A bit . . . oh yeah, I nearly forgot, some guy called by to see you.'

David placed the glass on the bench. 'Who was he?'

'Dunno. Never seen him before. I asked for his name but he wouldn't leave it.'

'Odd. Did he say what he wanted?'

'No.'

'Sounds like he was selling something.'

'Don't think so.'

'Oh?'

'At first, he asked if you and Mum live here.'

David pressed his lips together thoughtfully as he removed the glass water jug from the fridge. 'Mum? After all these years? That *is* strange.'

'Yeah. Oh, there was something else too.'

'Mm?'

'He told me to say Alpha in Aquarius. Seemed to think it would mean something to you.'

Alpha in Aquarius.

The words acted like quicksand. David slowed, then came to a complete stop in the middle of the kitchen, unable to move any further.

'WHAT?' he gasped, the blood rushing from his face.

Then his hands began to shake. The jug slipped from his grasp and shattered into jagged shards on the floor. Water splashed his shoes and ran across the tiles.

Ignoring the mess, he said, 'What did you say?'

As a rule, David was glacially cold, at least on the surface. Kalen had never seen him flustered before. 'Alpha in Aquarius,' he said warily.

'They were his exact words?'

'Yes. What do they mean?'

Either David didn't hear the question, or he chose not to answer it. Instead, he said, 'You're quite sure, Kalen? I mean, there's no chance you misunderstood?'

'I didn't misunderstand. You can ask him yourself if you don't believe me. He'll be back around half past seven.'

David leaned back on the bench, massaged his temples then buried his face in the heels of his hands.

'It can't be!'

♦

Thirty minutes later Kalen had disposed of the broken pieces of jug, mopped up the spillage and made short work of the lasagne and chips. Throughout, David just sat slumped at the end of the table, unspeaking, head hung low, hands resting limply in his lap. His meal sat cold on his plate. Occasionally, he prodded a chip with his fork but lost interest before it got to his mouth.

Three times Kalen had asked about the mysterious phrase but each attempt was met with a blank stare or, in the case of the last, a grunt worthy of some distant Neanderthal ancestor.

The clock on the wall chimed 7.00 p.m.

'He *did* say seven-thirty?' his father asked impatiently. 'Not seven?'

'Definitely half-past,' Kalen replied.

To which David nodded and went back to sitting quietly. The further the minute hand crawled down the clock face the more edgy he looked.

7.15 p.m. came and went.

Then 7.20.

And 7.25. Five minutes.

The doorbell rang.

Kalen got up to answer it.

'No, Kalen,' his father said peremptorily, 'this is for me to do.'

With heavy resignation, he pushed his chair away from the table and went out to the entrance hall.

From the table, Kalen heard the man come in. A muffled exchange of words. The soft tread of footsteps into David's study. The door closing.

Normally, Kalen would let the dishwasher deal with the mess, but tonight he was glad to have something to do. He ran the mixer and dolloped in some detergent. While the sink filled with steaming, sudsy water, he gathered up the plates and cutlery and began to wash them.

Alpha in Aquarius.

What could it possibly mean? Maybe something to do with the bureau? No, hearing it had knocked his father for six. He was a Doctor of Meteorology, for goodness' sake. Nothing at work could upset him like that. Kalen had heard of Alpha, of course. It was the first letter of the Greek alphabet. And Aquarius was one of the signs of the zodiac: the water carrier. But the two didn't fit together at all. The first water carrier? Nonsensical!

He worked at the sink in silence for a few minutes and despite making the chore last he was finished in no time.

Still on tenterhooks about whatever was happening in the study, he went into the lounge to kill time in front of the television.

'TV on,' he said. While the large screen came to life, he glanced at the clock on the mantel. It showed 7.40 p.m. which meant the *Red Dust Tales* had just started.

According to surveys, the show, a weekly newscast from the Martian colonies, was viewed religiously by 83 percent of Earth's population. David Rance wasn't one of them. He had never shown the remotest interest in Mars. In fact, whenever Kalen turned it on, he conveniently found something else to do and left the room.

Tonight's episode was about the recently commenced terraforming program. Camera drones swooped over a red desert and circled a factory-sized machine on caterpillar tracks, belching clouds of greenhouse gases into the air.

A minor politician with a paunch, a comb-over, and three chins came onto the screen and reeled off a string of obscure statistics on super greenhouse gases, CO_2 levels, mean temperatures and pressure gradients.

Obviously the most boring man on the planet, Kalen thought to himself as the politician lurched from one dataset to the next. The biopics on the Martian firstborn, which aired last year, were more his style. Especially the one on Nikel Pierce. Kalen smiled to himself as if she were a guilty pleasure. She was absolutely gorgeous! Every guy on Earth, Mars and the moon saw that one. And recorded it.

She was one of those people who seemed to have it all. When she wasn't working as a teenage supermodel, she was out exploring the wilds of Mars with her father. No doubt part of her appeal for Terran kids lay in the fact that she was completely out of their league, and beyond their reach. Apart from being unable to fly to Earth due to its stronger gravity, she was Adam Wolf's girlfriend.

The most famous of the Martian born, Adam Wolf was the first human being to be born off Earth. Along with Nikel's, his perfectly formed face was a constant fixture in promotions for anything from Martian life to spacesuits to ranges of kids' toys. He was the sort of teenager parents wanted as a son, guys wanted to be, and girls wanted to be with.

Yes, definitely the It Couple. And there were lots more like them.

The study door creaked open.

'TV off,' Kalen said. The sound of softly spoken voices drifted into the lounge room. Then came the pad of feet on the carpet. The front door opening. The stranger's voice saying, 'Goodnight, Doctor Rance. Sorry to have been the bearer of . . . well, goodnight.' The front door closing.

Then silence. Stillness.

'Dad?' Kalen rose to his feet. 'You okay?'

His father shuffled in slowly. To say he was stunned didn't do justice to his expression of stony-faced disbelief. He could barely place one foot in front of the other. His glassy eyes passed over Kalen, but it was plain he didn't really see him. Slowly, he made his way out to the kitchen. Kalen followed him as he opened the back door and staggered down the steps into the back yard.

It was quite dark outside now. From the top of the steps, Kalen watched him stumble into the garden. He fell to his knees in the wet grass and started to throw up.

Kalen rushed to his side. Unsure of what to do, he just hovered over him, looking on helplessly.

When David had finally stopped retching, he wiped his mouth, spat a couple of times, and then pulled himself up using the clothes hoist for support. He cast his eyes up into the night sky. By now, the rain had passed, leaving behind a few telltale wisps of cloud.

Methodically, he scanned the black vault of the heavens. Low on the eastern horizon, some feathery streaks of cirrus parted to reveal a small, red dot. He homed in on it and stared hard, nodding slowly to himself.

Then he turned to his son and said gravely, 'We have to go to Mars, Kalen.'

Chapter 1

'That's it,' David said quietly, 'we're through.'

Kalen just grunted, not even bothering to look at his father in the adjacent padded seat. This wasn't a moment for talking. Or other people. He just wanted to sit quietly in these final moments of the journey, thinking, staring through the window, and listening to the faint sound of the wind rushing past.

For the five months of the transit aboard the Earth/Mars Cycler, *Isaac Newton*, there had only been silence outside. Silence, stillness, and blackness in an infinite void. Now, after the savage buffeting and scorching heat of atmospheric entry, he was bathed in a soft light.

The burnt-orange glow of Mars.

He closed his eyes, imagining he could feel the sun's warmth on his face. But it *was* only his imagination. Mars was a cold world on the edge of the Goldilocks Zone. The only heat he could feel came from the air-conditioning nozzle hissing quietly above his head.

The broad-wing shuttle jolted as its elevons bit into the thin air and the nose pitched down. Kalen opened his eyes again and blinked in the glare. He tugged a pair of sunglasses from his breast pocket, flicked some wayward brown hairs out of his eyes, and slipped them on. Twisting in his harness, he pressed his face up against the window.

They were coming in from the west, he saw, across the Tharsis Bulge with its line of three enormous volcanoes, over the canyons of Noctis Labyrinthus, and on to the planet-ripping gash of Valles Marineris. Streaks of high cloud brushed past, temporarily obscuring the view. By the time they dissipated, the rugged canyon region had given way to broad, dusty plains pockmarked with craters.

'Impressive, isn't it?'

Another intrusion.

'Kalen, are you alright?'

His father was becoming tediously insistent, but Kalen understood why. He had been unwell for the past week and had woken this morning especially pale and squeamish. One of the physicians put this down to some lingering effects of the four months he had spent in cryosleep, or possibly pre-landing nerves, and had prescribed a pill to settle him. Now, half an hour after they transferred to the landing shuttle, his nausea had abated, but his face still retained some of its ghostly pallor.

'I'm okay,' he replied curtly. 'It's just that I left my stomach back on the cycler.'

'It'll catch up with you,' his father said, adding lamely, 'In the meantime, just think nice thoughts. We'll be down soon.'

Think nice thoughts? Who was he trying to kid?

All his nice thoughts, such as they were, had been left behind on that faint blue dot in the sky two hundred million kilometres distant, so there was little point trying to think about them. Instead, he gave his attention to the tracking display on the overhead bulkhead. Racing by below was a flattish wasteland called Hesperia Planum. Scattered across its surface were some minor landforms with names like Bunkum Fall, Pike's Run, Ivan's Folly, and The Ditch.

The broad-wing banked to the north-east. The image on the display turned accordingly, and Kalen saw they were on final approach to their destination near the edge of the planum, the cloaked city of Asheton.

Over the intercom one of the pilots told them they were now subsonic and that the crew was making final preparations for landing. The sixty or so passengers stirred, sat up, and adjusted their harnesses. A whirring sound under their feet indicated that the wheels were down, and through the window Kalen could see the wing reshaping itself as they slowed. Then came the thump of touchdown.

As the shuttle decelerated and bumped off the runway, Kalen gazed out across the red plain. An aircraft had just leapt off the ground and was rising into the eastern haze. Another was positioning for its take-off run. And he could count three airships nosed up to docking masts.

But this was all to be expected at a spaceport.

What really caught his attention was something far more subtle and quite unexpected. At first, he couldn't quite make out what it was. But then . . . the light.

The illumination on Mars was like nothing he had ever experienced. Not pink or salmon as described in the brochures; these were terrestrial names given by people from Earth. It had, rather, an inherently Martian quality. The colour of rust on a grand scale;

evocative of epochs gone, secrets hidden, and mysteries unsolved.

'This is weird,' Kalen said, 'I've never seen—'

But the words choked in his throat. Silvery tears were glittering on his father's eyelashes.

'Dad, what is it?'

David turned away quickly and wiped his eyes. 'Nothing.'

'But—'

'Nothing at all, Kalen. It's just been a long journey.'

Kalen knew *that* tone of voice only too well. It said, 'Close enough, you've crossed the line'. Seeing his father shed a tear was a rarity, and Kalen was still puzzling over it when, some minutes later, his ears popped as the crew opened the forward hatch. People rose from their seats, bled out into the aisle, and shuffled out onto the concourse of Asheton Spaceport.

By the time they passed through Immigration and arranged delivery of their hold baggage, David had recovered his calm, unaffected self.

♦

The Maglev train swung smoothly around a rise in the land and gave Kalen his first close-up view of Asheton. It bubbled off the desert like an enormous blister. He remembered from a familiarisation session a couple of weeks earlier that it was the biggest city of its kind anywhere in the solar system. A cluster of clear, interlinked, geodesic domes—known locally as cloaks—sealing in the homes, businesses, walkways, parks and bodies of water that made life possible for the colonists. Some of the taller buildings protruded through the top of the largest dome, and, in the west, a cloak shaped like an enormous, half-buried slug wound away several kilometres over hilly woodlands.

The train neared the city and swung north to skirt the marscrete and steel perimeter base. Kalen noted a number of small maintenance buggies moving about near a large airlock.

Eventually, the train reached its entrance further around the perimeter, passed through the air seal, and cruised into the colony.

'We're here,' David sighed in a tone that could have been either relief or apprehension. 'What do you think?'

Kalen could barely find the words. He felt as if they had passed through a portal into a different world.

'It's—it's mind-boggling,' he finally managed to gasp.

'Yes. Mind-boggling. I suppose it is. Good.'

Hidden vents automatically opened, and fresh air flooded into the cabin. Kalen inhaled deeply.

'Grass!' he said, unable to contain the surprise in his voice. 'I can smell grass. And water. And trees. It's just like Earth.'

'Good,' David said again.

The train raced across a bridge spanning a roadway and began to wind through lush parklands dotted with trees and dissected by a stream. Some low-lying buildings swept past, and then the city proper rose around them. At the speed they were travelling, it was difficult to gain more than an impression, but it seemed to be a mishmash of sharp spires, tall buildings, and the more adventurous, skeletal architecture possible only in low gravity. Curving walkways threaded around and through it all on multiple levels. Everything looked clean and bright and exotic, quite different from anything on Earth.

At last, they slowed into Asheton Metro Station in the middle of the city.

'This is us,' David said.

Hand luggage slung over their shoulders, they walked along the platform and out into a pretty thoroughfare lined with tall elms. Just down from the entrance waited a rank of transit pods, small white vehicles with clear, bulbous cabins. David led his son to the first. They threw their luggage onto the front set of seats and sat in the back two, facing forward.

'Galactic Tower,' David said to the pod.

'You have requested Galactic Tower in Viking Way,' it confirmed. 'Please fasten your seatbelts. Estimated travel time is twelve minutes. Departing now.'

With that, the pod, humming quietly, engaged the magnetic field generated beneath the roadway, levitated a few centimetres, then accelerated smoothly into the moving traffic. Through the window, Kalen noticed people everywhere, coming and going from shops, carrying parcels, or chatting in cafés. Some walked; others travelled in transit pods like them.

Mingling with them all were a variety of robots.

'Artificial Companions,' David explained when he noticed his son gaping at them. 'Not very common on earth—too expensive—but here you'll see quite a few out and about.'

Built on fine frames with strong but flexible humanoid bodies, the Artificial Companions averaged about two metres in height and came in a variety of different models and colours.

'I know,' Kalen replied. 'ArComs, for short.'

David raised his eyebrows in surprise and allowed himself a half-smile. 'Been reading up, have you?'

'I saw it on the *Red Dust Tales* last year.'

'The *Red Dust Tales*. Yes, I see. Very good.'

Suddenly, Mars seemed more welcoming. They'd only been on the ground for a couple of hours, and already his father was different. It was as if he had managed to throw off some enormous, suffocating weight.

As promised, the pod dropped them off twelve minutes later outside Galactic Tower.

While David paid for the journey with a funds transfer via his wristwatch, Kalen dumped their luggage on the pavement and looked up at Galactic Tower. While technically not a cloak scraper, the building was still tall enough to probe the upper reaches of the metrosphere.

'So we're gonna live here, are we?' he said.

His father closed the pod door, and the vehicle hummed off along Viking Way. 'That's the plan. Come on, let's find our apartment.'

They climbed the broad steps and walked through a pair of large glass doors into the bright foyer. When David had entered their details in the guest database, the pleasant, grey-haired concierge at the desk completed the arrival process and handed him two key passes.

'Room four twenty-eight,' he said. 'I hope you enjoy your stay.'

Galactic Tower had four high-speed elevators that climbed the exterior of the building. Lugging their bags into one, Kalen peered through the clear panel of glass that formed the outer wall and watched the streetscape drop away beneath them.

Their two-bedroom apartment on level four was neat and spacious. Now that the long transit, his week of feeling unwell, and the morning flight into Asheton were behind him, Kalen suddenly felt the weight of a crushing tiredness. He was unable to stifle a long yawn.

'It's been a busy time,' his father said with a sympathetic smile. 'Why don't you lie down for a couple of hours? Do you the world of good. I've got some things to do anyway.'

'Yeah, I might,' Kalen replied.

His room, square and ivory white, was starkly furnished with a large bed, a dresser, and some built-in robes. A large window offered a wonderful view of the city. It was comfortable, certainly, but it lacked homeliness. No doubt this would improve when he had surrounded himself with his personal effects after they were delivered in the morning.

He dropped his bag on the floor, shrugged off his jacket, threw it over a chair, then collapsed on top of the soft bed covers.

For a few moments, he lay there face down in the softness and quiet, feeling the rush of the previous hours fall away.

Dreamily, he allowed himself to mull over the frantic blur of the past six months. He had been living a normal, if small and lonely, life on Earth with his widowed father. Then, after a stranger's visit, he was pulled out of school; his father resigned from his job; their house was rented out fully furnished; transit and immigration data had been hastily sent to authorities and approved; they travelled to the spaceport in Queensland and flew into orbit to meet the Cycler to Mars.

And all for what?

Was his father running from something that had finally caught up with him? Something so diabolically bad that he had to leave the planet? Is that why he has always been so secretive? And had the stranger, whoever he was, come to warn him he was about to be caught? Or worse?

Once or twice throughout the transit, Kalen had tried to raise the matter, but as usual, his father had skilfully dodged his questions. Instead, he had extolled the virtues of the red planet—Mars, the new frontier; the way of the future; a place of unlimited possibilities for someone on the cusp of manhood; and a wonderful environment for someone working in the field of weather science.

But Kalen saw these for what they were. Excuses. Evasions. They were so clichéd, they could almost have been taken from one of the many Martian promotional campaigns.

Kalen's last thought before sleep finally took him was that he had never felt so frustrated, so powerless.

♦

The room was quite bright when he awoke. That curious Martian light poured in through the window, tinting the walls faintly butterscotch. A glance at the bedside clock showed it was just after 7.00 a.m. Morning! He'd slept away what remained of the previous afternoon, then on through the night. Obviously, he'd been more tired than he realised. He jumped into the shower to freshen up, threw on some jeans and a light cotton shirt from his bag, then went out into the living room.

His father was sitting at the kitchen bench, perusing some documents. 'Ah, welcome back to the land of the living,' he said, gathering up the papers and putting them away. 'Hungry?'

'A bit.'

'Good. After you went to bed, I nicked out and got some things for breakfast. When you've had a bite to eat, I thought we might head out for a look around.'

Kalen was a little taken aback. He couldn't remember the last time he and his father had gone out together—just the two of them, hanging out. 'Sure,' he said. 'But what about our stuff from the shuttle?'

'All in hand. I spoke to the concierge earlier. He said they don't usually deliver before nine. If we're not around when they come, he promised to arrange a drop-off in the apartment. Now, get yourself around some breakfast, then we'll make tracks.'

The ex-pat community of Australians on Mars was fairly small, which meant Vegemite wasn't readily available. Kalen had packed four jars, but as they were tucked away securely in his undelivered luggage, he had to make do with some sort of tasteless locally made marmalade on his toast, which, washed down with a mug of tea, fuelled him for the morning.

'Want to get a pod?' he suggested when they stepped out into Viking Way.

'Where to?'

Kalen hadn't planned that far ahead. 'Dunno. Somewhere.'

'Let's just wander around for a bit,' suggested his father. 'I always think the best way to see a place is on foot. It might help us get our Mars legs too. With some practice, we might even pass for locals.'

'That's important, is it, passing for locals?'

When his father didn't want to discuss something, he had a knack of pursing his lips and looking away. He did it again now. 'Come on. There's lots to see.'

David quite naturally adopted that peculiar loping, striding gait of the locals. 'Martian gravity is only a third of Earth's,' he explained when Kalen queried him. 'The trick is to take small steps and push forward, not up.'

Of course, Kalen knew about Martian gravity. Everybody did. But he hadn't given much thought to the art of walking in it. Obviously, his father had. And no surprise in that. David Rance was intelligent and clever, and usually well-prepared. That's why, in spite of all his personal failings and his secretive nature, Kalen always felt safe in his company.

The morning proved interesting enough. Upon turning off Viking Way, they found themselves in a wide mall, which took them to the Central Business District. Spindly, winding walkways led them past, up, and sometimes through the skeletal, twisted, and spidery buildings so common on Mars. In them were the offices of government, law, finance, real estate, agriculture, and all those other businesses that kept the colony functioning. Busy people rushed to and from them in their droves.

Never one for crowds, David led Kalen across the city square, past a large hologram of the red planet floating above a pedestal, and out of the main centre. At the northern edge of the CBD, they came upon the famous Hesper Reach, the tallest building in Asheton. Its tapering lines climbed to the cloak, where the upper storeys burst through to an enclosed observation deck. Father and son stepped out of the express elevator at the top and looked around at the bleak, dust-blown plains of Hesperia Planum. To the east sprawled a vast solar array, while to the south sat the spaceport linked to the city by the snaking Maglev track. In the far west lay the more heavily cratered wastes of Terra Tyrrhena.

By now, rumbling stomachs were calling them to lunch. The level below, still above the cloak, was occupied by the revolving restaurant, Hespers. They stood peering through its large double doors at crisp white tablecloths, gleaming cutlery, and pompous-looking waiters. Too formal, they decided, not to mention expensive, so they returned to street level and wandered to a narrow lane where they'd earlier noticed an assortment of little cafés. One offered quiet seclusion amid a riotous yet carefully crafted garden; unfortunately, it only served vegan food, which they didn't eat. Another looked promising, but a large group of diners noisily celebrating some milestone drove them away. In the end, they chose a quiet little hamburger joint, barely half full and boasting a number of tables in private booths.

They seated themselves near the back and attacked two enormous open hamburgers with salad washed down by coffee.

'Oh, that hits the spot,' David said gratefully.

"Oo' 'ucker.'

'Manners, Kalen!'

Kalen tugged a half-chewed lettuce leaf out of a gap in his front teeth and swallowed it noisily with a chunk of bun. 'Sorry. I just said good tucker.'

'Ah, yes. So it is. Obviously, you're feeling better.'

'Yeah, much.' Kalen wiped some drips of runny egg from his chin. 'The doc must've been right. Just arrival nerves.'

'Good to hear. If you were still off colour, I'd have to, well, do things differently. Postpone plans for a few sols.' He paused uncertainly for a moment, then continued. 'I haven't said it before, Kalen, but I do appreciate your forbearance over the past few months. You've shown patience above and beyond.'

Appreciation? Softness? This wasn't his father at all. For some reason, Mars was bringing out his long-hidden, warmer side. Kalen decided to take advantage of their new-found camaraderie. 'Why are we really here, Dad?'

David hesitated.

Before he could say something evasive, Kalen jumped in with, 'No, don't do that again. I think I deserve to know, now that we've landed.'

David picked up a napkin thoughtfully, wiped his mouth, and replaced it neatly on the table.

'Yes. Yes, of course you do. And a lot more, besides.'

This was promising! Still, there was that familiar tone of hesitant deferral. 'But?'

David sighed. 'Yes, there's always a but, isn't there. It must be enormously frustrating for you, but I can tell you this much: there are some things happening that I have to attend to; some very complicated things which I simply can't talk about.'

'Things that stranger came to the house to tell you? Something to do with Alpha in Aquarius?'

'That's part of it.'

'Who was he, that stranger?'

David held back, but Kalen pushed harder.

'Dad, who was he?'

'A friend.'

'No, he wasn't. He didn't even know Mum was dead.'

'He was still a friend.'

'Why? What did he say?'

'He made me realise some things.'

'What things?'

'Things that didn't go the way they should have. Not with me, not with Mum, not with our family.' He stared into his son's eyes with a kind of gentle desperation. 'Look, I know it's been just the two of us for a long time, and that makes it difficult, but you must understand family ties are everything. And they're forever, Kalen. Whatever happens, we're never completely apart.'

His father had never spoken so earnestly about family before. It was refreshing, but unsettling too. 'Are you alright, Dad?'

'Of course, yes. I'm sorry, but I needed to say that. And I must ask you to bear with me just a little longer. Believe me, it's for your own good that I don't tell you just yet.'

'Okay, but can I ask one more thing?'

'Go on.'

'Why did *I* have to come to Mars?'

'Because even though none of it's your fault, it concerns you as much as me. Maybe even more so in the long term.'

Another typical dad non-answer. Intriguing, pointing to something vague in the distance, but completely lacking in detail.

'What do you—?'

'I can't say any more. It's not . . . well, I just can't. But I promise you this: after solmorrow night everything will be different.'

'What's happening then?'

David sipped a mouthful of coffee and leaned back in his chair. 'I've got to go away in the morning.'

'We're already away.'

'I mean away from Asheton. I'll be gone first thing. Just for the sol. But when I get back, everything will be clear.'

'Right. So, what am I going to do while you're away?'

David looked at his son and smiled with unfamiliar affection. 'You're fifteen now. Old enough to be your own person, to make some decisions for yourself. Try pretending you've come here on your own. Then, when I get back at the end of the sol, you'll understand everything.'

'That's the third time you've said that.'

'What?'

'Sol.'

'It's a Martian day.'

'I know what it is. Huh, sol. And what was the other one? Solmorrow? You're even speaking the local lingo now.'

'As I said before, it's better if we try to fit in.' A clock on the wall caught his attention. 'Oh, is that the time? I'm going to be late.'

'What for?'

Again, those pursed lips and evasive eyes told Kalen not to expect an answer.

David paid the bill, and they walked along the lane to a broader street. By now, lunchtime was in full swing. People bustled about everywhere. They hadn't been in a rushing crowd for many months, and inadvertently, David stepped off the edge of the pavement without looking.

A tyre screeched. A horn beeped. Then a small, canary yellow unocycle swerved and flashed past, missing him by centimetres. David threw himself backwards and stumbled onto the pavement.

'Watch where you're going!' the rider bawled over his shoulder, barely slowing. 'You got a death wish or something?'

Then he was gone. Kalen was immediately at his father's side, helping him to his feet. Some people nearby stopped too.

'You alright?' an older man asked.

'Yes, yes, thanks. I'll be fine.'

'Idiot,' said a young woman, shaking her head. 'Honestly, they seem to give licences to anybody.'

'You should report him,' another man was saying.

'I would,' agreed a fourth person.

'No, no. It's fine,' David said quickly. 'No problems.'

'I didn't get its number,' the man persisted, 'but the MSA would soon track it down for you.'

'No, really. It's my fault. I should've looked first.' David seemed nervous, his hands shaking, his eyes darting around uncertainly at faces in the crowd.

'Well, if you're sure,' the man said.

'Yes, quite. Thank you. I don't want any trouble.'

With the fuss over, the small clot of do-gooders quickly broke up.

'Now, I'm running late,' David said.

'You sure you're not hurt?' Kalen asked.

'Yes, I just got a bit of a shock, that's all. Now, where will I meet you? Back at the city square, maybe. Say, in an hour? That should give me time.'

'I'll find it.'

Kalen watched his father rush across the road and disappear around the corner. What could he be up to? Whatever it was, there was nothing he could do about it at the moment, so he put it from his mind and headed down the street on his own.

◆

Kalen first suspected he was being followed about half an hour after he and his father went their separate ways. Initially, he dismissed it as mild paranoia; understandable given that he was alone for the first time in a foreign city on a new planet.

Once or twice, he jerked his head over his shoulder but saw nothing suspicious. Just people, transit pods, and a few ArComs. All very ordinary and expected. On, he walked. But still, he couldn't shake that uncomfortable, cloying sensation.

A few minutes later, he drifted into a large store that retailed unocycles. His fears of being followed were replaced for a time with dreams of riding one of these sleek, brightly coloured machines.

He first heard of them a couple of years earlier on an episode of the *Red Dust Tales,* but apart from his fleeting glimpse of the machine that had nearly flattened his father, he had never seen one up close. Odd-looking vehicles, they were essentially a seat and pillion with handlebars mounted on a single wide wheel, powered by batteries, and kept upright by a powerful gyroscope inside the body. A few Terrans owned them, but mainly for the novelty. Not so on Mars. The lower gravity here made them very popular.

'You look like you wanna try it out.'

Kalen turned to see a gaunt, twenty-something sales assistant with long hair dyed green and tied in a ponytail. He was leaning on a nearby counter. 'Thanks, but I better not.'

'Go on. Take your pick.' The man straightened up, walked over, and pointed to a sporty machine in fire engine red. 'How about that one?'

'I don't think so,' Kalen replied. 'I'm just filling in time.'

The man shrugged but wasn't to be deterred. 'No harm sitting on it. Fab little machine, that. Got all the latest tech. Power brake, City Locator with Auto Ride, seat warmer, acceleration to pin your ears back. The advertised range is four-fifty Ks, but between you and me, it can do four-sixty.' He pressed a button on the machine's console. It began to hum quietly, then sat erect on its single wheel. 'Jump on. Get a feel for it.'

'No, it's alright,' Kalen said.

'Go on. It won't bite.'

'Look, I'm really not in the market.'

'Come on, man! Everybody on Mars's in the market for one of these babes.'

Kalen didn't respond, so the man tried a different tack.

'Got a girlfriend?'

'What's that got to do with anything?'

The man flashed a suggestive smile, which revealed a pair of blue studs embedded in his front teeth. 'Nothing. It's just that the girls love a guy on a Unitrek 6. That's what this is. A babe magnet. A status symbol.'

'Status symbol. Right.' *The guy really was laying it on thick!* 'No, I haven't had time to think about a girlfriend yet. I just got here.'

'When?'

'Yesterday. I mean—how do you say that here?'

'Yestersol.' The man smiled and leaned back on the bench. 'So you're a real newbie, then. You'll definitely need one. But I don't want to be pushy. When you're ready to buy, come back and . . . hey, what're you doing?'

An ArCom, charcoal-coloured with light grey trim, had stepped into the shop. It propped itself inside the doorway and silently scanned the scene.

'I'm talking to you!' yelled the sales assistant. 'Clear off, or I'll report you. You're blocking the entrance.'

The ArCom, which had fixed its cold gaze on Kalen, glanced at the man, then turned and walked back outside.

'Huh, never seen that before,' said the man. 'Since when do ArComs go shopping? Must've blown a circuit. Anyway, where was I?'

Kalen took the opportunity to make his escape. 'I was just leaving,' he said. 'Gotta meet my dad soon.'

'Right. Well, bring him in solmorrow. No, wait, I'm off. Better make it the sol after. I can do you a great deal on two. Set you both up with the latest. Just ask for Victor.'

'Sure. Thanks. I'll let him know.'

Kalen finally extricated himself and headed out of the store. The wayward ArCom was standing on the street. Kalen ignored it and walked off. It followed.

By the end of the block, Kalen realised it was the stalker! He walked a little faster. So did the ArCom. He slowed down. So did the ArCom. Warning bells clanged in his head. There was no doubt about it. Something in the machine's neural circuitry had fixated on him.

Kalen fought down the impulse to call his father. Not an hour earlier, David had talked up the fact that he was fifteen now, able to start making decisions for himself.

A decision! Okay, here comes the first one.

He bolted off along the pavement. At a break in the traffic, he sped across the road and around a corner. The streetscape flew past. Literally! In low gravity, he became airborne with his long strides, much longer than those on Earth. On he ran, like a gazelle, swerving around corners, right, left, right, left.

At last, panting heavily, he came to a halt and turned to look behind him. To his dismay, the ArCom was still in pursuit. And, worse, it had reconfigured itself and was bounding along on all fours like a big cat.

What's wrong with this thing?

Kalen turned to run again. But suddenly, in a moment of clarity, he stopped himself. What did he really have to fear? It wasn't like he was being hunted by a dangerous human psycho. The ArCom was only a machine, an assembly of nuts and bolts and circuitry run by software, and as such, it was subject to the Laws of Robotics. Its programming would prevent it from harming him. He could pelt rocks at it all week, and it would just stand there, taking it.

With renewed confidence, he waited for it to reach him. A few metres short, it came to a stop and stood back up on its hind legs. The pale blue optical sensors on its faceplate, where human eyes would've been, scanned him impassively.

'Well?' Kalen said in his bravest voice. 'What do you want? Why are you following me?'

The ArCom remained mute.

Maybe he should try giving it a command? These things were supposed to obey humans.

'Okay, play dumb then. But I'm going now, and I don't want you to follow me. Do you understand? DO NOT FOLLOW ME!'

He walked off. The ArCom let him get about ten metres ahead, then set off again, matching his stride. Kalen started running. Once more, the ArCom went down onto all fours and picked up speed.

Sprinting through unknown streets in an alien city, Kalen's courage started to falter. Was the machine really malfunctioning? Or was there something more sinister in play?

On his right, a walkway climbed to the first floor of a shopping centre. Kalen followed it and found himself dashing past colourful, brightly lit shops. He skidded sideways around a corner, then headed down a declining walkway. He was outside again, in a quieter part of the city. Somewhere north of the CBD, he thought.

But he couldn't be sure. And he was starting to tire badly. In spite of the daily running sessions in the cycler's gym during the last week of the transit, his months in the cryogenic chamber had sapped much of his fitness. What he needed was a place out of sight to catch his breath. He passed what looked like a small warehouse on the left, a plumbing supply store on the right. Beside that was some sort of shop with drills and spades and barrows displayed in the window. And just beyond was the entrance to an alley. Now that was promising!

He ducked inside. It was narrow and bordered by walls so high that they shaded out much of the sunlight. As his eyes adjusted to the dimness, he noticed it had a dead end.

Hopefully, the ArCom, when it arrived, would just run harmlessly past. Kalen summoned the last of his energy and dashed across the stone pavers to the far end. If he was lucky, there would be an unlocked door or a stairway leading up to the roof.

But it wasn't to be. All he found were a couple of dead rats and a waste compactor against one wall.

On tiptoes, he pushed his nose over the edge of the compactor to look inside. It was half-empty. Plenty of room for him. He vaulted nimbly over the lip and landed on something furry and wriggling. It squealed abuse at him, then took a flying leap out of the compactor. A couple of its well-fed, glossy-coated rodent cousins followed. Scrambling across a layer of crumpled boxes, old vegetables, and empty bottles, Kalen reached the end and lay there, peering over the lip at the alley entrance.

His breathing was rapid-fire, the pounding pulse in his ears deafening. Then he saw the ArCom appear at the entrance. It stopped, stood up, and remained there, as unmoving as a sentry.

Kalen's heart skipped a beat. Somehow, it knew he was in here.

Moments later, there came a humming sound. A transit pod. It stopped at the entrance to the lane and settled to the ground. Its door opened, and a figure stepped out to stand beside the ArCom.

Twisting in the garbage to get a clearer view, Kalen saw a very tall, chunky figure. Silhouetted by the brighter light in the street behind, details were difficult to make out, but it appeared to be a man wearing a long, black coat with an upturned dark collar beneath a head of white hair. Kalen couldn't quite put his finger on the reason, but there was something scarily menacing about this lump of humanity.

Moving slowly, deliberately, the man placed a large hand with a set of thick, meaty fingers on the much shorter ArCom's shoulder and hunched to confer with it. Apparently, he was issuing instructions; for now, the ArCom strode into the alley towards Kalen.

That's it! Enough decision-making. Time to call Dad!

Kalen tapped his watch to bring the phone system on line and spoke his father's name. It rang twice, then connected.

'Hi.' His father's voice sounded a little impatient. 'We said an hour, Kalen. I'm not quite finished yet.'

'Someone's following me,' Kalen blurted out.

There was a momentary pause, then: 'Where are you?'

'Some alley just out of the CBD.'

'But where exactly?'

'Dunno. I've been running around the city like a mad thing.'

'Think Kalen.'

'I don't know!'

'Alright, don't panic. What about your locator?'

'I haven't downloaded the Asheton app yet.'

'Damn!'

For David Rance, this amounted to swearing. He was definitely worried.

'Wait! I just remembered. There's some sort of junk shop on the corner.'

'Junk shop?'

'Well, maybe not junk exactly. It had lots of things in the window. You know, for digging. Like the stuff old miners use. That's it, yeah. It was like an old prospector's shop. And there's some plumbing place beside it.'

'Okay. That helps. I'll find it.'

'You gonna send the police?'

'The MSA? No, no. I'll deal with it.'

'You?'

'Hold on. I'll be there soon.'

The call disconnected abruptly.

The alley was suddenly silent. Then Kalen heard the ArCom's feet crunching on the pavers nearby. It dragged itself up the outside of the compactor with a scraping, clattering sound. Kalen cowered lower, trying to bury himself under some sheets of packing. But it was futile. He felt something grab the waistband of his jeans, then his left arm.

'Leave me alone, you metal moron!' he bellowed.

It had no effect. The ArCom hoisted him effortlessly out of the compactor and dropped him on the ground.

'Are you the son of David Rance?' it asked in a nondescript, synthesised voice.

'None of your business!'

'Where is David Rance?' it persisted.

'I'm not telling you, you great—'

'Please answer the question.'

'What d'you wanna know for? What's he done?'

'Good enough!' This was the large man's voice calling from the alley entrance. He had obviously been listening. 'Come.'

Kalen lay limply on the ground while the ArCom left him and marched back to the transit pod, climbed in, and drove away with the man. When they'd disappeared, he climbed back up into the compactor to wait for his father. It was dirty and smelly, but in there, he felt safer.

After what seemed like an eternity, that familiar humming sound approached the end of the alley. Fearing his stalkers had returned, Kalen huddled lower in the trash. There came the faint whine of the door opening, followed by another set of footsteps chattering along the pavers.

To his relief, a familiar voice rang along the alley. 'Kalen?'

He sat up. A used pizza box slid off his head. He climbed out and stood beside his father.

David placed a reassuring hand on his shoulder. 'Are you alright?'

'Well, it wasn't the way I planned to spend my first sol on Mars,' Kalen replied, plucking a cold anchovy off his cheek, 'but yeah, I'll live.'

'Can you describe this man who was following you?'

'Actually, there ended up being two of them.'

'Two?'

'The first one—the one I told you about—was an ArCom.'

'What sort was it?'

'Very annoying.'

'Okay. Never mind that. What about the second one?'

'He was some bloke; rocked up in a pod soon after the ArCom got here. Now he was seriously creepy.'

'In what way?'

'Well, he didn't come close enough to get a good look at, but he was tall—and I mean mega-tall. The ArCom was bigger than me, but this guy towered over it. And I think he had white hair.'

David's shoulders slumped noticeably. His lips twisted into a grimace.

Kalen misread the expression as anger. 'It wasn't my fault!'

'What? No, of course it wasn't, Kalen. I blame myself for this. If only I hadn't been so clumsy.'

'What?'

'Nothing. Come on, let's—'

'There's something else too. The tall guy got the ArCom to ask about you. He wanted to know if I was your son.'

David paused for a few moments, then said with great gravity, 'And what did you say?'

'Well, I didn't tell him—not exactly—but it might've, um, you know, slipped out. Accidentally.'

'I see.'

'What's going on, Dad? How did he know your name? Are you in some sort of trouble?'

David instantly looked every one of his fifty-eight years. Tired, haggard, and drawn, his eyes brimming with sadness.

Quietly, he said, 'Come on. Let's get you back to the apartment.'

♦

The pod dropped them back at Galactic Tower a little after two. The concierge raised his eyebrows at Kalen's soiled, dishevelled appearance. His nostrils twitched at the stench of rubbish wafting over his desk.

'Boys will be boys,' David said, forestalling the inevitable question.

'Indeed, they will, sir. Got two of my own.' His eyes went dreamy. His mind drifted off to far gone days of young fatherhood. 'All grown up now, of course. Both working on Luna. Why, I remember when my late wife first—'

'Yes, yes. I'm sure.' David was in no mood for nostalgic reflections. 'Did our luggage turn up?'

'Er.' The man's mind tripped back through the years to present-sol Mars. 'Luggage? Oh, *your* luggage! Yes, of course. It arrived at around ten-thirty. As promised, I had it delivered to your apartment.'

Sure enough, the four transit cases were sitting just inside the front door when they entered.

Kalen had a quick shower to wash off the alley, the garbage compactor, and the rats, then returned to the lounge. His father had already begun to unpack. Kalen followed suit and dragged his two cases into his bedroom.

Unlatching the first, he set to work. There was something therapeutic about handling his familiar clothes and possessions. By being locked away, they somehow retained the normality of his former life. He could almost smell the Earth on them.

Two pairs of jeans were folded onto shelves. Socks and jocks were placed in drawers. A smart pair of trousers, some shirts, and a jacket were hung in the wardrobe. Shoes and runners were neatly laid side by side at the bottom.

In the second case were his possessions. He took out the four jars of Vegemite and threw them on the bed. Then came his e-reader and music list, which he placed on the bedhead shelf. His crucifix was next.

With due reverence, he stuck it to the wall above his bed. Then came his photomontage, which he set running on the bedside table. Snaps appeared and faded: the kids at school; his father; a family photo of him as a baby in his late mother's arms, father leaning over them proudly. His father was much younger then, in his early forties. So different from the man in late middle age who had brought him to Mars.

When he was finished, he slid the cases to one side and paused to look out the window at Asheton's afternoon skyline. From this perspective, it was a city imaginatively conceived, ingeniously planned, meticulously engineered, and courageously realised. Picture perfect, the subject of many a postcard.

But there was, as he now knew from experience, a different, darker Asheton too. An Asheton of people with hidden agendas. People who wanted to know about his father. Why? He was a weatherman, for goodness sake. How could he possibly be of interest to them?

Then a dark realisation struck him. His father had been running from something on Earth. Now it had found him on Mars.

Chapter 2

Early next morning, Kalen jumped out of bed feeling much refreshed. While he had gone to sleep the previous night understandably troubled, he had settled into a heavy slumber and woken more upbeat.

His father was going away for the sol to sort everything out. When he returned, he would bring with him some long overdue answers. That's what he had promised.

After showering quickly, Kalen dressed and went out into the lounge.

'Ah, you're up,' his father said. 'Good. I was hoping to catch you before I went.'

'Oh?'

'I've uploaded our debit facility to your watch.'

'Really? Why?'

'I just think it's prudent for us both to have access to it. It's in an account at the Bank of Mars I set up in transit. I'll trust you to be sensible with it. But if I come back and find you've bought a unocycle, there'll be some explaining to do. Are we understood?'

Kalen recognised the humour in this and responded in the same vein. 'Well, if I can't have a unocycle can I at least book a first-class shuttle fare back to Earth?'

'Sure. And I'll arrange for some officers from the orphanage to take you into custody when you arrive.'

'Okay, so no first class ticket to Earth either.'

'Got it.' David turned business-like again. 'Now, I nicked out before to pick up some things. There's fresh milk in the fridge; I forgot to pick up cereal, but there's still bread in the cupboard from yestersol, so you can make some toast.'

'With Vegemite.'

'Yes, I noticed our pantry's grown by four jars. I got orange juice, too, and tinned fish for your lunch.'

'I could've done that myself.'

His father frowned. 'I know I said to pretend you're here by yourself, but after what happened, I'm wondering if it might be safer if you don't go too far afield while I'm gone.'

'Oh,' he replied glumly.

'What's wrong?'

'It's just that I was going to go for a run this morning. I've gone to flab. I couldn't even lose that ArCom yestersol.' Kalen saw that his father was doubtful. 'Are you worried I'll come across that tall guy again?'

'Honestly, I don't think that's an issue, but let's play safe and not take any unnecessary risks.'

'Well—'

'Kalen?'

'Yeah, okay.'

'Good.' He glanced at the time on the wall clock. 'Now, time's marching on. I'd better get cracking.'

He picked up his travel bag. A blue plastic document holder, which Kalen hadn't seen before, slipped off it onto the floor. Some papers fell out. David scooped them up hastily and tucked the lot safely away inside his jacket.

Father and son stood facing each other. Suddenly, they were awkward in each other's company. Overt affection didn't come easily to either, and now, at the moment of separation, words completely failed them.

'Well,' mumbled David, clearing his throat.

Kalen nodded and said, 'Um, I'll be alright.'

'Yes,' his father replied softly. 'I know you will.'

Then he was gone.

For the first few moments after the door shut, Kalen stood staring at it. He felt his heart rate start to climb. His breathing became short and erratic. He recognised the beginnings of a panic attack. As a small child, after the death of his mother, he'd experienced them for a few months. But that was such a long time ago. He was no longer that small child.

No, I'm not doing this, he reprimanded himself. *He's gone for thirty seconds, and I'm already losing it. He'll be back tonight. Then I'll know everything. In the meantime, I've got to do something. Take my mind off it.*

The bag of groceries on the bench caught his eye.

Breakfast!

He boiled the jug and placed two slices of bread in the toaster. When they were brown, he slathered them in margarine and thick lashings of Vegemite. He had to make up for all those Vegemiteless mornings he'd spent on the cycler.

When he'd washed the dishes, he went back to his room and rearranged the doona over his bed. Then he selected some music and set it playing quietly so as not to disturb the neighbours.

At around 9.00 a.m., he went out to the lounge and decided to sample some Martian television.

There were fifteen channels, he discovered. Six were devoted to current affairs, one broadcast re-runs of old films from the 2030s, one showed only advertisements; and the rest had anything from sports to soaps to any number of talent contests.

It was all very yawn-worthy, so at around 10.00 a.m., he switched it off and boiled the jug to make some morning tea. But then he remembered a coffee shop they'd seen in their travels yestersol. It was just down the way from Galactic Tower. In its windows, he'd seen a tempting assortment of muffins, cakes, buns, and pastries. What could be the harm in sitting there for an hour or so? Surely he couldn't get into any trouble with people all around?

♦

Mrs Mack's Muffin Bar wasn't busy at that time of the morning, and through the open doorway, Kalen saw several free tables. But the butterscotch Martian light and the soft breeze blowing along the avenue reminded him of lazy summer mornings on Earth. So he ordered a Mugaccino/Strawberry Chocolate Muffin combo, then settled himself comfortably among the *al fresco* tables on the pavement.

His memory flashed back to the events of yestersol. He cast his eyes warily up and down the avenue. There were lots of people around, but none who even remotely resembled that menacing lump of a man and his ArCom stalker. He sucked in a couple of deep breaths and relaxed.

In no time, a matronly woman somewhere in her mid-forties came out with a tray and unloaded his morning tea onto the table.

'There we are, dear,' she said brightly. 'Enjoy.'

When she left, he sampled both the muffin and the coffee. Mm! The muffin had been warmed and was light and tasty, the coffee was hot and not too strong, just how he liked it. Mrs Mack's was definitely going to be a regular haunt while he was on Mars.

He just lazed in his chair and casually watched the people go by, alone, in couples, and in larger groups. All on the way to somewhere, with things to do. And they were all adults, which made him feel more alone than ever.

Twenty minutes later, he was still there, scraping up the last of the muffin crumbs with a licked finger and spooning froth from the bottom of his mug. Just as he had decided it was time to head back to the apartment, a disturbance along the avenue made him look up.

A white ArCom with dark blue trim had raced around the corner into view. In close and determined pursuit was a girl of about his age. Her blond hair was long, pulled tightly back off her eyes, and clipped up in a bouncing fountain at the top of her head. And she was taller than any of the other girls he had known. From that, he assumed she was a Martian; most of those born on the red planet were tall, their growth unrestricted by the much heavier Terran gravity.

'I'm warning you,' the girl yelled at the ArCom, 'if you don't stop this instant, I'll zap you.'

The ArCom looked back over its shoulder as it fled. 'No, you won't. You forgot your zapper.' If it was possible for an ArCom to sound smug, this one did. 'And I'm not stopping anyway. Your father will only tinker with me again.'

As the ArCom's head swivelled back to face forward, its toe caught the lip of the gutter, and it stumbled. Momentum carried it through the air in a curving arc.

'Look out!' the girl cried.

Too late. The ArCom came crashing down onto Kalen's table. Kalen dived to one side and ended up lying on the pavement under the shop window. His coffee mug clattered in another direction.

The ArCom didn't fare so well. When it tried to regain its feet, a silver bracket around its neck sprung loose with a loud *twang*. Its head came adrift, hit the ground, then tumbled along the pavement. Without the electronic brain attached, the body just collapsed like a rag doll.

Mrs Mack must have heard the commotion, for she stormed to the doorway and stood there on the threshold with hands on hips.

'Jenna Quill!' she roared. 'What do you think you're doing?'

'Really sorry, Mrs Mack,' Jenna cried. 'I'll—that is, Dad will pay for any damage.'

'You can be sure of that, my girl! Now get this bucket of bolts away from my shop or it'll be losing more than its head.'

Jenna looked despairingly at the decapitated body.

'I can't move him like this,' she moaned.

Behind her, Kalen got to his feet, dusting himself off.

'Don't mind me,' he said. 'I can pick myself up.'

Jenna turned a big pair of brown eyes towards him. 'Oh, really sorry.' Then she saw his overturned mug nearby. 'Looks like I owe you a coffee too.'

'Don't worry about it. I was finished anyway.'

'Well, that's something. He didn't hurt you, did he?'

'He?'

'Sorry?'

'You called it he.'

'Well, he's a machine, obviously, but he's called Mal.'

'Short for Malfunction?'

'Huh. More like Maladjusted and Maladroit.'

'They're his brothers, are they?'

'If he had any, they probably would be. Listen, you couldn't do me a favour, I suppose?'

'Like what?'

'Get his head.' She pointed along the pavement. 'I think it ended up over there somewhere.'

'Sure. Hang on a sec.'

In no time, Kalen found the ArCom's head lying face down in the gutter. He picked it up carefully with both hands.

'Are you my body?' it asked.

'Do I look like your body?' Kalen retorted.

'No, but I can't really afford to be fussy at the moment.'

'Give it here,' Jenna instructed. 'He's just talking gibberish.' When Kalen passed it to her, she fiddled with some of its circuitry. 'There, that should stop him running off. Think you can lift the top half for me? If you can, I should be able to put it back together. At least enough to get us home.'

Kalen knelt beside the prostrate machine.

'Careful, he's heavy,' Jenna warned.

Slipping his hands under the back, Kalen easily sat Mal up.

'You're strong!'

Jenna was clearly impressed. She reconnected some fine cables, twisted the head into place, and tightened the screws of its neck bracket with her fingers. Red lights flickered in Mal's eyes.

'Now, you better behave yourself,' she said.

'I exist to serve, Mistress,' said a more compliant Mal.

'Much better. Stand.'

Mal obediently got to his feet.

'So he's not going to run away again?' Kalen said.

'Not now,' Jenna replied with a shake of her head. 'I disengaged his autonomy software.' With the immediate problem solved, she ran a curious eye over Kalen. 'I'm guessing you're a Terran.'

'Is it that obvious?'

'Well, I haven't seen you around before. And your muscles are a bit of a giveaway.'

Kalen's chest immediately puffed out at what he took to be a compliment.

'No, no, don't get the wrong idea,' Jenna continued, faintly blushing. 'I just meant it's obvious you didn't grow up in Martian gravity.'

His chest deflated. 'Oh, right.'

'So what are you doing here? Your parents brought you, I suppose.'

'My dad did, yeah.'

'What's your name?'

'Kalen.'

'I'm Jenna.'

'I know. Jenna Quill.'

'Oh yes.' Her eyes dropped briefly in embarrassment. 'Mrs Mack *did* tell the whole street, didn't she. Can't blame her, I suppose. This's the second time in a month one of Dad's jobs has messed up her tables. I wish he'd use the restraints.'

Neither were given to lengthy bouts of small talk, so their conversation lapsed quickly into an awkward silence.

'Well, anyway, we'd better be getting back,' Jenna said. 'Dad'll think I'm chasing him around the city. And you've probably got things to do.'

'Yeah, right,' Kalen said, putting on his most bored expression. 'Muffins and coffee, coffee and muffins; then maybe another coffee or two, followed by a muffin—or three.'

'So a full schedule, then.'

'Yep. My dad's deserted me.'

'What?'

'Just for the sol. He's, er, busy.'

'Right.' Jenna looked at him, hesitated, then said, 'If you want, you can come with me. Once we get Malfunction here back to the shop, I could show you around. I'm meeting my friend Nikki later. You could join us.'

♦

Asheton Robotics was located in Wells Lane, a quiet, winding thoroughfare running off Viking Way. Jenna's father, Jules, had opened it many years earlier and built a reputation as a talented and reliable robotics engineer, Mal's behaviour that morning notwithstanding.

Parked on their stands outside the shop were a couple of unocycles. Jenna led Kalen and Mal past them and in through the door. The shop was a dingy hodgepodge of electrical hardware, components, circuit boards, and reels of wire. In glass cabinets and on wall shelves were a variety of robotic components: arms, legs, heads, and a couple of torsos with tangles of coloured wire trailing from them. A broad counter ran the length of the back wall.

Kalen, Jenna, and Mal were barely inside when a plum-coloured, battered old ArCom with one arm strutted up to Kalen on rickety, squeaking legs. 'How do you do?' it said, reaching out its hand. 'I'm a vanilla-flavoured walrus. Can I be of service?'

'You're not supposed to be up, Scratch!' Jenna said, raising her eyes in disapproval. 'Go back to your shelf and lie down.'

'Certainly, Miss. May I tell you a joke first?'

'Don't bother.'

'Did you hear the one about the blonde and the AI?'

'No.'

'She asked how she could get artificial intelligence.'

'So?'

'The AI told her to dye her hair brunette.'

Jenna glared at the ArCom angrily and tugged at a tuft of her own hair. 'See this, you misfit?'

'Yes, Miss.'

'What colour is it?'

'Fair to light brown with just a hint of honey in this morning light. Of an evening, it changes to—'

'Blond, Scratch! And I hate blond jokes. Besides, that wasn't the teensiest bit funny.'

'Everybody's a critic.'

'Last warning! If you don't go back to your shelf—'

'I'm going, I'm going. Nice meeting you, sir.' Scratch twitched, then collapsed in a heap on the floor.

Kalen said dryly, 'I'm guessing he's not quite ready yet.'

'The only thing he's ready for is the scrap heap.' She looked at Mal. 'And that's where you're headed if things don't improve. Now go and put yourself on the charger while I take Kalen out the back.'

The ArCom toddled over to the corner and stood on the wireless charger while Jenna led Kalen through a doorway behind the counter. They found Jules Quill sitting on the arm of a chair in his cluttered workshop, his eyes glued to a television screen on the bench.

'Did you catch him?' he asked without looking up.

'Not exactly. He caught himself on one of Mrs Mack's tables.'

'Not again!'

'Afraid so. At least no one got hurt this time.'

'Give thanks for small mercies, I say.'

'I think there's still a glitch in his autonomy software.'

'Shouldn't be. I've reloaded it twice—' Then he noticed Kalen. 'Oh, I see it wasn't just Mal you caught.'

Jules got to his feet while Jenna made the introductions. He was a short man in his early forties. His face was pleasant and lit by a pair of brown eyes. A fair, wispy goatee hung off his chin.

'I don't normally sit out the back,' he said, almost apologetically. 'I just wanted to see this newsflash.'

'What's happened?' Jenna asked.

'Terrible news! Just terrible. There's been a shuttle come down on the way to Touchdown.'

'Oh, passenger or freight?'

'Passenger apparently. This week's service out of Asheton.'

'You mean it's crashed?' Kalen said.

'That's what they're telling us. No survivors, by all accounts. A freighter's been diverted from South Cap to the site. Supposed to be sending some live coverage any moment now.'

Jules turned up the volume, and all three watched.

'This is MarsAir LTA freighter, *Forever Sky*. You seeing what we're seeing, Asheton?'

'Not yet,' a woman's voice replied, presumably from Asheton Control Tower. 'Wait . . .'

The screen flickered, then some moving aerial footage of an ochre desert juddered into focus. Everywhere were craters, red hills, and patches of darker rocks. Then, from the top of the screen, some scattered pieces of white material drifted into view on a gentle slope.

'Coming through now, *Forever Sky*. What do you make of it?'

The pilot said, 'From what I can see, both engines have separated from the wings.

'And the cabin section?'

'Stand by. We're still too far out.'

Kalen, Jenna, and Jules watched in silence as the freighter flew in closer and the white material resolved into pieces of equipment.

'This is horrific,' the disbelieving pilot reported. 'It's been completely blown apart. I can see at least five major pieces. And there's a wide debris field scattered across the plain.'

'Any signs of movement?'

'Only what the wind's stirring up.'

Shortly after, the *Forever Sky* slowed to a stop, hovering only metres above the scene. Its belly cameras panned across sheets of mangled metal, twisted pipes, torn hoses, and pieces of what looked like seats and tables. Shards of broken glass twinkled in the morning light. Here and there were broken environment packs, helmets, and torn sections of biosuits, macabrely waving in the breeze.

'Whatever happened, it was catastrophic,' the pilot said. 'The poor devils never stood a chance. Do you want us to drop some people onto the ground for a closer look? I've got a couple of tech crew suited up and ready to go.'

The garbled sounds of consultation could be heard in the background, then the woman's voice rose above them: 'That's a negative, *Forever Sky*. Just stay on site until rescue arrives.'

'Roger. Got an ETA on that?'

'They've already scrambled. Forty minutes, approx.'

The feed disappeared and was replaced by a talking head in the studio. 'This is Courtenay Rayne at Ares News in Asheton. You've been watching live coverage of our breaking story this morning. MarsAir flight 14 has—'

'What is it, Kalen?' Jenna asked.

She had noticed the worried expression on his face.

'Nothing.' He was staring blankly at the screen. 'Probably nothing at all.'

Then she remembered what he'd told her about his father being away for the sol. 'You don't think your dad . . . I mean, was he going to Touchdown?'

'No. At least he never said he was.'

'Your dad's travelling, is he?' asked Jules, catching up.

'I'm not sure.'

'Well, *could* he have been going to Touchdown?'

'I suppose,' Kalen shrugged, 'but I don't even know if he was *flying* anywhere. For all I know, he could've been going by land.'

'Unlikely,' said Jules, stroking his beard thoughtfully. 'Touchdown's too far from here by rover. When's he due back?'

'This afternoon. Or tonight, maybe. It was left open.'

Jenna could tell that Kalen was unsettled, in spite of his best attempts to hide it.

'You don't want to wait until then to find out,' she said. 'Are you set up for MarsNet?'

The phone! Kalen nodded, a little sheepish that he hadn't considered the obvious. He tapped his watch and waited for the display to appear. 'Dad,' he said. It connected quickly, rang a few times, then went to the message service. Kalen disconnected. 'He's not picking up.'

Jules scratched his chin. 'Well, let's not jump to conclusions. He could still be in Asheton with his phone off. Still, why don't I get in touch with MarsAir for you? They'll be sure to have a passenger manifest. I've got a contact in their maintenance division. Did some work for them last year.'

'Thanks,' Kalen replied. 'I'd appreciate that.'

'What's your dad's name?'

'David. Doctor David Rance.'

'Okay. Give me a few minutes. Now, where did I put their number? Oh yes, out in the shop.'

Jules left them to make the call from the front counter. Jenna and Kalen stayed in the back room in case a further update came through.

'So your dad's a doctor,' Jenna said.

'Yeah. But not a medical doctor. Everybody thinks that when I say it.'

'So what's he a doctor of?'

'Meteorology. Weather.'

'I know what meteorology is. Didn't know anybody could be a doctor of it, though. He must be really clever.'

'Probably. I don't suppose I've thought about it much.'

A chime on the wall sounded.

Jules called, 'Shop, Jen.'

'Just a customer,' she explained. 'Come out with me if you like.'

In one corner, Jules was talking on a handset. A woman stood at the counter, waiting for service. Somewhere in her late thirties, she was well-dressed with a coiffed hairstyle and heavy make-up.

'Not very good advertising, is it!' she said sharply, turning up her nose at the plum-coloured jumble of ArCom on the floor.

'No, sorry about that, Mrs . . ?'

'Xynthropileops,' replied the woman.

'Er, right. It's not yours, is it?'

'That thing? Goodness no. Giles and I wouldn't own anything like *that*.'

'Of course you wouldn't. No, we're just, er, having a tidy up. Now, how can I help?'

'Our Omicron Four's in for repair,' she replied.

'Oh yes. What was Dad doing to it?'

'Fixing it, I hope.'

'Yes, but what was wrong with it?'

The woman peered down the considerable length of her shiny nose at Jenna. 'You're asking me? I'm not one of those robot fix-it-thingies. All I know is that every time we put it away at night, it climbs out the window and runs off.'

'Little wonder,' Jenna muttered under her breath.

'Sorry?'

'Er, I said it's a little wonder. The Omicron Four. Great model, normally very reliable.'

'I see. Well, obviously, ours *isn't* normal. Anybody'd think it was trying to escape back to its previous owner.'

Jenna smothered her uncontrolled snigger with a cough. 'Right. I'll just see if it's ready.'

With the handset jammed to one ear, Jules was stabbing a finger at Mal, still standing obediently on its wireless charging pad in the corner. 'Only a glitch, Mrs . . . er. Its ownership-transfer software just needed reloading . . . yes, hello? Is that MarsAir? Just a moment, please . . . that's it over there, Jen. It's still under warranty . . . MarsAir? Sorry.'

Kalen said, 'That's Mal—'

'Colm,' Jenna finished. 'That's right. Malcolm belongs to Mrs er.'

'He *is* ready, isn't he?' asked the woman.

'Yes, yes, raring to go. I took him out for a trial run just before. He really knows how to move. I bet he could dance on tabletops if you let him.'

'On my expensive imported walnut tabletop? I think not!'

'No, of course. I didn't mean . . . Kalen, Dad wants you.'

Jules was waving madly for Kalen to join him. 'On this morning's flight to Touchdown,' he was saying. 'Yes, the one that crashed. Okay. Just a moment.' He passed Kalen the handset. 'They'll only speak to next of kin.'

Kalen snatched the handset to his ear. 'Hello.'

'Name, please?' said an officious voice on the other end.

'Kalen Rance.'

'Thank you. Name of the passenger?'

'David Rance. Doctor David Rance.'

'Thank you. Relationship to passenger?'

'I'm his son.'

'Thank you. Checking now.' A short pause followed, then the operator returned. 'Mr Rance? Our system isn't showing anybody by the name of David Rance or Doctor David Rance listed for that flight.'

Chapter 3

T hank you, Mrs er.'
'Xynthropileops. Why does everybody have trouble with that?'

'I can't imagine,' Jenna replied.

Jules said, 'If it gives you any further trouble, don't hesitate to pop it back.'

'You can be sure of it. Now come along, Malcolm.'

Hand in hand, they edged around the crumpled ArCom like it was something messy that had just dropped from the sky and walked briskly out of the shop.

'I'd be climbing out the window every night too, if she owned me,' Jenna muttered after them.

Kalen placed the handset on the counter. 'Good news,' he announced, 'Dad wasn't on it.'

'There you are,' Jules said. 'I told you not to jump to conclusions. Now, since you're here, would you mind giving me a hand to move Scratch? It's not good for business to have him lying here in the doorway.'

Together, Kalen and Jules dragged the decrepit ArCom to the side of the shop. 'I really don't know what I'm going to do with him,' the repairman muttered.

'The word 'scrap' comes to mind,' Jenna suggested.

'Mm, but I hate waste. Maybe I could replace the logic system. I seem to remember there's an old unit down in—'

'Boring!' Jenna interrupted with a sigh of exasperation. She looked at Kalen. 'Come on, we'd better get going.'

Jules looked up. 'What's this? Where are you off to?'

'The trekker bay. Nikki's due in. I promised Kalen I'd take him to meet her.'

'Oh yes, you did mention it. I didn't realise it was tosol. Off you go, then. But be careful. Kalen probably hasn't been on a unocycle before. At least not in our gravity.'

'You know what I'm like, Dad.'

'Precisely why I said it.'

♦

'Ever ridden one of these?' asked Jenna.

'Not yet.'

She handed him one of the helmets hanging from the handlebars, then straddled the seat. 'It's easy, but I haven't got time to teach you just now. Jump on behind me. And don't scratch it. I've only had it a month.'

'Very nice,' said Kalen, admiring the shining pearl-white vehicle as he fitted his helmet.

'A Unicruze 4,' explained Jenna proudly. 'High definition dash, GPS with auto-ride, heated seats.

Four-fifty Ks on a charge. Everything a girl could want.'

Kalen nodded his helmet in approval, then settled onto the pillion seat.

'Right, make like you love me,' said Jenna.

'What?'

'You're not shy, are you? Wrap your arms around me. That's unless you want to fall off.'

'Oh right.' He leaned forward and slipped his arms around her fine midriff.

'Not too tight. I've got to breathe.'

'Sorry.' He loosened his grip a little.

The gyro hummed to life between their legs. She kicked the stand up into its housing, and the machine settled, freestanding on its single, wide tyre.

'Hang on,' she called as they accelerated away.

Rolling along on one wheel was at first a strange and unnerving experience. Kalen felt like they were falling down the lane. Jenna banked into Viking Way. His reaction was to fight the movement.

'Not like that,' she said. 'Lean with me when I turn. Try it again.' She swerved the other way, and he transferred his weight accordingly. She flashed him a thumbs up sign. 'Much better. You're a natural.'

They rode past Galactic Tower, slowed at the entrance to Cloak Way, then powered up and raced out onto the two-lane thoroughfare.

It was out here that Kalen realised he wanted a unocycle. The silent speed was addictive, and as his confidence in the gyroscope grew, his fear of falling diminished. He slid up the helmet visor and tilted his head back. The air rushed over his face and roared in his ears. Any residual memories of his claustrophobic months on the cycler were blown away in the wind.

'So, do you know much about Nikki?' Jenna called.

'Nikki?'

'Oh sorry. You probably know her as Nikel.'

Nikel? NIKEL! He leaned forward and rested his chin on her shoulder. 'You don't mean Nikel Pierce?'

Jenna's helmet nodded.

'*The* Nikel Pierce? She's your friend?'

Again, she nodded. 'Anything wrong with that?'

'No, of course not. It's amazing. All the kids at home have wallpapered their rooms with pictures of her.'

'Huh. Them and every other male under twenty.'

'You're jealous!'

'What's there to be jealous of? She's only beautiful, intelligent, artistic, sensitive, and, worst of all, nice.'

'Nothing at all, obviously. Wow! Nikel Pierce!'

They rode on, clockwise around the cloak perimeter, and in no time they had arrived at Dome 3, which housed the trekker bay. A pair of tall trees stood like sentinels at the gated entrance. Jenna swung through and came to a stop in the parking area. In one of the bays sat another unocycle. It looked much older than Jenna's and had accumulated a number of dents and scratches during what must have been a hard life.

'I should've guessed,' Jenna said. 'He's already here.'

'Sorry?'

'Nothing. Just a lovesick friend of mine.'

She led Kalen through a set of sliding doors, and they came upon a fence bordering the rectangular parking area. Through the fence, they looked over an inner guard rail to a broad, flat staging area on which sat a variety of heavy all-terrain vehicles. To their right, a steep ramp declined to an underground garage where vehicles were kept when not in use.

'Jen!'

Someone of about their age was waving at them from further around the fence line. They wandered over to meet him. He was wearing a pair of khaki canvas jeans and a lemon T-shirt with "Next Stop Jupiter" printed across the front.

'Hi Tye. This is Kalen. He's just landed from Earth.'

'Hello,' Kalen said.

Tye Brindle nodded uncertainly. He was considerably taller than Jenna, and his scruffy hair was dark brown, tinted with sandy streaks. His eyebrows were upturned, which gave him a permanent look of surprise.

'Not too late, are we?' Jenna asked.

In answer, Tye pointed at a large six-wheeled vehicle lumbering into the bay through an airlock on the far side. When it had come to a stop, they walked out to meet it. On its front corner was emblazoned the name *Rebecca*.

'It's massive,' Kalen said.

Tye nodded. 'A Nomad J Class. Basically, a land-going spacecraft. It can stay out for months if it has to.'

A door high on the front behind the driver's windows swung open. A middle-aged man stepped out and clambered down the inset rungs of a short ladder. He jumped to the ground from the bottom rung.

'That's better,' he said, inhaling deeply. 'I haven't been outside without a biosuit for six weeks. Dunno why I keep doing this.' Then he winked at Jenna. 'Oh yeah, the money.'

Kalen thought he was probably the same age as his father, maybe a little older. His complexion was swarthy, his eyes dark, the corners creased by crow's feet. Under the sweat-stained, loose-fitting coveralls, his body was lithe and muscular. A greying stubble coated his cheeks, and his hair was longish, tied in a ponytail at the back. A diamond stud glinted in one earlobe.

'How're you all doing?' he said in a slow drawl. Then he noticed Kalen. 'Haven't seen you before!'

'I only just got here,' Kalen replied.

The man extended a leathery hand. 'Pleased to meet you. Krip's the name. Krip Winters.' The firm grip squeezed his fingers painfully, but Kalen did his best not to wince. 'I recognise that accent. You're from Oz.'

'Yep.'

'Which bit?'

'Melbourne. You?'

'Nowhere you would've heard of. A little place called Boort.'

'I know it. In central Victoria. The Wimmera.' Krip was clearly surprised, so Kalen added, 'My grandma and grandpa lived in Charlton for a time.'

'Right. Not too far away at all. Small solar system, isn't it. Still, that was a long time ago. Been around the world four times since then. As well as a stint on Luna.'

'So you're not Nikel's dad?'

'Heavens no! Don't do that to me. I'm way better looking.' Then, turning back to the Nomad, he sighed reluctantly. 'Now, I've got this to look forward to. I better get started.' He popped open an access panel and operated some levers. Doors on the sides of the Nomad began to hinge upward, revealing cargo bays stuffed with dusty containers.

'So what brings you to the fourth rock?' he called over his shoulder.

'My dad.'

'Huh. Doesn't he like you?'

'He's a weatherman.'

'Oh great! Someone else to get the forecast wrong. He got a name?'

'David Rance.'

Krip stopped what he was doing. 'Rance,' he said. 'That rings a bell. This his first stint on Mars?'

'Yep. First time for both of us.'

'Fair enough. Must be thinking of somebody else.' A rising clamour near the edge of the bay caught his attention. He grimaced and said sourly, 'Oh, on your knees, everybody. Here comes God's gift to the universe.'

Kalen turned to see a crush of people filing through the gate under a swarm of flashing camera drones. They moved as one towards the *Rebecca* like a multi-legged creature. Kalen recognised the figure in their midst immediately. So confident was his stride that he seemed to almost float on the sycophantic adulation of those around him. Taller than the rest by at least half a head, with a swimmer's physique, cool, deep blue eyes, and a flawless complexion, Adam Wolf, the famous Martian firstborn, was everything Kalen had expected.

'Just one more, Adam,' cried a woman with purple hair.

He turned to face her handheld camera with a white, straight-toothed smile.

Snap! Flash!

'Perfect.'

'Hi Krip,' Adam called. 'Has Nik come out yet?'

Krip bellowed up at the open door of the vehicle. 'Nikki, luv, you're wanted outside.'

Kalen recognised the second most famous person on Mars the moment she appeared at the top of the ladder and began to climb down. As she neared the ground, her father pushed his head through the doorway and called, 'Finished in here?'

'Yep,' Krip yelled, 'close it up.'

With the door shut, Alan Pierce joined his daughter on the ground. He headed over to help Krip at the cargo hold while Nikel waved at Jenna, mouthed 'Sorry, won't be long,' then joined Adam in the middle of the media scrum.

Snap! Snap! Flash!

She and Adam hugged automatically.

Snap! Flash! Flash! Snap!

A man wearing a bleached mohawk yelled triumphantly, 'That's great, my darlings. Now let's have a cutesy, lovey one.'

Adam and Nikel embraced each other and grinned cheek to cheek with practised happy, white smiles.

Snap! Snap! Flash! Flash! Snap! Flash!

'Beautiful! There's our cover shot. Great work, people.'

Nikel whispered something to Adam. He nodded and said to the group, 'Thanks everybody; that'll do for now. See you in an hour or so.'

The paparazzi retreated as one across the bay while the two most famous Martian born walked hand in hand to join Jenna and friends.

'Welcome back,' Jenna said.

'Thanks,' Nikel replied. 'Good to see you, Tye.'

'You too.'

Kalen wasn't normally shy of girls, but there was something achingly overwhelming about Nikel in real life. While tall like most of the Martian born, she was less so than he had expected; but she was more beautiful in the flesh than in any of the myriad photos he'd seen, even in the shapeless coveralls and waisted jacket she wore. His mouth went dry. His pulse started to race. His heart felt like it was going to pound right out of his chest.

Nikel Pierce! I'm meeting Nikel Pierce!

Her head swivelled on its elegant, shapely neck to face him. The deep blue almond eyes summed him up. The full mouth curled into an easy, natural smile, quite different from the manufactured grin she presented to the cameras.

'I see you've multiplied,' she said in a voice like warm honey.

'Hello, I'm from Earth,' Kalen said stiffly.

Ugh! Cringe!

Here he was, standing in front of the most perfect, the most beautiful girl in the universe, and the best he could come up with was, 'Hello, I'm from Earth'. On the list of embarrassing things to say, it was right up there with 'Take me to your leader.'

But if Nikel noticed, she didn't say anything. Instead, she looked questioningly at Adam. 'Have you two met?'

'Not that I remember,' the firstborn said with a shake of his head. He looked down coldly upon Kalen from his two metre plus height with what could have been either disinterest or disdain. The famous, penetrating blue-eyed stare of his photos became, in real life, a cold, superior glare.

'We need to be going,' he said.

Nikel looked surprised and disappointed. 'What? Now? Straight from here?'

He smirked arrogantly and swept Kalen, Jenna, and Tye with his eyes. 'She forgets everything.' Turning back to Nikel, he added, 'I told you last week. They've brought it ahead.'

'Oh, you *did* mention that. So when do they want us?'

'Just under an hour from now.'

'Well, that's annoying,' she replied with a sigh. 'I'll have to come, then. Sorry, Jen. I was looking forward to catching up.'

'You doing a shoot?' asked Tye.

'Afraid so.' She turned to Adam. 'Something for Martian tourism, isn't it?'

'Apparently,' he nodded. 'Some sort of push for the northern Terran summer. A bit of a drag, but that's our job.'

Jenna's face lit with a passing thought. 'Maybe we could come and watch? Kalen probably hasn't been to a photo shoot before.'

Kalen certainly hadn't, but just as his hopes skyrocketed, Adam shot them down. 'It's invitation only.'

'So, invite us,' Tye snapped.

'Not up to me,' Adam replied, coolly shaking his head.

'They're very protective,' Nikel explained with an apologetic shrug to Kalen. 'But there'll be other times. You're not missing much anyway. Just a whole lot of wannabe's prancing about.'

'No, that's fine,' Kalen said, burying his disappointment. 'No problems.'

'Right,' Nikel said to Adam, 'I'll just let Dad know we're going.'

Mr Pierce's legs were protruding from one of the lower cargo bays. He had crawled in after Krip to loosen some containers that had shifted during the journey and wedged themselves in tight.

'I've got to head off, Dad,' Nikel called. 'Something's come up.'

'What? Ow! Blast!' came from inside the cargo hold.

Her father wriggled out, sucking his thumb. 'Okay luv. See you at home. I'll arrange for the ArCom to bring your things. Oh, and if I'm late, don't worry. I might go to the Black Hole for a while with Krip when we finish.'

Adam and Nikel crossed the bay and disappeared through the main entrance.

'So what d'you think?' Jenna asked.

'She's even better in real life,' Kalen replied, unable to hide his admiration.

'And Adam?' asked Tye.

'Well, he's, um, sort of, er—'

'Yeah, that about sums him up.'

'I suppose it goes with being a celebrity,' Kalen said.

Jenna turned on him sharply. 'Oh, that's just a cop out. The first ten are all celebrities of a kind. But he's the only one like that.'

'Obviously, it doesn't bother Nikel.'

Tye shook his head. 'Nah, she can't see past the whole Martian firstborn thing.'

Jenna sprung to her defence. 'That's you being jealous, Tye. Nikki's much deeper than that, and you know it.'

Suitably admonished, Tye fell quiet.

'Besides,' Jenna continued for Kalen's benefit, 'she's one of them. The ninth born. She's got no reason to be in awe of any of them. Anyway, firstborn or not, Mister Wolf's seriously messed up my plans for the afternoon. I was going to take you and Nikki out for a spin in the hills.'

'Actually, things might have worked out for the best,' Kalen replied. 'I'm not sure what time my dad's coming back. He promised he'd have some important news, and I want to be there when he gets in.'

So Jenna and Kalen parted company with Tye and arrived at Galactic Tower a few minutes later. After exchanging contact numbers and making vague plans to meet up the next sol, Kalen dismounted Jenna's unocycle and headed into the building.

Chapter 4

Kalen spent the entire afternoon on his own in the apartment. Unhappy with the way he'd set up his room that morning, he rearranged it and then sat down to see if the television viewing had improved. Channel 4 was playing re-runs of *Lost in Space*. He had seen all the episodes before, but he still got a laugh out of them.

After wiling away much of the afternoon in the company of the Robinson family, he turned it off and went to his room, where he lounged on the bed, reading an e-article on the local girl band, Rona's Riders, and listening to their latest album, *Deimos Dreaming*.

Five p.m. passed with no sign of his father. Admittedly, they hadn't discussed a specific time for his return, but in his mind, Kalen had expected him home for dinner. He purposely held off eating in anticipation, but at around 6.30 p.m., his rumbling stomach told him it was time for some toast and vegemite with a glass of orange juice. It wasn't the most creative meal, but as a filler before dinner with his father, it was adequate.

By 8.00 p.m., Kalen was becoming very concerned. He began pacing back and forth across the lounge room. Then 9.00 p.m. came and went.

He decided to try calling and was surprised to hear a familiar ringtone from his father's bedroom. Following the sound, he went in and found his father's wristwatch ringing in the drawer of the bedside table.

He sat on the side of the bed, looking at it, mystified. Could his father have somehow forgotten to take it with him? Unlikely. He never went anywhere without his watch, especially when he was travelling. Besides, it was in the drawer; he must've placed it in there intentionally. Kalen flicked through the call register. The phone hadn't been used since they'd arrived on Mars. And the only incoming calls were Kalen's: his attempt to make contact earlier in the sol, and the one just now.

As often happens when worry sets in, his mind flashed to worst case scenarios, like the crashed shuttle out near Touchdown. But the call to MarsAir confirmed his father wasn't on that flight. So, where was he? Kalen waited another hour, then a little after 10.00 p.m., he phoned Jenna. She was still up. While he waited, she went to consult her father. Jules came on the line and told him, once again, not to jump to conclusions. But this time, he *was* concerned enough to suggest they contact the MSA.

'Who?' Kalen asked, remembering that his father had mentioned it the sol before.

'The Martian Security Agency,' Jules explained. 'Sort of a cross between the police and army. Their headquarters is on the edge of the CBD. Go down to the foyer of your building. Galactic Tower, isn't it? We'll come by and run you over.'

Kalen went downstairs straight away, and within ten minutes he was on the pillion seat of Jenna's Unicruze 4, with Jules riding alongside on his older machine, something called a Monoroller according to the decal on its side.

Compared to other buildings in the city, the headquarters of the MSA was more robust in design, as if its grey, squat features were meant to suggest the organisation's strength and reliability. Parking their unocycles out the front, they walked up the broad steps into the reception area. At this time of night, there was only a uniformed agent on duty at the front desk.

'We'd like to report a missing person,' Jules said without preamble.

When she stood up they saw she was a thin but obviously athletic woman of around thirty-five. The name on her badge identified her as Agent Ellen Jonquil.

'Who's missing?' she asked.

'My dad,' Kalen replied. 'At least he's late home.'

'Late home from?'

'I don't know where he went.'

This sounded a bit lame, and Jules felt further explanation was necessary. 'Kalen—that's this lad here—and his father only arrived on Mars a couple of sols ago. Apparently, he had to go away on some sort of business. Said he'd be back early tonight, but he hasn't turned up.'

'And who are you, sir?'

'He's my dad,' Jenna replied.

'And you?'

'Jenna Quill.'

'I see.' The agent opened up the log sheet on her computer and started to type. 'How old is your father, Kalen?'

'Fifty-eight.'

'Can you describe him?'

Kalen did so.

'Any distinguishing features?'

'None.'

'What does he do; for a living, I mean?'

'He's a weatherman.'

'So, a meteorologist?'

'Yep.'

'And what time did you last see him?'

'This morning, early. Around eight o'clock.'

'So he's been gone' – she glanced up at the wall chronometer – 'fifteen hours, give or take.'

'Yep,' Kalen agreed.

'I assume you've tried to call him?'

'Yeah, but he didn't take his watch with him.'

'Does he know anybody in Asheton? Or anywhere on Mars, for that matter? Friends, family, business associates?'

The confused matters of the stranger on Earth all those months ago, that curious phrase 'Alpha in Aquarius' and the alleyway encounter spun about in Kalen's head. None of it made any sense to him, separately or together. Deep down, he realised he should have made Agent Jonquil aware of these facts, but he was worried she might think him paranoid.

'None,' he said.

She lifted her eyes from the computer screen and stared at him. 'You hesitated before answering.'

'Yeah, just tired, I suppose.'

'I see. Is your dad on any medication?'

'No.'

'So he has no health issues?'

'No.'

'Right. And you heard about the shuttle crash this morning?'

'He wasn't on it,' Kalen said. 'We checked.'

The agent closed the file. 'Okay. I've logged it.' Formalities over, she leaned forward and rested her elbows on the counter. 'Anybody unaccounted for on Mars is always a cause for concern. But we don't normally consider people missing in anything under a sol. That allows for delays, missed communication, and that sort of thing. So unless you've got any specific reason for concern, I'll pass it onto the morning shift. By that time, he'll have been missing a full sol, so we'll be able to raise an official Missing Person's Report from the information you've given me and start inquiries.'

Kalen nodded tiredly.

The agent could sense his worry and realised her official line didn't sound terribly reassuring. She offered Kalen a soft smile. 'Misadventure on Mars does happen sometimes, but it's rarely fatal. Most people reported missing eventually turn up okay. If you want to expedite things, you can send through a recent photo of him. That'll start the ball rolling if we need to get involved. Here's my card. Contact's on the bottom. If he turns up in the meantime, I'd appreciate you letting us know.'

'Sure, thanks,' Kalen said, taking the card.

He left Agent Jonquil his contact number and address at Galactic Tower. Jules left his too, as a backup, then they thanked her for her help and walked out.

As Kalen dismounted from Jenna's unocycle at the front doors of his apartment building, Jules asked him to phone them first thing in the morning to let them know what was happening.

Kalen watched them ride off. Then he entered the foyer and caught the elevator upstairs, hoping that his father had returned while they were out. But the apartment was empty.

From the montage at his bedside, he uploaded a photo of his father to his watch and transmitted it to the e-address on Agent Jonquil's card. It was about five years old, but he hadn't changed much in that time, so it would serve the purpose.

She acknowledged receipt of it promptly, then he stretched out on the bed and drifted off into a troubled sleep.

♦

Not only was it troubled, it was also very short.

At 12.10 a.m., he was woken by the door chime. Its soft musical sound dragged him into wakefulness. The urgent, energetic banging that followed hauled him out of bed. He staggered sleepily into the lounge.

'Dad?' he croaked.

Then, somewhere in the back of his mind, he remembered that his father had a key pass. He wouldn't be ringing the door chime or banging to get in.

'Who is it?' he called through the closed door, trying to focus his sleep-deprived eyes.

'It's the MSA. Open up, please.'

He was wide awake immediately. His breathing tightened to short gasps. His pulse thudded loudly in his ears. He pulled open the door and was confronted by two people in dark business suits with gold MSA badges clipped prominently to their belts. The older of the two was a large, slightly overweight man in his forties with jet black hair swept backwards over his scalp. The other, a woman probably in her late twenties, was petite in build and had closely-cut red hair. She was carrying a red folder.

'Kalen Rance?' said the man.

'That's me.'

'I believe you reported a David Rance missing earlier this evening.'

'My dad, yeah. Have you found him?'

'I'm Agent Ron Hilbride. This is Agent Bess Telford. Sorry about the late hour. May we come in?'

Kalen stood aside wordlessly as the two agents entered.

'Over here, okay?' Hilbride gestured at the lounge suite.

'Sure. Um, what's happened?'

The two agents sat down. Reluctantly, Kalen joined them.

'Before we get into that,' Hilbride replied, 'we need to be clear on something. Bess?'

The younger agent inserted a freckled hand into her folder and slid out a photograph. She showed it to Kalen and asked in a quiet, no-nonsense voice, 'Is this the photo you sent to our office earlier?'

Kalen nodded slowly. A dark cloud descended on them.

'Then I'm terribly sorry,' Hilbride said gravely, 'but I have to inform you that the man in this photo has been found deceased.'

Chapter 5

Fifteen minutes later, with unhurried efficiency, the two agents escorted Kalen up the steps and into MSA headquarters.

Their shoes clicked on the hard floor as they crossed the reception area and headed through a door into a broad office. Even at this time of night, there were people about: working at desks, strolling around, chatting at a water cooler in one corner. Kalen followed Hilbride into the centre of the office and stopped at a desk littered with documents, lists, papers, graphs, maps, and some photographs of the barren, red desert.

'We'll be right,' Hilbride said dismissively to his colleague.

Telford moved to an adjacent desk and sat down in front of her computer, close enough to hear but not to appear intrusive.

Hilbride positioned a chair on castors at the other side of his desk. 'Take a load off,' he said. 'Can I get you something? Tea? Coffee? Water?'

Coffee, Kalen thought, clutching at something familiar and comforting. 'Mrs Mack makes good coffee.'

It didn't make sense in the context of the conversation, but Hilbride recognised shock when he saw it and played along.

'Mrs Mack's, eh? Her Portuguese custard tarts aren't half bad either.' He rubbed his swollen girth lightly. 'I know from experience.'

Then he fell quiet, giving Kalen the opportunity to reply. Or to say something else. But the teenager was mute.

'You're fifteen, I believe,' encouraged Hilbride.

Kalen just nodded dumbly.

'With somebody your age, we'd normally have a responsible adult sit in with us, but I understand it was only you and your dad on Mars.'

Kalen didn't need to be reminded.

'What about the man who came with you to report him missing?' Hilbride suggested. 'Jules Quill. Would you like him here?'

'I hardly know him,' Kalen replied, his voice not much louder than a whisper. 'What time is it?'

Hilbride glanced at his watch. 'Twenty-five to one.'

'The middle of the night.' Kalen looked at his hands, flexed his fingers. 'Don't bother him,' he said. 'There's nothing he can do anyway.'

'Quite. So are you okay talking to me by yourself? Because if you're not, I can get somebody over from—'

'No, it's okay,' Kalen interrupted, more sharply than he intended. He didn't want some bureaucrat from an obscure government department sitting in, offering pretend sympathy. 'I can talk for myself.'

'I'm sure you can.' Hilbride seemed relieved. He smiled kindly and leaned back thoughtfully in his chair. 'This business about your dad, then.'

'Why's he dead? I mean, how was he killed?'

Hilbride looked surprised. 'You really don't know?'

'How could I?'

'I'm sorry if this is upsetting, Kalen, but your father was one of the passengers on board MarsAir flight 14 to Touchdown.'

The words didn't seem real at first. Kalen wanted to be sure he'd heard correctly. 'You mean the one that crashed yestersol morning?'

'Yes.'

'But that can't be!' Kalen said.

'Why do you say that?'

'I checked.'

'Yes, so you told the agent at the desk.' Hilbride placed his elbows on the chair armrests and steepled his fingers in front of him. 'Why?'

'Sorry?'

'Why would you check? You say he didn't tell you he was flying out to Touchdown. Or flying anywhere, for that matter. What would make you think he was on that flight?'

'Nothing. I didn't know what he was doing. I just heard about the crash and needed to be sure.'

'I see. So, just to clarify, two sols after you both arrive on Mars, your dad leaves you alone in Asheton to fly to Touchdown—but he tells you nothing about it.'

Kalen nodded flatly.

'Did he often do that? When you were at home on Earth, I mean.'

Kalen's head rocked slowly from side to side.

'So why would he do it here on Mars?'

Again, Kalen shook his head.

'Well, why do you *think* he was flying to Touchdown?'

'I haven't got a clue. To be honest, I still can't believe he was. The lady I spoke to at MarsAir said there was no one by the name of David Rance listed on board.'

Hilbride looked closely at the teenager sitting limply in the chair before him. 'There wasn't,' he said soberly.

Kalen's eyes flickered, wondering if he had somehow misunderstood. 'But you said—'

'The man in the photo you sent us was travelling under the name of one Robert Whelan.'

Kalen looked at him dumbfounded, confused.

'I take it you haven't heard the name before,' Hilbride continued.

'No.'

'Did your dad ever use other names back on Earth?'

'Of course not! Why would he?'

'So you don't know anybody by that name?'

'I already said so, didn't I!'

Hilbride, an experienced agent who'd spent many years on the New South Wales police force before moving to Mars, rode the outburst of anger easily. He leaned his bulk forward and rested it on the desk. Very deliberately, he said, 'When he left, do you remember what he said? Think before you answer. Be as specific as you can.'

But Kalen couldn't think straight, let alone be specific about events that happened the previous morning. Everything was spinning around in his head. Hilbride looked at him with an unwavering gaze. Kalen knew the man was trying to help, so he squeezed his eyes shut and tried to remember. But remember what? There was so little to tell.

'Dad was never much for words,' he said vaguely. 'It was just silly, unimportant stuff. You know, things about groceries and making sure I could get my hands on the money in his account.'

'He said that? He wanted you to have access to funds?'

'Yeah, but he was only being . . . prudent. That's what he said.'

'With good reason, it seems.'

'Then we joked a bit about me buying a unocycle while he was away. Huh, we actually joked!'

Hilbride picked up on Kalen's incredulous tone. 'Why do you say it like that?'

'Oh, no reason. It's just that I don't remember Dad joking much before. He was always so serious. Then, the one time he does lighten up, he goes and gets himself killed. It's so unfair.'

Hilbride nodded heavily. 'In this job, I see a lot that's not fair. Was that all he said before he left?'

'Yestersol morning it was. But the sol before, we had lunch in the city. In a little hamburger joint. He told me there were some things he had to—how did he say it?—attend to, I think. Yeah, there were some things he had to attend to. He said they were complicated, and he couldn't talk about them. He was going to explain everything when he got back. Huh.'

'What is it?'

'Well, that was the thing about my dad—he was always big on promises, just not so big on keeping them.'

Hilbride nodded noncommittally.

'There was something else, too,' said Kalen.

'Oh?'

'I had an hour to kill on my own in the city. An ArCom started to follow me.'

'Follow you?'

Kalen nodded. 'I couldn't shake it, so I hid in an alley. But somehow it found me. Then a man turned up. Gave me a hell of a fright, I can tell you. Definitely not someone you want to meet in a—'

'Dark alley?'

'Right.'

'So what happened?'

'The ArCom asked me if I was David Rance's son.'

'It actually said that; it knew your father's name?'

Kalen nodded.

'Where is this alley, Kalen?'

'I don't know exactly. North of the CBD somewhere.'

'Can you describe him, this man with the ArCom?'

Kalen shrugged as he cast his mind back. 'He was big. Taller than his ArCom.'

'Really?'

'Yeah. And heavyset. Not fat. More like big-boned.'

'How was he dressed?'

'Not sure. It was dark, you know, with shadows. All I can say is he had on some sort of long coat.'

'Good. What about his general colouring?'

'Couldn't tell.'

'His hair?'

'Like I said, it was dark. But I got the idea it was very fair, even white.'

'White?'

'Maybe. I can't be sure.'

Kalen sighed heavily. He knew this was of little help, but he was doing the best he could. He also knew this would be a good time to mention the odd events that presaged their journey to Mars. The stranger who came to their house. The mysterious phrase *Alpha in Aquarius*. The hasty travel arrangements. Maybe it was the late hour or the shock, but at the moment he wasn't in a trusting mood, so he kept it to himself.

Anyway, Hilbride was quickly moving off in a different direction. 'According to the log, your dad was a meteorologist.'

'That's right.'

'Could those things he had to attend to have anything to do with his work?'

'I doubt it.'

The agent sighed. 'Yeah, me too. There's a small weather recording station at Touchdown. We spoke to the guy who runs it.'

'What'd he say?'

'Nothing of any use. He'd never heard of Robert Whelan or David Rance. Nor was he expecting a visitor from Earth. And their work certainly doesn't involve any of the cloak-and-dagger stuff your father seemed to be caught up in. To be honest, it beats me what it is meteorologists do on Mars anyway. Cold and dry, sol in, sol out, with the occasional dust storm thrown in. That's it.' He began to forage through the clutter of papers on his desk. 'Now where's it gone?' he muttered to himself. 'I gotta do something about this mess.'

Telford looked up from her computer. 'What've you lost?'

'Passenger manifest.'

'Here, borrow mine.' She passed over a sheet of paper from one of the neatly stacked piles on her own desk.

'Thanks.' He gave it to Kalen. 'Have a look at this.'

Kalen took the page and ran his eyes through the list of names: Raymond Gibbs, Damian King, Ping Lu, Robert Whelan, Jenny Wannamaker.

'There are five people here. How do you know Dad booked the flight as Robert Whelan? Why not Raymond Gibbs or Damian King, or—well, I suppose it wouldn't be Ping or Jenny, would it.'

'Good! Clever lad! You're thinking clearly. Not bad for this time of night. And given what's happened.'

Hilbride plucked a clear ziplock bag from the shelf behind him, then took out the blue document holder Kalen had seen his father stuff into his jacket pocket. It was dirty, blackened, and wrinkled at the edges, like it had been burnt. The agent opened it and took out a small plastic, burgundy-coloured card.

'Because of this,' he said, handing it across the desk.

It was a Planet of Mars passport. On the front was a photograph of his father, identified as Robert Whelan.

'Where did you find this?' Kalen asked.

'On the bod . . . er, with your dad.'

'Now you're telling me he had a false passport.'

'Yes. I'm guessing you know that's highly illegal.'

Kalen nodded slowly. 'So, are you saying Dad travelled to Mars on a false passport?'

'No, we checked that with the immigration people. They confirmed his journey here was all legit, but for some reason he saw fit to obtain a second passport.'

'Here on Mars?'

'Maybe, but not necessarily. It could've been arranged on Earth before you left.'

'But why?'

Hilbride shrugged. 'Same reason anybody gets a false passport, I suppose. To move around unnoticed.'

'He didn't need to hide!' Kalen protested.

'Clearly your father thought otherwise, Kalen. And we need to find out why.'

Kalen's eyes flashed to the folder. He asked timidly, 'Is there anything else in there?'

The man looked up sharply. 'Why do you ask?'

'Dunno. Just curious.'

'I see,' Hilbride said, settling back. 'Well, apart from his passport, we found a key pass to your apartment and some maps of Touchdown and the surrounding region. The maps are available online; any computer could have printed them out. They don't tell us anything we don't already know.' Suddenly, he was caught in the grip of a deep yawn and glanced at his watch. 'Let's have a break. Need the conveniences?'

'No, no, I'm okay.'

'You won't mind if I nick out and splash the boots, then? Grab a cuppa if you like. Bess will show you where everything is.' He looked at his colleague. 'Dead time.'

Kalen watched him weave his way through the desks and disappear through a doorway. Then he looked over at Agent Telford, working at her desk.

'What was that Agent Hilbride just said?' he asked.

'Sorry? I wasn't—'

'About dead time.'

'Oh, that.' She placed her scribe on the desk and eased back into her chair. 'You probably know that a Martian sol is longer than a Terran day.'

'Yeah, of course.'

'Well, when Agent Hilbride first came to Mars a few years back, the government was trialling a different system of timekeeping. Every morning at one o'clock, time officially stopped for about thirty-nine minutes so Earth could catch up. This kept the two planets in sync, which was good for business communications and such.'

'Time stopped?'

She smiled. 'The clocks did. It was called 'dead time'. Naturally, night workers hated it—it made their shifts longer—so they decided that if the clocks stopped working, they would too. In the end, common sense prevailed, and Mars went back to the old system of uninterrupted twenty-four-hour sols. But the habit of stopping work for a time at night stuck. Officially, it's frowned upon, of course, but no one seriously polices it. Those night shifters old enough to remember, like Hilbride, still take their long break.'

Kalen nodded slowly to himself. 'Huh, dead time.'

The poignancy of the name wasn't lost on him.

Bess Telford also made the connection, if belatedly, and her smile vanished. 'Oh, that was a bit tactless, Kalen. Sorry. Come on, let's get a cuppa.'

♦

Hilbride returned in around twenty minutes, not the thirty-nine Kalen expected.

His questions continued for several more hours. They seemed largely irrelevant to Kalen, covering aspects of their life on Earth. David's work. His social contacts, scant as they were. Kalen's late mother. When she died, and how. What events had transpired to bring Kalen and his father to Mars.

The longer they continued, the more uptight Kalen became. Each new question to which he didn't know the answer highlighted how little he really knew about his father's life.

By the time they were finished, it had just gone 5.30 a.m. Kalen was exhausted and very frustrated. Hilbride slumped back in his chair and rubbed his eyes. 'I think that'll do for now,' he said. 'I really appreciate your cooperation, Kalen, and at such a difficult time too. You've been a trooper. But you must understand why I've had to ask all these questions.'

In truth, Kalen did, but by now he wasn't feeling very agreeable. 'Can I go home?'

Hilbride exchanged an awkward glance with Telford.

'That's the other thing,' he said. 'Something of a complication, I'm afraid.'

Kalen wondered what could be more complicated than being orphaned on Mars and then finding out his dead father had been leading some sort of secret life.

Hilbride quickly brought him up to speed. 'Technically, you're an unaccompanied minor.'

So that was why he'd been dragged out of the apartment and carted down to MSA headquarters in the middle of the night! He was incensed by his treatment. His father getting killed wasn't his fault, and he said so in no uncertain terms.

'No one's saying it's your fault,' Hilbride said, patting the air in a placating manner, 'but it does put you in a difficult position. Thing is, we can't let you go back to your apartment alone.'

'So what am I supposed to do? Live on the streets?'

'We don't have street people here, Kalen. While I was out earlier, I got in touch with Jules Quill. You're friendly with his daughter, I believe.'

'I haven't known her very long, but yeah, I suppose.'

'Good. They've agreed to come and take you back to their place. You don't have to go with them, of course, but I would encourage you to. The alternative is detention downstairs.'

Outwardly, Kalen was a little peeved that he was losing control of his life and that even his accommodation details were being rearranged without his consent. Inwardly, though, he realised the MSA had a job to do, and that those who didn't know his father would naturally look upon his behaviour as suspicious. And by association, he, Kalen, could be viewed in the same way. Yes, they had an obligation to be careful.

'When will they be here?' he asked.

'In about a quarter of an hour.'

'Can I wait out the front?'

'As long as you promise not to run off.'

Where could I possibly run to?

He just grunted and got to his feet, eager to be out of the office, which suddenly seemed claustrophobic. As he was leaving, he turned and said, 'Just one other thing.'

'Yes?'

'When can I see him?'

The agent looked introspective for a moment. 'It's not necessary from our point of view, Kalen. The photo you sent is good enough for identification purposes.'

'I want to. One last time.'

Hilbride nodded slowly. 'I can understand that. And it's your right, of course. Come by later in the morning. That should give us time to, er, prepare. Let's say 11.00 a.m.'

'I'll be here.'

'Ask for Bess or me. And make sure you bring someone with you.'

Chapter 6

Sitting on the steps at the front of the MSA building, Kalen was completely alone for the first time since being given the terrible news.

He squirmed to get comfortable, then sat very quiet and still. Gradually, those deeper emotions he'd been suppressing rose to the surface. Tears welled into his eyes, and an uncontrollable trembling shook his shoulders. He drew his knees up under his chin, wrapped his arms tightly around them, and felt himself sinking into a deep, black well.

He didn't know how long he'd been down there when a familiar voice called his name. Lifting his head and squinting into the early pinkish light of the Martian morning, he saw Jenna and Jules standing over him.

'Poor lad.' Jules placed a comforting hand on his shoulder. 'You should've called us.'

'You would've been asleep.'

'We'd still have come,' Jenna said.

They would've too, Kalen realised. They were kind people. He smiled weakly in appreciation.

'Come on,' Jules said, 'let's get you back home.'

Kalen walked between them down the steps to the two parked unocycles and threw a leg over the pillion of Jenna's.

'Do you need anything from your place?' she asked, handing him a helmet and pulling on hers.

'Not just now,' he replied quietly.

In no time, it seemed, they had arrived at the shop. Kalen was led upstairs to the little apartment over the store Jules and Jenna shared. It was pokey but comfortable.

'You must be exhausted,' Jules said. 'You probably want to lie down for a few hours.'

'Maybe something to eat first,' suggested Jenna.

In truth, Kalen wasn't very hungry, but when she pushed a bowl of Wheat Sticks drowned in milk in front of him, he forced himself to consume half of it. When he could eat no more, he pushed the bowl away, and she showed him up to her room, where he settled himself on her single bed and fell into an exhausted sleep.

♦

His internal biological alarm woke him. For a time, he just lay still in a surreal, dreamlike state, thinking about his life on Earth. Then events on Mars came rushing back. A crushing feeling filled his chest.

The MSA had told him his father was dead!

He jerked up into a sitting position, his pale face plastered in a cold sweat. He looked around. He'd been so tired when he collapsed onto the bed that he hadn't taken any notice of where he was. A small room, he saw, simply furnished with Jenna's bed, an inbuilt robe, and a dressing table. A watercolour of a Martian landscape on one wall. Beside it, a photo of a smiling Jules with his arms around a couple of ArComs he'd presumably repaired. On the dressing table stood a framed photograph of Jenna's family. In it, she was no more than four or five years old, standing between Jules and a roundish woman he assumed was her mother.

Then he glanced at the clock on the bedside table. 10.15 a.m. The morning was half gone. He threw off the light coverlet Jules or Jenna had kindly laid over him, slipped into his clothes, and headed out into the lounge room. There was no one about, so he raced downstairs, through the workroom, and out into the shop.

Jenna was sitting on a stool behind the counter, perusing a magazine on her e-reader. At his arrival, she looked up.

'Hi. How're you feeling?' she asked.

'You don't want to know.'

She nodded, understanding. 'We didn't expect to see you for hours.'

'I wish you'd woken me. I'm gonna be late.'

'What for?'

'The MSA. I'm due back there at eleven o'clock.'

'They can't expect you to spend half the night there and then come back the next morning as well.'

'It's my choice, Jenna. For my dad. I need to see him.'

She looked away, faintly uncomfortable. 'Oh, right.'

'They told me not to come alone.'

'Ah, then there's a problem. Dad had to go around to see Mrs Mack about my accident. She threatened him with lawyers if he didn't come straight away.'

'Well, can *you* come? You don't have to go in, but you could just hang around and wait while I do what I have to do.'

'I could,' she said hesitantly, 'except that Dad's got me minding the shop. I can't just walk out and leave it.'

'But if I turn up on my own, they'll probably put me in detention,' explained Kalen.

'What?'

'I dunno. Something about being an unaccompanied minor. Seems stupid to me.'

'Hm. Just a moment.' Jenna tapped on her watch. 'Dad,' she said. 'Yeah, it's me. Oh, are you? So you shouldn't be long, then? Okay. It's just that Kalen's up. Yeah, as good as can be expected, I suppose. He says he's gotta go back to the MSA at eleven o'clock. Not by himself, no. You sure? Alright. See you soon.' Terminating the call, she said, 'He's on his way.'

'Thanks,' said Kalen.

While waiting for Jules to return, he decided to save time by going back upstairs to shower. It only took a few minutes, and just as he walked back into the shop, Jules returned.

'Well, we're not being sued,' he announced proudly.

'You really will have to put on the restraints while you're working on them,' said Jenna.

'You sound like Mrs Mack. You know how much I hate doing that. It seems inhuman somehow.'

'But they *are* inhuman, Dad! They're machines.'

'I know that, Jenna.'

'Do you? Sometimes I wonder. Anyway, we haven't got time for this. Kalen's running late.'

'Okay, go, go,' he said.

'And don't forget, I'm having lunch with Mum.'

'Oh, she's back in town, isn't she!' he replied grimly. 'I thought I felt a chill in the air. Give her my, er—'

'Best?'

'No, on second thought, I already gave her that. It wasn't enough. Just say hello. And the same to her toy boy.'

'Dad! Not in front of Kalen!'

'Sorry.'

♦

'Just thinking,' Kalen said as he settled onto the back of the unocycle behind Jenna. 'Maybe I should brush my teeth and get my jacket. We got time to go to the apartment first?'

'It'll be a rush,' she replied, glancing at her watch, 'but if I ride like a mad thing, we should just make it.'

She backed the unocycle out of the stand, spun about on the spot, and accelerated away, ducking and weaving through the traffic. Seven minutes later, they pulled up outside Galactic Tower.

'Wanna come up?' Kalen asked, leaping off the pillion.

'Sure. If you like.'

Jenna locked the unocycle and followed him inside. The concierge at the desk had obviously heard about the shuttle crash and wanted to make some expression of sympathy, but Kalen had neither the time nor the emotional strength to face it just now, so he led Jenna past without stopping.

The elevator doors opened on level four. They rushed along the corridor and burst into the apartment.

'Won't be long,' he said, disappearing into the bathroom.

While she waited, Jenna looked around in admiration and just a trace of envy at the plush apartment. Then she stood before the window, taking in the expanse of Asheton.

'Great view you've got from up here,' she called.

Kalen mumbled back something incomprehensible through a mouthful of toothbrush, then, moments later, reappeared and raced through to his room, calling, 'Nearly ready.'

Jenna followed him and propped herself in the doorway. On the wall opposite, she noticed his wooden crucifix. She had been wondering about the stoic way he was handling the sudden loss of his father. Maybe that was the answer.

'I didn't pick you for somebody religious,' she said.

'I'm not,' Kalen replied, shrugging on his jacket and twiddling with the collar. 'Why?' Then, in the mirror, he saw her point at the crucifix. 'Oh that. No, it belonged to my mum. Dad gave it to me after she died. Said she wanted me to have it.'

'Like an heirloom.'

'I suppose. Partly anyway'

'Why only partly?'

He raked a comb through his hair. 'Well, having it close makes it seem like she's never far away. I think she knew that, and that's why she wanted me to have it.'

'That's sort of religious, isn't it?'

Kalen's father was never a spiritual man, and, with the passing of his mother and grandparents buried deep in his past, the question of whether something was religious or not was one Kalen had never been forced to confront.

He had no answer for Jenna.

And she didn't demand one. Her attention had moved to the photomontage on his bedside table. She stepped into the room to examine it more closely. Three people were pictured there: a man in his mid-forties, and beside him, a woman holding up a wobbly toddler.

'I'm guessing this is you with your mum and dad.'

Kalen knew without looking which photo she was talking about. He gave himself a final inspection in the mirror and joined her. In the image, he and his father looked perfectly ordinary. But not his mother. Her face was twisted and blurred. It lacked definition, and the fingers of one hand were fused together.

'She was burnt,' Kalen explained, sensing an unspoken question. 'Really badly. Third degree.'

Jenna absorbed this for a moment. Finally, she asked, 'In an accident?'

'I suppose.'

She turned to him in surprise. 'You mean you don't know?'

'It's something Dad never talked about.'

'When did it happen?'

'Don't know that either. Not exactly. Sometime before I was born. I was only four when she died, so I don't remember much about her. But I do remember the burns. They're not something you forget.'

'No, I suppose not.'

◆

They arrived at MSA headquarters with just under five minutes to spare.

There was a different person on duty at the reception desk: a broad-shouldered, thirty-something man identified by his name tag as Agent Louis Delaney.

'Can I help you?' he said

Suddenly, Kalen looked unwell. The gravity of what he was about to do had finally hit him. He had trouble thinking of the right words, and when he finally managed to, he couldn't assemble them in any sort of coherent order.

Jenna realised what was happening and took the initiative. 'My friend here needs to see . . . what are their names, Kalen?'

Kalen pulled himself together and forced the names out. 'Hilbride or Telford.'

'I'll just check for you,' replied the agent. 'Kalen, is it?'

'Kalen Rance,' Jenna confirmed.

Delaney made a quick call, then replaced the handset. 'If you'd just like to wait over there, Agent Hilbride will be with you shortly.'

But they hadn't even reached the chairs on the wall before the doorway to the inner office opened, and Ron Hilbride came out to greet them.

'Very punctual,' he said. 'Excellent! And this must be Jenna.'

'Yes,' she replied.

'How do you do?' He shook her hand with a gentle formality. 'You can come through part of the way if you like, but the actual viewing will need to be conducted in private.'

Jenna understood and joined them as they headed through another door and along a pale corridor that had several rooms off each side. Hilbride led his visitors through one on the left. Hung on the walls inside were several pieces of art—nondescript watercolours, no doubt chosen for their abstract calming qualities. Beneath the largest were clustered some soft chairs, and opposite was a door labelled "Viewing Room".

Hilbride said, 'You can take a seat there, Jenna. We shouldn't be long.'

Jenna lowered herself into one of the chairs and watched Kalen and the agent disappear through the door.

♦

The viewing room was short and narrow, with a large rectangular window on one wall. Through the glass pane, in the middle of the floor, Kalen saw a gurney set at waist height. On it lay a figure shrouded by a plain, mint green sheet. An older woman in a white isolation suit stood waiting to one side.

Hilbride explained, 'I'm afraid your father's been exposed to the atmosphere, so it's too dangerous to go into the room with him. But you'll be able to see him perfectly well from here.'

Kalen felt a trembling sensation rise deep in his core. He tensed his entire body, then released it suddenly. That seemed to help. But now his arms and legs felt like lead weights. His breathing laboured.

Experience had made Hilbride sensitive to these signs of discomfit. 'Are you quite sure you want to do this, Kalen? It's very gutsy, but, as I said earlier, not strictly necessary.'

Kalen nodded with sharp little jerks of his head. 'I have to. It's not for the MSA; it's for me.'

'Then, of course, you must.'

The agent sidled closer in a gesture of professional comfort and nodded through the glass to the woman. She approached the sheet and carefully folded back one end to reveal the head and face.

Kalen gasped, then exhaled slowly.

In spite of the news reports, the false passport, and Hilbride's explanation of events, he had been tenaciously clinging to the hope that someone had made an error, that they'd become confused and labelled the body incorrectly, or made some other mistake that would at least admit the possibility his father was still alive somewhere.

But as his eyes settled on the cold, pale body displayed before him, that possibility evaporated.

His first thought was how small and thin his father looked under that sheet. He recognised the features, of course. The curve of that proud nose, the stern swell of the brow, the line of those thin, unsmiling lips, and the close-cropped hair streaked with grey. But there in that room, they seemed diminished somehow. The nose was no longer proud; it was just a nose. The brow was no longer stern; it was just a brow. The lips no longer unsmiling; just lips. The body's essence had departed, leaving only a characterless, empty husk.

'Death takes everything away,' he whispered.

'Not everything, Kalen. We still have our memories.'

He turned to face the kindly man. 'But that's the thing, Agent Hilbride. We didn't make any memories. It was only in the last couple of sols that I thought—'

'What?'

'Well, that I was starting to get to know him. But I was wrong. I didn't know him at all.'

♦

Ten minutes later, Jenna was still trying to work out if the paintings on the walls were portraits, landscapes, or some combination of the two when the door reopened and Hilbride ushered Kalen back out.

He looked utterly drained, like he had run a marathon.

She got to her feet and approached him timidly. 'Are you alright?'

He nodded wordlessly.

'Is it, um . . ?' she began awkwardly.

'Yeah. It's him—was him. But—'

'But what?'

'Dunno. It's not how I imagined it would be.'

'Did he look asleep?' Jenna asked. 'I heard my dad say that about my gran when she died.'

'Not exactly. Peaceful, maybe. Like someone who's—'

'Found all the answers?' Hilbride ventured. 'I quite like the idea of that. Tell me, are you religious? It can be a help if you are.'

Jenna had touched on the same question not an hour before. Maybe that's what death does: it forces us to ask the big questions, to look for more, to confront our own mortality.

But Kalen still had no answer.

And, like Jenna, Agent Hilbride didn't insist on one.

'It doesn't matter,' he said. 'Most people eventually find what they need.'

Chapter 7

Kalen said little as Jenna threaded her arm through his and walked with him down the steps to her parked Unicruze. She mounted, and Kalen climbed on behind, curling his arms around her. He was drawn to her warmth after the coldness of the viewing room.

The unocycle's gyro hummed to life, and they rode off down the street towards the city. Several blocks along, Kalen realised they weren't going to her apartment.

'Don't you remember?' she said when he queried her. 'I'm having lunch with Mum.'

'Oh yeah, sorry. Forgot. You sure you want me there? I mean, I'm not invited.'

'Well, not strictly, maybe. But Mum won't mind.'

'To be honest, Jenna,' he said, 'I'm not really in the mood.'

She swung her helmet around to face him. 'You mightn't realise it, Kalen, but you need people around you. And you've got to eat. Besides, I'd like someone there with me. I'm always outnumbered at these lunches, even when it's just me and Mum.'

Kalen acquiesced. He didn't feel remotely like being sociable, but neither did he have the fight to decline.

Jenna turned off Cloak Way and followed a road that bordered a broad, grassy area on their left. They turned through a gate with a sign that read "Sojourner River Park" and came to a stop in a section of the parking area set aside for patrons of The Boathouse.

Kalen dismounted while Jenna locked the Unicruze, kicked out the stand, and pulled off her helmet. Her long blond hair tumbled out into the breeze. She noticed Kalen looking at her.

'What is it?' she asked.

'Sorry?'

'You're staring.'

He looked away hastily. 'Oh no, it's just—well, I'm glad you're here.'

'Me?'

'Someone. Anyone.'

'Oh.'

She seemed disappointed, and he realised how he had sounded.

'No, I didn't mean it like that.' He paused for a few moments, then continued. 'I feel disconnected, Jenna. Like everything's been ripped away from me. It's good having you around, you know, to talk to.'

She touched him lightly on the arm and smiled sympathetically. 'Come on. You'll feel better with some food inside you.'

They walked beneath the shade of some large, knobbly oak trees and joined a winding path that descended through thickly planted garden beds to a terraced area with tables and chairs. The rich smell of wet soil and plants filled Kalen's nostrils, so he wasn't surprised when, a little further down, they came upon the green Sojourner River. A fleet of small boats was moored side by side to a landing at its edge.

To their left, a two-storey building rose out of the greenery, its upper level surrounded on the three sides in view of the water by a veranda crammed with table settings.

'Looks expensive,' Kalen said.

'Don't worry, Mum's new partner's rolling in it,' Jenna replied. 'He'll shout. If he doesn't, Dad'll cover it.'

The Boathouse had that bright and breezy informality common to many waterside eateries. The furniture was made of synthetic wood, and the tables were draped in blue and white chequered tablecloths set with gleaming silver cutlery. On one wall was a bar with a backdrop of colourful liquor bottles.

A young woman, in her late twenties and neatly attired in a black skirt and pastel pink shirt with matching spiky hair, saw them enter and positioned herself at the booking desk.

'Table in the name of Erica Paton,' Jenna said, adding in an aside to Kalen, 'Mum uses her maiden name now.'

The clerk checked her booking system and said, 'Yes, for three.'

'That's right, but can we squeeze in another one?'

The clerk tapped in the adjustment. 'No problems,' she replied crisply. 'You're upstairs. Table seven.' She waved her hand vaguely at a staircase. 'Straight up there and around to your left.'

The breeze was more blustery on the upper balcony. Cooled by the river below, it swirled around them and gently fluttered the tablecloths. In the back of his mind, Kalen knew it was merely the result of some vast artificial circulation system, but with the nearby water, the boats, and the profusion of plant life, the illusion was impressive.

Business wasn't especially brisk, and as he followed Jenna across the floor, he spotted her mother sipping a cool, fizzy drink with a small plastic umbrella stuck in it. Ten years older than the woman in the photo on Jenna's bedroom wall, she had aged into a buxom lady with makeup plastered on with a trowel and fair hair left long in a soft flowing style which was rather too young for her. Her grey blue eyes darted about, perhaps with uncertainty, until they settled on her approaching daughter.

'Ah, there you are, dear,' she said when they reached her. She spoke loudly, making sure everybody around could hear her. 'I was starting to think you'd changed your mind.'

'Not if Richard's shouting,' Jenna said.

Erica's eyes said, *Don't be cheeky*, but in deference to Kalen, she bit her tongue and pecked her daughter on the cheek. 'This is a face I don't know.'

Jenna introduced them, adding, 'I didn't think you'd mind if I brought him along.'

Erica ran a critical eye over the wiry, rather glum teen with dark eyes standing a little behind Jenna. Is he a suitable friend for my daughter, she wondered? Why is he so pale? So tired-looking? For one horrified moment, she suspected he had been taking something. Kids on Earth managed to get their hands on illicit substances. But no, this was Mars. Controls here were much tighter. Eventually, she decided to reserve judgement until she knew more about him. She broke into a bright smile. 'Not at all,' she said. 'I'm very pleased to meet you, Kalen. You're not Martian born, are you?'

'He's just arrived,' Jenna explained.

'Excellent! The more, the merrier,' she enthused, adding with an impatient glance at the door, 'And we could do with another one still. What *can* be keeping him?'

On cue, a tallish and quite handsome man appeared at the top of the stairs and walked easily towards them. Erica got to her feet, her eyes alight, and waved to him with little-girlish enthusiasm. 'Yoo-hoo! Over here, Richard. Richard, this way.'

A couple at a nearby table looked at her and hid smirks behind raised hands.

'Alright, Mum,' Jenna said, cringing, 'he's old enough to find his way over.'

Barely, Kalen thought. *He can't be much past his mid-twenties.*

In fact, Richard Albright was thirty-five, but he was blessed with one of those boyish faces that had people guessing his age at anything between twenty-five and forty.

'Don't fuss, Erica,' he said before planting a kiss on her eagerly-offered cheek. 'Hello Jen. Great to see you again.'

'Hi, this is my new friend, Kalen.'

Richard sat down, extended a friendly, well-manicured hand across the table, and shook Kalen's warmly. 'Good to meet you.'

Up close, he wasn't quite as handsome as he'd seemed from a distance. His nose was a little too large, and seemed to roam all over his face. The brown eyebrows were bushy, the mouth fleshy and pouting.

'Did you get everything done?' Erica asked.

'Pretty much. The guy I've been dealing with wasn't there, but I spoke to his offsider. He seemed to be across our contract. Main pump production's running to schedule. A slight hitch with a batch of spares, but as long as there are no major hiccups in the first few weeks, I dare say we can make do.'

Kalen had picked up the spoon from the sugar bowl and was stirring the crystals absentmindedly.

Erica noticed, and she seemed affronted at his lack of exuberance for her partner's pump.

'Richard's in water, Kalen,' she boomed.

'Usually of the hot variety,' Richard laughed, 'but that's another story. I'm a hydrologist.'

'Such important work,' put in Erica, rubbing his back affectionately. 'Richard's so clever.'

He smiled at her indulgently. 'Not so clever, really. I'm just part of a team working down on South Cap. We're trying to free up some of that ice so we can pump it up here to Asheton. Should keep us supplied for the next century or two.'

Then mercifully, before he started recounting the history of water distribution on the red planet, a prim waitress arrived to take their orders.

'Barbequed steak for me,' Richard said. 'Medium rare. And I think the spring vegetables.'

'And I'll have the vegetarian pasta,' chimed in Erica. 'Small, please, with a side salad.' In an aside to Kalen, she added lightly, 'I do try to watch what I eat. We might weigh two-thirds less here, but we still burst out in all the wrong places just the same.'

'You're just right for me, Erica,' said Richard, who sensed she was fishing for a compliment.

Erica giggled with loud delight and looked around to see who was watching.

Jenna slumped lower and groaned behind her menu.

Erica heard. 'And what's that for, Miss?'

'Nothing. Just my stomach rumbling.'

'Right, well, we're here to fix that,' Richard said. 'Order up.'

Jenna splashed out on a plate of fish and salad.

'Good choice,' Erica said. She turned to Kalen. 'And what about you, dear? Don't stint yourself. It's on Richard tosol.'

'Thanks,' Kalen mumbled, 'but I don't feel like eating.'

'Nonsense, a growing lad like you!'

'Mum.'

'Don't let the light gravity fool you. You've still got to keep up your strength.'

'Mum!'

'When I first arrived here, I thought I'd be doing away with diets, but—'

'MUM!'

Erica turned to her daughter impatiently. 'What is it, Jen?'

'Kalen said he's not hungry.'

'That so?' Richard, like Erica, had noticed Kalen's gaunt condition, dark eyes, and now, lack of appetite. In a tactful tone, he asked, 'Not feeling so good?'

'Something like that,' Kalen replied quietly.

Erica, who thought all teenagers were permanently hungry, tried to make light of it. 'Just the excitement of arriving on Mars, I expect. Not to worry. If you do get peckish, I'm sure Jen won't mind sharing her chips.'

Richard turned back to the waitress, who had been standing patiently to one side. 'Just the three mains, then. Can we have a couple of glasses of the house red too? And maybe a jug of iced water.'

It all arrived with pleasing speed.

Richard forked a large chunk of slightly bloody steak into his mouth. 'Mm, up to their usual standard,' he said, forcing his syllables around it. 'Now, what's your story, Kalen? I assume you're not here by yourself.'

Jenna looked daggers at him. They struck home.

'What is it?' he said, swallowing hurriedly. 'Have I put my foot in it? Something I'm famous for, unfortunately.'

'Don't worry,' Kalen replied with an understanding shake of his head. 'You couldn't have known. I came here with my dad.'

'Oh yes.'

'But I'm on my own now.'

'How so?' asked Erica, loading her fork without any inkling of what was to come.

'You heard about the shuttle that crashed, I suppose?' This got their attention. He braced himself for the flood of sympathy that was sure to follow. 'My dad was on it.'

Forks paused mid-flight, then floated slowly back onto plates.

'You don't mean to say . . . oh, how terrible!' Erica exclaimed. 'Jenna, why didn't you warn us?'

'My!' said Richard, followed by, 'Goodness.' Then he finally managed to string the complete sentence together: 'My goodness me. No wonder you're not eating.'

'So what's happening?' Erica asked. 'I mean, do you have somewhere to stay?'

Jenna prised loose an unexpected bone from her fish and laid it on the side of her plate. 'With us,' she said firmly.

'Your father's looking after him!' Erica cried. She couldn't keep the outrage out of her voice. 'He can't even look after those tin pot machines he—'

'Don't start, Mum!' Jenna didn't like anybody demeaning her father, especially not her mother, now that she'd abandoned them. 'We're *both* looking after him.'

'Ah, then you're in good hands,' Richard said diplomatically. He wasn't quite sure what else to say, so he renewed his onslaught on the steak and headed off in a different tack. 'So what have they told you about the crash?'

'Not much.' For something to do with his hands, Kalen reached over to Jenna's plate, stole a chip, and pushed it into his mouth. 'Just that it went down not far from Touchdown.'

Richard nodded in agreement. 'That's what I heard. Eighty-two kilometres south-west, I believe. And what are they saying about the cause?'

Kalen shrugged. 'Just an accident, as far as I know.'

Richard's eyes narrowed. He picked up his wine glass and leaned back, swirling the cherry-coloured liquid about thoughtfully. 'So that's the official line.'

Something about the man's tone disturbed Kalen. 'Why do you say it like that?'

'I probably shouldn't say anything, really.'

Kalen wasn't going to let him get away with that. 'But?'

Richard scratched his chin, still hesitating.

Kalen pushed harder. 'It was my dad who got killed out there. I've got a right to know.'

'Yes, yes, of course you have.' Richard replaced his glass on the table and wiped his mouth with a napkin. 'Well, as it happens, I know the pilot of the freighter that was first on the scene.'

Kalen remembered it from the newsflash: 'The *Forever Sky*.'

'That's the one. I should explain that I'm an amateur pilot. Comes in handy out in the field. Anyway, it wasn't reported in the news, but he said he'd swear on a stack of Bibles that it was no accident.'

'Why?'

'A couple of reasons. Firstly, there were signs of heat damage in the wreckage.'

'It crashed. There should be, shouldn't there?'

'Not in this case. The Cloud Master—that's the model of the shuttle—is electrically powered. No fuel on board whatsoever. You with me? There's no fuel to burn. And secondly, Mars's atmosphere is mainly CO_2. Carbon Dioxide. If anything was inclined to burn—say the batteries, though that's unlikely the way they're made now—the atmosphere would snuff it out before it got started.'

'But there *was* heat,' Kalen protested. 'I saw my dad's document holder. It was all singed.'

'Heat, yes. But not from the crash.'

'Then what?'

Richard lowered his voice a little. 'According to chatter around the flying community, there were hints of charring on some pieces of the fuselage. Know what I'm saying?'

Kalen thought he did, but he needed to be sure.

'There was an explosion?'

Richard nodded soberly. 'Not just an explosion, I'm afraid. Someone blew it out of the sky.'

Kalen froze in his seat, not even drawing breath for long seconds. He just sat staring at Richard in disbelief.

Then, almost of their own accord, his legs thrust him into a standing position. His chair crashed backwards. The tablecloth snagged on his belt, upsetting the wine glasses and jug of water. Erica ended up nursing her bowl of pasta.

In one swift motion, he ripped the tablecloth free, then bolted across the balcony, weaving around the tables, ignoring the stares of strangers. He raced down the stairs, two steps at a time, and out to where the boats were moored. Without slowing, he leapt into the nearest one, unclipped the mooring line, and pushed away from the river landing.

An attendant working in the maintenance shop beneath the restaurant heard the commotion and rushed out. He saw the teenager in one of his boats and dashed out to stop him, yelling something about having to pay. But he was too late.

There were pedals for propulsion in the bottom of the boat, but Kalen ignored them. He just wanted to drift away from The Boathouse. Away from all the people who were crowding the terrace rails to watch. Away from all these things that were happening to him. As far away from everything Martian as he could get.

In the middle of the stream, where the current was stronger, the boat began to float along more quickly. It rounded a dogleg in the channel, and The Boathouse disappeared from view.

Here the stream was wider, and the craft began to turn slowly on itself. Watching the banks spin dizzyingly around him, Kalen started to feel sick. His temples began to throb, his face turned a greenish, pallid hue, and his mouth filled with foul-tasting saliva. He slipped off the seat and slumped onto the floor. He felt absolutely terrible, wishing he could throw up to relieve it. But he hadn't eaten enough and just lay there, dry-retching.

Deep down, he knew it wasn't just the motion of the boat. It was the culmination of everything that had happened over the previous sols. His arrival on Mars. The encounter with that ArCom stalker. The tall stranger. News of his father's death followed soon after by the discovery that he had been leading a secret life. And now, to top it off, a suggestion that the accident that had killed him wasn't an accident at all. It was murder.

His father had been murdered!

That was unofficial, of course. Richard had only passed on unconfirmed information, maybe even gossip. But given everything else that had happened, it seemed quite plausible. The man and his ArCom in the alley had somehow known his father was here. They just wanted confirmation, and he, Kalen, had unintentionally given it to them.

The sunlight faltered, flickered, and coated the inside of the boat with dappled shade. He blinked a few times, then squinted upward. A leafy branch had drifted overhead. The boat bumped to a stop. He sat up and saw that it had run aground on the riverbank. Grabbing the gunnel, he stepped out. The water here was shallow, but the mud under the surface was soft. His feet sank up to the ankles. He pulled one free with a sucking feeling. But the effort cost him his balance, and he toppled over onto his hands and knees, mud clouding in the water around him. With some effort, he struggled to his feet and managed to stagger out onto the sloping bank.

All about him, wild greenery grew thickly. He slowly made his way upward, past prickly brambles, slipping occasionally on the carpet of moist and rotting leaves. Eventually, he reached the top and pushed his way out into the neatly maintained grass of Sojourner River Park.

He realised that if he just followed the edge of the park, he would meet up with the path that led back to the restaurant.

By now, Jenna and the others would no doubt be concerned. None of this was their fault, and he didn't want them worrying about him.

He set off. It was a large, expansive park, and he must have drifted further than he realised, for the surroundings weren't at all familiar. The pathways ran in different directions around unfamiliar garden beds overhung by tall, broad trees he didn't recognise.

And over there, what was that? A couple of hundred metres away, he guessed. A grassy mound crowned by some sort of metallic monument. Curious, as well as thinking he might be able to get his bearings from its higher elevation, he detoured towards it.

Up close, he saw that it rose about two metres above the rest of the park. A narrow, gravel path with some steps at the very top took him to the summit. Displayed there beside a large rock was a small gold cart on six silvery wheels. It was primitive and tiny, only about thirty centimetres high, and its flat top was covered in old solar panels with a rod antenna on one corner.

An information panel bolted to the rock identified it as a full-size replica of the original *Sojourner* robotic rover, namesake of the river and park. He read how the courageous little machine had been flung to Mars in the last years of the 20th century; how it had bounced in a balloon contraption onto the Northern Hemisphere plains of Ares Vallis and been left there to trundle about by itself until it stopped working.

'You had us worried, Kalen.'

He looked over his shoulder. Jenna mounted the final steps and stood beside him. He nodded wordlessly.

'What are you doing here?' she asked.

'I think I've found myself.' He gestured morosely at the little rover. 'We're two of a kind. Both thrown off Earth, flown all the way out here, and abandoned.'

Chapter 8

They walked in silence back to the path that led down to The Boathouse. Erica and Richard were coming the other way and met them at the top. The adults exchanged a glance at the sight of Kalen's ragged state and drenched arms and legs but thought it best not to pass comment.

Instead, Richard was all apologies. 'That was terribly tactless of me, Kalen,' he began. 'Jenna told me that you'd been to, er, see your father this morning. If I'd known, I wouldn't have prattled on like I did.'

'It's okay,' Kalen said. 'What you said sort of fits with some other things that have been happening.'

Richard didn't understand, but realising he'd put his foot in things once that sol, he decided to adopt a safer line. 'I think I've smoothed over the boatman. He wasn't very happy about having to go and fetch his boat, but it's amazing what a small donation can do.'

'I appreciate it,' Kalen said sincerely. 'And thanks for lunch. I feel a bit better.'

'But you only had one chip,' Erica said doubtfully. 'Still, if you'd wanted more, I'm sure you would've ordered it. I hope the company helped anyway.'

'Yes,' agreed Richard as they ambled across the park towards the parking area. 'I don't know what your plans are, but we're up in Asheton every few weeks, so we might see you again. Of course, if you find yourself down on South Cap feel free to look us up. We're in McKinnon Base. That's the big one down there. Jenna's got the address.'

'Well, we best be off.' Erica turned to Jenna. 'Give our wishes to your father.'

She gave her daughter a parting peck on the cheek, clutched Richard's arm, then steered him across the grass towards the city.

'Sorry about all that,' Jenna said.

'No problems. If that's as hard as it gets, I'll be okay.'

'I hope you're right.'

'So where to now, then?'

Jenna looked at his wet, muddy jeans. 'The first thing you need to do is get cleaned up. Come on. I'll run you back to your apartment.'

They arrived at the unocycle, but, just as Jenna fitted her helmet, her watch flashed. She glanced at the display and transferred the call to her helmet.

'Bad timing, Tye. We're just leaving The Boathouse. Pardon? Oh, right. I'll put him on.' To Kalen, she said, 'It's Tye. I'll transfer him to your helmet.'

Kalen pulled it on and spoke into the com. 'Hi.'

'I've been trying to call you,' came Tye's voice. 'You got your watch off?'

'Don't think so. Hang on.' Kalen tapped his device. Nothing happened. He tried again a couple of times. Some coloured lights on it flickered feebly but failed to resolve into the usual bright display panel. 'Looks like I've killed it,' he said to Tye. 'Obviously, it's not river-proof.'

'Sorry?'

'Don't worry.'

'Right. Well, I was going to see if you wanted to meet up at Mrs Mack's, but if you've just been to The Boathouse, you won't be hungry.'

'Don't be too sure. Lunch was cut a bit short. Just a sec.' To Jenna, he said, 'He wants to meet up at Mrs Mack's. Will she let us in?'

'You mean after Mal demolished her table? Not sure. I think Dad smoothed her over, but there's only one way to find out. Um, that's if you feel up to it?'

Kalen nodded. 'Actually, I could do with one of her muffins.'

'Tell him half an hour, then.'

♦

Showered and changed, Kalen dismounted with Jenna outside the crowded *al fresco* dining area of Mrs Mack's.

'It's busy.'

'Good,' Jenna replied. 'We might be able to sneak in without being noticed.'

The shop hummed with private conversations and the clutter of cutlery on plates. In one of those coincidences of timing, a group vacated a table near the front window just as they stepped inside.

'Perfect,' Jenna said, grabbing a chair. 'We should be able to keep a low profile here.'

Immediately, there came a *crash!* followed by a *thud!* from outside, and Tye's lanky figure went cartwheeling past the window, followed by an airborne unocycle, a chair, a table, and a couple of clattering rubbish bins.

'So much for a low profile,' she muttered with a disgusted shake of her head. 'He would have to be the clumsiest Martian! Sit tight. I'll go and see what he's broken this time.'

'You sure you don't need a hand?'

'Yep. Just stay here and mind the table.'

She darted out the front door just as Mrs Mack burst in through a pair of rear saloon doors marked "Staff Only", looking for the cause of the disturbance. Kalen hastily plucked a menu off the table and hid behind it as the woman scanned the shop for troublemakers.

Jenna reappeared, walking past the window with Tye, who was limping and cradling his arm.

'There should be a law against bins out there,' he whinged as they came inside.

'I don't know about that,' Jenna retorted, 'but there *is* a law against riding on the pavement.'

'So there should be. It's dangerous. You could do yourself an injury with all those people walking about.'

Mrs Mack confronted them. 'Jenna Quill! I might have guessed. Why does everybody you know end up flat on the ground outside my shop?'

'Don't know,' she replied. 'I just seem to attract them. Um, will it be okay if we stay and have something to eat? I promise we won't break anything.'

'I'm not sure I can afford too many customers like you, but—alright. For goodness sake, be careful, though. And you!' She glared sternly at Tye. 'No more acrobatics!'

'Sure, Mrs Mack. Right. Absolutely.'

So they gave their order, and she toddled off to the kitchen to fill it.

Fortunately, Tye's accident hadn't left him with any permanent injuries. The only sign of his encounter with the pavement was a grazed elbow and a dirty scuff mark on his T-shirt, which was emblazoned with "Fourth Rock".

'You're lucky you live on Mars,' Kalen commented. 'Where I come from, you'd probably have broken something.'

'Maybe,' he replied, 'but it'd still be worth it.'

'What's that supposed to mean?' Jenna said.

Tye leaned back in his chair, grinning like the cat that got the cream. 'Ask me why I crashed.'

'You mean you need a reason?'

'No, seriously. Ask me.'

Jenna played along. 'Okay, why did you—?'

'Nikel rang,' he said, unable to keep it in any longer.

'So? She's rung you before.'

'Yeah, but this time it was different.'

'You mean she's gonna throw herself outside the cloak without a biosuit if you don't go out with her?'

'Not exactly, but at least I'm on first base.'

Jenna's head snapped up to face him. 'What?'

'She wants to see me,' he said with enormous gravity.

'But you see her every week. At least when she's not trundling around the desert.'

Tye flashed her a look of annoyance. She wasn't giving his news the required importance.

'You don't get it, Jen. She wants to *see* me.'

'Yes?'

'Get it? See me as in *be with* me.'

'Like on a date, you mean,' Kalen said.

'Exactly.' He looked appreciatively at the Terran. 'Obviously, it takes a guy to understand these things.'

'What's the big deal?' Jenna said. 'You make it sound like you just discovered the Big Bang.'

Tye smirked mischievously. 'Not on a first date.'

'Tye!'

'Sorry.' He backed down sheepishly.

'But what about Adam?' Kalen asked. 'I thought they were together.'

'Obviously, she's finally come to her senses about him.'

'Oh, dream on,' Jenna said. 'She probably only wants to, um—'

'What?'

'Just, er—'

'Yes?'

'Well, I can't think of anything. But there'll be a reason. When's this all going to happen?'

'Tonight. I'm meeting her at seven outside the holoplex.'

'What are you seeing?'

'Who cares? I mean, this is Nikel Pierce we're talking about. *The* Nikel Pierce.'

'I know, Tye. My best friend, remember?'

'Huh. Can you believe this?' He shook his head in wonder at his luck. 'Nikel Pierce has actually asked me out!'

He looked back and forth between Jenna and Kalen, expecting them to shower him with praise and wishes. Instead, Jenna just stared at him uncertainly. And Kalen—well, Kalen looked positively glum.

Maybe he *was* overdoing it?

'Sorry,' he said, fighting down his elation. 'It's just that I've liked Nik for—'

'It's Nikel,' Jenna said firmly. 'Or Nikki. Whatever you do, don't call her Nik.'

'Adam does.'

'Adam's Adam. You're not.'

'Right, okay. Thanks for the pointer. Anyway, I've liked her for ages. With Adam around, I never thought she'd even notice me, let alone ask me out.'

'I'm pleased for you,' Kalen said flatly.

'Thanks.' Tye paused for a moment. He looked at Kalen more closely. 'If you don't mind me saying, you seem a bit down in the dumps. Everything alright?'

'I was wondering when you'd notice,' Jenna said. 'Kalen's had some serious stuff of his own to deal with this morning. Haven't you, Kalen. Do you want to tell him, or will I?'

'Tell me what?' Tye looked curiously from one to the other.

So they relayed the news about David Rance and the shuttle crash. When they'd finished, Tye sat rigidly in his chair, not sure what to say or even if he should say anything at all.

Finally, he managed, 'Oh, I'm really sorry. That must be so tough. What are you going to do?'

'Not sure yet,' Kalen answered with a shrug.

'You'll probably have to stay on Mars for a while, at least until they sort everything out. You know, investigate the accident, see what caused it. It could take months.'

'It gets worse,' Jenna said.

'How can it get worse?'

'It might not have been an accident.'

Tye fixed his gaze on Jenna as she related Richard's thoughts over lunch.

'You've got to be kidding!' he exclaimed when she'd finished. 'BLOWN UP!'

'Sh! Not so loud,' Jenna said. She scanned the people around them for signs someone had overheard. Fortunately, Tye's voice had been lost in the ambient shop noise.

He leaned in conspiratorially. 'You mean, it was shot down?'

'Or bombed,' Kalen replied. 'We don't know for sure.'

'Wow! I thought that sort of thing only happened on Earth. And you think your dad was the target.'

'Dunno. Could be.'

'But why? What's he done?'

'Don't know that either. All I do know is we left Earth in a big hurry. I got the feeling he was running away from something.'

'And that something's followed him here.'

'Looks like it.'

'Well, now that whoever it is has got what they want, you might be safe.'

'Maybe. *If* they got what they want.'

'What's that supposed to mean?'

'Not sure. I just can't imagine how killing my dad would solve anything.'

At that moment, a guy arrived with their orders, deftly served them, and left. They ate in silence for a while, then, stuffing his mouth with the final third of his apple and cinnamon muffin, Tye said, 'So are you staying in your apartment?'

'No, at Jenna's. For a while, at least.'

'Above the shop?' Tye spooned some cappuccino froth into his mouth leaving himself with a white moustache. 'That must be a tight squeeze.'

'Wipe your mouth, Tye,' Jenna said.

He ran the back of his hand across his upper lip, leaving a chocolatey streak on his cheek.

'Now it's on your face,' Jenna said. 'You'll have to do better than this on your date.'

'Don't worry, I will.' Tye took out a handkerchief and wiped his whole face to make certain he hadn't missed anything. 'Better?'

Jenna nodded approval, stirred her coffee, picked up the cup in both hands, and leaned back in her chair.

'Listen, Kalen,' Tye said, stuffing his hanky back into his pocket, 'if you like, you could move in with us at Brindle Farm. Plenty of room out there. And Mum won't mind.'

'Thanks, but I'd better just stay where I am and do what I'm told for now. If the MSA comes looking for me and I'm not there, things might get worse, if that's possible.'

'Okay. Well, if plans change, let me know.' Tye checked his watch. 'Time I wasn't here. I promised Dad I'd clean out the chicken run before tonight.' He picked up the menu. 'What am I up for?'

'Don't worry about it,' Kalen said. 'It's on me.'

'You sure?'

'Yeah. Shout Nikel supper with it. I want to try out the debt facility my dad gave me anyway.'

Tye nodded his appreciation. 'Thanks. I owe you.'

Jenna watched his back thoughtfully as he walked out the door and disappeared around the corner.

'What *is* that girl up to?' she muttered to herself.

'Nikel? Does she need to be up to something?'

Jenna sighed. 'Not normally. But this time she is.'

'Why do you say that?'

'There are two guarantees in life. The Martian born can't travel to Earth. And Nikel isn't interested in Tye.'

'What happened to death and taxes?'

'Well, there are four then, but I wasn't going to mention the death one. Not after what happened to your—well, you know.'

Kalen felt a sudden pang in his chest. He would probably have to get used to it, at least until the initial rawness began to subside. In the meantime, he would ride the pain and confront it head-on. The way he handled most things.

Kalen drained his cup of coffee. 'I don't see why it has to be so sinister. Maybe Nikel's just decided she likes him. I mean, he seems okay.'

'Of course he's okay. He's my friend. But he's Tye. You saw him just now. He doesn't park a unocycle; he crash-lands it; he ingests food like a corpuscle; *and* he leaves half his cappuccino on his face; *and* he cleans up chicken poop. On the other hand, Nikel was voted the most beautiful teen model for the past two Terran years. She meets all the important people in the colony, has her face in the media every second sol, makes official appearances at civic functions. Can you seriously see them together? No, something's not right.'

'She's your friend. Can't you just ask her?'

Jenna scrunched up her nose. 'It's not really any of my business, is it.'

'Well, I don't know either of them, but I think you're making too much of it. It's only one date. Now, are you finished? Let's get out of here.'

The debit facility his father had left him worked fine. The balance left after the three coffees and three muffins was M$38,867.32. It wasn't a fortune, but it was far more than he had expected. Whatever his problems, he wouldn't run out of funds in the short term.

For what was left of the afternoon, he put himself in Jenna's hands. They cruised around the city. She showed him some of its main points of interest. The arts centre, the concert hall under its striking spire, and the multi-faith chapel. All the prominent civic buildings he didn't get to see with his father. Then they sat for a while on the shores of Lake Curiosity and watched some people on skimmers go through their paces above the mirror-smooth water.

Afternoon became early evening, and they returned to the apartment above Asheton Robotics. When they walked in, Jules, wearing an apron and oven gloves, was juggling a steaming concoction of meatballs and vegetables from the oven onto the bench.

'Ah, perfect timing,' he said.

He wasn't the best cook on Mars, but his casseroles were quite passable, and Kalen, while still not overly hungry, forced down a plateful along with a slice of cheesecake. When he had finished, the sol's events began to catch up with him.

He leaned back in his chair and yawned. 'I think I better have an early night.'

'Of course,' Jules replied from the dishwasher, where he was stacking the crockery and cutlery. 'Think of this place as your own. You can have Jenna's room again tonight, and then solmorrow we'll make some other arrangements for the rest of your stay.'

Kalen felt bad about putting his friend out of her room, but, after a weakly argued debate, he let himself be persuaded that he wasn't being any trouble. So, when she had changed the sheets and removed all those things she would need for the night, Kalen collapsed into her single bed and fell into an exhausted sleep.

♦

For the umpteenth time, Tye looked up nervously at the sign flashing above the doorway:

Live your dreams at HAL'S HOLOPLEX

He certainly hoped to live his dreams tonight. But that wasn't going to happen if Nikel didn't turn up.

He looked once again at the pavement outside. It had just gone seven o'clock, but there was still no sign of her. Should he go back outside and wait? No. She'd told him to stay in the foyer. She would find him.

Deep down, he wasn't really concerned about missing their session; it could be rebooked. He wasn't even worried about losing face should news get out that he had been stood up. No, it was more the fact of having his hopes raised, then dashed.

Impatiently, he tapped his watch to check the time again. Three minutes past seven! Now, she really was late. Nervousness turned to mild annoyance. The session would already have begun. How could she do this to him? Especially since it was she who had proposed they meet.

He looked down at the small posy of wildflowers grasped in his sweaty hands. His mother's idea. She had selected them from her garden plot near the front of the house. If Nikel didn't turn up soon, they would start to wilt. So would he!

Then, just as he was about to call to see why she was delayed, a transit pod pulled up outside the foyer. The door opened, and Nikel got out.

His heart leapt. His doubts evaporated. So did all the peevish thoughts rumbling about inside his head. She hadn't let him down after all. How could he ever have doubted her?

The pod closed its door and abandoned her on the pavement. He took a moment to admire her in the bright lights under the awning, not as some unattainable goddess but as his date-to-be. Even in informal clothes, away from the catwalk and the cameras, she looked striking. Casual, heeled shoes. Cream jeans. Perfectly matched short-sleeve top. Gold designer jewellery flashing at her delicate throat, dangling from her earlobes. Honey-blond hair flowing wild and free.

She turned towards the main doors, but before she had taken two steps, a group of kids hanging around outside realised who she was.

A voice rang out, 'Look guys! That's Nikel!'

It was enough. She was one of those A-list celebrities who needed only a first name. Bianca, the French romantic actress; Sludge, the lead singer of American punk group, Rats in the Sewer; Fabiano, the Italian football star; and Nikel, the Martian supermodel.

And Nikel was the most famous of them all, at least in this part of the solar system.

The kids, most of whom looked to be about thirteen, his sister's age, stopped what they were doing and gaped, heads tracking her slowly as she headed towards the foyer doors. One of their number, more courageous than the rest, broke away from the group and took a few tentative steps in her direction. He said something Tye couldn't make out. Then the others joined in and surrounded her adoringly.

She was well used to intrusive attention and blinked those almond eyes, gave that famous toss of the head, and stopped to chat politely.

Tye was mortified. She was his date! This was their night, just the two of them, to the exclusion of everybody else. Thrusting the posy before him like a fragrant lance, he trotted out, a medieval knight defending his maiden's honour.

She saw him coming, politely disentangled herself from her young admirers, and extended a long-fingered hand to accept the offered posy.

'For me, Tye? I love flowers,' she purred, waving them under her nose, inhaling deeply. 'Mm. African daisies, cornflowers, phlox. They're all my favourites.'

He couldn't help but smile. *Good one, Mum!*

'But how could you have known?' she asked.

'Er, you look like someone who loves flowers.'

Was that a bit over the top?

'How lovely.'

Phew! Sometimes a guy just knows what to say.

'And they're freshly picked.'

'Yep. I chose them myself.'

What's a little white lie between friends?

'So thoughtful.'

Holding the posy in one hand, she clutched his arm tightly with the other, and they walked inside.

Behind them, Tye heard jealous mutterings from the group.

'Who's her date?'

'It's not Adam!'

'No.'

'Who's *that*?'

'She's dumped Adam for *him*?'

'Unbelievable!'

Riffraff! What would they know?

'I was pleased when you invited me,' he said. 'And a bit surprised.'

'Surprised? Why?'

'Not sure. I suppose I thought it'd never happen.'

'Well, it has. Really sorry I'm late, by the way. We're still doing that shoot I told you about.'

'The one for Martian tourism?'

'Yes. I couldn't get away. There was a glitch with one of the lighting pods.'

'No problems. The session's probably already started, but if we're lucky, they won't have locked the doors yet.'

'Oh, didn't I mention? I've booked us a private suite.'

'Private?'

'That's alright, I hope?'

'Wow! I mean, yes. Of course. Great.'

'You've never been in one before?'

'Not really.'

'Good. Then you're in for a real treat.'

Hal's Holoplex had two private suites, both located on Level 3 at the top of the complex. Stepping off the escalator, Nikel unlinked Tye's arm and went to the service desk.

The girl behind the counter knew who she was without asking, but Tye's presence caught her off guard. It was usually Adam in her company. Still, Nikel's choice of date was entirely her own affair. She could have anyone she wanted.

'Evening, Miss Pierce,' she said, trying hard to keep the prickly jealousy out of her voice. 'You're in Suite 2. Would you care for refreshments afterwards?'

Nikel looked askance at Tye.

'Maybe a coffee,' he suggested.

'Fine,' said the attendant. 'That includes snacks as well. So, show and refreshments for two. Comes to ninety-six dollars.'

Tye silently baulked at the price. It was a lot of money for a humble farm boy. Sessions in the lower-level theatres only cost half that. Obviously, the private suites were in a different league. But he needn't have worried.

'I've got this,' Nikel said.

'Sure?'

'You're my guest. I can't ask you to pay. Unless it makes you feel bad.'

It did seem a bit unfair, but to avoid awkwardness on their first date, he offered a compromise. 'Let me get the afters.'

So, with the payment sorted, they headed along a carpeted corridor to a heavy door marked Suite 2. An attendant ArCom ushered them through, then closed it firmly behind them.

They found themselves alone in an empty room about twenty metres wide and thirty metres long. The high grey walls curved into the ceiling and were covered in acoustic panels, holographic projectors, and the ultrasonic transmitters that produced the touchies. Elsewhere were air blowers, audio speakers, vents for the smellscape system, and nozzles that generated fine sprays of water for wet effects.

'I hope you don't mind,' Nikel said, 'but I chose the main feature for us.'

'Yeah, sure,' Tye replied. 'I didn't get a chance to look at the program anyway.'

'It only runs for about twenty minutes. You can pick the chaser if you like.'

Before he could reply, the room dimmed to pitch black. Tye felt like he was being sucked into a black hole. Then a soothing male voice from nowhere in particular said, 'Welcome to *Morning in the Rainforest*.'

'Here we go,' Nikel said with an excited tremor in her voice.

Directly ahead, a faint glow thinned the blackness. In it, the silhouettes of some enormous trees took shape—only grey shadows at first, but still tall and upright with branches reaching out like leafy arthritic fingers.

The glow intensified. Now the trees surrounded them; they became three-dimensional, some nearby, and others marching off into the distance. Grey became pastel pink. Tye realised he was witnessing a sunrise. But not one he'd ever experienced before. Not a Martian sunrise where the sky started blue and turned to pink during the sol. This was pink at first, changing slowly to a beautiful deep azure.

His breath caught in his throat. This was a Terran sunrise. He was on Earth!

Now, the colours became a storm. Torrents of light poured over them, pooled at their feet, eddied around their bodies, and seemingly gained texture. Photons combined magically to become moist brown soil tufted with green dew-beaded grass; mottled plants; shrubs hung with red and blue berries; and ferny tendrils uncoiling in dank, shaded nooks. Above swelled a vast canopy, which, through clever optical trickery, extended beyond the height of the room. Through gaps in it, they glimpsed a blue sky with scudding fluffy white clouds. Now a rugged mountain track materialised before them and wound its way among the moss-covered rocks that had erupted from the ground.

A rainforest.

'What do you think?' Nikel asked.

Tye was speechless.

She understood. 'According to the program, we're somewhere in South America. Come on, let's go for a walk.'

They wandered off along the track. Curiously, the ground felt uneven. Their feet crunched in the soil. And all around them were the smells and sounds of a living forest. The sweet fragrance of tropical flowers, the earthy scent of drenched wood and greenery, the plop of water, the buzz of tiny wings, the click of an insect, the hiss of a snake, the screech of a tree-dwelling primate, the growl of a small creature defending its territory, the roar of a predator followed by the scampering of its fleet-footed prey, raucous squawks, and choirs of birdsong. A light breeze blew up, rocking branches, rustling leaves, kissing their faces, and teasing their hair.

'Oh, over there!' Nikel squealed in delight.

A brightly plumed bird with an overlarge beak hopped back and forth on a high branch.

Tye finally found his voice. 'Look at that!'

'I think it's called a toucan,' Nikel replied. 'And there!'

Tye caught sight of a long-tailed, furry creature vanishing into a burrow. But, in truth, he was more interested in watching her.

She looked up and caught him staring. A little self-consciously, she said, 'Sorry if this isn't the me you're used to seeing.'

'Don't be. That's why people go on dates, isn't it? To get to know each other?'

She looked away, as if afraid to meet his eyes. 'I suppose. Not sure exactly what you're seeing at the moment, though. Probably just a frustrated artist.'

Tye knew she painted in her spare time.

'Watercolours, isn't it?'

'When I get the chance.'

'No need to be frustrated.'

'You don't think?' She went quiet for a moment then continued, 'I've travelled all over the planet, but there's only so much you can do with the Martian pallet.' She moved her hand around in a grand, sweeping gesture. 'I wish there was somewhere I could go to see things like this.'

'You could always set up your easel in here.'

She laughed, though with little humour. 'Believe me, I've thought about it. But it wouldn't be real. I mean, this is all great, but it's been designed and built by holographic engineers. I'd just be copying someone else's work. I prefer real things.'

He looked at her more closely, liking what he saw. 'Me too,' he said.

But she either missed his hidden meaning or ignored it.

He forced his attention back to the illusory forest. 'I had no idea it would be so real. It's just like being on Earth.'

'Is it?'

The question tripped him up. He back-pedalled. 'Well, I don't *know*, obviously. But it's the way I imagine Earth.'

Nikel hesitated, as if about to broach a difficult subject. 'Your new Terran friend could tell us,' she said at last.

'Kalen? Yeah. We'll have to bring him here before he goes home.'

'He's not leaving so soon?'

'Don't know. He doesn't want to. But it's probably out of his hands.'

'Why?'

They passed under a thick, low bough hung heavy with beards of moss.

'You haven't heard, then,' he said.

'Heard what?'

'Something horrible.'

'Tell me.'

'You know the shuttle that crashed?'

'The one in the news, yes.'

'His dad was on it.'

'But there weren't any survivors!'

'Told you it was horrible. And Kalen's got no mum, either. Or brothers or sisters, as far as I know. Poor guy. He's staying with Jenna until the MSA sorts out what to do with him.'

They rounded a rocky outcrop. Before them lay a wide gorge cut deep into the mountains by a surging river hundreds of metres below. The thunder of its churning water reached them even at this height. Nikel stepped onto a narrow suspension bridge and began to cross. Tye joined her. He felt it shaking and swaying but managed to keep his balance.

'That's terrible,' Nikel said. 'Why did they come here?'

'Not sure,' Tye shrugged. 'I don't even think Kalen knows.'

'He comes to Mars and doesn't know why?'

'They just upped and left, apparently.'

'But there must've been a reason. People don't just move planets on a whim.'

'You'd have to blame his dad, I suppose. Whatever his reasons were, he never told Kalen.'

'Hmm, well, I think it's all very unfair.'

'It gets worse,' Tye said.

'How?'

'I shouldn't say anything, but there's no harm telling *you*, I suppose . . . they think the crash wasn't accidental.'

'That wasn't on the news,' Nikel said.

'No, it's just what Kalen's heard. He was talking to someone about it.'

'Who?'

'I shouldn't say any more.'

'Go on, you can tell me.'

'I can't. It's not official.'

They reached the other side, stepped off, and continued walking. A stone ruin lay in the undergrowth, wrapped in strangling creepers. They walked among the enormous blocks and pillars and came upon a sun-flecked bower with a tranquil pond in the centre. To their delight, drinking from the pond was a small, white horse-like creature. From its nose grew a long, pointed horn.

'A unicorn,' Nikel said.

Tye was dubious. 'I've heard of them. I don't think they're real, though. Not even on Earth.'

'No, but I like the idea of them. I put in a special request when I booked.'

They approached the creature. It lifted its head from the pond and looked at them with large, long-lashed eyes. Taking a couple of timid backward steps, it stopped and cowered before them. Nikel stepped closer and reached out to stroke its glossy coat. It tossed its head and nickered contentedly at her touch.

'Try it,' she said with an amused smile. 'The touchies in here are amazing.'

Tye ran his fingers lightly along its flank, across the side of its head, then down its nose and around the base of the horn.

'It feels just right. The horn's hard. The skin's soft. It's even warm.'

Then something unsettled the creature. It pulled back and turned its head to face Nikel. 'Pardon me for disturbing you, Miss Pierce,' it said, 'but *Morning in the Rainforest* is nearly finished.'

'Already?' She couldn't hide her disappointment.

'I'm afraid so. But your session still has nine minutes to run. Do you wish to make a second selection?'

'Might as well. Go on, Tye. Impress me.'

'Yeah, sure. Um, let's see. I've always wondered what it would be like to stand on a beach. Can they do that?'

Nikel looked at the unicorn. 'Can you?'

'Certainly. Your companion has made an excellent choice. Configuring now.'

Long seconds passed. Nothing seemed to happen.

'Ready when you are,' Tye said.

'*Golden Beaches* is now running,' the unicorn replied. 'Look behind you.'

They turned around. Gone were the stone ruins, the twining creepers, and the dank mountain greenery. The path by which they had approached the bower had become a sandy track leading off through some tall coconut palms. Kalen looked over his shoulder to thank the unicorn, but it had vanished.

They followed the track. Beyond the palms lay a sun-drenched beach. It curved away into the distance, finally disappearing behind a high, windswept bluff. A few metres from where they stood, waves chased themselves up a sandy slope, then retreated to a restless ocean.

'Let's take off our shoes and socks,' Tye said. 'I bet we can feel the sand between our toes. I heard that's what Terrans do.'

They sat down, stuffed their socks into their shoes and left them lying in the sand as they walked off.

Tentatively, Tye took Nikel's hand. To his intense delight, she didn't pull it away.

'It all seems so real,' he said.

She opened her mouth to speak, but decided against it.

Sunshine fell bright on their faces. They were forced to squint. The blustery wind smelt of salt and brought with it the roar of the sea and the crash of foamed waves. Still holding hands, they ran playfully down to the edge and stood there as cold water surged wetly around their ankles. Further out, where the water turned a deep blue, they watched a large wave build, then collapse on itself, spraying foam high into the air. Droplets floated to them and stung their faces. Tye wiped his free hand across his cheek. The water was real.

They returned to the dry sand and continued on.

Warmed by the sun, refreshed by the wind, energised by the relentless energy of the ocean, Tye felt strangely empowered.

'Can I ask you something personal?' He felt her hand flinch slightly in his, but he held on tighter, undeterred. 'Why are we here?'

'Aren't you enjoying it?'

He recognised this for the evasion it was. 'That's not what I'm asking. You go with Adam. The most famous of us. Why would you ask me out?'

She tugged her hand free. 'It's not all about fame, Tye.' She drew in a deep breath and added more forthrightly, 'Anyway, Adam doesn't own me.'

'Of course he doesn't. I know that. But you still go with him. I don't think you're someone who'd go behind his back to go out with the likes of me.'

'The likes of you? What's that supposed to mean? There's nothing wrong with you, Tye. I like you. If I want to ask you out, I can.'

Still, he wasn't satisfied.

'Has something gone wrong between you two?'

She turned away, her lips twitching. 'It's complicated. I don't really want to talk about him tonight. Do you mind?'

He realised he had overstepped the mark. 'Sure. Sorry. I didn't mean to . . . no, right. It's none of my business.'

In one way, he regretted being so honest. The last thing he wanted to do was upset her, especially on their first date. But, while honesty sometimes hurts, it more often reveals new truths. And the wonderful new truth revealed to him was that all wasn't well with Mars's famous It Couple!

A surge of joy rose from somewhere deep inside. Was that selfish? Probably. Was he sorry? No.

They continued on for a time and came upon a tiny beach hut erected near the tree line. No more than a simple, lemon-coloured box with a pink pitched roof and a lime green door, it looked quaint yet out of place.

Curious, they veered up the beach towards it. On the step up to the door sat their shoes and socks. Nearby, standing patiently as if guarding them, was the unicorn.

'Your session will end in one minute,' it announced. 'Please gather your property and exit through the door.'

They sat on the ground, pulled on their socks and shoes, and took a last look at the beach. Then Tye pushed open the door, and they stepped back into reality.

♦

'I hope you enjoyed it,' Nikel said, draining the last of her coffee and placing the cup back on its saucer.

'Loved it,' Tye replied. 'Best thing I've ever done.'

She nodded, satisfied, and glanced at her watch. 'I told my dad I wouldn't be late home, so maybe I should head off. You know what a bore dads can be about time.'

They left the dimly lit café and rode the escalator down to the foyer. Just as they got outside, a vacant pod pulled up.

'This is me,' she said as its door opened. 'Well, thank you for coming. We must do it again. Soon.'

She looked at him and, after a moment's indecision, leaned in close and brushed her lips across his cheek.

'Keep in touch,' she whispered.

Then she boarded the pod and was gone.

♦

Tye was in heaven. No hologram could be so perfect.

Swerving all over the road on the way home, he nearly crashed his unocycle twice. But he didn't care. All he could think of was Nikel's soft hand in his, her sweet breath when she'd leaned in close, the delicious burning on his cheek where her lips had kissed him, and her parting words echoing over and over in his brain:

Keep in touch. Keep in touch. Keep in touch.

Chapter 9

Disembodied voices came to Kalen in the night. He tried to ignore them, but they grew louder, more insistent. As he crossed the barrier between sleep and wakefulness, he found the voices still there. Distant, wafting faintly through the closed door. Jenna's, he recognised immediately. And Jules's too. But they weren't alone. A woman was speaking. Then came the deeper tones of a man. And another man.

His eyes found the bedside clock. The red numbers swam blurrily in his vision. He blinked hard a couple of times until they assembled into 2.37 a.m.

A flurry of thoughts filled his head. News of his father? No, his father was dead. A breakthrough in the investigation, maybe? Surely that could wait until morning.

Now came the sound of padding feet on the stairs. A knock at the door. Before he could answer, it was pushed open, and light flooded into the room. Then the ceiling lamp was turned on. The blinding glare burned into his eyes, and his hands flew up to cover them.

Jenna called his name, her voice tremulous, tentative.

'Do you know what time it is?' he asked grumpily.

'You'd better get up.'

As his eyes adjusted to the light, he could see that she was still in her nightie with her hair mussed, her normally bright face pale and frightened.

'What's happened?' he asked.

'Some people from the MSA have turned up. Get dressed and come downstairs.'

'In a minute.'

'Better make it now, Kalen. They mean business.'

Kalen could tell by her voice that she was deadly serious. Still half asleep, he threw on his jeans, a shirt, and some sneakers and made his way down the stairs to the shop.

Jules was standing near the counter with one arm around Jenna's shoulders. Scratch stood watching nearby. Opposite were three strangers. He had guessed correctly: two men and a woman. All were dressed in plain black business suits with the stovepipe trousers and mandarin collars currently in vogue on Mars. These gave the impression of no-nonsense severity, which matched their harsh, unsmiling demeanours. Beneath their jackets, Kalen noticed slight bulges, which he suspected were concealed firearms. Clipped to the belt of the woman's slacks was a silver badge with what looked like an official MSA insignia.

All eyes turned to Kalen as he came down into the shop.

'Kalen Rance?'

It was the woman who spoke. Her voice was brusque and matter-of-fact. In her late thirties, she stood about Kalen's height and looked impressively fit. Her arms were muscular, her eyes penetrating—

those of a predator. Her black hair was cut very short, which lent her sharp face a harsh, almost masculine appearance.

'I'm Agent Soryn Eckhart,' she continued. 'We're from MSA Special Investigations.'

Kalen just looked at her, unspeaking, as she continued:

'I'm afraid you'll have to come with us.'

'Why?' he managed. 'What's happened?'

'It's my duty to inform you that, as an unaccompanied minor, you are to be deported from Mars under Article Five, Subsection Nine, Paragraph Three of the Immigration Act of AD Two Thousand and Fifty-One.'

'WHAT?'

'Do you want me to repeat it, sir?'

'No, no, I heard what you said.'

'Good. If you'd be good enough to get—'

'But Agent Hilbride said I could stay here.'

'Agent Hilbride has no authority in these matters. Now, I understand you're here just for the night, and most of your things are back at your apartment in Galactic Tower. We'll go straight there so you can collect them.'

'You can't deport the boy at this time of night!' Jules protested. His face burned hotly with outrage, and a vein in his neck was throbbing.

'Normally you'd be right,' the agent conceded. 'But in this case, there's no choice.'

'Why?' Jenna asked, her lips starting to tremble. 'Kalen's not a danger to anyone.'

'It's not a question of danger, Miss. It's more about timing. There's a shuttle leaving for orbit later in the morning. Kalen needs to be on it. It's been decided.'

'*Who* decided?' Jules asked, adding, 'Surely you can tell us that?'

'I'm afraid we can't,' Eckhart said stubbornly.

'But the cycler only left a couple of sols ago,' Jenna reasoned. 'It's the one that brought Kalen here, for goodness sake. There won't be another one for months. You can't leave him in orbit until it gets here.'

'He won't be going on the cycler,' the agent replied coolly. 'The private cruiser *Star Rise* is in orbit, preparing for departure solmorrow afternoon. Arrangements have been made with the captain to take Kalen back to Earth.'

'No one arranged it with me,' Kalen snapped irascibly.

Now one of the men—Agent Rohan Neale, according to his badge—spoke up firmly. 'Let's not make this harder than it needs to be.'

'You can't burst in here in the middle of the night and take him,' Jenna protested. Tears of anger had begun to roll down her cheeks.

Jules looked from the agents to Kalen, then back to the agents again. Struggling to keep his voice reasonable, he said, 'Are you really sure this is necessary? Why can't we just bring him to your office in the morning? I'm sure we can sort something out.'

'It's all been sorted, sir. Now come along, Kalen.'

'Alright, alright.' Kalen was tired and confused, and faced with three armed agents, he felt completely defeated. 'Just let me get the rest of my things first.'

Eckhart nodded to her other male colleague. He had the stocky build of a rugby player, an olive complexion, and features that suggested a Mediterranean heritage, the latter confirmed by the name "Bernardo Rocco" on his badge.

'Go with him, Bernie,' she said.

Shadowed by Bernie's hulking form, Kalen climbed the stairs in something of a daze. He bundled up his pyjamas from the bedroom, and his toothbrush, towel, and soap from the bathroom, then returned to the shop.

Pausing at the counter, he ran his gaze over Jules, then Scratch, and finally Jenna. 'Looks like I mightn't be seeing you again,' he said numbly. 'I suppose all I can do is say thanks for everything. And tell Tye and Nikel that it was great meeting them.'

Then he was escorted out to a waiting pod commandeered by the agents and took a seat beside Eckhart.

'I thought the MSA was on my side,' Kalen said glumly as they pulled away from the kerb.

'It's just the law,' Eckhart replied distantly.

'I know, but I thought Hilbride was okay. So was Telford.'

'They are,' Eckhart replied, adding absent-mindedly, 'good men, both of them.'

Kalen sat thinking for a couple of seconds, not understanding why this sounded wrong. Then realisation struck him. His heart skipped a beat.

Good men, she'd said. *Both of them.*

Maybe he'd misheard? At this time of night, his concentration was bound to be a bit fuzzy. Or was it just a slip of the tongue on her part? He glanced sideways at Eckhart. She was looking straight ahead—cold and inscrutable.

They had turned into Viking Way. Galactic Tower was already in sight. Time was running out. He needed to test her.

'You know them both?' he said with outward calm.

'Of course.'

She had to say that now, of course.

'Well?'

Suddenly prickly, she turned to look at him. 'What?'

'I wondered if you knew them well.'

'Why?'

'Just curious. As I said, they were good to me.'

She nodded and, after a pause, said, 'Well enough.'

It was like extracting water from a rock, but Kalen kept pushing. 'I liked Telford better than Hilbride, though.'

'That so?'

'Yeah, he seemed, I dunno, more understanding.'

'He is,' said Eckhart, turning away.

So she *was* lying. She said she knew Telford well, but somehow she missed the fact that she was a woman! Bess Telford. Something was very wrong. Everything about their arrival in the middle of the night was wrong.

The pod hummed to a stop outside the imposing entrance to Galactic Tower.

'Wait here,' Eckhart commanded the pod.

'Standby status confirmed,' came the synthetic voice.

The agents climbed out, surrounded Kalen in a tight huddle, and marched in. Once inside the enclosed foyer, Eckhart and Neale relaxed a little and spread out, giving Kalen some room. Now was his chance. Maybe his only chance.

He looked around. Rocco was walking behind, cutting off any chance of escape through the front doors. Then he saw it. One of the elevators across from the concierge's booth. It had just returned from the upper floors, and its doors were slowly opening.

He shot forward suddenly, out of the agents' reach, his strong Terran muscles launching him right over the top of the concierge.

'Don't be stupid!' Eckhart bawled.

Kalen hit the ground hands first on the far side of the booth and somersaulted over his right shoulder. Keeping low, he scrambled into the elevator car, punching the button marked '4'. The doors began to slide shut with agonizing slowness.

To his terror, he saw through the narrowing gap that all three agents had rounded the booth in pursuit, hands inside their jackets, groping for firearms. Eckhart was the fastest. She pulled a hand weapon from her jacket and took aim. Luckily, the elevator doors closed before she could fire.

Just as the sound of pounding fists started dully on the metal, he was pressed to the floor when the elevator shot up the side of the building.

Cocooned in the safety of the car for a few moments, he took stock. Why was all this happening? What had he done wrong? He wasn't a criminal—at least as far as he knew. Surely an unaccompanied minor didn't present a danger worthy of an armed escort off the planet in the middle of the night. Or was there something else happening of which he was unaware?

The elevator slowed, stopped. The doors opened. He got to his feet, darted out into the carpeted corridor, and raced to his apartment. He swiped his pass key at the door and burst inside, locking it behind him.

At most, he had a few minutes before Eckhart and her cronies arrived. Exactly what they intended when they got here didn't bear thinking about. But whatever it was, he had no intention of being around to find out.

♦

Eckhart turned to the concierge's booth and barked, 'Do you have CCTV?'

The booth appeared to be empty. Then a thatch of grey hair rose slowly behind the desk. It was followed by two frightened eyes and a nose.

'Of course, sir, er, miss, er, madam. Agent?'

'So where is he?'

The concierge glanced down at one of the tiny monitors under the counter. 'Got out on level four.'

'And?'

'Just gone into his apartment. Number four-twenty-eight.'

'Good. Master pass key! Now!'

The concierge snatched it from a drawer and threw it to Eckhart. She and her colleagues scrambled into a second elevator and rode it to the fourth floor. Weapons drawn, they broke out into the corridor and ran along it until they reached a door marked "428".

Eckhart tried the door handle. It didn't give.

She swiped the Master pass key over it. The lock clicked open. All three stormed inside and fanned out into the lounge room. The light was on, and they scanned the room. There was no sign of their quarry.

'Armed agents, Kalen,' Eckhart bellowed. 'Show yourself now, and you won't come to any harm.'

No reply.

Then they noticed one of the bedroom lights was on.

Rushing in, they found the window wide open. On the off chance it was a false lead, Rocco wrenched open the wardrobe. It was empty. Kalen had given them the slip.

Neale raced to the window and peered down onto the street.

'Tell me you can see him,' Eckhart said.

Neale panned his eyes across the darkened street below, then pulled back into the room, shaking his head. 'No such luck,' he said, adding with grudging admiration, 'I don't know if that was brave or stupid. That's quite a climb.'

Eckhart shook her head in annoyance and muttered through clenched teeth, 'I forgot Terrans are more agile here.'

'We better organise a com trace,' Neale said.

'Good thought, but it won't help us,' Rocco replied. He was holding Kalen's watch, which he had picked up from the bedside table.

'Damn!' Neale exclaimed, turning to Eckhart. 'You think he left that intentionally?'

'Dunno. Maybe.'

'If he did, it means he's not a fool. Okay, so what are we going to do?'

'I'll have to call it in.' Into her wrist phone, she said, 'Sir? Eckhart. There's been a glitch. Yes, I'm afraid so. Through a window. Yes, but it's four storeys up. We thought of that, but he's left his watch here.'

Neither Neale nor Rocco could hear what the man on the other end was saying, but they knew he wouldn't be happy.

Eckhart was placating. 'Yes, sir. Of course, sir. Will do. Yes, we'll keep you updated.'

'I'm guessing that wasn't congratulations on a job well done,' Neale said when she'd disconnected the call.

'Top of the class.'

'So what does he want?'

'Well, the kid doesn't know anything yet, so deportation's still the goal.'

◆

Kalen ran like he'd never run before.

He was under no illusions about his predicament. The MSA would no doubt be unimpressed about being given the slip, so it was only a matter of time before the area was crawling with agents keen to get their hands on him. At most, he had only minutes to get clear of the area.

It didn't matter that climbing around the outside of the building had torn his right hand until it bled. It didn't matter that he'd jarred his ankle painfully, first as he landed on the roof of the descending elevator, then again as he dropped three metres into Viking Way. Either jump on Earth could have broken bones, but on Mars, he'd gotten away with it—just.

At first, he'd considered taking the transit pod, which was waiting outside the foyer. But that was too risky. It would probably be traceable or, worse, capable of being centrally controlled.

So he ran.

And ran, stumbling breathlessly from one shadow to the next. Although it was late, he thought it best to avoid areas like Asheton Square, the restaurant precinct, and the holoplex—where late-night stragglers would likely be found—so he slunk blindly along dim laneways like an abandoned dog, body hunched, face down, until he found himself at the intersection of a broad thoroughfare. On the other side, he could make out the smooth, black expanse of Lake Curiosity, which lapped the southern edge of the city. He'd ridden along here with Jenna yestersol, but it looked different at night.

Making certain no one was about, he crossed the road and began to skirt the shoreline along a gravel path. Regularly-spaced lamps threw pools of light onto the ground. Nervous in their illumination, he pulled off to the left and continued along the spongey grass in the darkness near the water's edge.

Now that the immediate danger was over, he felt his right hand stinging badly as it pumped out warm, wet blood. It needed to be seen to. He stopped and bathed it in the shallows, then pressed his handkerchief firmly over it. The stinging continued, but the pressure began to staunch the flow.

He knew he had to keep moving, so he tied a primitive knot in the handkerchief, fitted it firmly over the wound, and walked on slowly, wondering vaguely what he would do when it got light.

Further around the shore, the sounds of splashing and voices interrupted by bouts of giggling reached him. He dropped into a crouching position to listen more closely. It was a couple of twenty-somethings frolicking in the water after a night out. The sounds of harmless fun continued, so he assumed they hadn't noticed him.

He walked on. A shape materialised in the darkness. It was a unocycle parked on its stand near the water's edge. Two helmets, a bag, some discarded clothes, and a couple of towels sat folded on its seat.

He came to a stop, looking around about warily. There was no one in sight. The voices in the water continued unabated.

He looked more closely at the unocycle. It would certainly enable him to put some distance between himself and the authorities. That would give him more time to think.

Coming to a decision, he removed the helmets, bag, clothes, and towels, placed them carefully on the grass, and straddled the seat. The vehicle wasn't exactly the same as Jenna's, but it looked easy enough to operate. He pressed a button marked "Power". The digital display glowed. It showed a remaining range of one hundred and twenty kilometres, maybe a bit less if he used the headlight. More than enough to get him out of the city. With another glance across the black water, he punched the "Start" button. The gyroscope began to hum, and the vehicle sat up by itself.

The laughter and splashing in the water stopped abruptly, and he heard a woman cry, 'Marty! There's someone near our things!'

Then a man yelled more loudly, 'Hey, you! Get off that!'

Committed now, Kalen, heart racing and adrenalin pumping into his veins, kicked up the stand and turned the throttle on the right handlebar. The machine surged forward to the boggy water's edge. He leaned to the right, as Jenna had taught him, and banked hard into a U-turn. The wheel spun in the mud, then gained traction; he bumped back up onto the grass.

In the mirrors, he saw a couple of pale, naked figures splash out of the water and give chase briefly. But they were too late. He re-joined the path, turned on the headlight and sped off around the lake.

♦

On the far side, about five minutes later, he came upon a parking area. It was empty at this time of night. He slowed, cruised across it to a gate, then swung left onto a road that took him westward away from the city.

Rushing along in the cool darkness without a helmet, the wind filled his ears. The smell of grass and wet soil filled his nostrils. He felt free and unrestrained. Gone were the claustrophobic city streets, the towering buildings, and the bright lights. Even the cloak high overhead was invisible.

Hedgerows flashed past; gateways, too, and bridges crossing streams. Occasionally, as he steered left and right, he saw in his lights gentle hills rolling away on both sides. They were riven here and there by small valleys, spiked by trees and bushes. Out here, it wasn't hard to imagine that he was safely back on Earth.

But no. It was all merely a clever illusion to make life more tolerable for the colonists.

On he rode.

Soon he would have to stop and find somewhere to bed down during the light hours. A concealed hollow, maybe, or a thick copse of trees. Even an abandoned farm. No, this was Mars. There would be no abandoned—

A farm!

Tye told him he lived on a farm! What was it called? Brindle? Brindle Farm!

He checked his mirrors. There was no sign of anyone following, so he slowed and braked to a stop on the roadside. Looking at the instruments, his eye was caught by a familiar display. A GPS system. He fiddled with the touchscreen, quickly located Brindle Farm, and set up the most direct route to it. He also noted a system marked "Auto Ride". Jenna's had that feature as well. It enabled the unocycle to guide itself. But he left it off, preferring to steer himself. Everything in his life had been wrested from his control. Feeling the unocycle respond willingly to his touch gave him a sense of power, false and fleeting though it may have been.

◆

Brindle Farm was located twenty-three kilometres away in the far west of the colony, not far from where the cloak reached the ground. Kalen cruised through the hamlets of Golding's Point, Middlefarm, and Tokbyrne, then under the sandstone bridge, which formed the main feature of Underbridge. Windows were darkened in all the houses he passed. Nothing stirred.

Finally, following the road up the side of a steep hill, he came to a front gate signposted "Brindle Farm".

According to the clock on the handlebar display, it was just after 4.00 a.m. Kalen knew that farmers generally rose early. But this wasn't Earth, and he thought it unlikely anybody would be up yet. He swung off the road, through the gate, and bumped along a snaking driveway.

When he came upon it in the first glimmer of dawn, the farmhouse was quite unexpected. It was a small stone cottage at the base of a gentle, grassy slope. A porch enclosed a front door, and there was a window on either side. A path lined with wild flowers led to a clearing where vehicles could park.

Kalen brought the unocycle to a stop a couple of hundred metres from the building. Much as he wanted to go straight to the door and ask for Tye, he knew that would be unwise. No doubt news of his escape would soon be common knowledge, and, while Tye might understand, his mother and father probably wouldn't. No, he would have to find some way to attract Tye's attention, unbeknown to the rest of his family.

◆

Nikel's long, silken hair fluttered gently in the breeze behind her as she ran carefree through a field of wildflowers. He loved the way Martian girls ran with their long, effortless, slow-motion stride. Powerful and athletic, yet graceful and feminine. And Nikel was the most feminine, the most beautiful of them all. Still running, she turned her head to look at him. Eyes soft, sultry, and adoring. Full lips upturned in a perfect smile, the one she reserved for him only. Then from those perfect, kissable, rosebud lips came the heart-stopping words he'd always wanted her to say . . .

'Psst, Tye. Open the bloody window!'

'Wha'?'

The Martian born lay sprawled on his back, his long arms and legs hung over the sides of the single bed. He stirred and hacked a dry cough into the room. He'd been mouth-breathing again, and his tongue tasted like the floor of the chicken run. He forced his eyes open. Framed blurrily in the pre-dawn glow of the partially open window was a head on a pair of shoulders.

Clinging hopefully to the last vestiges of the dream, he moaned, 'Nikel.'

'You wish! Come on, wake up. It's me, Kalen.'

'Ugh,' he croaked, sitting up and scratching his head. 'Anyone ever told you your timing's terrible?'

'What?'

'We were just about to get it together.'

'Huh?'

'Never mind.' He tossed off the covers and staggered sleepily to the window, where Kalen was leaning on the sill. 'What're you doing out here at this time of morning?'

'Long story. Let me in, quick.'

'Don't you have doors on Earth?'

He pushed the window fully open and dragged his visitor inside. They sat on the side of his bed while Kalen related the events of the night. When he finally stopped talking, Tye just stared at him, mouth agape.

Eventually he managed, 'So you're a fugitive.'

'You could say that.'

'How much does Jenna know?'

'Only that I got arrested last night. She was there when I got carted away. Everything else has happened since. It's been the worst night of my life, I can tell you.'

'She'll want to know what's happening. Better call her.'

'Can't. My watch's in the apartment.'

'That wasn't very clever.'

'It doesn't work. I told you, remember?'

'Oh yeah.'

'Anyway, that wasn't the reason. The MSA could use it to track me.'

Tye nodded solemnly. 'Okay, I'll ring her. But listen, you can't stay here.'

'Well, where am I supposed to go?'

Tye ran a hand over the fine stubble on his cheek. Then he dragged Kalen back to the window and pointed. 'See that pond out there?'

'Yep.'

'And the apple trees behind it.'

'Yeah.'

'And the hill behind them, rising up to those big trees.'

Kalen peered through the early dawn and fixed his eyes on a copse of what appeared to be pine trees about three hundred metres away.

'I see them.'

'Right. Well, on the other side of those is a small dale with a brook. You should be safe there for the sol. Go and wait for me. I'll be as quick as I can.'

'Thanks. Could you bring something to eat when you come? I'm famished.'

'I'll see what I can scrounge up.'

'Great. Oh, and one more thing. I need something for this.' He raised his wounded hand, bound in the dirty handkerchief.

'That looks bad!'

'It is, but I'll live if I can get some cream on it.'

'Yeah, okay. I'll see what I can find in the bathroom. Now, for goodness sake, go.'

'Thanks. I really appreciate this, Tye. Coming here was the best decision I've made all night.'

'Depends on your point of view. Now get moving before you wake up the whole house.'

He shoved Kalen back out through the window and watched him ride off.

♦

The unocycle still showed a range of ninety kilometres. Good; the battery was lasting well. Leaving the headlight off, Kalen rode around the pond, disturbing some irritable geese as he went, then made his way through the apple trees and up the hill. When he reached the top, he saw that the far side ran down to a little brook.

The trees were mainly conifers with some willows mixed in, all growing taller in the weaker gravity. Under their sheltering branches, the wheel crackled over fallen pine cones and needles, as well as dry twigs, leaves, and tufts of grass. He came to a stop, dismounted, and kicked out the stand. Then he made his way down to the slowly flowing brook, knelt on a mossy rock at its edge, and scooped a few handfuls of water into his mouth. Cool and refreshing, it flowed easily down his throat. At least he wouldn't dehydrate while waiting for help.

He slipped the bloodied handkerchief off his hand and rinsed it clean. The wound had stopped bleeding, but the skin around it was red and tender to the touch. Hopefully, Tye wouldn't forget the disinfectant. He sat back, removed his shoes and socks, and immersed his feet in the water. The soothing fluid trickling between his toes took his mind off things, and he settled in to wait.

♦

It was several hours later that the sound of footfall came to him through the trees. He thought it was probably his friends, but, erring on the side of caution, he scrambled quickly behind a thick, nearby willow.

Relieved, he saw Tye first, then Jenna.

'Over here,' he called, brushing himself off as he stepped out into view.

'Here's your breakfast,' Tye said, handing him a small bag. He jerked a thumb at the stolen unocycle. 'Nice wheel. How'd you get hold of it? Or shouldn't I ask?'

'Probably best that you don't.' Kalen fossicked inside the bag and found a couple of cold sausages, which he began to chomp on ravenously. 'Oh, I needed this. You're a lifesaver.'

'Thank Keire. They were going to be her lunch.'

'Who's Keire?'

'My sister.'

As Kalen made short work of Keire's lunch, Tye noticed the makeshift bandage on his hand and remembered the disinfectant. 'Do you want to put some stuff on that cut?'

'Did you bring it?'

'It's in the bag.'

When Kalen had finished the sausages, he pulled out the tube, squeezed a gob of white gunk onto the wound, and massaged it in.

'Thanks,' he said, screwing on the top and throwing the tube back into the bag. Then he noticed Jenna looking at him with a combination of wonder and disbelief. She seemed to be lost for words. 'What?'

'Do you have any idea what you've done?'

'Probably broken half the laws on the planet.'

'And then some. People have gone to prison for less!'

The last thing he needed was to be reprimanded. 'At the moment, Jenna, I don't care. I'm completely fed up with Mars. It's a stupid planet with stupid laws.' What began as a trickle of anger and frustration began to gush out in an unstoppable torrent. 'Nothing here's real. You do know that, don't you! You all think you're so clever with your cloak, your city, your forests, and your farmhouses. Your farmhouses! Seriously, what're they about? I mean, stone houses on Mars? Come on! It's all so artificial.'

Neither Jenna nor Tye reacted to the outburst. Kalen's eyes darted wildly from one to the other. In the end, their silence forced him to back down.

With gentle disappointment, Jenna said, 'I'm not artificial, Kalen. Neither's Tye. If you think that—'

'No, no, of course I don't.' He realised how unfair he'd been to his only real friends on the planet. He lowered his head shamefully. 'I'm sorry. I didn't mean any of that. It's just . . . well, I've had a really bad night.'

'We'll forget you said it, then.'

'Thanks. I'm not used to being on the run. Huh, speaking of which, it's probably all over the news by now.'

'Curiously not,' Jenna replied, squirming into a comfortable fork of a nearby tree trunk. 'But it's only a matter of time. What were you thinking, escaping from the MSA like that?'

He leaned back on an adjacent branch and looked deeply into her brown eyes. There was anger there, certainly, but anger tempered by sympathy. Her anger, he could handle. But her sympathy burrowed deep under his skin and forced him to speak honestly. 'I'm tired of being pushed around, Jenna. And of not knowing. If I get sent back, I'll never know what really happened to my dad or why he had to leave Earth in the first place. And he did have to leave, you know. He didn't give *me* a choice because *he* didn't have a choice. I don't know why, but that's the truth. The answer to everything lies here on Mars. I need to stay until I find out what it is.'

Jenna pushed herself out of the tree and moved over to sit at the edge of the brook with her knees tucked up under her chin. Kalen and Tye followed and sat, one on each side of her.

'I don't expect you to help me,' Kalen continued. 'I just want to be left alone to do what I have to.'

'Left alone?' She frowned at him. 'Are you sure that's what you want?'

'No.' He hung his head. 'No, I'm not. I'm not sure of anything.'

'So what are you going to do? I mean, do you have even a vague plan?'

'I told you. I'm gonna find out why my dad's dead.'

'Right, but how will you do it?'

Kalen shrugged sheepishly. 'Haven't got that far yet.'

'So there're some holes in your plan, then,' Tye said.

'Huh, just a few.'

Jenna sighed. 'Maybe I can help.' She lay back on the slope, resting on her elbows. 'After you were taken away last night, I didn't sleep a wink. But as I lay awake, something occurred to me.'

'What?'

'Do you remember when we all went to see Nikel come in from her last trek?'

'Of course.'

'And when you told Krip your name, he asked if your dad had been to Mars before?'

'I told him he hadn't,' Kalen said.

'Right, but are you absolutely sure about that?'

'I think I'd know if my dad had been to Mars!'

'Well,' she retorted, 'pardon me for saying, but he didn't tell you he was going to Touchdown either.'

'She's got a point,' Tye agreed. 'You gotta admit your dad did seem partial to a secret or two.'

That had to be the understatement of the millennium.

'Yeah, okay,' Kalen conceded. He looked at Jenna. 'So where are you going with this?'

'You said he was a meteorologist.'

'Right.'

'And I'm guessing he's always been one.'

'Far as I know. Certainly since before I was born.'

'Okay. So, if he was on Mars a long time ago, the chances are he worked here as a meteorologist.'

'Makes sense, I suppose.'

'Good. Then there should be some record of him at the Met Bureau.'

'That's brilliant!' Tye enthused as he caught her train of thought. 'But how can we get hold of their records?'

'We can't. At least not the official ones. But there might be another way.' She jumped to her feet.

'Kalen, you stay here out of sight. We'll be back as soon as we can. Come on, Tye. I'll need your help.'

♦

'Where're we going?' Tye cried as his bent, twisted, and scratched unocycle rattled along through Underbridge beside Jenna's.

'My place,' she yelled back.

'What for?'

'You'll see.'

They slowed into Tokbyrne, turned right at the crossroad, and got onto Cloak Way. Its higher speed limit made for a faster journey.

They arrived outside Asheton Robotics within twenty minutes and parked their unocycles in the rack out front. Jenna pressed her face up against the front window and peered in. Her father was busy serving a woman at the counter.

'Good, he's in the shop,' Jenna said. 'Now, listen carefully. As of now, you're interested in robotics.'

'I am not! Dad needs me on the farm.'

'I told you to listen, Tye! From this moment on, you're interested in robotics. Madly, keenly, insanely in love with robots of all kinds. You want to know everything about them. How they think, move, speak. Everything.'

He stared at her suspiciously. 'Haven't been outside the cloak recently, have you? Sniffed a bit too much CO_2? Does funny things to the brain, I hear.'

Ignoring him, she continued, 'While you're in the shop telling Dad about your sudden love of all things robotic, getting him to show you some units he's fixed, asking which study courses you should apply for, I'll be out the back on his repair database. Don't ask why. I'll explain later.'

Tye was about to tell her what he thought of her idea but was cut off when the front door of the shop opened and the customer, who turned out to be Mrs Xynthropileops, stepped into the lane.

'Oh, hello, Mrs er,' Jenna said brightly. 'How's Malcolm going?'

'Ask your father,' she snapped. 'Someone turned off his autonomy software.'

'Really? How annoying.' Jenna tried not to look guilty. 'I wonder who did that.'

'No idea. Luckily, my husband managed to turn it back on.'

'Great.'

'No, it's not! This morning, it tried to get into bed with us. Dressed in my nightgown.'

'Mm, it must've gone into sleep mode. Not to worry. Leave it with Dad. He'll get to the bottom of it sooner or later.'

'Sooner rather than later, I hope,' the woman replied threateningly as she turned and stormed off down the lane.

'Regular customer?' Tye said.

'Huh, too regular. Now, come on. Let's do this. And don't forget to sparkle with intelligence and curiosity.'

He followed Jenna into the shop, wondering how to sparkle, when Scratch—or more precisely, his upper half, for Jules had been working on him and hadn't gotten as far as reattaching the legs—took matters out of his hands. 'Hello again!' he said from a shelf on the wall. 'May I tell you a joke?'

Tye looked askance at Jenna, who had begun to make all sorts of encouraging eyes at him.

He took the hint reluctantly.

'Yeah, sure. Why not? We could all do with a laugh.'

'Thank you. Are you ready?'

'Fire away.'

'Two robots go into this bar, you see. The first one orders two screwdrivers.'

'Right.'

'So the second one says, "I'm nuts and bolts about you, but I'm not that kind of robot", and storms out.'

An awkward silence fell over them.

At last, Tye said, 'Um, was that it?'

'Yes sir. I am sensing a lack of laughter. If you didn't like it, I've got lots more.'

'No, no, that's fine. I got it. You might be better telling it to an audience of ArComs, but, yes, very good. Hah. Screwdriver. Not that kind of robot. Ha Hah.'

'You asked for it,' Jules said humourlessly.

'He did,' Jenna said, giving Tye a none too subtle shove towards the counter. 'Didn't you, Tye! And that's not all you want to ask about, is it.'

'Er, no, that's right,' Tye said with a nod. 'See, thing is, I want to work in robotics. I want to be a robot engineer.'

Jules's lower jaw hit the bench at the same time as the component he was tinkering with. 'You what?' he said.

'Robotics. Artificial Intelligence. Mechanical men. I live and breathe them. They're, huh, so-o-o me.'

'I see,' said Jules, who didn't. 'And when did you trip over this life-changing revelation?'

'Seems like only a few minutes ago. Just sort of hit me, you know? I think it comes from working with drones on the farm.'

'The drones!' Jenna cried. 'That's brilliant!'

Tye's confidence rose. 'And I was hoping you could give me a few pointers. If you don't mind, that is.'

'Well,' Jules said, suspecting something was afoot but playing along anyway. 'It's true; we can never get enough engineers.'

'Good, you two keep talking about that,' Jenna said. 'I'll just be out the back.'

She went through to her father's work room, made sure the curtain was drawn all the way across, then plonked herself at the bench in front of his repair computer and began to interrogate its archives.

Chapter 10

When his friends had disappeared from sight, Kalen drank some coffee from a thermos Tye had also thoughtfully placed in the bag. It was a bit weaker than he preferred, but it was steaming hot, and it warmed him through. His hand was still stinging, but not as badly as before. The ointment was starting to work.

Now that he was fed and medicated and feeling relatively safe, for the moment at least, he became aware of another, deeper pain throbbing in his core. An all-encompassing pain that dwarfed the dull ache of his torn hand. It had been there all the time, just under the surface. Not a physical pain. Not the sort of ache a thermos of hot coffee can wash away or a dob of ointment can alleviate. It was the anguish of being alone, of being orphaned, of being far from home, and of being pursued by dangerous strangers for reasons unknown.

He shook his head, trying to toss it all loose. But it wouldn't budge. He wrapped his arms around his shoulders as though trying to squeeze it out like toothpaste from a tube. Or was he holding himself together?

Gradually, mercifully, the gentle breeze curling up the slope and the rhythmic bubbling of the nearby brook numbed him and carried him away in the soft, comfortable arms of sleep.

♦

It was raining when he woke around sunset. At first, he thought he was imagining things, but when he saw large drops pitting the surface of the brook and felt them splashing on his face and clothes, he crawled up under the cover of some willow branches to watch. It was eerily beautiful as it tumbled downward through the dying light and soaked the hills.

When it finished, a cacophony of buzzing, and croaking, and warbling rose from reeds in the shallows and tufts of grass at the waterside. And the water plopped occasionally as some small fish jumped out bravely in search of food, then disappeared. The activity continued into the evening hours.

Eventually, a little before eight o'clock, the sound of those tiny, unseen creatures was joined by the scuffling of feet behind him. Then a light came bobbing through the trees.

'Psst, Kalen,' Tye hissed.

Kalen stepped out of cover. 'Over here.'

'Did you get wet?' Tye asked.

'Water does that.'

'Sorry, I forgot it was rain sol. Should've left you an umbrella.'

'Rain sol?'

'Yeah. Not rain like on Earth, obviously,' he explained. 'It's artificial . . . er, like everything here.'

Kalen rode the jibe. 'I suppose I deserve that.'

'Yeah, couldn't resist. No, it's just an automatic sprinkler array up on the cloak. It switches on every two weeks. Keeps the plants watered and freshens everything up. Breaks up the monotony too.' He placed a bag he was carrying in the fork of the tree. 'There's some more food in here.'

'Great, thanks. I think whatever's down near the water is hungry too.'

'Oh, they're nothing. Just some fish and a few frogs and bugs. Dad says it helps with the ecology.' He unzipped the bag, shone his torch in, and produced some wrapped sandwiches.

Kalen was impressed. 'You made these?'

'Mum did. For Keire's lunch solmorrow.'

'She's gonna hate me.'

But he was hungry and took them anyway, tore open the plastic, and began to scoff them down. 'Mm, ham and cheese.' With some food inside him, he started to feel a little more optimistic. 'So, did Jenna find out anything?'

'Not sure, but I think she might be onto something. You can ask her yourself when we meet her in the city.'

Kalen paused mid-chomp. 'I can't go back there! I'll get arrested again.'

'So what are you going to do? You can't spend the rest of your life out here with the frogs.'

Kalen just shrugged and continued with his sandwich.

'Anyway,' Tye continued, 'no one will recognise you in this.'

Again, he delved inside the bag and held up a bright pink slop top with an attached hood. Emblazoned on its front was a cartoon of a Terran astronaut entreating a little green man to "Take me to your leader".

'And I suppose you think this is my colour,' Kalen said.

'No. Keire's.'

'Of course. I should've guessed. First, I steal her food. Now it's her clothes.'

'She won't miss it,' Tye replied dismissively. 'It's one of her old ones. I was thinking, since you're a bit shorter than most of us and she's only thirteen, it might fit you better.'

His foresight was commendable. The result wasn't. When Kalen had finished eating and had managed to squeeze into the top, he found that while the length was fine, the body was too tight. It made him look like a raw sausage with legs. But the fabric stretched sufficiently to make it wearable, and if he was going to hide his face from prying drones and whatever else the MSA might be using to search for him, the attached hood might prove useful.

'Perfect fit,' Tye said. 'Now come on, I promised we'd be there at eight thirty.'

Together, they walked back to where the vehicles were parked. Tye climbed onto his. Kalen mounted the other one.

'You're taking that, are you?' Tye said.

'Yeah. Why?'

'Well, it's probably been reported stolen. The MSA will be on the lookout for it.'

'I only borrowed it, Tye.'

'Without asking.'

'Yep, and that's exactly why I'm going to return it.'

Tye powered up his cycle. 'For a thief and fugitive, you're amazingly honest.'

'Huh, tell that to the judge at my trial.'

To avoid attracting attention in the farmhouse, they left their headlamps off until they reached the front gate, then accelerated down the country road towards the city. Through Underbridge, they raced, then on to Tokbyrne, Middlefarm, and Golding's Point.

In no time, they reached the entrance to the Lake Curiosity parking area. Kalen slowed down. 'I want to make a detour around the lake,' he called.

'It's out of our way,' Tye protested.

'Not if I'm going to return this machine.'

He swung through the gate and led Tye across the parking area. They reached the smooth body of black water, then turned onto the lakeside gravel path and accelerated again.

When, shortly after, the brightly illuminated buildings of the city reared up on his left, Kalen began to look more closely at his surroundings. 'I think it was along here somewhere,' he said. 'The place where I found it.'

Cruising on a little further, he saw what looked like a sheet of paper attached to a lamp post. He pulled up beside it. The light above showed it to be a photograph of the unocycle covered in scrawled handwriting smudged from the rain shower. It read:

Stolen! If you see this unocycle, please contact Marty at ASHETON-1196003 or the Martian Security Agency.

Kalen kicked out the stand, dismounted, and then climbed onto the pillion of Tye's machine. 'Sorry, Marty,' he muttered to the photo. Then to Tye, he said, 'I feel better now. Come on, let's make tracks.'

They crossed the main road and entered the city, ducking and weaving through dark, winding lanes and alleyways, swerving around ArComs running nocturnal errands and overtaking the occasional transit pod.

At a T-intersection, they turned onto the Trans-City Feeder. Supported by huge trestles, it climbed away from ground level, passed a tall spire, ducked under a building shaped like an inverted 'U', then snaked around the lower storeys of some cloak scrapers to join up with Cloak Way on the far side.

Somewhere in the north of the city, an off-ramp appeared out of nowhere. Barely slowing, Tye turned onto it. They followed it down until it levelled at a road that ran along beside a grassy area. An illuminated sign told them that North Woodlands Park lay ahead.

Before they reached that, though, Tye swung onto a clearing covered in stone pavers, on which was built an awning covering some escalators that disappeared underground.

When they'd dismounted, Tye pushed his unocycle into the border of bushes until it was barely visible.

'You took your time,' said an adjacent tree.

Jenna appeared from behind it.

'My passenger had an errand to do,' Tye explained.

'I don't want to know.'

'No, it was a good errand. He was unstealing the cycle he took. Unstealing? Is that a word?'

'Not if you just made it up.'

Jenna had changed into a pair of dark overalls with braces and had tucked her hair up inside a cap. From under its visor, she was now eyeing the vision of pink, which was Kalen. Her nose screwed up in disapproval.

'That's one of Keire's!' she said accusingly.

'Er, yeah,' Tye mumbled.

'Not exactly inconspicuous, is it!'

'Don't you start! Pink's her favourite colour.'

'Really, Tye! Sometimes I wonder.'

'I thought the hood was a good idea.'

'It is. A pity the rest of it makes him stand out like a passing comet.' She shook her head despairingly. 'Still, you've got this far, so something must be working. Come on.'

'Where to, exactly?' Kalen asked.

'The undercity,' she replied, adding to a nearby shrub, 'You too, Scratch.' The shrub shook and rustled, then the ArCom stepped out of its branches on a pair of newly-fitted legs.

They crossed the clearing in a tight huddle and stepped onto the downward-moving escalator.

'So what did you find out?' Kalen asked.

Jenna leaned on the moving handrail behind her. 'Well, I went back through twenty-five years of archived data on Dad's repair system. Turns out that he did repair ArComs used by the Met Bureau way back then, and some of those have been decommissioned.'

'Decommissioned? That doesn't sound good!' Tye exclaimed.

'No, it's great. It means they've been dumped in the decom facility.'

'I assume we can get in there?' Kalen said.

Jenna produced a pass key and dangled it before him on a thin length of cord.

'Silly question,' he muttered.

♦

The descent seemed to take forever. When the escalator finally levelled out at the bottom, they stepped off and began to make their way along a tunnel.

"Undercity" was something of a misnomer—a grandiose name for a series of excavated caverns linked by rock-walled tunnels, all lined with pipes, ducts, and cabling. Down here, deep beneath the surface, were storage areas, battery stations, monitoring systems, and the infrastructure of water, air, and power, which authorities had decided was an eyesore best kept from public view.

The cold rock walls brought out prickling goose bumps on Kalen's skin. He shoved his hands deeper into his pockets.

'Who turned off the heater?' he grumbled, breath clouding in the air.

'It's not off,' Jenna explained, 'but it turns down automatically at night after everybody goes home. That's why I waited so late to come down. There's less chance of being disturbed.'

Rounding a corner, they passed an electronics bay, then what looked like a pumping station. At last, they came upon a door marked in bold black lettering, "Decommissioned ArCom Facility". Jenna had been to it many times with her father when he had ArComs to dispose of or, more often, to scavenge for spare parts.

She ran her pass key over the lock. The door slid aside with a hiss. Before them was what looked like the scene of a bad accident. Stacked on high racks, leaning two and three deep against the walls, lying on the floor—prostrate, bent, twisted, on their backs with arms and legs stuck up stiffly in the air—were the assorted bodies of the city's old, discarded ArComs.

'What a mess,' Kalen muttered.

'We've been meaning to clean it up all year,' Jenna said a little defensively. From her pocket, she took a scrap of paper on which she had neatly written some numbers. 'Now, we're looking for three models: an Athena Two, a Zeus One, and an Apollo Six.'

'How do we know which is which?' Tye asked.

'By their ID plates.'

'And where do we find those?' said Kalen.

'Mostly on the back of their necks. If you can't find one, call me. I've written down the serial numbers here. Now, this could take a while, so let's get to it.'

In no time, Kalen and Jenna were busily scrambling over the jumble of old, worn-out machines on the floor, while Tye scaled the wall racks to search higher up.

'So, have you only got one sister, Tye?' Kalen asked conversationally as he pried apart two ArComs, which looked like they were hugging each other to keep warm.

'Yeah. Any more, and we'd be illegal.'

'Martian families are only allowed two kids,' Jenna explained.

'I did read that somewhere, I think,' Kalen replied. 'But you're an only child.'

'Mm,' she nodded. 'Mum and Dad realised they couldn't improve on me, so they stopped.'

'Huh! Dream on,' Tye said. 'More likely it was the shock of . . . here, found one! It's an Apollo.'

'Type six?'

'Ah, yeah, Apollo Six.'

'Good. Just a second.' Jenna pushed aside the unit she was examining and consulted her list. 'And the serial number is?'

'A-one-oh-six-dash-nine.'

'Nope, no good.' She stuffed the paper back in her pocket. 'Keep looking.'

'Nothing wrong with being an only child,' Kalen continued. 'I'm one.'

'But I thought Terrans could have as many kids as they wanted,' Tye said.

'Earth's pretty crowded these days, but, yeah, we can. Trouble was, my mum died not long after I was born.'

Tye realised he'd blundered into sensitive territory. Fortunately, just at that moment, his watch *beeped,* and he retreated thankfully to the back of the wall rack to take a call.

'Just ignore him,' Jenna muttered, glaring daggers up at his shelf. 'He's a bit like Richard. Spends half his life with his foot jammed in his mouth. I wonder who's ringing him.'

'Maybe his mum, wanting to know where he is.'

Then they heard Tye snigger quietly in the shadows.

'Doesn't sound like it. Never mind; I think I can guess.'

They continued their search for a time. Finally, Tye terminated the call and reappeared with a supercilious grin on his face.

'How's Nikel?' asked Jenna with a knowing smile.

'What? Oh, good. Great. Fine,' he replied, trying too hard to sound indifferent. 'Just rang for a chat.'

'About?'

'Nothing in particular.'

'Wow! Definitely one of the great romances.' She didn't know whether to be jealous or annoyed. 'Anyway, mind back on the job. In case you've forgotten, we're trying to help . . . ah, here's an Athena Two. Kalen, can you hold it?'

Kalen grabbed the torso and held it firm while she checked its serial number.

'No good either.' She scrunched up her nose in disappointment and brushed the dust from her hands. 'This could take longer than I thought.' While surveying the room, she noticed some older machines heaped against the back wall and waved generally in their direction. 'Those look more promising. Let's try over there.'

'Sure,' Kalen replied. 'I'll just finish—WHAT!' He dropped the ArCom he was holding as if it had bitten him and staggered backwards. His foot tripped on the corner of a rack, and he ended up lying in the embrace of an old catering unit.

'What is it?' Jenna cried in alarm.

'There's a body in there! A *human* body.'

'No! Can't be!'

'Yeah, over there. Behind that green one without an arm.'

Jenna pulled Kalen to his feet. He pointed at a perfectly formed figure of a man leaning against the wall. It stood a little under two metres tall and had bright blue eyes, a chiselled chin, gaunt, flesh-coloured cheeks, and a thatch of jet-black hair.

'Mm, dishy. But it *is* only an ArCom, Kalen.'

'*That* is? You're kidding!'

'Nope. And even better, it's a Zeus One. One of those on my list.'

'But it's so lifelike.'

'All the Zeuses are. Or were. They don't make them anymore.'

'Amazing.' Kalen approached to look at it more closely. 'Why did they stop making them?'

'*Too* lifelike, apparently. My dad says they were a bit creepy to have around. Most people like their machines to look like machines, not their hunky

Uncle John. So they were discontinued. Come on, let's check its serial number.'

Kalen climbed over to the Zeus and pulled its head forward, exposing the identification plate.

'It's a bit rubbed, but I can just make it out,' he said. 'Zed-six-seven-one-dash-five.'

'It's here!' Jenna cried triumphantly, stuffing her note into a pocket. 'Found one, Tye.'

Tye broke out of his swoon and monkeyed down from the racks to join them while Jenna and Kalen cleared some space around the Zeus.

'Now, let's see if we can get Uncle Hot Stuff here working.' She found the power-up button on the side of its head and pressed it. Nothing happened. 'How annoying,' she said, sitting on the chest of a unit lying nearby.

'What is?' Kalen asked.

'No power. I forgot that Dad brings a portable charger down here with him.' She sucked her teeth thoughtfully, then her face lit up with an idea. 'Scratch, come here, please.'

The ArCom had been standing quietly near the door. When he heard his name, he made his way across to them.

'Yes, Miss?'

'Time to go bye byes. I need your battery.'

'Not as much as I do, Miss.'

Jenna scowled at him. 'Like to live down here permanently, would you?'

'No, Miss. Shutting down now.'

Scratch braced his legs, locked them, and powered down.

'Tye, you do him, and I'll do this one,' Jenna instructed.

So, while Tye set about opening the access panel on Scratch's back, Jenna pried open the Zeus's chest.

When the two batteries had been removed, they were seen to be different sizes, but by using a trick of her father's, which involved bending the Zeus's terminals, along with some serious pushing and prodding, Jenna clicked the good one into place, and the old ArCom slowly came to life.

'Looking good,' she said as it started to run through its power-up protocols.

Fingers flexed, arms and legs twitched, lips pouted, eyes blinked, the nose wrinkled, and finally its handsome head swivelled to face her.

'Good morning, and thank you for activating me,' it said cheerfully. 'My name is Jonty. How can I be of assistance?'

'Pleased to meet you, Jonty,' Jenna replied. 'We need your help. Did you work for the Bureau of Meteorology?'

'I had that pleasure.'

'Good. We need to get into your archived memory.'

'Of course, Miss. Please wait just a moment.'

The ArCom fell quiet for a few seconds as its processors, unused for a generation, went to work. At last, it announced, 'The archive is available for interrogation.'

'Right. Search for name David Rance. All entries.'

Electronically stored data stirred in the deepest recesses of the ArCom's memory and rushed around its stale circuits.

In under a minute, it had an answer: 'Data accessed.'

The words hit Kalen like a couple of bricks.

'You mean you've found it?' he gasped.

'I have.'

Still not quite believing his ears, Kalen asked again, 'You've really got a record of my dad? On Mars?'

Jonty looked quizzical. 'Please clarify: your dad.'

'He means David Rance,' Jenna explained.

'That is correct. I have a listing for David Rance.'

A numbness spread through Kalen's whole body like cold water. His mind went blank. The blood drained from his face.

'You alright?' Jenna asked. 'You've turned green.' Then suddenly, she understood. 'It's the shock. You sure you wanna hear this?'

'I have to,' he replied soberly.

Jenna turned back to the handsome ArCom. 'Jonty, tell us everything you know about him.'

'Certainly. David Rance originated in Melbourne, Australia. Employed as a Level Two Forecaster, Martian Bureau of Meteorology, on the tenth of Mina, AD, two thousand and fifty-six. Promoted to Level Three in AD, two thousand and fifty-seven. Employment terminated on the eighth of Rishabha, two thousand and sixty-one. Reasons unspecified.'

'Is that it?' Jenna asked.

'Yes, Miss. Information complete.'

It wasn't the most thrilling or complete portrait of a life, but it was more than enough for Kalen. 'Five years!' he exclaimed. 'Dad was here for five years!'

Deep down, he had believed this journey into the undercity would just be a means of eliminating an unlikely possibility. But no. His father had been on Mars before he was born. For five years. And he had kept it a secret. Kalen didn't know whether to feel excited. Or angry. Or disappointed. Or some combination of all three.

'A bit of a shock, that,' Tye said.

'Huh, just a bit.'

Kalen shoved his hands deep into his pockets and walked slowly around the room like a yacht in the doldrums.

At last, he said, 'All his life, my dad seemed to be running away from something. So when he brought me here, I thought it was just more of the same. But it wasn't. He wasn't running *away from* something on Earth at all. He was running *back to* something on Mars.'

Chapter 11

As they made their way with Scratch, his battery refitted, back through the cold tunnels towards the escalators, Jenna noticed Kalen had gone very quiet. His colour was starting to return, but he had developed a bad case of the shakes.

'We'll be back topside shortly,' she said.

'Sorry, what?'

'You're shivering. It'll be warmer up there.'

He shook his head. 'It's not the cold. Jonty's just made me realise what I've gotta do.'

'What's that?' Tye asked.

'Go to Touchdown.'

'Touchdown? Do you even know where that is?'

He didn't. Not exactly. But he shrugged as if the matter were only a minor inconvenience.

'A third of the way around the planet,' Tye explained. 'You'd never make it.'

'Well, I've got to find a way,' he replied doggedly. 'It's where my dad was headed. Whatever made him drag me to Mars must be there.'

The thought of Kalen heading outside the safety of Asheton on his own worried Jenna. Deaths outside the cloak weren't as common as they'd been in the early years of the colony, but people sometimes still got themselves killed. Even people with long experience of the red planet—people who understood the dangers.

'I don't know much about Earth, Kalen,' she said softly, 'but I do know it's nothing like Mars. Here, you can't just decide to travel around on a whim. Especially with the MSA looking for you.'

'Even so, I've got to go,' he replied stubbornly.

'You don't understand, Kalen—'

'No, *you* don't understand!' he countered, frustration bubbling up. 'I'm in so much trouble now; a bit more won't make any difference. I'm on the run from authorities; I stole a unocycle—'

'Which you returned,' Tye said.

'I stole food and clothes.'

'Technically, that was me,' Tye said again. 'And that was from my sister. She won't mind.'

'I broke into that decom room.'

'No one broke in,' Jenna corrected him. 'I had a pass key.'

'Which you stole from your dad.'

'Borrowed.'

'Without his permission, Jenna! And you were doing it all for me. I'm the problem. It's up to me to fix things.'

They reached the foot of the ascending escalator, stepped on without breaking stride, and headed up out of the undercity.

'I admire your determination,' Jenna said, 'but on Mars it'll get you killed. Look what happened to—'

She cut the sentence short too late.

Kalen finished it for her: 'My dad?'

'Sorry, I didn't mean to be insensitive.'

'You never met Dad, Jenna,' he said earnestly. 'All my life, I thought he was just a dull, boring nobody. Someone who never did anything remotely exciting. Then I find out he once had a secret life on Mars. I need to know why he kept it secret. And what brought him back. And what got him killed. I'm going to do it, and nobody's going to stop me!'

The two Martian born looked at each other in bemusement at what seemed like Kalen's blind determination to put himself in danger. But the firm set of his jaw told them that no amount of dissuasion was going to change his mind.

'So how will you get there?' Jenna asked.

'A shuttle, I suppose. That'd be fastest.'

'Forget it,' said Tye. 'You won't get near one, not with the MSA crawling all over the spaceport. No, it's worse than that. You won't even get near the spaceport. They'll be watching the station.'

Kalen leaned back, elbows on the moving handrail.

'Possibly.'

'Why only possibly?' Tye asked.

He didn't answer immediately, ordering his thoughts before continuing. 'I've been declared an unaccompanied minor, right?'

'Apparently.'

'And that's supposed to be a big deal on Mars.'

'Not supposed to be,' Jenna said. 'It is.'

'Okay, so why haven't I made the news?'

'Maybe they don't want to panic you into doing something stupid,' Tye suggested.

Kalen shook his head doubtfully. 'From what I've seen of Asheton, it's big—but not that big. If my face was plastered all over the news, somebody'd see me, and I'd be arrested before I could say, "It wasn't me, officer." And, anyway, why aren't there any patrols out looking for me? I mean, we rode all the way here from your farm, but I didn't see a single MSA agent.'

'That *is* a bit strange,' Tye conceded. 'Remember what happened last year, Jen? When that miner from Tharsis ran amok in Asheton Metro.'

'Larry Doolan. Yeah, they splashed his face over every public vid in the city and shut down the transit pod system. He was in custody within two hours.'

'Less,' Tye said. 'Huh, he was so surprised they didn't even have to draw their weapons.'

'I should be so lucky,' Kalen said darkly.

Jenna picked up on that immediately. 'You mean they shot at you?'

'Not quite, but they would've if I hadn't been diving into an elevator at the time. I'm lucky I'm not on my way back to Earth in the freezer section of the *Star Rise*.'

'The *Star Rise*?' Tye queried.

'Oh, some cruiser they were holding for me in orbit.'

Jenna chewed her lower lip thoughtfully. 'But I don't get it, Kalen. The MSA wouldn't shoot at you. And Eckhart *was* from the MSA. I saw her badge. So did you.'

'Well, we saw *a* badge, but I'm not so sure about it now. Anyway, even if it was legitimate, there's something else. She lied about knowing Hilbride and Telford.'

'Why do you say that?'

'In the pod on the way to my apartment, she told me she knew them. But she doesn't. Unless Bess Telford's a cross-dresser.'

'So what're you saying? Eckhart and her cronies really work for someone else?'

'I don't know. Maybe. But whoever they are, I've got to keep my head down until I can find out what's going on.'

The escalator reached the surface. They stepped out into the night. Warm air, sweetly perfumed by flowers in the surrounding shrubbery, entered their nostrils and filled their lungs, dispelling the cold sluggishness that had seeped into them underground.

They returned to where they'd hidden their rides.

'There's something I need to mention, Kalen,' Jenna said delicately as she wheeled her cycle out into the open.

'What's that?'

'We can't come with you. Not if you're going outside Asheton.'

If he'd had time to think, Kalen would've seen this coming. But he hadn't. A knot formed in his gut. This might be the last time he saw either of them. Surely the moment called for a grand speech—some poignant remark that could be added to the annals of Martian history—something future generations could look back on and read with awe.

What actually came out was, 'Oh, um, er, right.'

Jenna was underwhelmed. She didn't even seem to be listening. Or looking at him, for that matter. Her eyes had drifted to some point in the air behind his right shoulder.

'Kalen!' she said.

Her voice was aquiver. He thought she was about to burst into tears.

'I know it's hard,' he said, 'but I've got—'

'Kalen!' Tye said.

He sounded emotional, too. And he was staring over Kalen's left shoulder in the same direction as Jenna.

'Not you too! Look, the last thing I need now is a—'

'Duck,' Jenna said.

'A duck? No, I was gonna say a scene.'

'DUCK!' Tye yelled.

The next thing Kalen knew, he had been tackled to the ground and was lying in a tangle of arms and legs under his two friends. A blinding light flooded the scene. Then a sound like a giant, angry mosquito filled their ears. A pair of boots swooped low over their heads, streaked across the pavement, and then climbed rapidly, leaving a wake of swirling dust and leaves.

'Scratch!' Jenna cried, clambering to her feet.

The ArCom had stayed upright. 'Yes, Miss. I saw it.'

'Well, that's reassuring. Analysis please?'

'Flight pack, Miss.'

'I know that, you idiot. I meant, where from? The MSA?'

'The model is not known to my database, Miss.'

'It's a Dart,' yelled Tye, who spent much of his spare time reading about such things. 'A military model.'

'Mars hasn't got a military!'

'Yeah, it's a worry, isn't it.'

'So it's armed?'

'One pulsar. One cannon.'

'Great. Scratch, any suggestions?'

'Run, Miss.'

'Don't you love machine logic!' Tye groaned, scrambling to his feet and hauling Kalen onto his. 'Let's get out of here.'

In a mad flurry of movement, Jenna and Scratch mounted her cycle. Tye dragged his out of the bushes, but before he could even get the gyro spinning, another unocycle raced off the boulevard and slowed to a halt on the pavers, blocking their way.

Squinting into the glare of its double-headlamps, they were able to make out the rider. Like his machine, he was all in black. But even though his face was hidden in a helmet, Kalen recognised the rider's broad shoulders and lumps of muscle.

It was Bernardo Rocco, one member of the squad sent to deport him.

Rocco extended his left leg to the ground and slipped a hand pulsar out of his thigh holster. His arm came to the horizontal, aimed at Kalen, steadied, and . . .

Instinctively, Kalen jammed his eyes shut and braced himself. When it came, the flash was lightning-bright. Even his closed eyelids couldn't completely block it out.

Tye yelled. Jenna screamed.

Then . . . nothing. No impact. No burning. No pain.

Surely Rocco couldn't have missed from that distance?

Kalen forced one eye open, then the other. Scratch was swaying drunkenly in front of him. His back had been ripped open, the exposed electronic innards flashing and sparking.

Responding to some deeply entrenched part of his programming, the ArCom had rushed in front of him and absorbed the shot. Somehow, he was still standing. And not only standing. He began to stagger towards Rocco, who hadn't moved from his unocycle.

Rocco fired again. The night flashed, and the air crackled. This time Scratch took the blast in the chest plate. He stumbled backwards. Threads of energy leapt and looped and chased themselves around his body, then dissipated. Instantly, his shorting systems rerouted, software rebooted. He regained some motor function and began to lurch towards the man like a macabre, mechanical Frankenstein's monster.

'Call it off!' Rocco bellowed.

That was the last thing on Jenna's mind. Anyway, ArComs weren't usually capable of violence. Their built-in protocols were supposed to prevent it. Yet Scratch was looking very menacing. He kept moving forward.

Rocco retreated a step. 'Last warning before I—'

Too late. Scratch lunged forward unexpectedly. He grabbed the weapon, wrenched it out of Rocco's hand, crushed it in his vice-like fingers, and threw it into the bushes. Then he grasped the man by an arm and leg, hoisted him effortlessly into the air, and body-slammed him onto the hard stone pavers. The thud was sickening. Rocco's helmet cracked. He groaned, raised his head slightly, then fell back and lay still.

Scratch turned slowly to face Jenna. His whole inner torso was exposed, hissing and arcing. Recovering herself, Jenna jumped off her unocycle and rushed forward with some vague idea of helping him. But quickly, she realised the damage was too great.

'Threat to life averted, Miss,' he said.

'Yes.' She stroked his damaged shoulder affectionately, then looked down in wonder at the fallen man. 'But you're not supposed to do that, Scratch. You're not supposed to harm humans.'

'I am sorry, Miss. I am in error. Energy surge has rendered my behavioural protocols non-functional. Detected threat had to be eliminated, but I have done harm. I am in error.' Suddenly, he twitched violently.

'Regret I am—regret I am now suffering complete systemic breakdown, Miss—breakdown, Miss. To preserve basic—basic neural capability. I need—need—need to power—power down imm—immed—'

Black smoke belched from his chest. The smell of ozone filled the air. Then he toppled over and collapsed stiffly beside the motionless Rocco.

Now something else whooshed over their heads. A tree on their left exploded into flames. The two Martian born dived to the ground. Kalen dropped to a crouch as the Dart jetted over him again.

He glanced across at Jenna and Tye, slowly recovering from the shock. 'We need to be gone,' he called.

Neither of his friends argued. They scrambled to their feet, and in a matter of seconds, they had boarded their machines. Jenna's was already powered up, so she reached Kalen first.

'Get on!' she yelled.

He leapt onto her pillion while it was still moving and threw his arms around her waist.

Tye joined them, juggling his helmet onto his head.

'What do you think?' Jenna said to him. 'Back onto the City Feeder?'

'No, too exposed. We'll never outrun a Dart in the open.'

Looking around frantically, Kalen noted the dark expanse of the adjacent parkland.

'In there!' he cried.

Chapter 12

At night, North Woodlands Park was a place of blackness. Black grass sprinkled with black bushes, black shrubs, black garden beds, and the occasional black bench seat. Towering over them was an assortment of trees, tall, slender, and black with twisted branches. And through it all meandered a not-quite-so black path of fine stones, which threw off a number of tributaries in different directions.

Unocycles, of course, were permitted on the paths. Signs limiting their speed to 15 kph were large and numerous, but as Jenna was bolting along at 70 kph with her headlights off, she couldn't see them.

She couldn't see much at all.

Neither could the Terran, clinging nervously to her back.

'I hope you know where you're going,' he said.

'Someplace where we won't get blown to smithereens.'

Kalen threw a glance over his shoulder. Above the park, several hundred metres back, was a bright light. The Dart's spot lamp. He could tell by the way it was zig-zagging across the treetops that the pilot had lost sight of them. But this wasn't a time for complacency. Anybody in charge of one of those flying machines wouldn't be confused for long. It was only a matter of time . . .

They came to a Y-intersection. Jenna took the right arm. It turned out to be a straight stretch, and she was able to increase speed. The wind ballooned Kalen's hood, tunnelled up his sleeves, and flapped the legs of his jeans. In spite of the cover of darkness, he felt very exposed. He tightened his grip around Jenna, pressing closer into the warmth of her back.

Jenna! Poor Jenna. And poor Tye, riding close behind.

What had he done, getting them involved in this mess?

The Dart would eventually find him, and when it did, his friends would likely be caught in the crossfire.

And now there was no Scratch to defend them. His mind whirled with visions of the ArCom's violent end. If a hand pulsar could blast holes in that tough, artificial body, what would the Dart's more powerful weapons do to their living flesh?

Their parents would have to identify what was left, just as he, Kalen, had been forced to identify his own father. No, he couldn't be responsible for that. He had to put a stop to it. Now.

'Jenna!' he yelled at the back of her helmet.

'What?'

'Let me off.'

'Here?'

'Yeah. Quick. That goon's lost sight of us for the moment.'

She hit the brake, and they pulled up beside a large tree. As Tye rolled to a stop beside them, Jenna turned to look at Kalen, her face full of questions.

'It's me he wants,' Kalen explained. 'I'll take my chances.'

Jenna stared hard at him for a moment, as if he had taken leave of his senses. But then she began to nod slowly. 'Yes. Of course! You're right. It *is* you he wants. That's brilliant!'

'It is?'

'Yep. Tye, we need a few minutes of privacy.'

'Er, now?'

'Right now. Any suggestions?'

'What about the bridge?'

'The one we all used to play under?'

'Yep.'

'Good enough. Can you find it? I've lost my bearings.'

'I think so. What're you gonna do?'

'I've got an idea. Just lead the way.'

As an explanation, 'I've got an idea. Just lead the way,' didn't exactly make Tye feel warm and fuzzy. But he had known Jenna all his life. She was clever. She had imagination. Her ideas usually bore fruit. Ripe, juicy fruit. He wheeled his unocycle around, hunched over the handlebars, and raced off through the darkened park, his friends close on his tail.

'What have you got in mind?' Kalen yelled into Jenna's helmet.

'You'll see.'

Orienting himself via a couple of park benches whooshing past on his right and a water fountain on the left, Tye swerved around the gnarled trunk of an old tree he remembered falling out of as a small kid and came upon a bridge that forded a small stream. He veered left and bumped down a rocky slope, past its pillars, and skidded to a stop under the span. Water, looking syrupy in the Martian gravity, lapped thickly across the smooth pebbles beneath his feet.

He slid up his visor. Runnels of sweat dribbled down his face. His breath came in fearful gasps.

'Your few minutes start now,' he said to Jenna as she and Kalen pulled up beside him. 'I hope this is good.'

Jenna had already dismounted her cycle. She pulled off her helmet. Her ponytail came free at the same time. Long hair flicked around her face.

'There's one of him and two of us,' she explained hastily. 'If we split up, he'll have to make a choice. And I think I can guess who he'll follow.'

'Me,' Kalen reasoned.

'You said it. You're the one he wants.'

Tye's face wrinkled with confusion. 'I think I'm missing something. So we're going to—?'

'Hand him over.'

Tye had been anticipating some ingenious scheme of escape. An act of selfless daring. What he was hearing sounded more like betrayal.

'Not quite what I expected.'

'You know me. Full of surprises. Now, Kalen, give me your top. It's about to become useful.'

'No, Jen! You can't,' Tye cried, suddenly thinking he had fathomed her plan. 'I mean, you're a great rider, but even you couldn't outrun a Dart!'

'He's right,' Kalen said. 'You saw what happened to Scratch. Whoever these people are, they mean business.'

'What *are* you two on about?' Then she realised. 'Oh, I see. No, no, I'm not that brave. Come on, Kalen—your top. There isn't much time.'

More out of curiosity than any understanding of her plan, Kalen slipped off the pillion and tugged the top over his head. Jenna snatched it from him. Then she stopped suddenly. She looked at Tye's machine.

'How much range have you got left?'

He glanced at the dash. 'Forty-three Ks.'

'Hmm, I've only got eighteen. Better use yours. Jump off. Er, do you mind?'

It was a rhetorical question. The moment Tye was off his seat, she draped the pink top over it and secured the sleeves to the handlebars with her ponytail ties.

Kalen and Tye watched on with questioning looks.

'Auto Ride's a wonderful thing,' Jenna explained.

Auto Ride! Kalen had forgotten about that. The cycle could drive to a pre-set destination by itself! The seeds of hope took root.

'Is this really gonna work?' he asked.

In Tye's head, possibilities tripped over themselves and turned into probabilities. He nodded with rising enthusiasm.

'Actually, it could. If it gets a decent head start.'

Kalen frowned. 'But what happens when the guy flying that Dart gets a close look at it?'

'He'll know we've given him the slip,' Jenna said. 'But by then, it won't matter. He'll be kilometres away. And we'll be long gone from here. Anyway, at the moment I'm not exactly overflowing with ideas, so unless either of you can do any better . . .'

I can't, boomed Kalen's deafening silence.

Don't look at me, said Tye's blank expression.

'Thought not.' She brought up the Auto Ride menu on the cycle's dash display. 'Now, where to send it.'

'Jupiter sounds good,' Tye muttered. 'Or Saturn.'

Jenna ignored him. 'I know: Solis Park. That should give us time.'

Solis Park was Asheton's biggest sports stadium, located in the middle of a broad grassed area on the opposite side of the city.

Jenna's fingers danced nimbly across the destination settings until she was rewarded with a *beep!* 'There, all set.' She flicked on the headlight and stepped back out of the way.

Tye's unocycle hummed to life, then drove itself out from under the bridge, up the slope, and began to chase its light across the park.

The pilot of the Dart immediately caught sight of it and swung around in pursuit. From under the bridge, three pairs of eyes watched it disappear over the treetops.

◆

The Labyrinth was a shopping strip just east of Asheton's centre. During light hours, it was considered trendy—the place to be seen, to browse, to shop, to chat, to eat pastries, and to drink coffee. But at this early hour, vacated and lit only by light poles, it was as quiet as a morgue. A dead place of empty shops, winding pavements, dark corners, and shadows.

And a drunk.

He was slumped in the entrance of a poky little Italian restaurant called Alphonso's. An ageing, weedy man, his face was prickly with stubble; his salt-and-pepper hair was long, pulled back, and tied with a ribbon at the nape of his neck; and he wore a brown bomber jacket of good quality but mottled with liquor stains.

His glassy eyes bounced up and down in delight as a tribe of warrior fairies in pink tutus paraded past ahead of a dancing herd of striped elephants. They always put on quite a show after his weekly session in the Black Hole bar around the corner.

Then something spooked them. The warrior fairies dived for cover. The elephants stampeded out of sight. The man peered out into the street with squinting eyes.

Voices reached his ears. Shadows stirred and shifted. A blurred shape tottered into view and resolved into the strangest creature he had ever imagined. It had six arms, six legs, three heads, and a wheel. And it was arguing with itself.

'Hooshat?' he rattled.

The argument stopped abruptly.

One of the creature's heads whispered, 'Did you hear something?'

'Nope,' replied another head.

'Hooshere?' the man said.

'Heard it that time,' said the second head. 'What is it?'

'Dunno. Squat down a bit. I can't see a thing past you.'

'I'll have tyre marks across my face if I get any lower,' came the terse reply.

'Come on, you two!' chimed in the third head. 'Sort yourselves out. You're behaving like a pair of six-year olds!'

'When was the last time you tried sitting on the handlebars of one of these things?' the second head retorted.

'Never.'

'Thought so. That's it. I'm walking.'

Kalen jumped off and stopped to massage the feeling back into his numb buttocks. The choking smell of strong alcohol hung thickly in the air. It wafted off a lump in the adjacent doorway. The lump moved and grew limbs. It was a man.

The man struggled to his feet, leaned forward, and froze at an impossible angle, as if facing a gale force wind. Unfortunately, there was no gale force wind. His nose fell into the gutter. So did the rest of him.

Concerned, Kalen approached and kneeled beside him.

'You alright, Mister?'

'Ugherrrzzz,' the man dribbled.

Grabbing him under the armpits, Kalen half-dragged and half-carried him across the pavement into the entrance and sat him down comfortably against the locked door. Dishevelled and drooling, reeking of grog, the man looked and smelled like a complete loser. Except, perhaps, for the logo sewn proudly to the breast of his bomber jacket. It was a yellow roundel enclosing the letters 'PAF' in dark blue. What it meant, Kalen had no idea, but somehow it gave the man a place to belong and pulled him back from the depths of complete worthlessness.

The man coughed thickly and snorted. Blood trickled from a nostril.

Kalen took out his clean handkerchief.

'Here, use this,' he said.

The man's eyes spun in all directions. Finally, one settled on the handkerchief. The other followed shortly after. He took it and pressed it to his face, roughly where his nose was.

'Hoo yoo?' he asked.

'Nobody,' Kalen replied, waving away a gust of alcoholic breath. 'Nobody at all.'

'Righ'. Er, yer sure?'

'Very. We're not here.'

'Wha'! None of you?' His eyes flicked to Jenna, then Tye. 'Who'm I talkin' to, then?'

Through the man's drunken slur, Kalen heard an accent. American, he thought.

'No one,' he said.

'Okey Dokey. Thanksh . . . thanksh for helpin' a man down on, down on, um . . .' His forehead wrinkled as the pickled brain behind it fumbled for the right words. 'Down on—'

'His luck?' Kalen suggested.

'Nope. The groun'. Thash it. Down on the groun'. Don' like bein' on the groun'. Better in the air. Flyin'. Thash the thing. Goin' flyin' toshol. Yup. Nuthin' like it. Up into the wild pink yonder.'

He struggled to his feet and flapped about madly as if trying to take off. Then he wobbled forwards and threw his arms around Kalen's neck, clutching him in a sloppy hug.

'Yup, yer a good kid,' said the drunk. 'Can shee that. Want your hanky back?'

'No, keep it,' Kalen replied, waving him off. 'Good night.'

'I owe yer, then,' the man replied. 'Nigh'.'

He stuffed the soiled handkerchief into one of his jacket pockets, then staggered backwards and slid down the door into oblivion.

'And I thought things were bad for me,' Kalen muttered.

Jenna rode on at a walking pace with Tye propped on the pillion. Kalen kept pace at their side. The encounter with the drunk had put an end to the argument that had been raging ever since they left the park. Now that tempers had cooled and they were thinking more clearly, they realised they were all tired, angry, hungry, and frightened.

'So where to from here?' Tye asked.

'Well, they obviously know who Kalen is,' Jenna reasoned, 'so his apartment's a no-go zone. And they saw him with me at our place, so they'll be watching the shop too.'

'I'm not hiding anymore!'

Kalen glared at his friends defiantly. They glared back.

'I mean it,' he continued. 'I've had enough. I'm going to Touchdown!'

'How?' Jenna asked in her most reasonable voice. 'As Tye said, they're probably watching the train station.'

'Forget the station. I'm gonna try the trekker bay.'

'But they could be there too,' Tye said. 'I mean, they were obviously waiting for us when we came up from the undercity.'

'I was wondering about that,' Jenna said. 'How did they know we were there? It's like they're tracking us somehow.'

An idea struck Tye like an uncharted meteor.

'Kalen, your watch!'

'Relax,' he said, holding up his bare wrist for inspection. 'I told you out at the farm; it's still in the apartment! What about yours?'

'No, they don't know anything about me.'

Jenna suddenly realised they did know about *her*. She snatched her watch from her wrist and held it before her like something with too many legs she'd found crawling in her bed.

'I didn't think of that,' she gasped.

She was about to throw it under the wheel to be crushed when Kalen held up his hand. 'No, wait. If they were tracking that, the guy on the Dart wouldn't have left us to chase Tye's cycle.'

That made sense. Jenna was relieved. Her wristwatch was a glitzy, Swiss-made gift bought by her parents for her last birthsol; not one of those cheap models made locally on a 3D printer. She slipped it back onto her wrist, and they moved on.

She gazed at the passing shop windows. Familiar and comforting in their normality, they brought to mind her regular appointments at Chantelle for Hair, the meals she'd eaten at Noh's Noodles, the designer wear she'd bought at the Miss Mars Clothing Boutique, and the visits to the Little Green Man, a male clothing store to which she occasionally dragged her reluctant father for clothes.

Tonight, all these places seemed to belong to a different world. A kinder, simpler, more civilised world where strangers didn't shoot at them.

♦

With its three passengers once more piled on board, the Unicruze rolled warily into the trekker bay's parking area about twenty minutes later. It was empty and dimly lit. They waited quietly for a few moments to make sure they weren't about to be ambushed, then, leaving the unocycle in a dark corner, they walked inside and came to a stop beside the guardrail.

The *Rebecca* was no longer in view.

'It'll be in the underground garage,' Tye explained. 'To make room for that.' He gestured at a smaller, four-wheeled vehicle, which now sat in the middle of the staging area. 'It's a Wanderer. A short ranger. Looks like it's going out soon.'

Kalen had guessed as much from the active charging cables snaking to it out of recessed ground ports. A sudden idea prompted him to ask, 'Are they hard to drive?'

The heads of both Martian born whipped around to face him.

'Don't even think about it!' Tye said.

'No, seriously, how long would it take to get to Touchdown?'

'You can't steal it!' Jenna warned him sternly.

'How long?' Kalen persisted.

'A week,' Tye said. 'Maybe more.'

'What if I get someone to take me?'

'Forget it. You'd never talk them into it.'

'I could pay them,' Kalen suggested.

'To carry a fugitive? On Mars? Not likely.'

Kalen sighed and looked a little crestfallen. They were probably right. 'A week's too long, anyway.' He panned his eyes curiously around the bay. 'I thought there'd be people about.'

Jenna glanced at her watch. 'Not at one in the morning.'

'Ah, the dead time break.'

'You know about that? Well, yes, the prep crew'll probably be in the restroom.'

'Good timing, then,' Kalen said.

His eyes drifted from the Wanderer across to the large airlock door. Immediately, he saw its possibilities.

Pointing, he said, 'I need to find a way through that.'

Tye looked at him. Twice.

'Sorry, must've misheard. I thought you said you were going through the airlock.'

'I did.'

'You do know what's out there, don't you?'

'Mars.'

'The real Mars, Kalen. Wild Mars.'

'I know.'

'Airless Mars.'

'I know.'

'Pressure-so-low-your-blood-will-boil Mars.'

'I know.'

'Radioactivity-so-high-you'll-burn-to-a-crisp Mars.'

'I know all that. Anybody with half a brain does.'

Tye swallowed the obvious retort.

'So?'

'So I'll get a biosuit, won't I!'

'Oh really? Where from?'

'Dunno, but this is the trekker bay. There's gotta be one around here somewhere.'

'Just lying around, eh? Ready and waiting for you.'

Jenna was equally disbelieving. Convinced that Kalen didn't fully understand the dangers, she decided to lead him through his argument. 'Okay, you'll find a biosuit. Then what?'

'Sorry?'

'Martian biosuits are different from the spacesuits on the cycler. Do you know what size you are? How to fit it? How to set the coms? The air flow? The temp controls?'

'They're that complicated, are they?'

'Ugh!'

'Don't be like that. I'm new here. Anyway, I'll work it all out when I find one.'

'You'll work it—?' Jenna bit the sentence off before saying something she might regret. Instead, with forced patience, she asked, 'Okay, then what?'

'The sol we arrived, I saw some little buggy things working just outside.'

'Buggy things?'

'He probably means the PICs,' Tye said, adding to Kalen, 'Perimeter Inspection Carts.'

'Whatever. They'd get me to the spaceport, wouldn't they?'

'Don't know. Maybe. If you're lucky.'

'Good.'

And before his friends could protest further, he had climbed the guard rail and began to make his way across the staging area.

'Definitely gonna kill himself,' Tye muttered with a shake of his head.

Jenna wasn't sure whether to be scared of Kalen's naivety or impressed by his courage. Or both. He was the first Terran of her age she'd had anything to do with. Surely they couldn't all be as impulsive as him? No, of course they weren't. Kalen's situation was unique. Maybe she should try to be more understanding.

'We can't really blame him, you know,' she said.

'Speak for yourself.'

'No, think about it, Tye. He's dragged all the way to Mars without being told why. Then his dad is killed in a shuttle crash, and the authorities try to deport him for being an unaccompanied minor. And when he escapes, they start to hunt him down. What does that all sound like to you?'

'A really bad year.'

'Tye! This is serious!'

'Okay, okay,' he shrugged contritely. 'It's like they're, I don't know, scared of him somehow.'

'Right! Or of something he might find.'

'That still doesn't qualify him to go trekking across the planet by himself.'

'What choice does he have? He hasn't got anybody else.'

They locked eyes for a few long moments and achieved the sort of silent connection that, between good friends, is more eloquent than any words.

'So we're it, eh?' Tye said.

'Afraid so. And, like it or not, we're involved. In what exactly, I don't know. But we're in it up to our necks.'

'Not me. They don't know who I am.'

'Er,' she said, looking at her boots sheepishly.

'What?'

'They mightn't know who you are yet, but it's only a matter of time.'

'Huh?'

'When the pilot of that Dart catches up with your cycle, he'll run the registration and—'

Tye's heart crashed to his boots, then bounced up into his throat, where it got stuck.

'It's in my name! Thanks very much!'

'Really sorry. I thought you would've realised.'

'Yeah, well, I'm a bit new at this whole being-on-the-run thing.'

He started to pace back and forth, nervously weighing up options. One by one, he dismissed them. He muttered something unmentionable. More options fell into place but were dismissed just as quickly. His lips mouthed a whole string of words, many of which would have made his Terran granny blush.

'Tye?'

He stopped mumbling and pacing.

'I haven't got a choice, have I!'

Jenna shook her head.

'Well, it's a good thing my walker creds are up-to-date. Are yours?'

She flashed him an appreciative smile. 'Of course. I did a refresher last year and passed with honours, if you remember.'

He did. At the time, he'd been very envious.

'And you're really sure about this, are you?' Tye said. 'I mean, it'll be seriously dangerous out there.'

'Not as dangerous as it was in here tonight. Huh, it might even be safer. For a while, at least.'

Voices and some laughter drifted up the ramp from below.

The prep crew was returning.

♦

Rounding the bulk of the Wanderer, Kalen passed a first aid room on the far wall, then came to a door marked "Walker Room". He pushed it open. Inside were racks of biosuits and shelves stacked with thermal under-gear, helmets, gauntlets, boots, torso rigs, and enviro packs. A number of changing booths lined one wall. Without pausing, he plucked a powder-blue suit from a hanger and walked along the shelves, selecting an assortment of gear he thought he would need. He lugged it all into one of the changing booths and started to dress.

In a matter of minutes, he realised it wasn't going to work. The suit was too big, the boots too small, the helmet wouldn't clip into the neck lock, and, as for the pressure hoses and cabling, they ended up in a tangled mess that didn't mate with any of the ports.

Then he heard the door open. He froze.

'You in here, Kalen?' Jenna whispered.

He stepped out into full view. The bottom half of the biosuit slipped down around his ankles.

'Nice knees,' Tye muttered. 'You need a belt.'

'More like an instruction vid.'

Jenna shook her head in disgust. 'You got that right. Take it all off. We'll start again.'

He fixed his eyes on her.

'What?' she said.

'You said we.'

'Well, it's pretty obvious you need help.'

'Thanks,' he said, 'um, very much.'

'Now don't go all soppy on us,' Tye said. 'We're only coming because those looney friends of yours seem to have taken a dislike to us too. Now, what do you think, Jen? Size five?'

She sized up Kalen and pursed her lips. 'He's not as tall as you. Better make it a four.' Looking along the racks, she selected a set of thermal under-gear and handed it to the Terran. 'Take this into the booth with you. Strip everything off, put this on, and then come back out. We'll help you with the rest.'

While Kalen disappeared back into the booth, Jenna and Tye each selected a set of under-gear for themselves and went into adjacent booths to change.

'When you said strip everything off,' Kalen called over the partition, 'did you mean my underwear too?'

'Everything means everything,' Jenna replied. 'While you're outside, the stuff I gave you *will* be your underwear. It plugs into your suit to keep you from freezing.'

Kalen was the last to emerge. He saw that Tye and Jenna, dressed like him in under-gear, had scrounged through the shelves and assembled three piles of equipment on the floor.

Jenna gave Kalen the once-over, untwisting some fabric here and there and making sure the power connectors were accessible.

'Okay, that looks pretty good. Now,' she added, pointing at the middle pile, 'that's yours. It's gonna keep you alive, so do as we do. *Exactly* as we do.'

They set to work. Watching his friends carefully, Kalen squeezed into the grey, form-fitting suit. The matching boots. The torso rig to which the enviro pack was clipped. The panoramic helmet. The gauntlets. The power leads were connected, and the hoses were fitted and pressure-checked.

Finally dressed, he paced up and down the room, flexing his legs, rolling his shoulders, and working his fingers in the gauntlets. The biosuit was designed to be worn skin-tight, but he was surprised to find it comfortable and easy to move about in.

Tye's voice boomed in his earpiece: 'Coms check.'

'Agh, not so loud!' Kalen groaned.

'Sorry, my fault.' Jenna adjusted a slide switch on a control panel on his left forearm. 'That better?'

'Much.'

While Tye kept an eye on things outside, she worked a little longer on Kalen's suit settings, tweaking the thermal control system, the gas flow, and the fuel cell settings. When she was finally satisfied, she and Kalen bundled up all their clothes and rammed them into a bin.

Jenna held onto her expensive watch. Reluctantly, she said, 'I suppose this better stay, too.'

Kalen nodded at her. 'I don't know if those goons will be able to trace it outside the city, but, yeah, better leave it.'

'Oh, Mum's so going to kill me.'

'She won't get a chance to if those goons find us first,' Tye said.

'Good point.' She tossed the watch into a nearby bin, and then they joined Tye at the door. 'Anything happening?'

Tye peered out. 'Could be. The prep crew's gone back inside. I think the Wanderer's about to head out.'

Lights inside the vehicle had come on. People could be seen moving about in the cabin, and someone had taken their place in the driver's seat.

'This might be our chance,' Kalen said. 'If we can shadow it into the airlock, no one'll know we're gone.'

It was a good idea. Their only other option was to go through the smaller walker airlock, but Tye and Jenna knew that was connected to a safety alarm. The moment the outer door opened, an alert would sound. Clearly, they didn't want that.

The Wanderer's hydraulic brakes hissed. Then its powerful motors hummed and heaved it forward.

'Quick,' Kalen said. 'It's now or never.'

Double-checking to make sure the coast was clear, they raced around to the far side of the Wanderer, out of sight, and kept pace with it as it edged forwards.

The inner airlock door opened ahead of them. The vehicle manoeuvred inside. They huddled beside one of the large front wheels as the door sealed behind them.

'Pressure drop,' Jenna warned Kalen. 'Brace yourself.'

Vents on the outer wall opened. The Terran atmosphere roared out. Motes of fine dust swirled into the air. The temperature dropped. Fog formed all around them as the air pressure plummeted. A sheen of vapour coated each of their visors before the suit demisters kicked in.

Now the heavy outer door began to rise into its housing. The fog dissipated. The Wanderer's powerful headlights came on and blazed out into the Martian night. Then it edged slowly outside and trundled off across the landscape.

Nobody on board noticed the Terran and his two Martian born friends dash away into the darkness behind them.

Chapter 13

The world had turned pitch black. It was as if all the light in the universe had been snuffed out.

'I can't see a thing,' Kalen said.

'Me either,' agreed Jenna. 'We need some lights.'

Tye glanced around nervously. 'Okay, but low beam only. And keep them down. We'll stick out a light year if anybody looks this way.'

His helmet lamp came on, followed moments later by Jenna's. With some fiddling, Kalen brought his own lamp to life. Still, there wasn't much to see. Just the three of them facing each other on a patch of frost-encrusted dust speckled here and there with small rocks. The cloak base formed a two metre high backdrop. Everything else beyond their little bubble of light was shrouded in darkness.

'How much air have we got?' Kalen asked.

'Enough for ten hours.'

'Plus a half-hour reserve,' Jenna added.

'Let's not waste it, then.' Kalen gestured north along the perimeter. 'The carts I saw were this way.'

He headed off counter-clockwise around the base of the cloak with his friends close behind. In a matter of minutes, they came upon a cluster of four small vehicles. Simple and practical, they were little more than a chassis on four wheels. Kalen was reminded of go-carts, though these were larger, more robust, and had two seats and a load tray on the back.

Tye went to the first one and walked his gloved fingers across the console. Nothing happened. He groaned in annoyance.

'Trouble?' Kalen asked.

'It's out of charge. What's the next one like, Jen?'

She climbed into the seat of the second cart.

'The same,' she said.

Through their visors, Kalen saw the beginnings of concern on Tye's face. The Martian born seated himself in the third machine.

'This one's got a few volts,' he said.

'Enough to get us to the spaceport?' Kalen asked.

'Not even close. What about the last one, Jen?'

She was already sitting in its seat, playing with the controls. They could see by the way her shoulders slumped that the news was bad.

'I can't believe this.' Tye sounded as exasperated as he felt. 'Four carts, and not one of them any good.'

'But we must be able to recharge one,' Kalen said.

'Sure—if we had a charger.'

Jenna said, 'Whoever used them last obviously didn't notice they were so low.'

Kalen turned away and stared out into the black nothingness. He was annoyed at lots of things, but mainly himself. 'I should've tried my luck at the station.'

'The train,' Jenna said. Then more exuberantly, 'Yes, the train! Tye, when you say 'a few volts' on that one, exactly how many Ks range are we talking?'

'It's virtually dead, Jen.'

'But how many?'

He looked again at the display. 'One point eight.'

'Good. Should be enough. Jump on the back. Kalen, into the front beside me. We're going for a ride.'

'Where to?'

'You'll see.'

While Kalen climbed into the front, Tye tossed aside some loose tools to make room for himself, then clambered onto the tray. Jenna backed out, and they headed away from the city.

'Do I need to remind you the spaceport is twelve Ks from here?' Tye said.

'We're not going to the spaceport,' she replied.

They drove on for a time, watching the red surface roll past and listening to the faint hiss of air feeding into their helmets.

'Everything looks so different at night,' Jenna said, peering hard into the blackness. 'It can't be much farther.'

'What can't?'

Suddenly, the beams of her helmet lamp bounced off a drab wall-like structure that had reared up out of the ground ahead. It stood three metres high and extended left and right, beyond the range of their lights.

'That,' Jenna said, a hint of triumph in her voice.

'The Maglev track.' Tye sounded mystified. 'I'm not with you.'

'Not the track, exactly. The runner rail.'

Their lights glinted on a metallic rail embedded in the side of the Maglev structure.

Tye said, 'What do you—? Oh, I see! That's clever!'

'Glad you think so,' said Kalen. 'You've lost me.'

'Maintenance crews ride the runner out to service the track,' Jenna explained. 'It goes all the way to the spaceport.'

She drove in close, swung sharply left, and began to follow it.

'There's a boarding point just along here.'

'And you know all this, how?' Tye asked.

'Emi's dad works for Maglev Mars. You haven't met Emi Tamura, Kalen. She's a friend of ours. Her dad took her to work a couple of times when she was younger. We had to sit through her boring presentation on it at the Learning Centre.'

'I don't remember that,' Tye said.

'You wouldn't. You snored all the way through it.'

The cart's console began to flash red.

'Battery's dying,' Kalen said.

'Doesn't matter. We're here.'

She pulled up.

The runner, a box-shaped assembly of panels, hung off the rail beside a boarding plate about head height off the ground. It was accessed by a ladder. One by one, they climbed into it and found themselves facing a simple control panel with a joystick.

'And I suppose Emi told you how to drive it, too,' Tye said with a mixture of cheek and hope.

Jenna shook her head. 'No such luck.'

'Well, it can't be that hard.' Kalen had unintentionally propped himself between his two friends, directly in front of the console. He ran his eyes over the controls. 'It looks like it's basically stop and go.'

He pressed a button marked "Power". Lights on the console glowed. A standby indicator showed the machine was ready.

He slid the power lever forward, and they shot off along the rail in the direction of the spaceport.

It was still hours from dawn, so the only real indication of movement was the Maglev track whizzing past on their left and the rocking motion of the runner. It surged, slowed, jerked, and lurched along. So much so that Kalen began to feel quite sick. He'd read about people throwing up inside space helmets. The only advice they'd had to offer was: don't.

Fortunately, in under ten minutes, the landscape ahead lit up with the foreglow of the spaceport. Shortly after, the facility itself came into view.

Kalen pulled the power lever back, and they slowed to a halt just outside the boundary.

'What are we stopping here for?' Tye asked.

'It just occurred to me, if we go inside the terminal, people will start asking questions. I mean, what reason do we have for being here at this time of night?'

'But we've got to get inside,' Jenna protested. 'There's no other way to board a shuttle.'

'And the moment we try, we'll be arrested; or if we do somehow manage to get onto one, we'll be picked up at Touchdown. I might as well just deport myself.'

Much as it pained Tye and Jenna, they had to accept that Kalen was probably right.

'We should have thought of that before we came out here,' Tye said.

'No, it doesn't change the plan,' Kalen replied firmly. 'We're still going. We just need to rethink how.'

They leaned quietly against the back of the runner for a few minutes, mulling over possibilities.

Oddly, hidden there in the quiet darkness between his two friends, Kalen felt safe. The nausea had faded, and he was warm. His suit had plenty of air and power. Only Tye and Jenna knew he was here. There was no need to rush into anything.

He calmly scanned the length and breadth of the spaceport. Rectangular in shape, its borders were delineated by red lights placed every so often along the boundary. The main terminal building sat nearby. Other buildings were scattered about too, all connected by enclosed walkways. Service vehicles lay idle on the ground near the fence. Pieces of stray equipment were strewn everywhere, awaiting the start of operations later that sol. And everything was bathed in the dreamy amber glow of sulphur lights.

His gaze drifted to a freight yard on the right. In it stood half a dozen inactive exoskeletal lifters amid orderly lines of containers ready for loading.

Air freight! A possibility sprung to mind.

'Jenna,' he said, 'can we access flight schedules from here?'

'Uh-huh. Should be able to.'

Her nimble fingers played across her suit controls. A few seconds later, a flight list from the spaceport database was showing on her visor HUD.

'Got it,' she said.

'Okay, call out all the flights to Touchdown.'

'Um, let's see.' She ran her eyes up and down the list. 'Only two passenger services. One MarsAir flight at thirteen hundred—that's an airship. Another one at fifteen-thirty: a plane. Nothing at all this morning for MarsAir.'

'We'll be running low on air by then,' Tye said doubtfully. 'It doesn't have to be MarsAir, does it?'

'Suppose not. Here's one. Departs at six this morning. Flight PAF03 on the *Blue Dawn*.'

Kalen's head snapped up. 'Did you say PAF?'

'Phipps Air Freight,' Tye explained. 'Why, have you heard of it?'

'Not exactly. It's just something I saw before. So it's a freight company. Plane or airship?'

'Airship. Phipps Air only flies airships. That's probably it over there.'

He pointed to an enormous, pale, elongated shape, curved on top and flat on the bottom, resting on landing skids in a clearing beyond the freight yard. Spot lamps on its sides illuminated the company insignia on the tail fin, a blue "PAF" on a yellow roundel.

'The *Blue Dawn* at six o'clock,' Kalen said. He glanced at the time on his own suit HUD and nodded slowly. 'That's our ride. We've got four and a half hours to find a way on board.'

◆

Tye's battered, riderless unocycle lay on its side in the middle of the road, just outside the gated entrance to Solis Park. The pink slop top lay twisted on the ground nearby, one sleeve still attached to the handlebar. Three people were gathered around it, heads lowered as if mourning its loss.

One was Soryn Eckhart. The second was Rohan Neale.

'How could you let them get away?' asked the third.

He was Thaddeus Wolf. Though his bearing suggested someone younger, he was a man in his early sixties who wore a long coat with an upturned collar, which hid the lower half of his large face. Standing a good head and shoulders above the others, he was very imposing. His voice was deep, quiet and deliberate, the words carefully crafted. And he spoke them with the confident leisure of a man who knew he wouldn't be interrupted.

Neale, the pilot of the Dart that had landed on a nearby grass verge, said, 'He's not acting alone.'

Thaddeus stared down at him menacingly.

'Sir!' he insisted.

'He's not acting alone—sir,' Neale repeated, the last word hissing through his teeth.

Thaddeus looked at him a little longer, then turned away, choosing to ignore the hint of disrespect.

'How many are there?' he asked.

'Three, sir.'

To Eckhart, Thaddeus said, 'Do we know who they are?'

'One's the Quill girl. We know that for sure. The Terran's staying with her. They seem quite chummy.'

'I have no interest in how chummy they are.'

'No, sir. Of course.'

'And the third?'

'We don't know yet.'

He stared at her gravely.

'Given the fee we're paying you to make all this go away, I don't ever want to hear you say you don't know.'

'No, sir. Yes, sir.'

She swallowed hard. Few men could instil fear in Eckhart. But this one did. There was something menacing in the quietly controlled voice, the large hands with thick fingers, and the small, narrow-set eyes that never wavered. Cold shivers ran up her spine. She broke out into a clammy sweat. Yes, something primal and instinctive told her this was a man not to be crossed.

'Yes, sir,' she said again. 'We're running the registration of this machine against our database. It's only a matter of time before we identify the owner.'

'And then?'

'I'm thinking I should involve the parents.'

'No. You won't involve the parents. Not under any circumstances. You won't involve anybody else at all. And when you find these kids, I don't want them in a position to talk about any of this. Do I make myself understood?'

'You mean—?'

'I mean, Mars is a very dangerous place. Accidents are bound to happen from time to time. While we do our best to avoid them, we're not to be held responsible if a recently arrived Terran leads two of our foolhardy Martian born astray with—how shall I put it—tragic consequences.'

'I understand, sir.'

'No, you don't. Nor are you supposed to. All you need to know is that if we fail, if anybody learns why David Rance returned to Mars, lives will be irrevocably changed. And that would be most unfortunate.'

'Yes, sir.'

'Most unfortunate indeed.'

♦

Kalen edged the runner forward and brought it to a stop just inside the perimeter fence. Here, the drop to the ground was about three metres. Even in Martian gravity, it was still an impressive leap in full biosuit gear.

Kalen and Jenna scrambled out of the cage and alighted catlike on their feet. Tye tripped on the edge as he jumped and landed on his head.

'You okay?' Jenna asked.

'Yeah, of course,' he said, gaining his feet and dusting himself off. 'I'm always doing that.'

'Honestly, Tye. I wish you'd be more careful. One sol, you're really going to hurt yourself.'

She inspected his helmet and fittings for damage. There was a small dent in the pack casing, but not enough to cause concern, so they headed off towards the freight yard.

Kalen wanted to run, but it was dark, and, as Tye pointed out, it was too risky to use their helmet lights. So, for a little over half an hour, they skirted the sides of buildings, skulked through shadows, and, when they couldn't avoid them, trotted with hunched backs across swathes of open ground. Finally, they reached the freight yard fence.

They sneaked along its base until nothing stood between them and the *Blue Dawn*. Nothing, that is, except the freight handlers busily working around the open cargo hold doors.

They presented a problem. One for which Kalen didn't have an immediate solution.

He looked along the fence line. About one hundred metres away was a gate. It opened onto a marscrete apron stacked with containers, obviously awaiting transfer to the airship.

'There,' he said.

Without waiting, he ran off towards them. He didn't break any land speed records, but he reached the closest one swiftly and crouched at its base to catch his breath. Jenna joined him moments later.

Their breathing quickly quietened and steadied. In his earpiece, though, Kalen could still hear the sounds of heavy gasping.

'Who's that?' he asked.

'Not me,' Jenna replied. 'Tye, you alright?'

They twisted to look behind them. Their friend wasn't there. He was staggering about in the open, about ten metres away, apparently not sure where he was.

'Don't know,' came his gasping voice. 'My air—'

Then his legs buckled, and he collapsed in a heap on the hard surface. Immediately, Jenna and Kalen launched themselves across to his fallen body, and, taking an arm each, they dragged him back behind the containers and out of sight.

Kneeling at his side, Jenna examined his suit's environment displays.

'Your CO_2's way too high. Hang on, I'm just going to tweak your gases.'

Her fingers played frantically across his forearm controls. While she did, Kalen switched his lamp onto low beam and stared hard through Tye's visor. His lips were tinged blue, and his eyes were closing.

'He's not looking good, Jen.'

'Stay with us, Tye,' Jenna pleaded. 'You should be feeling better in a second.'

Several passed. Almost a minute. Finally, Tye's breathing quietened and became less laboured.

'CO_2 level's dropping,' Jenna said, the relief in her voice palpable.

Tye's eyes flickered, blinked, then opened.

'Ugh, I hope someone got the name of that comet,' he groaned.

Jenna sighed in relief. 'What happened?'

'Dunno. It just started. Maybe I jarred something inside my pack when I fell.'

Recovering quickly now that regular airflow had been restored, he sat up and leaned against the wall of a container.

'Could be,' Jenna said. 'I can't do anything about it here, but first chance we get, I'll check your scrubbers.'

'Another reason to get on board that ship,' Kalen said.

Jenna looked at him intently. 'Assuming it's the right one. We don't know for sure that it is.'

She'd made a good point. One worth checking. He peered around the corner and stared hard at the vessel. There was some lettering on its nose. At this distance, it was barely decipherable, but he just managed to make out the words *Blue Dawn*. He got to his feet and wandered a few paces along the neat row of cargo. It was a mixture of tightly wrapped pallets and sealed containers. Running his helmet lamp over them, he saw that each was labelled with printed shipping instructions: "AIR CARGO - FLT PAF03, ASHETON-TOUCHDOWN 10/4".

'We're in luck,' he said, the relief in his voice obvious. 'And we shouldn't have to wait long.'

They didn't. A small tractor with a train of carts in tow soon pulled away from the *Blue Dawn* and snaked its way towards them.

The three friends ducked into a space between some containers. The vehicle arrived shortly after. The two handlers on board climbed off, disappeared for a few moments, then returned, each clumping along in an exoskeletal lifter. The powered lifters, with their huge mechanical claws, made light work of the loading.

One by one, the carts were loaded.

When he was happy he understood their routine, Kalen said, 'Okay, when they come back for the next two, follow me.'

Again, both lifters clumped back among the freight. They stopped beside a couple of pallets one row along and started to grapple them into the air. Unseen, three figures dashed out, around the front of the tractor, and jammed themselves in between two containers on the fourth cart.

Confinement in the tight space was very uncomfortable. Fortunately, the loading was completed quickly. In no time, the handlers had parked the lifters and begun the bumpy drive back across the dust towards the airship.

From a distance, the *Blue Dawn* didn't look very impressive. Up close, it was a different matter. A vast, streamlined fuselage containing a series of cavernous cargo holds. Four engines hung off its sides, wings and fins were fitted at the tail, and a small, clear bubble for the pilot hung under the bottom towards the nose.

As they wound their way towards the vast vessel, Kalen noticed that the loading crew was working on the far side. The cargo bay doors on the near side were still open, their ramps reaching to the ground like tongues. This was going to be easier than he had anticipated.

'Get ready to jump,' he said.

The tractor reached the tail. As it swung around to the left under the lower vertical fin, Kalen, Jenna, and Tye jumped off and dashed to the shelter of the nearby large landing skid. From there, it was a simple matter to run up through the nearest cargo door and into the safety of the hold.

Chapter 14

The cavernous cargo bay lay in darkness. Luckily, the vessel's outer lights shone far enough inside for Kalen, Jenna, and Tye to find a place behind some pallets to sit down and wait. They didn't dare turn on their helmet lamps for fear of attracting attention.

As it turned out, their fears of discovery were unfounded. In the two hours it took the loading crew to complete the job, only one wandered down their end of the vessel, and he didn't even stop at the door, let alone come inside.

They were all starting to get quite stiff from sitting still when, at around 5.30 a.m., they heard the faint whining of machinery. The door by which they'd entered hinged slowly upward until it sat flush with the wall. Heavy bolts slid into place, sealing them inside.

'At last, Touchdown, here we come,' said Tye, flicking on his suit lamp.

They got to their feet, stretched their muscles, and looked around.

At over two metres high and ten metres long, the cargo bay was more spacious than Kalen had expected. But the amount of cargo crammed in there, secured to the floor and walls by webbing nets, didn't give them a lot of room to move about.

Tye clambered over a couple of pallets and made his way to the door. Beside it was a small control box. He turned a switch, and small lamps flooded the bay with light.

'Might as well save our suit power,' he said, turning off his helmet lamp.

Then the room lurched. Pitched upward. They all skittered across the slippery metal floor, bounced off pallets like balls in a pinball machine, and came to a jarring halt against the back wall.

'We're climbing,' Tye announced.

'Good,' Jenna said, picking herself up. 'Come on, let me have a look at your suit. I don't want you passing out again.'

Tye found a spot on the corner of a pallet and sat down. Jenna knelt behind him and unclipped an access panel on his enviro-pack. Inside were spherical cells, bottles, and boxes linked by tangles of cables and coloured metal tubes.

With nothing else to occupy him, Kalen found a comfortable spot nearby and settled down to watch her work.

'I meant to ask, Tye,' he said, 'how did the big date go?' In his earpiece, he heard a deep sigh, almost like a moan. 'That good, eh? What did you do, or is that too personal?'

'Nothing much. She just took me to some mountains in South America, where we visited her pet talking unicorn.'

'Er.'

'Then I took her to the beach.'

'So there was drinking.'

'Oh, don't listen to him,' Jenna said. 'They only went to the holoplex.'

'Not *only*,' Tye said. 'She booked a private suite just for the two of us.'

This surprised even Jenna. She stopped working for a moment. 'But that would've cost a fortune.'

'She paid.'

'What?'

'You heard me.' Tye signed deeply. 'She had it all planned.'

'And now, I suppose you're in love.'

'Well—'

'Oh, give me strength! Kalen wouldn't be so gullible, would you, Kalen?'

'Don't know. I suppose it would depend on the girl.' He flashed Tye an encouraging smile. 'Good for you.'

It was kindly meant, but he was unable to keep a tinge of envy out of his voice. Not envy of a date with Nikel, though that would have been understandable. He was jealous of its normality. That's what he should be doing. Going out. Having fun. Not running for his life on this dustball of a planet.

He sighed and forced himself to refocus on Jenna's work. She was probing here and prodding there with what seemed to be expert hands.

'Where did you learn all this stuff?' he asked.

'Oh, I don't know that much, really,' she answered with a modest shrug. 'What I do know I mostly got from watching my dad in the shop. And we were taught some basic biosuit repairs on the walker course. Two full sols of theory before they'd let us loose outside.'

'Huh. And I was just going to wander out in that blue thing I pulled off the rack. I'd probably have exploded.'

'Don't believe that old wives' tale!' Tye said, twisting a little to face him.

'Keep still!' said Jenna.

'Sorry. I'm just saying, people don't explode.'

'It might be better if they did. At least it'd be fast. Remember the first sol of our course? We were shown a photo of an old guy they found dead outside the city.'

Tye nodded at the memory. 'Dusty? The old outbacker who walked outside, sat down on a hill overlooking the city and pulled off his helmet.'

'That's him.'

'What was his real name?'

'Drummond, I think. My dad knew him.'

'That's it. Wal Drummond.'

'And he killed himself!' Kalen said. 'Why?'

'Who knows! Although one rumour has it that he was trying to sniff the sunlight.'

'Sounds like he was off his nut.'

'Maybe. I don't think anybody really knows. He was a bit of a recluse. Anyway, like I said, they showed us his photo. It wasn't pretty: blackened, bleeding from the eyes, freeze-dried. He went through a couple of minutes no one should ever have to go . . . ah, here's the problem, Tye.'

She pressed her helmet up close to his pack to get a better look.

'Can you fix it?' he asked.

'I think so. One of the scrubbers has come loose.' Her fingers began to work on it. 'If I can . . . get a grip . . . I might be able to . . . screw it back—'

Suddenly, her hands slipped. She fell forward. Her visor struck the back of his pack with an audible clicking sound.

'Oh no!'

'What is it?' Kalen asked.

She didn't answer immediately.

'Jen?' Tye said. Then the HUD on his helmet began to flash with red warnings. 'Woh! What's happening?'

'I've broken it,' she gasped.

'What?'

'This.' Slowly, she withdrew a small disk-shaped component from inside his pack. The threaded port on its side was cracked. 'I can't believe it. It snapped off in my hand.'

Tye tried to get to his feet, but Jenna placed a gentle hand on his helmet and pushed him down.

'Better not move,' she said. 'Your air's not cleaning properly. In fact, go onto your reserve. Now.'

'Yeah. Good idea.'

Tye was clearly shaken. He switched to his emergency air supply and slumped back down onto the pallet.

'I'm so sorry.' Jenna huddled close to him and linked a comforting arm through his. 'I really am, Tye. It was right near the dent in the outer case. Must have got knocked when you fell.'

Kalen glanced from one to the other.

'Silly question, but is this as serious as it sounds?'

Tye nodded slowly. 'Put it this way: if we don't do something in the next half hour, I won't be seeing Touchdown—or anything else. Not ever.'

So it *was* that serious!

'Then we better do something,' Kalen said.

His mind racing, he wandered off around the bay, as if a solution might be found among the numerous containers and pallets of freight. At the far wall, he tried to slide his gloved fingers in behind a metal panel. If he could pry it loose, he might be able to break into another compartment, maybe one with access to a pressurised section of the vessel.

But that was too much to expect. It wouldn't budge.

He backtracked along the outer wall and came to a stop at the entry hatch. It was tightly sealed and held in place by three latches. They were power-driven, but because the cargo bay wasn't pressurised, they weren't designed to be especially sturdy. An interesting possibility occurred to Kalen. His eyes drifted to the floor beside the hatch, where a winder handle was marked with a sign reading, "Manual Door Access – Emergency Use Only". Kalen thought it was probably to allow the escape of any loading crew unfortunate enough to be trapped inside before take-off.

Tosol, it would serve another purpose.

'What is it, Kalen?' asked Jenna.

She and Tye had been watching and moved over to join him.

'If we could break the hatch open, the pilot's controls will probably light up like a Christmas tree.'

'Just before we fall out of the sky! Great thought.'

'No,' Tye said. 'This is a vacuum airship. As long as the bladders hold, it'll stay airborne. One little hole in its fuselage wouldn't necessarily be a disaster.'

'Exactly what I was thinking,' Kalen said. 'But the crew would want to investigate it. Urgently.'

'They would!' Tye enthused. 'And these ships can land anywhere. They'd take us straight down. But how would we do it? I mean, I can see the emergency crank handle there, but the latches are power-locked. There's probably a failsafe mechanism in place, too, to stop them opening mid-flight.'

'What if we cut the power to it?' asked Jenna.

Kalen and Tye shared a hopeful glance.

'Worth a try,' Kalen said.

Jenna looked more closely at the control panel on the wall. 'If I had a screwdriver on me, I'd shut it down in a flash.'

'There might be something in here almost as good.'

'What?' asked Tye.

'Never you mind. Just sit down and save your air. Come on, Jenna, help me look.'

Tye sat back quietly on a pallet and listened in to his friends' conversation.

'What are we looking for?' Jenna asked.

'Around here somewhere—I remember seeing . . . here! Help me.'

Working quickly, they unclipped a cargo net from a pallet, dragged it aside, and ripped open the plastic wrapping. Underneath, lay some neat bundles of digging tools: picks, rakes, crowbars, shovels, and spades.

'Garden supplies,' Jenna said. 'You've lost me.'

Ignoring her, Kalen unstrapped one of the shovels and hefted it into the air. In the light gravity he could swish it about like a club.

'A shovel?' Jenna said.

'Yep. It's gonna dig us out of trouble. But first, help me with this net.'

Tye had been following the conversation avidly and seemed to understand what Kalen was up to. He got to his feet and joined them.

'You're supposed to be sitting still,' Jenna said.

'It'll be faster with the three of us,' he replied. 'If this works, we'll be on the ground in plenty of time to get me help. If not . . . well, it won't matter.'

Neither Kalen nor Jenna could argue with that, so all three manhandled the cumbersome net into the open space near the hatch. Kalen stepped into the middle of it while his friends drew it up and around him like a coat, leaving his arms and legs poking out between the webbing straps, free to move.

'That's it,' he said. 'Now clip it to the floor here and stand away from the door.'

When all was ready, Kalen started to rain down blows on the door control panel. The first cracked its display, and the second caused the bay lights to flicker and die. They switched on their suit lamps. He struck again. The fourth blow sent the panel tumbling across the floor, trailing torn wires.

'That should've killed the power,' he said.

Throwing the shovel to one side, he grabbed the first latch and slid it back into the open position. The sharp clunk was faintly audible even through his helmet. Then he retracted the remaining two.

'Okay,' he called. 'Keep back against the far wall and grab hold of something. It's about to get windy.'

He knelt before the crank handle and gave it a twist. It moved slightly. Applying all of his Terran strength, he turned it again. It was becoming easier. A sliver of light appeared in the crack at the door seal. Again, the handle turned. The crack widened. Beams of bright morning light streamed inside. He kept cranking, and the hatch pushed out into the jet stream.

Suddenly, the atmosphere rushing past outside caught the hatch and wrenched it fully open. A vicious gust blasted into the cargo bay. It swirled around Kalen. Gripped him with icy fingers. Then it lifted him off his feet and carried him headfirst out through the doorway.

♦

Clang! Clang ! Clang!

The pilot's eyes jerked open blurrily. Daggers of pain erupted behind them. His red eyeballs spun about. He uncrossed his ankles and kicked his feet off the instrument console. A warm, half-drunk cup of coffee went flying.

'Wossat?'

Instrumentation swam in and out of focus, settling finally into semi-clarity. A red warning indicator flashed on the overhead display. He stared at it and sat up.

'Breach in cargo bay five. What's that all about, Canis?'

The old German Shepherd curled up in the seat beside him, lifted its hoary muzzle, and looked at him. Then it lowered its head sleepily back onto its front paws.

The pilot's flight bubble was hung off the bottom of the craft about a quarter of the way back from the nose. Accessed by some steps from the observation deck concealed within the fuselage, it provided a 270-degree view of the landscape forward and below the crew and observer seats.

The pilot looked out through his side windows. Even now, after many years of flying across the Martian desert, he took a moment to marvel at the landscape around eight hundred metres below.

Directly beneath him stretched the western rim of Herschel Crater. Good. They were on course. A veteran of the run between Asheton and Touchdown, he knew by heart the names of every major crater and many of the larger landforms they crossed. It was his favourite route, mainly because it was one of the shortest in the company's network, but also because he could fly it alone and nothing ever went wrong. Well, not usually.

'Never known one of these things to breach,' he muttered to the dog. 'Something's not right.' He brought up the vessel's cargo manifest on a screen and scrolled through the entries. 'Let's see: raw materials, foodstuffs, tools, mining supplies, a spare drill engine, some general hardware. Nothing to worry about in that lot.' A fresh thought upturned his bushy eyebrows. 'Unless that crook Phipps is up to his old tricks again.'

'That crook Phipps' was Woden Phipps, the owner of the company. Known across Earth as a "colourful character", he led his life in that shadowy divide between the legal and the illegal. Rumours of diamond smuggling in Africa, money-laundering in the European Union, people-smuggling across Asia, and gunrunning in South America followed him wherever he went, as did a number of jealous husbands intent on murder. But neither the law nor any of the miffed husbands ever managed to catch up with him, and he had arrived on Mars about six years earlier, ready to do business. Within a year, Phipps Air Freight was established and trading.

'Blasted Phipps!' the pilot cursed. 'Boss or no boss, if he's stuck something nasty on my ship, I'll be volunteering him for the Nudist Spacewalking Society.' He sighed heavily. 'Still, we got to deal with the here and now. Don't we, boy.'

Canis burped in reply.

The pilot pulled on his earpiece.

'Asheton control, Asheton control. This is the *Blue Dawn,* tracking from Asheton to Touchdown.'

The crackling in his earpiece was replaced by a male voice.

'Good morning again, *Blue Dawn*. Thought we'd heard the last of you this week.'

'No such luck. Listen, I need to make a slight detour.'

'Didn't know there were any bars out that way.'

'Huh. Don't mention bars around my liver. It's been waving a white flag all morning. No, I'm showing a breached cargo door.'

The voice immediately became all-business.

'Understood, *Blue Dawn*. Are you declaring an emergency?'

'What? Don't be ridiculous! Too much paperwork. It's probably just a faulty warning light, but I need to check it out. I'm gonna drop down for a looksee on the eastern rim of Herschel.'

'Roger that. You're still in the Asheton control zone, so we are tracking you. Let us know when you're ready to uplift so we can revise your ETA at destination.'

'Yeah, whatever. *Blue Dawn* out.'

♦

Kalen had never shown any piscatorial ambitions, but right now he was flapping about like a trout on a line. The Martian atmosphere might have been much thinner than Earth's, but at this speed, the airstream was still knocking him about. The only positive about still being attached to the *Blue Dawn* was the fact that he wasn't plummeting to his death. At least not yet.

Looking back at the net, he could see that his arms and legs were still safely entangled. Good! He wouldn't be falling out of it in a hurry. Further along, beyond his feet, he saw a single, thin strip of webbing stretched tautly up to the open hatch in the fuselage. It looked frighteningly thin for a lifeline.

He turned away to look at the scene below.

And was immediately filled with an urge to pee into his biosuit.

No, no, it's okay, he told himself.

The webbing was holding. How high were they? Several hundred metres, maybe more. A lot more. At the bottom of those metres was a vast world of ochre, splashed with darker rock. It was folded, creased, twisted, and pocked with craters all the way to the hazy horizon. Definitely nothing down there that a fifteen-year-old Terran had any business dropping in on.

What would his father have advised at a time like this?

Probably something like, 'Think nice thoughts.'

Okay. In the absence of any other advice, it was worth a try.

Beautiful morning up here . . . great view . . . wish I had a camera . . .

Nope, as usual, it was no help whatsoever.

He closed his eyes and cleared his mind to make room for inspiration. Instead, an image of Tye and Jenna popped into it. They were probably working feverishly inside the cargo bay to pull him back. The trouble was, with the net snapping about so violently, he couldn't tell. Then he remembered his radio. Why didn't he just ask them? Idiot!

'Jen? Tye?'

'KALEN!' came Jenna's frantic voice. 'Are you out there?'

Which was the silliest question of the morning.

'Yeah, but I'd prefer to be inside with you. Can you pull me up?'

'We've been trying. You're too heavy. It's probably the airstream.'

'You guys need to spend more time in the gym.'

'What?'

'Nothing. Look, I'm okay for the moment. But we *really* need to land.'

'We are!' That was Tye's voice.

'What?'

'We've been descending for the last couple of minutes. Can't you tell?'

Which was the second-silliest question of the morning.

'Sorry, got a few other things on my mind,' Kalen said.

'Well, look at the ground.'

He twisted himself around and looked downward. The features below *did* have more definition than before. Yes, he could make out some large individual rocks now. Dark lumps of scoria, half buried in red sand. Fine plates of layered sandstone. And he could tell by their shadows that some of the ridges were quite high. Over there! What was that? The wall of a crater.

And now the vicious juddering of the net seemed to be diminishing. They were slowing.

A few minutes later, the *Blue Dawn* came to a stop about ten metres above the frosty surface, a little east of the crater's rim.

This morning, there was little wind at ground level, so Kalen found himself hanging upside down from the cargo hatch, swinging like a used teabag as the vessel gently alighted onto its skids.

The moment it had settled, Jenna and Tye jumped out and bounded back to where Kalen sat in the dust, busily disentangling himself from the net.

'You okay?' Jenna asked.

'I think so,' he replied, pulling the webbing straps free and brushing himself off. 'We might have some explaining to do, though.'

He gestured back towards the airship. His friends spun about to see a man in a bright orange biosuit striding purposefully in their direction along the length of the vessel. He came to a stop a few metres from them, looking at each in turn.

Their earpieces crackled, and then the man's voice broke through. 'All I can say is, this better be good!'

'It is,' Kalen replied, 'but I don't suppose we could tell you inside? My friend here's been on reserve air for nearly half an hour.'

'Which one?' the pilot replied.

'That'd be me,' Tye said.

He held up his forearm display so the man could see his now dangerously depleted oxygen levels. Red alarms were flashing as the last litres of air were used up.

The man had been on Mars long enough to recognise an emergency when he saw it. 'Inside, all of you,' he said. 'Quickly now. Don't touch anything, and don't mind the dog. I'll be in shortly.'

Not wishing to antagonise the pilot any more than they had already, Kalen, Jenna, and Tye raced along the length of the ship and climbed the short ladder into the airlock.

The pilot, meanwhile, gathered up the net, carried it back to the hold, and used it to secure the door closed. It was only a temporary fix, but it would last until they reached Touchdown. With a satisfied nod at his handiwork, he returned to the airlock and cycled through.

Into chaos.

Kalen was staggering around the floor in a kind of drunken waltz. Tye's legs were wrapped around his waist, his arms around his neck, yelling, 'Look out for its teeth.' And Jenna was perched on his shoulders, screaming, 'Get it away! Get it away!'

This was the first time either of the Martian born had encountered a dog, and they weren't enjoying it.

But Canis was. And he was milking the moment for all it was worth—jumping up and down, yapping, growling menacingly, and baring an impressive set of fangs.

'What the?' the pilot cried as he twisted off his helmet. 'That's enough, Canis! You've made your point.'

Canis snarled at him indignantly.

'Do you want to go for a walk outside?'

The dog recognised *that* tone. It was usually followed by a large boot in the jaws. Or the other end. His hind quarters obediently dropped to the floor, and he sat flicking his tail, admiring the tottering pile of panicked humanity he had created.

With the immediate danger passed, Jenna and Tye slithered down Kalen onto the floor. Keeping the Terran between them and the dog, they tried to compose themselves.

Kalen, meanwhile, stood perfectly still, staring intently at their rescuer.

The pilot noticed.

'What're you eyeballing me like that for?'

'Don't you remember us?' Kalen asked.

'No,' he replied, squinting suspiciously. 'Should I?'

'You're the man from last night.'

'Am I? Could be, I suppose. Last night's a bit of a blur.' A worried expression crept like a shadow across his face. 'I didn't do anything stupid, did I?'

'Don't know,' Jenna replied, still with one eye on Canis. 'We found you lying in the Labyrinth. Outside Alphonso's.'

'Kalen dragged you out of the gutter,' Tye added.

'Really?' The pilot shook his head, trying to recall the hazy aftermath of his hours in the Black Hole bar. 'It must've been a seriously good night.'

'You had a blood nose,' Kalen said. 'I gave you my handkerchief.'

The fog of the man's memory cleared a little. He went to a cabinet on the wall, pulled open the door, and tugged his brown bomber jacket from a hanger. He thrust his hand into one of its pockets and withdrew Kalen's blood-stained handkerchief. Memories of a three-headed creature on a wheel trickled back.

'This yours?' he asked.

'Not anymore,' Kalen replied. 'You can keep it.'

'Humph. So that was you.' The last traces of hostile suspicion dissipated. 'Well, I suppose I owe you some breakfast then, don't I.'

♦

The ship's galley was a small room tucked in between the airlock room and the large observation deck. The pilot placed himself at the end of a table, with Kalen on one side and the two Martian born on the other. Jenna sat with her feet tucked up underneath. She was still worried that Canis might start gnawing on them if they were left dangling. But the dog had lost interest and just dozed quietly beside its plastic water bowl.

Everything was canted backwards as the *Blue Dawn* flew itself up to cruising altitude.

The pilot leaned back in his chair, a mug of steaming black tea cupped in his hands.

'The name's Asheton,' he said.

Kalen hungrily swallowed a mouthful of toast.

'As in the city?'

'As in Bob.'

'So the city wasn't named after you?'

'Well, it was, but I don't talk about that much.'

Kalen swallowed hurriedly, nearly choking on a hard bit of crust. 'So you're *the* Bob Asheton? The first person to walk on Mars.'

Astronaut Bob Asheton was as famous as Neil Armstrong, the first man to walk on Luna, Earth's moon. Everyone learned about him at school, wondered at his heroic exploits, and dreamed of being him.

Everyone, it seemed, except the man himself.

'Oh, that was all half a lifetime ago,' he replied dismissively. 'These sols, I'm just plain old Bob Asheton, freighter jock, tour guide, lover of the amber nectar, and this morning, to my surprise, a purveyor of stowaways. So what's your story?'

Over the next twenty minutes, Kalen recounted the past year of his life. He told Bob of the stranger's visit to his house, the journey to Mars, the death of his father in the shuttle crash, and the threat of deportation. Jenna and Tye chipped in now and then to describe their near-death experience at the hands of Rocco and Neale, their desperate chase across the park, and their escape to the spaceport.

'So, are you going to hand us in?' Kalen ventured when they'd finished.

The pilot's eyes played across his face as he quietly assessed the extraordinary story. Surely no dishonest person would admit to the foolhardiness and illegality of what they'd done. He could see that Kalen and his two friends were obviously tired, frightened, and mixed up in something way out of their control. But they were confronting it. Bob Asheton admired courage against the odds, particularly in young people. He had been the same once, so he was finding it difficult to hold any anger towards them.

'I'm inclined to believe you,' he replied, 'but I don't see that I have much choice. If the MSA thought I was complicit in any of this, I'd probably lose my licence. But on the other hand, if everything you say is true, I've got some serious doubts about the people chasing you. I think the best thing is to get you safely home to Touchdown. Then we can decide what to do.'

'You live in Touchdown?' Kalen said.

The pilot nodded.

'That's where my dad was headed.'

'So you said. And it's because I know it so well that I can't imagine why he would need to go there.'

Right, this was crunch time! Kalen felt as safe here above the Martian desert with his two friends and this ageing pilot-astronaut as he would anywhere on the planet. Maybe anywhere in the solar system. If he wasn't going to trust these good people, he might as well give up now.

'There's something else—' His voice broke nervously. He cleared his throat, took a swig of orange juice from his glass, and began again. 'There's something else I haven't mentioned. Not to anyone since I got here.'

Jenna and Tye leaned forward keenly on their elbows.

Bob peered over his steaming cup. 'What's that?'

'The guy who brought Dad the bad news, whatever it was, passed him some sort of code. Just three words. Dad never explained what they meant, but from the moment he heard them, he wasn't the same.'

'What are they, these three words?'

'Alpha in Aquarius.'

Jenna and Tye glanced at each other, none the wiser.

Bob pursed his lips and scratched the stubble on his chin as he considered the phrase.

Kalen held his breath. Would this finally mean something to someone?

'Alpha in Aquarius,' the pilot mused quietly. 'I wonder if he meant Alpha Aquarii.'

'What?'

'Sorry, just thinking out loud. Alpha Aquarii—it's one of the stars in the constellation Aquarius.'

'Ok-a-a-y,' Kalen said doubtfully. 'What's that got to do with my dad bringing me to Mars?'

'I can't imagine.'

'Me either,' agreed Jenna, scrunching up her nose. 'It's thousands of light years away.'

Bob shook his head. 'Yeah, forget I said it.'

'It must tie in with something closer to home,' Jenna said.

'What about Aquarius, the fifth month?' suggested Tye.

'Month?' Kalen looked at him, bemused. 'I thought Aquarius was the water carrier. Like in the Zodiac.'

'You're thinking like a Terran, Kalen,' Bob said.

'I am a Terran.'

'But you're on Mars now.'

'We use the Darian calendar here,' Jenna explained. 'Sagittarius, Dhanus, Capricornus, Makara, Aquarius, and the rest.'

Kalen did recall the Darian calendar from an early episode of the *Red Dust Tales*, but he'd never had any reason to commit the names of its twenty-four months to memory.

'Interesting thought,' Bob said, 'but without knowing what Alpha means, it doesn't get us anywhere. I'm sorry, Kalen; I don't think I'm going to be much help.'

A *beep* came from the flight bubble. Canis's ears pricked up. He got to his feet and padded out the door.

'Just someone on the blower,' Bob said. 'Stay there and finish your breakfast while I find out what they want.'

He stepped out, crossed the observation deck, and went down to the bubble. Sitting in his seat, he switched the radio to speaker and said, '*Blue Dawn* receiving.'

'*Blue Dawn*, this is Asheton Control,' a male voice replied. 'I thought you were going to let me know when you were on your way.'

'I knew you'd be watching,' Bob retorted.

'One of these sols you're going to get us all into real trouble, Bob Asheton. You can't keep living on your reputation.'

'Two divorces says you're probably right. That all you wanted?'

'Yeah. Oh, by the way, what was the problem? Faulty warning light?'

Bob felt a muscle twitch in his jaw.

'Not exactly. The door blew out.'

'Blew out! How? Your bays aren't pressurised.'

'No, it was something else.'

'Suspicious cargo?'

'In a manner of speaking. Nothing for you to worry about, though. I'll sort it out with my people in Touchdown.'

'Whatever you say. Now that you're on your way again, we'll slot you in for arrival at fourteen hundred hours.'

'Fourteen hundred works for me. *Blue Dawn* out.'

He turned off the radio.

'Thanks Bob.'

He turned to see Kalen, Jenna, and Tye assembled behind him.

'Yeah, well, one good turn deserves another. Anyway, I didn't exactly lie, did I.'

The *Blue Dawn* reached its cruising altitude and levelled off. It was largely automated, so there wasn't much for Bob to do in-flight. He spent most of the morning in the galley, sipping tea with his stowaways.

Like Kalen, Tye and Jenna had learned about him in their history classes. All the Martian born did. But there was a lot they didn't know, too. And Bob seemed happy to fill them in.

'Day I turned seventeen,' he began, 'I joined the Air Force to train as a pilot. That was in 'twenty-six. By 'thirty-two, I was flying sorties in the Somalian Uprising. Huh, boy, was I wet behind the ears in those days. Amazing I survived. But I did. When it was over, I joined NASA as a test pilot.'

'I didn't know that,' Jenna said with genuine surprise.

'Yeah. Did it for a few years. It was good training for what I wanted to do next.'

'The astronaut corps?'

'Yep. I moved to Germany and joined ESA, the European Space Agency. By age twenty-nine, I got my first space command, shuttling freight between Earth and the Armstrong Luna Base.'

'Wow!' Tye enthused.

'Think that sounds exciting, do you?'

'Ooh yeah!'

Bob snorted. 'Well, think again! Watching grass grow in the morning and paint dry in the afternoon's more exciting than sitting in those cramped cabins for days at a time. Lucky for me, I didn't have to put up with it for long. Friend of mine had contacts in the Mars Exploration Group back at NASA. I whispered a few words in his shell-like, and he got me an interview.'

'That's how you ended up in charge of the first crewed flight out here,' Jenna said.

'Well, it wasn't quite that straight forward. I had to work my socks off, but, yeah, I was finally chosen. Anyway, we did the mission without too many mishaps, but when I got back, things weren't the same. My first wife had moved out and shacked up with my life insurance agent. Can you believe that? I was worth a bit dead, too. They probably hoped I wouldn't come back at all. Me dying would've set 'em up for life. Huh, best thing I did that year was go home and disappoint them. Anyway, no point dwelling on that. What's happened has happened. For a time, I threw myself into work. There was no shortage of parties, public speaking engagements, dinners, and other stuff to go to. I was a sort of celebrity for a while.'

'*Sort* of celebrity!' Kalen cried in disbelief. 'You were the most famous man in the whole solar system. Everybody still knows your name.'

Bob raised his eyes dismissively. 'Yeah, probably. And I suppose, if I'm honest, it was fun for a while. Thing is, that sort of fun wears you down pretty quickly. When people have met the famous astronaut and he's posed for their selfies, what's left for the astronaut when they've gone? Answer: nothing, when he's not really an astronaut anymore. The man behind the astronaut goes back to his hotel room and sits alone, watching TV.'

Bob reached down and softly fondled Canis's ears. 'You're my only real friend these sols, aren't you!' Canis yawned. 'Good boy!' He swigged a mouthful of tea and continued. 'It was around that time I found the bottle. Flying my glass spaceship, I called it.'

'Is that what you were doing when we found you in Asheton: flying your glass spaceship?' Kalen asked.

'No! Goodness no! That was just a social drink. Me and some of the guys patronise the Black Hole once a week. Was I really that bad?'

'Before or after I dragged you out of the gutter?' Kalen said.

'Er, point taken. Want to hear the rest?'

Three heads nodded eagerly in unison.

'Right. It was at one of those celebrity dinners that I met my second wife Tami. She was a space groupie. We married six months to the day after we'd met. Seemed romantic at the time, but we both should've known better. I married someone far too young, and she married her hero. I couldn't keep up with her, and she couldn't reconcile her dull new husband with the astronaut she'd put on a pedestal. We divorced just over a year later. By that time, I'd had enough of the celebrity circuit. Anyway, Mars had gotten under my skin. The first colony had been established, and they were looking for people to come here. There was no shortage of volunteers, but I pulled a few strings and got shoved to the front of the line. So, here I am. Tried my hand at exploring for a while. It wasn't enough, though. Flying's in my blood. I joined MarsAir as a pilot, and later, when that crook Phipps arrived here and set up his freight company, Canis and I got a job with him. And the rest, as they say . . .'

He rambled on a little longer about his more recent time on Mars and revealed that he had worked briefly with Krip Winters. Tye and Jenna asked more about this and soon found themselves discussing other acquaintances they had in common.

Of course, they were all strangers to Kalen, so he lost interest. His attention drifted away. Using the excuse of a toilet break, he stepped out.

Both sides of the broad observation deck were lined with full-length windows. He settled into a swivel chair on the port side and stared out at the bleakly beautiful landscape drifting by far below.

His father had died somewhere out there. He remembered what Jenna had said about the old man, Drummond, who had taken his own life. About the two minutes it would have taken for him to die. Was that what it had been like for his father? He shook his head, trying to shake off the terrible images. It was a reminder that, although spectacular from the elevated safety of the *Blue Dawn*, Mars was a hostile place. Outside the thin window, life as he knew it simply couldn't exist.

He heard a scuffling sound behind him. Bob spun a chair around to face him and sat down.

'You okay, son?'

Kalen nodded. 'Just thinking.'

'Things on your mind, eh?'

'Yeah. My dad, mainly.'

'Right.' Bob squirmed to find a more comfortable position. 'Good man, was he?'

Kalen shrugged. 'I always thought so, even though I didn't really know him. Still, whoever he was, he didn't deserve what happened to him out there.'

'No one deserves that.' Bob nodded slowly. 'I heard about the crash. From all reports, it went in pretty hard. If it's any comfort, I don't think those on board would've known much about it. It would've all been over in a few seconds.'

'It happened somewhere out this way, didn't it?'

'Shuttle planes fly slightly different routes to the LTA craft,' Bob replied. 'The impact site's a bit further on, but quite a way south of our track.'

'I don't suppose we could detour and have a look?'

Bob shook his head. 'Not at the moment, I'm afraid. It's still subject to a no-fly zone. We wouldn't get close enough to see anything.'

Kalen turned back to the window and stared out glumly.

'Listen,' Bob said, 'I was thinking about what you said before—about what that stranger told your dad.'

'The code?' Traces of enthusiasm flooded back into Kalen's eyes. He sat up eagerly in the seat. 'Alpha in Aquarius?'

'Woh, settle down,' Bob said, patting the air. 'I didn't mean to get your hopes up. It might be nothing.'

'But what are you thinking?'

'Well, it seems to me your friend might be onto something about Aquarius being the fifth month. It's the only thing that makes sense.'

'Okay.'

'And this Alpha—there's something I—'

'Go on.'

'No, it'll be easier if you see for yourself. It's in Touchdown. If you like, I'll take you there when we land.'

Chapter 15

The *Blue Dawn* ran into a strong headwind just before lunch. That, along with the unsealed cargo bay door, made the journey to Touchdown slower than expected. However, the vessel still made good time, and it alighted on the rooftop landing pad of Finger 2 only ten minutes late. In no time, Bob was leading his three stowaways through a floor hatch into the assembly area beneath.

At one end stood a small counter. The attendant on duty, a pasty, bored-looking man in his early fifties, glanced up in surprise as Bob and Canis stepped off the spiral staircase with a teenage girl and two teenage boys in tow.

'Past's finally caught up with you, I see,' he said with a leery smile.

'Mind your manners, O'Rourke!' Bob retorted.

But he knew that wouldn't be enough. O'Rourke was a gossip. If Bob couldn't explain the presence of his three teenage passengers, a colourful story would soon be humming around the city grapevine. And that was something to be avoided.

Thinking fast, he said, 'You know how it is. I promised their parents I'd take them out to see the lander.'

This seemed to satisfy the attendant. It was a common enough occurrence for Bob Asheton to escort tourists out to the old Advena lander, from which, thirty-seven years earlier, he had first stepped onto the Martian surface and into history.

'Come on,' Bob said to his three charges. 'I'll just sign off the flight; then we can be on our way.'

A short walk along the terminal finger, between a business selling joy flights and a small regional exploration company, was the local branch of Phipps Air Freight. Bob went in while the friends waited outside, admiring a holographic display of the company's airship fleet in the front window.

Bob was in there for quite some time, and when he finally emerged, he didn't look happy.

'I sure am glad I never took that desk job they offered,' he complained.

'What's wrong?' Kalen asked.

'Bah, bureaucrats! They're gonna make a song and dance about that broken door in the cargo bay. Told me I should've called for help. I ask you! I landed the Advena with a faulty thruster and a malfunctioning landing radar, and they're worried about something as piddling as that. People have no sense of proportion anymore.'

'Sorry about that,' Kalen said.

'Oh, it's not your fault.' He flashed a sideways smile at the young Terran and slapped him on the back. 'Actually, it is your fault. But you had a good reason. Anyway, I've got until the end of the week to talk my way out of it. If I have to, I'll just blame poor maintenance. Now come on, I've ordered a pod. It should be waiting for us in the mall.'

It was. Canis bounded in first and decided he should have a whole seat to himself. Bob disagreed and dragged him, growling, onto the floor. But when they'd all sat down and the pod was moving, Canis pawed his way up onto Kalen's knee and shoved his snout out through the partially open window. The passing smellscape was a pleasure not to be missed.

In spite of their riotous introduction in the *Blue Dawn*, Kalen quite liked Canis. There was something comforting in his uncomplicated, furry warmth. So he sat there, absent-mindedly fondling the creature's ears as it looked out the window.

With the emotional build-up of the previous few sols, he had visualised Touchdown as a grand and exotic city, if not bigger than, certainly on a par with Asheton. A place where all his questions would be answered. But, now that he was here, he could see it was much smaller, and the ambling inhabitants, the drab, banal buildings, and the sparse traffic all left him feeling underwhelmed. What could his father possibly have been seeking in this Godforsaken place?

'Originally, it was to be Mars's main city,' Bob explained, apparently sensing Kalen's unspoken question, 'but when Asheton started to take shape, the powers-that-be realised this place would better serve as a hub for the surrounding mining settlements. So that's what it became: a distribution centre with an airfield.'

'Then you don't think it was my dad's final destination?'

Bob pursed his lips. 'Well, I can't be sure, of course, but I think it's probably unlikely. Touchdown just happens to be where all the flights to the region terminate. He could've been going on by land to almost anywhere.'

'So what was that stuff you said before about Alpha?'

'Yes, I haven't forgotten. We're on our way to see it.'

The pod soon left the built-up area behind and climbed into the hills to the east. Along the bottom of a valley, it raced, then up the side of a steep, wooded slope. At the top, it broke out into a flat clearing, slowed, and settled to the ground. A fenced-off area on the far side was accessed through a gate over which hung a sign reading, "Necropolis".

'A cemetery,' Kalen said.

'Yep. Come on.' Bob opened the door. Canis pushed past him and scampered off towards the gate. 'No, you don't!' his master bawled. 'The bones in there are strictly off limits to you. Come back here and wait for us.'

Canis obediently returned and plopped himself head-on-paws beside the waiting pod.

The gate squeaked as they pushed it open, and soon they were walking along a pathway between neat rows of memorial plaques. After the rush of the past couple of sols, it was a refreshingly peaceful place to be.

'Good morning.'

The voice was that of an older woman. Her complexion, they saw, was clear, the pale blue eyes bright, and her thick grey hair was short and low maintenance. She wore a set of khaki coveralls tucked into heavy brown boots, and in her hand she held a garden trowel. Damp patches on her knees showed she had been kneeling in the soil, probably weeding, which was why they hadn't noticed her.

'Morning,' Bob replied. 'Don't mind if I take the kids down to the grotto, do you?'

'The grotto.' The caretaker seemed a little taken aback. She looked carefully at each in turn and finally replied, 'No, not at all, Commander Asheton. We don't get many people asking for that. If I can do anything—'

'Yes. We'll call you. Thanks.'

♦

The caretaker watched them walk on. When they had disappeared behind a flower-covered mound, she put down her trowel and headed up to her office near the main gates.

Walking in the front door, she went through to the compact kitchenette out the back. In the middle was a small table with some chairs, a microwave cooker, a refrigerator, some cupboards, benches, and a metal locker.

From the locker, she removed a backpack and fumbled around inside it for her watch. She never wore it while working in the garden for fear of damaging it. Slipping it over her liver-spotted wrist, she tapped on the phone system.

It rang twice, then a male voice answered, 'Hi Lis.'

'That visitor you've been expecting,' she said without preamble.

'Yes.'

'I think he's here.'

'So soon! I'm on my way.'

'Okay,' she said, adding hastily, 'I should mention that he's not alone.'

'What?' The surprised inflection was obvious.

'Yes. There are three people with him. A boy and a girl around his age. And an older man.'

'That doesn't sound right. Could they be legit? Maybe a dad showing his kids around?'

'Only if Bob Asheton found some kids he never knew about.'

There was a pause then: 'Bob Asheton, eh! Okay. I'll be there soon.'

♦

'Even the caretaker out here knows who you are,' Jenna said with an impressed shake of her head as they approached a fork in the path.

'The price of fame,' Bob muttered.

Taking the right arm, they wandered into a narrow gully. Memorial plaques, gravesites, and shrubs mingled on the slopes on either side. Eventually, they arrived at a steep set of winding stone steps veiled in greenery. Treading their way carefully down to the bottom, they stepped out into a cool, shaded space.

The Grotto of Peace.

Embedded in the rock walls and spread across the moist, light-dappled ground were more bronze plaques mixed in with an assortment of lush shrubs and plants.

The group split up and ambled about, reading some of the names: Arcady Popov, miner, 68 years, had died accidentally on the 3rd Mina, 2056 AD; Leyla Dredd, geologist, 102 years old, had passed away peacefully on the 19th Kumbha, 2058 AD; Ernst Weiner, construction worker, had gone to meet his Maker on the 25th Scorpius, 2059 AD, at the age of 108 years.

Unknown people with forgotten lives. All, no doubt, had come to Mars with high hopes and grand dreams. Of adventure, perhaps. Or love. Even escape. Had any of them found what they wanted? Who knew? The only certainty was that they'd never left. In the end, Mars claimed them all.

A heaviness swelled in Kalen's chest. Would his father end up in a place like this? Would some stranger stand, one sol, looking at a plaque with his name on it, wondering who he was and why he'd come?

'Over here,' Bob called. 'This is what I wanted you to see.'

He was standing at the end of the grotto, in front of a coarse stone wall splashed with lichen. Before it, grew a line of four trees. Autumnally clad, they were some sort of dwarf variety standing only a metre high, and at the base of each was a plaque stained by verdigris.

As he and his friends gathered at Bob's side, Kalen's heart began to pound out a strong, silent tattoo. His mouth dried up, and he fought a sudden urge to shake. Falling to his knees, he looked more closely at the plaques.

Slowly, pausing between each, he read aloud, 'Beta in Aquarius; Gamma in Kumbha; Delta in Kumbha; Epsilon in Pisces.' Puzzled, he leaned back on his heels. 'I don't get it. There's no Alpha in Aquarius.'

'That's why I wanted you to see it for yourself,' Bob said. 'It's not what's here that's interesting. It's what isn't.'

'Kalen!' Jenna gasped, dropping to her knees at his side. 'That's why your dad was coming to Touchdown!'

He looked at her blankly.

'Don't you see?' she continued. 'Beta, Gamma, Delta, and Epsilon! They're all dead. But Alpha's not.'

'But who is Alpha?' he asked.

'Obviously somebody important enough to bring your dad rocketing all the way out here,' Tye said.

'And important enough to kill him for,' Jenna added.

'You got that right!'

The new voice caught them by surprise. Scrambling hastily to their feet, Kalen and Jenna turned with the others to see a man somewhere in his mid-twenties come to a stop a couple of metres away. The soft ground had dulled his approach. Wearing a cream-coloured, loosely-woven shirt with baggy canvas trousers, he was well-proportioned with a muscular chest and arms. His dark hair was stylishly unruly and prematurely thinning. A designer stubble coated his gaunt cheeks.

He looked at them with a pair of tired eyes, dark with uncertainty and doubt—an aberration on an otherwise impressive figure.

Yet none of these details particularly interested Kalen. What really caught his attention was the fact that the man seemed familiar. Maybe it was the shape of the nose, the set of the cheekbones, or the prematurely thinning hair. But whatever it was, Kalen was more surprised than threatened by the man's arrival.

'I wondered how long it would take you,' the man continued.

'Take me to what?' Kalen replied, for the stranger's eyes had come to rest on him.

'Find this place. You *are* Kalen Rance, aren't you?'

So the man knew his name. Could he be Alpha? Kalen's heart began to race. Was he at last going to learn what this was all about? But experience had taught him that things weren't always what they seemed. Best to play safe until he was sure.

'How could you know that?'

A friendly smile softened the man's face.

'Relax; I'm on your side.'

Kalen remained careful, noting that the man didn't answer his question. 'How do you know who I am?' he persisted.

'I spoke to your father the sol before he was to fly out here. He told me you knew about Alpha in Aquarius, so when he was killed, I guessed it wouldn't be long before you worked out where he was coming.' He paused, then added with a faint smile of admiration, 'You didn't disappoint.'

'Huh.'

'So I arranged for Lis—she's the caretaker you spoke to before—I arranged for her to watch out for a kid visiting the grotto. Not many come down here. When you turned up, she gave me a call.'

Jenna said, 'But that means you knew Kalen was on Mars all along.' There was an accusatory note in her voice. 'You could've just contacted him. It would've saved us a lot of trouble.'

'And probably got us all killed,' Lyle said.

He said it with such gravity that nobody questioned him.

'Okay,' Kalen said, 'so you know me. Who are you?'

'Name's Lyle Geyer. I was really sorry to hear what happened to your dad, by the way—if that means anything.'

'It doesn't.'

Lyle flinched at Kalen's abruptness. But he understood. Kalen would still be harbouring a lot of anger over his father's murder. A little curtness wasn't surprising. He nodded and said calmly, 'No, I don't suppose it does. But I wanted to say it, Kalen. He seemed a very decent man.'

'How did you know him?'

'I didn't. Not really. We never got the chance to meet. Not that meeting me was all that important to him.'

'But I thought . . . wasn't it you he was coming to see?'

'Only as a go-between.'

Kalen felt disappointment rising. 'You mean you aren't Alpha?'

'Me?' Lyle seemed darkly amused by the suggestion. 'Then your father didn't tell you anything at all.'

'He was going to when he got back to Asheton, but—'

'He never made it. Yes, I understand.'

Lyle looked away, trailing his eyes over the surrounding plaques, as if finding the dead easier to face than the living. The dead had no expectations. He shrugged and turned back to Kalen.

'It's only fair that you know in advance, I suppose.'

'Know what?'

'Alpha's your sister, Kalen. Your Martian born sister.'

Time in the grotto jolted to a stop. Minutes piled up against each other. Breathing stilled. Mouths gaped in disbelief.

The nearby trees shifted in a breeze. Some leaves broke loose and fluttered in a see-sawing motion to the ground between them. In that moment of distraction, Kalen's defences went down, and the full impact of Lyle's news struck him.

His first impulse was to be sick. The back of his throat burned as choking acid rose from his stomach. Wriggly things swam before his eyes as he swallowed hard, fighting down the urge.

Then he felt something warm and comforting on his shoulder. Jenna's hand. She was looking at him with a mixture of compassion and disbelief. Her mouth opened, but no words came. And who could blame her? What could anyone say at a moment like this?

Tye summed it up best of all when he whispered, 'Oh wow!'

In spite of their floundering inadequacy at this moment, Kalen appreciated his friends more than ever. Their presence gave him something to hang onto, prevented him from falling completely into madness.

In one way, he realised, the news explained so much: his father's inconsolable moods, his remoteness, his introverted nature. Long ago, in a different life, he had abandoned a daughter on Mars. It must have been a terrible secret to carry. He had probably tried to shut it away in a dark corner, to forget it had ever happened. But the stranger's arrival all those months ago had brought everything crashing back.

Yes, it made sense now.

But so much, too, remained unexplained. Why had he left her here? Why had he never spoken of it? Did he, Kalen, and his sister share the same mother?

Kalen knew he should be asking all these questions and a hundred more, but at the moment his thoughts were so jumbled and incoherent that all he could do was stand there, opening and closing his mouth like a fish on the surface of a pond.

In the end, it was Jenna—intelligent, practical Jenna—who was the first to recover. 'But that can't be right,' she said to Lyle. 'Kalen's dad left Mars around two thousand and sixty-one. That's twenty-one Terran years ago. There were no Martian born then.'

'She's right,' Tye chimed in. 'Adam Wolf's only sixteen, and he's the first of us—the Martian firstborn.'

Lyle was unmoved. 'Officially, maybe. But believe me, there were others before him. Five, to be exact. Four of them—Beta, Gamma, Delta, and Epsilon—died soon after birth. But the first one, Alpha, survived.'

'And Alpha's my sister,' Kalen managed at last, still trying to come to terms with the fact he had a sibling. 'But that can't really be her name.'

Lyle's mouth curled up in a half-smile. 'No, Alpha's just a code name. We know her as Cassandra.'

'Cassandra,' Kalen repeated, rolling the name around in his mouth, letting his tongue feel the shape of it. 'My sister Cassandra Rance.'

'Cassandra Loach, actually. She took Annabel's name. That's her foster mum: Annabel Loach.'

'Loach. Okay. Where is she? Can I see her?'

'Of course. That's why I'm here. But it'll have to be solmorrow now. I'll need time to organise a ride.'

'Ride to where?'

'A little place called Shadows Drift. It's not far away, but it is off the beaten track, so we'll need to make our own way out there.'

'Shadows Drift,' Tye said with a shake of his head. 'Never heard of it.'

'That's not surprising.' Bob, whose natural courtesy had kept him in the background, stepped forward, pleased he could at last contribute to the conversation. 'It's just a dot in the middle of nowhere.'

'On Mars, even dots have a reason for being,' Jenna said. 'What's there?'

'Not much,' Lyle replied. 'At least not any more. Some areologists set it up as a research outpost in the first years of settlement. They abandoned it decades ago. It's about thirty clicks from Stewart.'

'The deuterium plant?'

'That's the place.'

'I know where you mean,' Jenna said. 'But if it's abandoned, what's she doing out there? Is she a hermit or something?'

'Not quite. She lives with her foster mother and their ArCom.' Lyle noticed the bemused faces staring at him. 'Look, I know at the moment this must all seem very strange and confusing, but that's where she is. If you want to meet her, we need to head out there.'

Even though he had found his voice, Kalen was still inwardly reeling from the news. In the space of a couple of seconds, he had gone from being an orphan with no immediate next of kin to somebody with an older sister. It was, at the very least, a little surreal.

The initial numbing shock had begun to pass, and he started to think more clearly. His natural wariness of strangers clicked into gear. Warning bells clanged in his head. Was this all really credible? Who was Lyle, anyway? Why should I believe him?

'How do I know I can trust you?' he asked bluntly. 'I mean, for all I know, you could be working with those people who killed my dad.'

It was a question Lyle had obviously come prepared for.

He called up MarsNet on his watch, and a display popped into the air above it. He angled his wrist so Kalen could read it.

'So?' Kalen said, unimpressed. 'It's a hire confirmation. From some place called Touchdown Trekker Services.'

'Can I see?' Bob asked.

Lyle showed it to him.

Bob read it carefully. 'That's their page, alright. They've got an office in the middle of the city.'

'Who are they?'

'They hire out rovers and such,' Bob explained. 'I've used them a couple of times. Quite a good service, actually.'

'I still don't get why you're showing me,' Kalen said to Lyle.

'Look at the date.'

The date of hire was in a small square field at the top of the display. 'Two sols after we arrived,' Kalen said. 'The same sol my dad was killed.'

'Right, and look at the names on it.'

'The registered driver is—you, Lyle Geyer.'

'Yep. And the passenger?'

'Robert Whelan.' *Robert Whelan!* 'The name in my dad's false passport.'

'Exactly. If I was part of some conspiracy to blow his shuttle out of the sky, I'd hardly have left a record by arranging a journey for the two of us later on the same sol, would I?'

Bob pushed his hands deep into his jacket pockets and slowly nodded approval. 'Makes sense.'

'Yeah, it does,' Tye agreed. 'What do you think, Jen?'

'I believe him.'

Kalen was reassured by the confirmation of people he trusted. Something, though, was still niggling at him.

'If Dad was travelling as Robert Whelan, how did the people who killed him know he was on the shuttle?'

'He told me he had a near-miss in Asheton Metro the sol after you arrived.'

'He did. With a guy on a unocycle.'

'Yeah. It caused a bit of a stir, I believe.'

'No. It was nothing. Dad wasn't even hit. He just dived out of the way, and some people stopped to help. It didn't last more than a minute.'

'More than enough time. Security cams pick up on anything like that.'

Kalen's mind flashed back to the incident. The speeding unocycle. His father falling. The concerned crowd milling about to help. The ArCom in the unocycle shop. The confrontation in the alley shortly after. And he remembered his father's worried expression and the slumped shoulders when he'd described the tall man with the white hair.

'Yes,' he said. 'I think Dad knew.'

'Have no doubts about that. Now, there'll be time enough for questions solmorrow. Anyway, Cassie's better placed than me to answer them. Do you have somewhere to stay overnight? If not, there're some cheap rooms in Touchdown Central. I'm sure we can arrange—'

'No need for that,' Bob interrupted. 'I'll put them up.'

'Good. Then I'll meet you outside the trekker bay in the morning. Say seven forty-five for departure at eight. Are you all coming?'

Kalen looked askance at his two friends.

'We've come this far,' Jenna replied. 'Right Tye?

The Martian born nodded. 'If you want us to.'

'Of course I do,' Kalen said. 'I wouldn't have got this far without you.' He turned to Bob. 'Like to come?'

The pilot sighed. 'I must say this has all got me very curious, but unfortunately I've got a flight in the morning. Normally, I could swap places with somebody, but we're a bit short at the moment. Got people away. Scheduling won't be impressed if I pull out on such short notice. Anyway, after blowing out a door on the way in, I'm sort of in their bad books. If I want to keep my job, I'd better not let them down.'

'No problems; we can handle it.' Lyle ran a critical eye back and forth over the three teens. 'Are these biosuits yours?'

'Not exactly,' Tye explained. 'We sort of borrowed them on the way out of Asheton.'

'I see,' nodded Lyle with an understanding half-smile. 'Well, they look like they could do with a service. I'd better hire out some fresh sets for you. There's no rover dock at Shadows Drift, so you'll need them to get inside.'

'Thanks,' said Kalen.

'Right. And speaking of rovers, I'd better get back and arrange a Dust Rider. Until the morning, then.'

Chapter 16

Jenna looked at herself in the full-length mirror, admiring the waisted, navy blue jumpsuit and the pair of flat Velcro-strap joggers she had chosen. She was a perfect Martian size 3; clothes fitted her off the peg. Nodding in satisfaction, she pulled on a matching cap and tucked her hair up under it. Then she picked up her boots, bundled up the biosuit, stepped out of the changing room, and navigated the islands of floor racks to the counter.

The biosuits she, Kalen, and Tye had "borrowed" before fleeing Asheton were relatively comfortable, but they weren't by any means casual wear, and she noticed they had become quite whiffy after their long hours of use. When she raised the matter with Bob on the way down from the necropolis, he offered to bring them straight into Touchdown's main mall for a shopping expedition.

'I'll wear them out,' she said to the shop attendant. She dumped the discarded gear on the counter. 'And if I could have some bags for these?'

'Cerdainly,' the female attendant replied in a voice like a bassoon. She was in her early thirties, with a snooty manner and a bad head cold. She coughed thickly. 'Oh, exguse be. Now, how bill biss be baying?'

'I'm not sure exactly. Someone's buying it for me.'

The woman looked up suspiciously. 'I'b sorry?'

'He shouldn't be long. Ah, here he comes now.'

Bob walked through the front door with Kalen hot on his heels. While Jenna had been running riot in the local branch of the Miss Mars Clothing Boutique, her three companions were in the Little Green Man, which also had a small outlet just across the mall.

By now, Kalen was starting to come to terms with the idea of having a sister. The initial shock of the news had faded, and his choice of clothes reflected an upturn in his mood.

Jenna ran an approving eye over the new zipper jacket and double-breasted shirt, the light-weight jeans, and the grey and white runners.

'Clothes maketh the man,' Bob said. He glanced in a nearby mirror and saw reflected there his baggy-seated trousers and tatty old shirt with its unfashionably long collars. 'Not that I'd know anything about that.' Turning back to Jenna, he continued, 'We're told it's what all the best-dressed Touchdowners are wearing this season. Does he pass?'

'I think so.'

'Good. Now,' he said to the attendant, 'I'll fix this all up for the young lady.'

'I really appreciate this, Bob,' Jenna said. 'Dad'll pay you back when we get home.'

He gave her remark a dismissive wave. Even though Kalen, Jenna, and Tye weren't his responsibility, Bob was feeling a little guilty that he couldn't travel with them to Shadows Drift. But he was well off, and buying them each a new set of clothes made him feel like he was at least doing something to help.

'Will that be credid or dransfer, Cobbander?' the shop attendant asked, hastily plucking a tissue from her sleeve to catch a threatening sneeze.

'Transfer please.'

While Bob set about completing the transaction, Jenna looked around the shop and realised one of their number was missing.

'Where did Tye get to?' she asked Kalen.

'Not sure. He nicked out to do something while my jeans were being shortened. Promised he'd meet us here after.'

'Right. So, what did he end up with?'

'Maybe I should let him show you. But I can give you a hint: if he stands beside Lyle, you won't be able to tell them apart.'

'Don't you believe it.' Lowering her voice, she added, 'Between you and me, that Lyle's just a teensy weensy bit dishy. Mm, those dark eyes. Whereas Tye's—'

'Right behind you,' Kalen interrupted.

She clammed up. Their friend had walked into the store dressed in exactly the same outfit—both in style and colour—that Lyle had been wearing.

'Think Nikel'll like this?' he asked, strutting about like a model on a catwalk. 'Not bad for a farm boy from Asheton, eh?'

'Or a Lyle-wannabe,' Jenna muttered.

He stopped mid-strut. 'What?'

'Nothing. Where did you get to, by the way?'

'Nowhere!' He fired the word like a bullet, as if falsely accused of something. 'Just having a look around.'

'Alright! No need to snap. I was only curious.'

The attendant was just finishing with Bob.

'Thag you, Cobbander. *Ah-Choo!* Oh, bardon be.' She coughed and wiped her runny nose again. 'Ugh, I knew I should've galled in sick. I hobe you haff a dice sol. *Ah-Ah-Choo!*'

Out in the mall, they collected Canis, who had been sitting patiently on the pavement.

'I was thinking,' Bob said as they ambled along, 'it might be a good idea if you contact your parents. They'll be worried sick about you.'

A lump rose in Kalen's throat. That was something he didn't have to worry about. Not anymore. He swallowed hard and tried to focus on his friends. Bob was right. Jules would be worried about Jenna, and Tye's mother and father would no doubt be concerned about their son. But making contact with them at the moment was out of the question.

'We can't, Bob,' he said. 'At least not yet. Whoever those people chasing us are, they'll be tracing all the calls. We can't give ourselves away now. Not when we're so close to the end. I've seen what they can do. If they find out where we are, it could put them and us all in danger. Not to mention Cassandra and Lyle.'

Bob looked down thoughtfully at the pavement.

'I see,' he replied. 'Well, promise me when you get back, you will. Thing is, I could be in all sorts of trouble with the MSA if they think I'm mixed up in helping you keep hidden.'

'I thought being the famous Bob Asheton would keep you safe from that,' Jenna said.

'Don't you believe it. Anyway, Mars isn't somewhere you can hide forever. You'll have to surface sooner or later. Best to make it sooner.'

'Okay,' Kalen said. 'We'll call them the moment we get back solmorrow afternoon. It should all be over by then.'

'Good. Now, let's get some dinner before we head out to the apartment. I've been away for a few sols, and whatever I had in the pantry has probably grown legs and run off. I know a little Chinese takeaway along the mall. My shout, of course.'

'Huh, Chinese!' Kalen grunted.

'Don't you like it?' Bob asked.

'I love it. It's just that my dad promised us Chinese the night this all started. But he forgot to pick it up. We never had it.'

'Well, tonight you will.'

♦

Given that China was on another planet two hundred million kilometres away, the meal Mister Huang cooked for them wasn't half bad. The cold remnants of steak chow mein, lemon chicken, special fried rice, spring rolls, and dim sims lay on plates scattered around Bob's lounge room floor, along with Kalen, Jenna, and Tye.

Bob lounged in his recliner chair with Canis at his feet. 'Like another dim sim, boy?'

Canis's ears pricked up excitedly, and his tail began to wag as it was dropped into his bowl.

'He loves these things,' Bob said with an affectionate smile. 'Must be Pekinese somewhere in his family tree.'

Kalen said, 'Can't blame him. It's really good.'

'I'm a regular of Mr Huang's,' Bob admitted. 'He knows me well.'

'Like the Governor,' Jenna said.

A photograph on the wall had caught her eye. It showed a much younger Bob in heavily-medalled dress whites standing formally with the Governor of Mars, two men, and a woman.

'Oh, don't pay any attention to that,' he said. 'Typical politician. Just trying to get his face in the news with anybody even half-famous.'

'So that *is* Simon Galbraigh,' Jenna said.

'That's him. Much younger then, of course. That photo was taken just after he got the top job.'

Kalen peered closely at the photo.

'I don't know the others.'

'The short one shaped like a pear is Ewan Maidstone,' Bob explained. 'He's the CEO of the Bank of Mars. The tall one's Thaddeus Wolf; the doll with the plastic smile on his arm is his wife, Natasha.'

'Wolf?' Kalen queried. 'As in—?'

'Adam Wolf,' Jenna said. 'Thaddeus is his father.'

Thaddeus Wolf drew Kalen's closer attention. He was unusually tall—something over two hundred centimetres at a guess. His head was abnormally large, the forehead prominent, the jaw jutting, and the teeth gapped.

'He doesn't look . . .'

'He's a giant,' Bob said, anticipating Kalen's reaction. 'As in the medical condition, gigantism. Makes people grow bigger than normal.'

'So he's sick.'

'Not really—at least, not that I've heard. If he is, it certainly hasn't stopped him.'

'How do you mean?'

'Well, he would've been in his forties at the time of this photo. He was a professor of physics; rose to the upper echelons of Martian society; married a beautiful woman; and fathered a son.'

'Yeah? What about now?'

'Now, he's Mars's Chief Scientist. I also heard on the grapevine that he has the governor's ear in most of the important goings-on in the colony.'

Kalen pulled back from the photo. 'What's he like?'

Bob scratched his belly and belched loudly. 'Ugh. Excuse me. That's that third spring roll talking. What's he like? Can't say I really know him. Not personally. The likes of him and me don't usually mix. But appearances aside, he wasn't somebody I took to.'

He belched again.

Chapter 17

Next morning, Kalen was awake early. Dressing quietly so as not to disturb Tye, with whom he had shared Bob's spare room, he went out to the lounge.

Jenna lay cocooned in fresh sheets and a borrowed sleeping bag on the couch, where she had volunteered herself for the night.

Canis was there too, squeezed onto the couch with her. Sometime during the night, he must have realised she was a warmer, softer option than the blanket in his corner basket.

As Kalen tiptoed past, one brown, furry ear shot up, and Canis lifted his jowls off Jenna's feet.

The movement woke her up. She yawned and opened her eyes.

'Found a new best friend, I see,' Kalen said.

She coughed thickly, then croaked, 'He's actually very comfortable as long as he keeps his sharp end away from me.'

'What's wrong with your voice?'

'Not sure, but I feel horrible. *Ah-Choo!*'

'Rabies from your new friend, maybe.'

She cast a wary eye at Canis. 'Rabies? Not sure what that is. Does it make you feel *Ah-Choo!* like you were hit by a shuttle then force-fed broken glass?'

'Don't know. Never had rabies. But I think you're safe. It sounds more like a cold to me.'

'Me too. My nose tickles as well.' She suddenly jerked up into a sitting position, sucked in a deep breath, and held it on the brink of another sneeze . . . which didn't come.

'Oh,' she groaned in frustration. 'Don't you hate that!' She gave the dog a light push. 'Can you scram, please?'

Obediently, Canis jumped off and loped over to his basket, where he sat watching them curiously.

'Blame that woman in Miss Mars,' Kalen suggested.

'I do. She probably charged extra for it as well.'

'Probably.' A thought suddenly occurred to Kalen. 'You gonna be okay to travel?'

'I've come this far. You're not getting rid of me that easily.'

'You sure?'

'Of course. *Ah-Choo!* Anyway, I'll feel better after a shower and some breakfast.'

The hot, stinging jets of water did help a little, as did the cheese and ham omelette washed down by orange juice Bob prepared for breakfast. Overall, though, she still felt like death warmed up when they assembled at the front door to leave.

'Well,' Bob said, looking at them all, 'I hope things work out.'

Kalen heard the faint note of concern in his voice.

'We'll be fine,' he said reassuringly.

'I'm sure. Only I . . .'

'What?'

'It's just my old aviator's nose. It has a habit of smelling trouble.'

'Wanna swap?' said Jenna, wiping hers for the hundredth time that morning. 'At the moment, I can't smell anything at all.'

'You should be at home in bed, young lady,' Bob said with a stern voice, though one tempered by a half-smile. 'Not gallivanting around Mars.'

'Don't I know it!'

'No, we'll be right,' said Tye.

'Well, just don't take anything for granted.'

Kalen felt a sudden need to justify his actions. 'I've gotta go, Bob. It's why my dad came to Mars. Whatever he was doing, I have to finish it for him.'

Bob looked closely at the young Terran. An unfamiliar emotion swelled in his chest. He had no children of his own, but he imagined it was how a parent might feel in the same situation. 'Of course you do, Kalen. I'm just saying, keep your wits about you, that's all.'

'If it makes you feel any better, I'll radio through an update later in the sol.'

'I'd appreciate that. Lift-off's scheduled for nine thirty, so any time after then. Now, you best be on your way.'

'Right. See you this afternoon.'

'Bye,' added Tye.

'*Ah-Choo!*'

♦

Touchdown's trekker bay was located on the far side of the settlement, roughly a ten-minute journey by transit pod. As promised, Lyle was waiting for them outside the main door when they arrived.

Jenna saw him first, dressed in a snugly-fitted black biosuit, which showed off his muscular frame to good effect.

'There he is!' she gasped. '*Ah-Choo!*'

Tye noticed she was suddenly a little breathless, and her normally pale cheeks were blushing pink. 'Thanks for that, Jen,' he smirked annoyingly. 'We'd never have noticed.'

'What?'

'You're drooling.'

She understood what he was implying and stared daggers at him. Her pink cheeks glowed hotly, matching her raw nose. When they were small kids, Tye's humorous jibes at her expense often sent her running home in a flood of tears. As they grew older, though, she developed thicker skin and the knack of putting him back in his place. Now that they'd reached their mid-teens, she gave as good as she got.

'If you don't mind, Tye Brindle, I don't drool!'

'Right,' he said.

'It's just my cold. Not that it's any business of yours.'

'No business of mine. Absolutely. Understood.'

Lyle noticed her sniffling the moment they drew near.

'Are you okay?' he said. 'You don't look so good.'

'*Ah-Choo!* Yes, of course. Fine. *Ah-Choo!*'

'It's just a bug,' Kalen explained as Jenna fumbled a handkerchief to her nose.

'Yeah, a love bug,' Tye mumbled under his breath.

'I'm *Ah-Choo!* warning you, Tye!' she snapped.

'I know, I know. Just a cold!'

Thankfully, Lyle didn't hear Tye's remark, and he ignored the rest of the exchange as he led them inside.

'Your biosuits and boots are in the ready-room,' he explained. 'Best if you put them on before you board. I've stowed the rest of your stuff in the cabin. You won't need it until we get there. Come through to the big airlock when you're ready.'

Laid out on the dressing bench in the ready room were three charcoal-coloured biosuits, each with a pair of matching boots. While similar in style to those they had taken from Asheton, some of the accessory ports were arranged differently, so Jenna had to stop and help Kalen. Still, within fifteen minutes, their clothes were secured in a locker, the biosuits snugly fitted, and the boots fastened.

On the floor of the large airlock, accessed through a heavy door, they found the Dust Rider. It was a white, medium-range, six-wheeled rover, good for a couple of sols in the desert. The airtight cabin with its panoramic windows on the forward half could accommodate five people easily, six at a squeeze, which meant that the four of them had plenty of room to spread out.

Lyle was in the cabin. When he saw them coming, he moved to the hatchway, where he crouched, nodding approval.

'Looking good,' he said. 'Everything fit okay?'

'Perfect,' replied Jenna. 'You've done this before.'

'A few times,' he replied dismissively. 'Now the rover's prepped, so if you're ready, we should make tracks.'

He shuffled to one side as his passengers clambered up the short ladder and entered. Then he sealed them in, jumped into the driver's seat, and powered up its systems. The console glowed brightly with lights, displays, and touchscreens in blue, red, green, mauve, and amber.

This was to be Kalen's first ride in a Martian rover, so he had hoped to sit in the front. But as he threw one leg into the seat beside Lyle, Jenna pressed his arm and said with a look, *You do, and I'll never talk to you again.*

He took the hint, pulled back, and plopped himself into the position behind the driver's seat.

Tye had seen it all unfold. Taking his place directly behind her, he said, 'That's right, Jen, you sit up front with Lyle. We'll be right back here. Or if you want to be alone, we can jump outside and run along behind.'

Lyle looked up from the controls. 'Am I missing something here?'

'Just ignore him,' Jenna said, glaring over her shoulder at Tye. 'We don't often get to ride in these things. When you're fifteen going on five, it's a big deal.'

'I see. No problems, then. It usually takes a couple of hours to get there, so if you want to change around later, you can.'

If he noticed Jenna's undue attention and Tye's playful stirring, it didn't show. He was soon preoccupied with other things.

Once outside the settlement, they quickly left behind the lattice of wheel tracks, which lay thickly over the well-used ground near the entrance, and headed out into the desert, where the wind had blown away most signs of human transit.

True to its name, the Dust Rider made easy work of the journey. The wheels floated lightly over undulating red hills, dotted everywhere with lumps of dark volcanic rock. By the time Touchdown had receded to a mere speck in the rear windows, the small sun had climbed high into the hazy butterscotch of mid-morning. Everywhere, the land looked bleak and dead.

Apart from the few minutes spent near the edge of Hershel Crater, Kalen had only seen the remote regions of Mars from altitude, aboard the descending shuttle and Bob's airship. Rushing by thousands of metres above the surface, everything looked remote and surreal, like the moon viewed through a telescope from his home planet. But crawling along down here at ground level, among the dust and craters and frosted rocks, he got a greater sense of its wonder. He began to understand how people became attached to its sere, desolate beauty.

Jenna, meanwhile, had seen variations of it before and was chatting away amiably with Lyle. Her nose still felt stuffy, but to her relief, the other symptoms of her cold—the sneezing, the sore throat, and the headache—had waned with the advance of morning.

'What do you do out here when you're not running a taxi service?' she asked.

'I'm a bit of a Mr Fix-It, I suppose,' he replied. 'I qualified as a mechanic, but basically I just do whatever needs doing.'

'For yourself?'

'Huh, I wish! No, Mars Mobile Inc.'

'So, rovers and stuff.'

'Rovers, dozers, excavators, transit pods. Sometimes, even the Maglev, if it stalls in the region. We're contracted to support it out here. Pretty much, if something stops moving, I get to fix it. I'm based in a tech shop just around the corner from the trekker bay, but I spend most of my time out in the field.' He turned over his shoulder to include Kalen. 'That's how I met Cassie, actually. She was over in Alexandrina when I went there to work on a faulty excavator.'

Time passed quickly as they rolled along. At a little after 9.00 a.m., they rounded the edge of a large depression whose steeply sloping walls were lined with shattered layers of plated sandstone.

'Ferguson's Crater,' Lyle announced. 'Pretty close to the halfway mark. Time for a cuppa, I think.'

The silent electric engines, the soft suspension, and the gentle rise and fall of the landscape combined to make them all feel drowsy, and the promise of hot refreshments perked them up. They stirred in their seats and stretched stiffening muscles.

'You'll find tea and coffee in the storage compartment on the bulkhead behind you,' Lyle said, one eye in the overhead mirror, the other outside the forward window. 'There's chilled water, too, if you want it. And some biscuits. Whoever's doing it, can you make mine a coffee? White, no sugar.'

Loosening his seat harness, Tye turned to the small compartment and pulled open the door. Soon, four vacuum mugs had been passed around, each with a two-pack of chocolate cream biscuits.

'I usually pull up to eat somewhere around here,' Lyle explained while Jenna flipped open the cover of his mug and handed him a biscuit, 'but, if you don't mind, I'll drink and drive. I don't want to stop if I can help it.'

'No problems,' Kalen said. 'Jen?'

'What?'

'Do you mind if we swap seats?'

On any other sol she would've argued her case to stay up front with Lyle, but, given the doubts over Kalen's long-term future on Mars, she couldn't bring herself to refuse him. So, while the journey continued, they wrestled past each other, dropping only some biscuit crumbs.

In the new position, Kalen found he had a much broader view of the landscape through which they were passing. He sat there for some minutes, taking it all in, until Lyle burst into his thoughts.

'It must've been tough, Kalen,' he said. 'Losing your father like that.'

'Losing him? I never understand why people say that. It makes it sound like I was clumsy and mislaid him somewhere.'

'Sorry. None of this was your fault. Your father knew what he was doing. He knew the risks.'

'Mm.'

'I don't pretend to know what you've been going through, but I do know what it's like to lose a parent. My mum didn't see me into my teens. She passed away a couple of months before my thirteenth birthday. It really knocked me and my brother about for a while. I don't know how you've coped.'

Kalen's quest, along with his safety and that of his two friends, had been a major distraction over the past couple of sols. There simply hadn't been time to dwell on his feelings.

'Sometimes you've just got to keep going,' he said. 'I mean, it's there in the background all the time. Of course it is. Like a dull ache. I've just been pushing it down so I can keep going.'

'You've got your father's courage.'

'Huh, I don't feel very courageous. I'm just doing what has to be done in spite of everything that's happened.'

'Sounds like a pretty good definition of courage to me. Anyway, things will soon be a bit easier. You'll have a sister to share it with.'

'A sister! I still can't get used to hearing that. How long have you known her?'

'We met just after I arrived. That makes it a bit over four years—Terran years, obviously, not

Martian years. Been good friends for most of that time.'

'And does she know what's happened?'

'I made a special trip out here to tell her.'

'She was upset, I suppose.'

Lyle looked hard at the landscape outside. 'I'm not sure upset's the right word.'

'No,' Kalen said with a nod to show he understood, 'why would she be? It's been over twenty years since our dad was last here. She wouldn't remember him.'

'That's probably part of it, but it's not what I meant.'

'Oh?'

'Cassie can be a bit—how can I put it?—hard to read. She's different from other people.'

This snagged Kalen's interest. 'Different, how?'

'Well, the thing about Cassie is that she doesn't show a lot of emotion.'

'She's like our dad, then. I thought he might have been the way he was because he had to leave her out here. But maybe it was just him. You know, his genes.'

Lyle let that go without replying and turned his full attention back to the task of driving.

Now that they were into the second half of the journey, the thought of the upcoming meeting with his sister made Kalen thoughtful and less inclined to talk. He rested back in the seat and sipped his coffee, feeling the caffeine flood into his veins. His head rolled sideways, and he let his eyes wander over the landscape.

After more than an hour of travelling the view had begun to look much the same. Everywhere, fine red dust dotted with rocks rolled across the endless plains and disappeared into the hazy distance.

Suddenly, an odd movement caught his attention. Just a smudge on the outside of the glass, he thought at first. Then he sat back, rubbed his eyes, and squinted outside again. It was still there, moving of its own accord, independently tracking their progress.

Ever observant, Lyle had seen it too.

'A dust devil,' he explained.

Probably formed only minutes earlier, it twisted its way aimlessly across their field of view. Motes of ochre were sucked into its spinning funnel and tossed skyward. Kalen followed its wandering track across a flat expanse ahead, where it slowed, tottered back and forth for some moments, then dissipated. Through its dying swirls, Kalen saw the landscape suddenly fall away.

'Ma'adim Vallis,' Lyle announced as they drew nearer the edge of the vast canyon and turned to drive along its length.

Kalen opened his mouth to speak, but the sight of the breathtaking vista robbed him of words. Instead, he just leaned in close to the window and gaped.

In the late Noachian period, around 3.7 billion years ago, vast quantities of water and ice had flowed south across the surface of the planet, etching out a sinuous channel 700 kilometres long, 20 kilometres wide, and up to 2 kilometres deep in some places. The outflow came to rest in a large southern lake, named Gusev Crater after the Russian astronomer.

'Only Valles Marineris is bigger,' Jenna said.

Kalen turned to her. 'You've seen this before?'

'In photos. We've never come out this far. Nikel probably has. Don't you think, Tye?'

'Probably,' Tye replied, sitting up at the mention of her name. 'She's been everywhere, pretty much.' He gazed across the canyon, where the far wall, badly eroded but still sheer, was partially obscured by dust haze. 'How do we get across it, Lyle?'

'Don't need to. Shadows Drift sits down on the floor about a third of the way over.'

He hit the brakes suddenly as the rover reached a rough section of landscape strewn with small, eroded rocks. 'This is what I've been looking for,' he said, turning the rover sharply onto a broad, descending rut. 'I think it's what the experts call a sapping channel. It takes us right down to the canyon floor. Hold on. It can be a bit rough in places.'

The Dust Rider jerked and slipped and shimmied down the ancient channel until finally it broke out onto a plain of cracked mudstone. On the firmer, flat canyon floor, Lyle was able to accelerate to a quite respectable forty kilometres per hour. They cruised quickly around bluffs of wind-sculpted basalt and onto a broad flat strewn with volcanic rocks dumped there in some ancient eruption. It was then that they caught their first sign of the settlement.

If it could be called a settlement.

Initially, Shadows Drift made little impression. In fact, from the back seats, Jenna and Tye couldn't make it out at all. For the benefit of his passengers, Lyle pointed ahead at what appeared to be a mere swelling on the ground.

'That?' Tye said doubtfully. 'You'd hardly know it was there.'

'Why do you think they're out here?' Lyle replied.

It was only as they drew to within the last few hundred metres of the journey that Kalen realised what he was looking at. Seven cylindrical modules had been clustered together on their ends, six grouped around one in the middle, bricked over and daubed in clay made from the drab surrounding landscape. Rendered brick buttresses flew outwards from the gaps between the outer cylinders and sloped to the ground. Drifts of red dust, pushed up against them by decades of wind, made the whole construct look something like a large sea star wallowing in the mud at the bottom of an ocean. Four of the outer habitats were illuminated by windows, and a couple were fitted with access hatches. The middle cylinder, slightly taller and broader than the others, was crowned with a small communications mast stabilised by wire guys.

Lyle slowed the rover and pulled up a few metres from one of the sealed doors.

'That's close enough,' he said. 'Okay, gear on everyone.'

They opened the rear stowage bays and, for a few minutes, passed equipment to each other, twisting and squirming in the confined space as enviro packs were fitted and gauntlets, helmets, and hoses were locked into place. A few more minutes were spent on system and pressure checks, and then they were ready.

'That's it.' Lyle punched a button to depressurise the cabin. 'Pop the hatch, someone.'

Tye twisted the handle and pushed it open. They stepped down the ladder and gathered on the surface. The last out, Lyle pressed the hatch shut after him, then led his passengers across the short distance to the settlement's main entrance.

While not huge, the airlock was large enough to accommodate them all. A light on the wall panel changed from red to green. They pulled off their helmets.

'Agh!' Jenna cried suddenly, her shoulders hunched, and her face contorted in pain.

'What is it?' Tye asked.

'My ears!'

'Your ears?' Lyle said. 'Must be the air pressure in here. They set it higher to keep the dust out. It's not normally a problem.'

'It wouldn't be if I hadn't caught this bug,' Jenna whined, grimacing as she massaged her jawline. It's blocked me up.'

'Oh, sorry, I should've thought of that.' He looked at her sympathetically. 'Can you clear them?'

She worked her jaw up and down, left and right. Her eardrums felt like they were being pierced by hot needles, but the blockage remained. It wasn't working, so she closed her mouth, pinched her nostrils, and blew hard. The pain was terrible, but she rode it and tried again. At last her ears crackled, and then, with a whoosh only she could hear, the pressure equalised.

'Okay,' she said with a shake of her head, 'that's done it.'

The pain was quickly forgotten as the inner hatch opened. A woman waited there to greet him. Older, somewhere in her late forties, and short with a maternal figure, she was dressed in a pair of shapeless coveralls. Black hair sprinkled with grey was drawn tautly away from her round face into a bun on the top of her head, which made her look more severe than her red, frightened eyes suggested.

Kalen stepped out into the egress room after Tye and Jenna. He looked at the woman with his bright, green eyes. She gasped as if jabbed by a thorn. Her upper lip began to tremble. Her eyes filled with salty tears that trickled down her cheeks. Slowly, her head began to nod up and down.

'Yes, it is,' she whispered softly to some imagined question. 'After all this time, it really is.'

'I told you, didn't I!' Lyle said, stepping out behind Kalen and closing the door.

The woman wiped away her tears with the back of one hand and gradually managed to regain some composure. 'It's one thing to hear it. To be standing in front of him is something I—well, something I never thought would happen.'

'If you'd known what he's like, you'd never have had any doubts,' Lyle said. 'He's as determined as his father was.'

His father was!

References to his father in the past tense were still something Kalen was getting used to. The sense of loss once again sent a painful pang darting through his chest. But it was true. His father was gone. That was why he, Kalen, had come out here: as his father's representative. And right now, he had to live up to that responsibility. He felt he should say something.

'I'm Kalen,' was all he could manage. It wasn't much, but it broke the ice.

'Yes,' replied the woman. 'I knew that the moment I saw you. I'm Annabel. Annabel Loach. Lyle has told you everything, hasn't he?'

'Not everything.'

'No. No, of course he hasn't. That's why you're here.' Underneath, she was more flustered than she was letting on. 'Oh, but where are my manners? When you've got your gear off, come through. Cassie's in the Rec Room.'

Cassie! thought Kalen as he unplugged his suit hoses and cables and shrugged off his enviro pack. *Like Lyle, she called his sister Cassie. It felt right. They knew her well. Soon he would too.*

When their suit accessories had been hung on hooks and the helmets on the shelves with the settlement's spare suits, they followed Annabel out of the egress room. Shadows Drift was more spacious inside than expected. They turned right along a passageway called the "ring" which circled the entire central module and linked up to the outer modules through pressure hatches.

Passing a closed hatch marked "Sleeping Quarters" on the right, they came to an open doorway on the left.

'Through you go,' said Annabel, gesturing for Kalen to enter.

Beyond, he found himself in the recreation room, the largest in the cluster. Accessed by two doors—the one by which they had entered and another directly opposite—its interior had been fitted out with organically-shaped mouldings, which softened what would have been a stark, spacecraft-like interior. Small shrubs grew in planters placed here and there. Rivulets of water trickled down a glistening, wall-mounted panel of rock crystal into an aquarium containing four goldfish. On either side of it were hung some photographs of the dramatic Coprates Chasma in the faraway Valles Marineris. A section of floor on the far side recessed into a conversation pit with a low central table surrounded by a long, curving sofa scattered with plump cushions in bright colours.

Sitting among the cushions was a young woman.

Straight-backed, legs crossed elegantly at the ankles, hands folded in her lap, she stared straight ahead, apparently listening to some music on a set of wireless earbuds.

Kalen didn't need to ask who she was. Without being aware of walking, he drifted across the room and stepped into the pit in front of her.

The night before, he had dreamt of this first meeting. They'd greeted awkwardly, hugged, then relaxed and fallen into hours of conversation, stilted at first, then free-flowing.

But now that he had arrived, the reality was quite different. Cassandra just continued to sit, her eyes staring straight ahead as if she was unaware of his arrival.

She was dressed in a black jumpsuit similar to the one Jenna had bought, and her feet were clad in casual mauve runners. She looked to be in her very early twenties, with flawless skin stretched tautly over high cheekbones. It couldn't be said that she resembled him, but there was a similarity in the shape of her face, the fine features, and the way her head sat on her shoulders. Her blond hair, cut short, elfin-style, had a gentle wave and fell about her forehead in soft points. She had his eyes, too—deep green pools that glowed with intelligence and . . . something else.

If she had come from Earth, she would probably have been similar in build to their late mother, as he remembered her. But she had been born on Mars, so she would most likely be taller. He noted her long limbs. Yes, when she stood up, he knew she would be tall and fine in that low-G way Jenna and Tye, and all the Martian born, were tall and fine.

At last, she moved. With long fingers, she tugged out the earbuds and placed them on the table. Then she blinked those large green eyes and raised them to look at her brother.

'Forgive me, Kalen. I wanted to hear the end of that.' The voice was light, the words considered, evenly spoken and unhurried. 'Do you like Mozart?'

'Mozart. The composer. I've never listened to him.'

She nodded slowly. 'It doesn't matter.'

'I heard Rona's Riders the other sol,' he ventured. 'Their album is—'

'I didn't know,' she said suddenly.

'Sorry?'

'About you. I didn't know I had a brother. At least not until a few sols ago. It was never passed on to me.'

'I didn't know about you either,' he replied.

'No. That was the way they wanted it.'

'They?'

'The people who keep the secret.'

There was no regret in her voice. No anger. Whoever 'they' were, she simply accepted them. Like Mozart. Either you listened to him or you didn't. In the grand scheme of things, it didn't matter which.

She lifted her hand in a continuous fluid movement, her long, unadorned fingers trailing, and gestured at the empty space beside her. 'Would you like to sit with me? You must have lots of questions.'

'You've got no idea,' he replied.

'Oh, I think I do.'

Her eyes sparkled and widened imperceptibly. He saw in them what had eluded him before. Not mere intelligence, but understanding. An unfathomable understanding. Immediately, he loved her eyes. They were so welcoming. He wanted nothing more than to plunge into their green depths and swim to infinity.

He sat beside her.

'I'm not sure where to start,' she said.

'At the beginning. I need to hear it all.'

'Yes. Of course, you do. Before I begin, though, I'd like your friends to join us. What I have to say goes far beyond you and me. Eventually, it will affect everybody.'

Everybody? Had Kalen been thinking clearly, he might have questioned this. But he wasn't. He was overwhelmed by the moment. He hadn't even noticed that his new friends had stopped at the door, leaving him to enter alone.

They were being kind, of course, giving him and his sister some privacy in their first moments together. But without these brave people, he might never have found Cassandra; this meeting might never have taken place. They were his friends; they should be by his side.

He turned to wave them in.

They gathered in the conversation pit. Cassandra got to her feet. As Kalen had guessed, she was statuesque and striking, taller than Jenna, as tall as Tye. One by one, Kalen introduced them. She shook each of their hands in turn, repeating each name carefully as Kalen said it.

'There we are,' said Annabel. 'Now, you all make yourselves comfortable while I go and get the refreshments.' Lyle offered to help, but she refused with, 'No need. You stay here with Cassie. If I need a hand, I can ask Benny.'

When Annabel had left them, Lyle reshuffled the cushions and sat on the sofa close beside Cassandra. She clasped his hand and entwined her long fingers loosely with his. Noting this with a little disappointment, Jenna sat on the other side of Lyle and hugged a cushion tightly in front of her. Kalen and Tye sat opposite.

'Thank you for everything,' Cassandra said privately to Lyle. 'I know it's placed you in great danger.'

He acknowledged her with barely a nod.

Then she turned to her guests, paused to gather her thoughts, and began.

'My name is Cassandra. I am twenty-one Terran years old. I am Kalen's sister. And I am the first human being to be born on Mars.

'All my life I've been known as Cassandra Loach, and until three Terran years ago, I believed that to be true. But when I turned eighteen, everything changed. Annabel told me she was not my natural mother; that, in reality, I had been born to a Terran couple, David and Elizabeth Rance, as part of a program run by the Martian government.'

'I've never heard of anything like that,' Jenna said.

'You wouldn't have,' Cassandra replied. 'It was never made public.'

'Why?' Tye asked.

'Because it was illegal. Twenty-one years ago, Mars was still under Terran rule, and it hadn't been granted permission to start self-populating. Terran officials still believed the risks were too great.'

'Risks,' Kalen said. 'You mean like radiation?'

His sister nodded. 'That's the best-known one. But there were others. Low-G bone weakness, the possibility of deformities, the unknown effects on children reared in sealed domes. Also, the colony was very young then, and there was talk it might not continue. It was thought too dangerous to create children in a colony that might fail, especially when no one knew if people born on Mars could survive in Earth's gravity.'

There was movement in the doorway as Annabel re-entered ahead of an ArCom carrying a tray. It was an old Prometheus model. Jenna remembered seeing one in her father's shop when she was little. While primitive compared to the more recent machines, it was efficient and quite reliable when looked after. Unfortunately, this one had been let go to rack and ruin. It was scratched and knocked about, one of its optical sensors seemed to spin around uselessly, and its limbs looked so stiff that it didn't walk so much as push its head forward in the hope its legs could catch up.

'On the table, please,' said Annabel, who seemed unperturbed by its clumsy gait.

She found a seat beside Kalen as the ArCom, in a moment of surprising deftness, balanced the tray on the fingers of one hand and, with the other, unloaded a coffee pot, sugar bowl, milk jug, some mugs, and a plate of biscuits.

'Would you like me to pour, Annabel?' it asked.

'Um, well.' She looked doubtful. 'If you think you can.'

'Of course.' The ArCom picked up the pot and started pouring coffee onto the floor.

'No Benny! Into the cups.'

Benny froze mid-pour. 'I am sorry, Annabel.'

'No, never mind; it's my fault. Why don't you go out and put yourself back on your charger?'

'Yes, thank you, Annabel. I am feeling rather rundown at the moment.'

The ArCom stood up and tippled its way towards the door.

'Benny?'

It stopped and turned to look over its shoulder.

'Yes, Annabel.'

'Leave the coffee pot, please.'

'Of course. If you wish.'

They waited. It didn't move. Annabel got to her feet, pried the pot out of its fingers, and gave it a push. Benny tottered through the door while Annabel returned to the table.

'A bit past his prime, that one,' she muttered. 'Still, he's quite a good conversationalist. It makes a difference on these long desert nights with only two of us here.'

She filled each of the mugs and distributed them. Then she picked up the milk jug, dolloped some into her own mug, and passed it to Lyle. 'I'll let you add your own,' she said. 'Help yourselves to the biscuits, too. Now, how far did you get?'

'I was just talking about Mars before the Martian born,' Cassandra said.

'Oh yes.' Annabel sat back in her seat. 'It was a very different time. And a matter of enormous frustration for the government. Mars wanted to stand alone, but that couldn't happen until it was allowed to populate itself. The colony's leadership team decided that it was time to force Earth's hand. If they showed that children could be carried and born here, that would be the end of the debate.'

'So they set up a secret birthing program?' Jenna said.

Cassandra nodded. 'Five young couples were chosen and removed to an isolated desert location where they could have their children. In time, five healthy babies were brought into the world: myself and my four birth kin.'

'Alpha, Beta, Gamma, Delta, and Epsilon,' Kalen said.

'Our codes under the program, yes. Of course, our parents gave us all names too.' She paused for a moment and panned her eyes over them all. 'I can show you, if you like.'

'Sure.'

'Pass me the holopad, Lyle. It's on the desk.'

Lyle collected the flat device from the desktop and placed it on the table before Cassandra. She opened its cover and selected a file. Five stars of coloured light formed in the air between them, then each expanded into the holographic image of a swaddled, newborn baby. All had floating labels attached, showing the applicable program codes and names. They began to chase each other slowly around in a circle so everybody could see them:

Alpha: Cassandra Rance
Beta: Oscar Wang
Gamma: William Durant
Delta: Elena Tarasova
Epsilon: Lloyd Nkosi

Listening to Cassandra relate the story was one thing. But seeing these little bundles of humanity in full colour brought the reality of it all much closer. Jenna was unable to keep her bubbling emotions in check. Her upper lip began to tremble. Her eyes filled.

She tried to cover it by blubbering, 'It's just my cold.'

Cassandra saw through her pretence.

'I'm sorry if you find this upsetting, but there's one more I'd like you to see.'

She selected a different file. The five pictures stopped spinning, merged into a ball of coloured light, and then reformed into a single larger image in which the babies lay in a row of sealed cribs before a smiling nurse who looked like a younger version of—

'Annabel!' Kalen said.

The woman nodded reluctantly at her floating likeness.

'Yes, I was the program midwife. I haven't seen these for a long time. They were taken in happier times, before the accident.'

'What accident?' Tye asked.

'We were never told exactly what caused it, but there was an explosion in the nursery. And a fire.'

'A fire!' Kalen exclaimed. 'My mum's burns!'

'She got burnt, yes,' Annabel acknowledged. 'But she was one of the lucky ones.'

'Lucky! How can you call what happened to her lucky?'

'She survived, Kalen; just, but she did manage to pull through. Only four of them did: Cassie, your mother, as well as your father and another of the men who were away in Asheton at the time.'

'My mum saved Cassandra?'

'She was very courageous. You probably haven't been told that before.'

'I haven't been told much about her at all,' he replied. 'She died when I was young, and Dad wouldn't talk about her.'

'So she died.' Annabel looked down at her feet for a moment to absorb the news. 'I should've realised when I learned it was only you and your father who had come to Mars. I'm really very sorry to hear it. She was a fine woman. With great inner strength. I liked her a lot. But I'm not surprised details were never passed onto you. Like all the others, your father was bound by the agreement.'

'What agreement?'

'Everybody involved was sworn to secrecy in the event of things going wrong.'

'But more than that, Anna,' Cassandra said.

The woman lowered her eyes as if she'd been reprimanded.

'Yes, you're right, of course. Much more.'

'What do you mean?' Kalen asked.

'They'd broken the law,' Cassandra explained. 'Terran law. Even if they decided to break their agreement with the Martian government and spoke out, under Terran law, they could've been sent to jail for a very long time.'

'Not to mention the public outcry,' Annabel added. 'They'd brought children into the world—an alien world—against all the prevailing legal and medical advice. What would people have thought of them? Said about them? They would have been pariahs. Their lives would have been unliveable.'

'But they must have known all that before they started,' protested Jenna.

'Of course they knew, but you can't blame them for wanting to continue,' Cassandra replied. 'Not really.'

'Sorry?'

'How can you? They were living on Mars. The program was set up by the Martian government. They were told they were doing something important for the colony—for the future of humankind. They didn't kill anyone on purpose. It was all just a terrible accident.'

Jenna opened her mouth to speak, but then thought better and slowly pressed her lips together again.

'So what happened after the fire?' Kalen asked.

'Your mother was treated, then returned to Earth with your father and the other survivor, Blair,' Annabel explained. 'The reasons for the burns were falsified. I think they were explained away as some domestic accident in a remote settlement. Something like that. Anyway, no one questioned it. Or, if they did, nothing ever came of it.'

'And Cassandra couldn't go home with them because she'd been born here,' said Kalen. 'Dead or alive, if a newborn baby had arrived back on Earth, the secret would've been out. The people who set up the program could never have allowed it.'

'Yes,' Annabel replied, adding hesitantly, 'but there's another reason too.'

'Oh?'

Cassandra explained, 'Our parents were told that I'd died.'

'But Annabel said Mum saved you!'

'And so she did,' said Annabel. 'But the accident left her in no condition to know anything about it.'

The group sat in silence for interminable seconds, trying to come to grips with this long-hidden, uncomfortable event in their history.

At last, Jenna muttered, 'It all seems so wrong.'

Annabel nodded with understanding. 'It's hard not to be judgemental, I suppose. But they were different times.' She looked for a moment at the fish tank, where a goldfish had gently broken the surface, sending out rings of tiny ripples. 'After they'd all gone, Cassie was put into my care. I was as involved as any of them, so they knew I wouldn't talk. I had no children of my own, so I was the best placed to do it. And the government promised to look after me if I didn't cause a stir.'

'We lived in a remote community where people didn't ask questions,' Cassandra continued. 'Just Annabel, myself, and some others around us. We were well looked after and wanted for nothing. But as I got older, I realised something wasn't right. Then I started to watch the *Red Dust Tales*. I heard of the others being born: Adam first, then the rest, including you, Jenna, and Tye. I saw you all and the lives you were leading, and I wondered why I couldn't be a part of it. After all, I was the real Martian firstborn, not Adam Wolf, as everyone believed. Then, on my eighteenth birthsol, Annabel had an unexpected present for me. The best and worst present anybody could be given. She told me everything.'

'It would've been unfair not to,' Annabel explained. 'I had been thinking about revealing the truth to her for a year or so. No one should live their entire life without knowing who they really are. So I did. I told her all about her father and mother and their roles in the program. And my role, of course. I took her to the Grotto of Peace and showed her the plaques for her birth kin. Naively, I hoped that might be the end of it, but deep down, I knew it was just the beginning.' She looked affectionately at Cassandra. 'And so it was.'

'Lyle and I had been close for some time by then, so of course I told him all about it,' Cassandra said.

She squeezed his fingers in her lap, and he took up the narrative.

'I had a brother working for the OEC—'

'The what?' Kalen asked.

'The Orbital Elevator Consortium.'

'Right.'

'His contract was up, and he was heading back to Earth on the next cycler. A couple of sols before he departed, we asked him to carry a verbal message to Earth for Cassie.'

'But that would've taken months,' Tye said. 'Why not just radio through?'

'Transmissions can be intercepted and traced.'

'It had to be kept secret,' Cassandra said. 'If I sent a message by word of mouth, no one except us would know about it. Anyway, I had time. I was prepared to wait.'

'Alpha in Aquarius! That was the message you sent.'

'Yes, my codename in the program and the month of my birth. Meaningless to most people.'

'But life-changing for Dad.'

'And you.'

'Yes. For me too.' To Lyle, he said, 'And that's why you look familiar. The stranger who came to our house. He was your brother!'

'Bryan, yes. People say there's a resemblance. I can't see it myself.'

They sat quietly for what seemed like long moments. Jenna shifted in her seat. A heavy frown weighed on her brow.

Cassandra noticed her discomfit. 'You have a question.'

'There's something I still don't get.'

'Go on.'

'Well, I can see why this would all have been hushed up years ago. I don't like it, but I can understand why. But the point is, it *was* years ago. What's to stop you from making it known now? If the current authorities knew what was happening, surely they'd protect you. None of it was your fault. Anyway, the people involved in the program can't be around now.'

If she expected this to be a world-shattering revelation, she was disappointed.

Cassandra exchanged a knowing glance with Annabel, then said, 'Let me show you something else.'

She tapped the holopad screen and retrieved another file. The image in the air blurred, turned into swirls of light, and then reformed into another rotating hologram. It was a static, posed shot. Four middle-aged people stood smiling at the camera.

'The program team, taken a few sols after we were born,' Cassandra explained. 'Before the accident, just before they intended to announce their success to Terran authorities. It was meant to be a record for posterity, but—'

'That's Professor Wolf,' Kalen gasped.

'Thaddeus,' Annabel said. 'Currently, Mars's chief scientist.'

Another of the men was familiar too. 'That's Simon Galbraigh.'

Annabel was clearly impressed. 'You're well informed, Kalen. He's kept a tight rein on the governorship for over twenty-four years.'

'What about the others?'

Cassandra said, 'The third man is Xavier De Witte.'

'At the time,' Annabel explained, 'he was only a middle-level operative in the fledgling organisation, which later became the MSA. These sols he's in charge of it.'

'And the woman?' Jenna asked.

'Constance Flint-Massey. She ran the birthing facility. Now she's back on Earth, working somewhere in Africa. Mali, I think. Or is it Malawi? Not sure.'

Kalen's head swirled as he tried to absorb what he was hearing. But, in the midst of everything, one important fact stood out: three of the four people who ran that illegal program years ago were still on Mars. And not only were they on Mars, they held positions of power in the current administration. If any of this got out, they would be returned to Earth. There would be public outrage, professional disgrace, and probably trials resulting in lengthy jail terms. Their lives and those of their families would be ruined.

Kalen reeled as the terrible realisation struck him.

'It was because of them that Dad was killed! He knew about all of this. And he came here to bring Cassandra out into the open. He was going to expose everything.'

Jenna squeezed her cushion more tightly. She looked worriedly from Kalen to Tye and back again.

'And now we know about it too,' she said.

Chapter 18

I hope I haven't frightened him,' Cassandra said. She and Lyle were alone in the sleeping quarters. They had left Kalen and his friends with Annabel to mull over what they had been told. There was a lot to process.

More importantly, they had a dark inkling that life as they knew it was coming to an end, that perhaps their time together was finite, and that they should make the most of this opportunity to be alone and to say things that needed to be said.

Lyle sat close beside her on the bunk and encircled her soft shoulders with a protective arm.

'That mightn't be a bad thing,' he replied. 'Fear's kept us alive. It might work for Kalen too.'

She tilted her head to rest on his broad shoulder.

'No,' she said gently. 'Fear isn't the answer. It's the problem. It's what's kept this all a secret. It forces people into hiding. It kills the truth. The time for all that is past. Everything must come out into the open.'

She was right, of course. She was always right. They lay back on the bunk in each other's arms.

'Do you think Kalen's up to it?' he asked. 'Clever and resourceful as he obviously is, he's not your father.'

She didn't reply for a long time.

Finally, she said, 'Yes, he's my brother. I feel only good things about him.'

He smiled at her. 'And your feelings are always right, aren't they.'

She heard the words and saw the smile. But in his voice, she detected a note of doubt. 'You *are* still worried.'

He looked away. 'I could never fool you.'

'You should know better than to try.'

'Yes,' he confessed. 'I am worried. But not about Kalen.'

'Then what?'

He paused, afraid to say what was on his mind.

She pushed her face close to his. 'What is it, Lyle?'

'I know we've hated having to keep this all quiet, not knowing from one moment to the next when these people would find us or if help would ever come. But throughout it all, we've had each other. I can't help wondering what's going to happen when it comes to an end.'

'If there'll still be an us, you mean?'

'Yes.'

She sat up and looked upon his handsome face. 'You should know better than that, Lyle Geyer! You've been important to me since we first met. If it weren't for you, I'd still be lost out here, wondering where to turn next. It's true; things will change. They have to. I think that's why I'm here. Why I was saved. And that's precisely why I want you close by. For your strength, your stability, your kindness. Your love.'

He stared into those bright, beautiful green eyes of hers. Windows to the soul, some people said. But not Cassie's. Oh, no. They were in a different league. They were portals to a universe of new and wonderful worlds, where only joy and hope and love were possible.

He held her close, and once again they travelled away, away, away to that fine place.

♦

At the moment, the conversation pit was anything but. Everybody was immersed in their own unspoken thoughts.

Annabel sat, savouring the fact that her long years on the run were drawing to a close. She knew that being complicit in the original cover-up meant she would likely have to face the legal consequences. But she was prepared for that, and she relished the possibility of soon returning to Earth.

Kalen was riding a rollercoaster of emotions ranging from grief over the death of his father, to fear of what might happen to them, to joy at the discovery of a wonderful older sister, someone who could connect him with that sense of family he had always missed.

Jenna was stewing over the fact that the horrendous events revealed by Cassandra had been allowed to transpire on the peaceful, wholesome Mars she had always known.

And Tye? Well, Tye was just hungry.

'Any more biscuits?' he asked.

'Of course,' Annabel said. 'I'll fetch the barrel.'

'No, I'll do it,' he said. As he got to his feet, though, a dull humming sound arose outside. He stopped to listen. 'Sounds like the wind's picked up.'

A mood of disquiet descended on Annabel. 'I've never heard the wind in here before.'

Suddenly, a violent *boom!* thundered overhead. Then came a loud metallic *crash!* on the roof. The room shook so severely that one of the pictures on the wall was dislodged and fell to the floor.

At once, they were all on their feet.

Eyes darted back and forth frantically in search of telltale cracks in the ceiling mouldings, the walls, and the windows. Ears were instantly alert for the terrifying hiss of escaping air. Lungs inhaled warily, bracing for a suffocating drop in air pressure.

But the interior atmosphere of the module was holding.

'We're okay,' Annabel said after a few tense seconds. 'If there was a breach, we'd know about it by now.'

'So what was it?' Jenna asked.

'The coms tower,' Lyle yelled as he and Cassie stormed through the door.

It was only a guess, of course. With no windows, he couldn't be certain. He ran across the room and out through the door opposite. Swinging left, he raced around the ring and into the storage module. It was filled with shelves stocked with plastic containers and disused equipment. The others rushed in after him, and together they crowded around a bench under the south-facing window.

'You're right,' Jenna said grimly.

The brick buttress to the window's immediate left lay demolished beneath the remains of the communications mast. It had been bent in the fall, its base frame blackened and twisted by the explosion that had toppled it. One of its three support guys remained attached and snaked limply across the desert to a securing pylon buried in the surrounding rock.

But shocking as it was, the mangled communications mast was quickly forgotten when they saw what had brought it down.

A gunmetal grey airship floated just above the desert surface, about two hundred metres beyond the rover. It wasn't anywhere near as big as the *Blue Dawn*, but even the smallest vacuum airships are huge. Its two cowled thruster fans were running hard, gimballing back and forth as they manoeuvred the craft to a soft landing.

'Expecting visitors?' Kalen asked darkly.

'Only you,' Annabel replied.

With a deepening frown, Lyle ran his eyes back and forth along the bare fuselage of the slowly turning vessel. 'No name, no registration number, no livery,' he said. 'They don't want to be identified.'

'I don't get it.' Kalen looked bemused. 'How did they know we were out here?'

'They must've followed us,' Jenna replied.

'No!' Lyle protested. Then, realizing the evidence was stacked against him, he added, 'I mean, obviously they have. I just don't see how. We've been so careful.'

'Well, they're here now,' Jenna said, 'so what do we do?'

'If we can get out to the rover, maybe we can make a break for it,' Tye suggested.

By now, the airship had landed. The dust churned up by its slowing fans was blowing away in the breeze.

Lyle quietly assessed Tye's idea but quickly decided it wouldn't work. 'We'd never reach it in time. Anyway, even if we did, we wouldn't get very far.' He jerked a thumb at the jumble of bricks and metal outside the window. 'They mean business.'

Tye's eyes darted frantically around the room as if a solution might be found on one of the shelves. 'Well, is there another entrance, then? Maybe we could sneak out the back before they get in here.'

'There is a back entrance,' Annabel replied. 'Out of the lab. But what then? We're in the middle of nowhere. The closest settlement is Stewart. To get there, we'd have to cross the canyon floor, climb the far wall, and then walk twelve kilometres across the desert. It would take hours.'

Hours they clearly didn't have.

'But don't you have some sort of rover?' Jenna asked. 'I mean, how did you get out here?'

'The same way you did,' Lyle said.

'You drove them! Great!'

Options were vanishing fast.

Kalen turned away from the window and leaned back on the bench with folded arms. The destruction of the settlement's coms mast had sent adrenalin flooding into his veins. He was starting to feel its effects. His heart raced, and his mind churned with a mishmash of half-baked thoughts. At last, a couple crashed together and melded into a coherent idea.

'Of course there *is* an upside,' he said.

Tye looked at him incredulously. 'What?'

'Think about it. One shot fired, one coms mast destroyed.'

'That's an upside?'

'It is.' Jenna had quickly tuned into Kalen's wavelength. 'Whoever fired that shot's a pro.'

'Exactly,' Kalen said. 'Anyone good enough to take out that mast so clinically could easily have blown a hole in the settlement.'

'But they chose not to,' Lyle nodded slowly. 'Makes sense. If they wanted us dead, we'd be dead now.'

'Okay,' Tye said. 'Assuming you're right, we've got about ten minutes before they walk over here, then maybe another two before they get inside. So where do we go?'

'Maybe we don't need to go anywhere.'

Jenna looked at Kalen quizzically. 'Sorry?'

'It might be enough if they just believe we have.'

The group huddled closer around him. At this moment, anybody with an idea was worth listening to.

'Go on,' Lyle said.

'Well, if we hide ourselves, they might think we saw them coming and abandoned the place.'

Tye screwed up his nose in disappointment. 'That's it? We hide and hope they don't find us?'

'If anybody's got something better, I'm listening.'

Blank looks bounced back and forth around the group.

'Thought so.' Kalen turned to Cassandra and Annabel. 'So, *is* there any place in here we can hide?'

'I don't think you realise how small Shadows Drift is,' Annabel replied with a shake of her head. 'Seven modules. That's it.'

'But there must be somewhere you store stuff you don't use all the time. You know, supplies, spare equipment?'

'Only in here,' she said, gesturing at the shelves around them.

It was too obvious.

'But nowhere else?' Kalen persisted.

'Well, there are cupboards, of course. And wardrobes.'

'No, they'd rat us out of those in five minutes.'

'What about the pit, then?' Cassandra suggested.

This sounded faintly promising, but Annabel was far from enthusiastic. 'We'd never fit. At least not all of us.'

'Let's have a look, anyway,' Kalen said.

So she led them back along the ring and through to the galley. While compact, it was cleverly designed with a bench for food preparation, a sink, a microwave cooker, some drawers, and overhead stowage cupboards.

Annabel knelt down, gripped a handle recessed into the floor, gave it a sharp jerk, then heaved open a trapdoor. Thin clouds of icy fog wafted up and over the lip and flowed around their feet.

Jenna joined Annabel, kneeling at the edge, and peered through the opening, which was about a metre square. The 'pit' was essentially a freezer built beneath the floor. It was three-quarters full of square plastic containers, neatly packed.

'You can't be serious!' Tye snapped. He turned on Annabel, almost ferociously. 'It's completely nuts to think anybody would be safe in there!'

Annabel was taken aback by his angry outburst.

So was Jenna. It was very out of character for him. And completely unnecessary. 'Tye!' she scolded. 'Annabel's trying to help.'

'I'm just saying—'

'Well, don't!' she retorted with a fiery glare. 'Don't say another word unless it's something constructive.'

He was about to fire back something completely unconstructive, but realised he had overstepped the mark and backed down.

Annabel understood that he was scared and let it go. Refocusing, she said, 'There simply is nowhere else. Shadows Drift was set up as a scientific outpost, not a refuge for runaways.'

Despair fell like a dark cloud upon them. Heads turned back and forth. Each hoped to see a flash of inspiration in the eyes of one of the others. Surely there was something they had overlooked? A missing piece that would solve the problem. Some tiny hook on which to hang an escape plan.

But all they got was a tense, impotent silence.

At last, passing her eyes softly over each of them, Cassandra began, 'I think—'

There was a collective gasp. Someone had an idea! They all leaned in eagerly.

'You think what?' Annabel asked.

'I think we all know it's me they're coming for. Why don't I just go with them quietly? They might leave you alone.'

As courageous plans went, it was right up there with those that led to the first manned moon landing and the inaugural group skydive from Deimos. As bad ideas went, it was right down there with the square wheel and the waterproof teabag.

'No!' Kalen said firmly. 'I can't let you do it. I don't know what Dad would've done if he was here, but *I'm* not going to just stand by quietly while they take you away. Besides, once you're safe with them, I've got a horrible feeling they're going to do nasty things to this place.'

'I'm afraid I'm with Kalen on that,' Annabel said.

'So am I,' nodded Lyle.

'I'm not.' Jenna's voice had a determined edge.

Kalen turned on her. 'What?'

'You heard me.'

'But you can't just—'

'Neither is Tye.'

Tye turned to her, startled. 'Um, aren't I?'

'No.' She stared back defiantly at the group of horrified faces. 'Well, go on. Ask me why.'

'Okay, why?'

'We're not with you because we're not here.'

Kalen was learning to recognise that tone. His mouth turned up in a hopeful smile. 'You've got an idea!'

'Well, half an idea at the moment.'

'Let's hear it.'

'Those loonies will be expecting to find at least three people in here. Cassandra and Annabel, because they're on the run; and Lyle, because they must've followed the rover. They might ever. be expecting you if they know you're Cassandra's brother.'

'Your point being?' Kalen asked.

'My point being that they won't necessarily be expecting Tye and me as well.'

Lyle looked at her uncertainly. 'So what are you saying? You and Tye want to hide in the freezer?'

'Maybe.'

'And do what?'

'That's the half I haven't quite worked out yet.' She looked more closely at Tye. 'You with me?'

'Why not,' he shrugged. 'Half a plan's better than no plan.'

Chapter 19

Rocco was first out onto the surface. He was dressed in standard Martian camouflage gear: a biosuit coloured with swirls of charcoal and dark red. His plain grey boots, matched to his combat helmet and gauntlets, kicked up tiny puffs of dust as he landed.

He paused to look at the fallen communications mast he had destroyed from the open airlock as they passed overhead. It had been a difficult shot, bringing it down without breaching the settlement. His sniper training and many hours on the firing range had paid off.

'Wait there,' Neale's voice boomed in his earpiece. 'You know what happened last time you took on those kids by yourself.'

Rocco didn't need reminding. Whenever he turned his head sharply, the staples in his skull pulled, sending swollen rivers of pain deep into the muscles of his neck and down into his shoulders.

In a twisted way, though, he appreciated the pain. It kept alive his memory of the Terran and those two Martian born who, with their ArCom, had nearly killed him. Yes, the pain was good; it kept him angry. And anger drove him to seek revenge.

Neale drew up beside him. 'All set?'

Rocco gripped the butt of his high-powered Strictor assault weapon more firmly. 'You bet.'

'Right, let's finish this.'

Side by side, they strode out of the shade cast by the craft's fuselage and closed in on the main entrance to the settlement.

Eckhart's voice came through their earpieces. 'Okay, gentlemen, suit coms are online, and I've got eyes on you. Take it slowly, and keep your wits about you. I don't want to have to explain any more stuff ups to the good professor.'

'Copy that, Boss,' Neale replied crisply.

'And don't forget the prime mission. We want the one called Cassandra alive.'

'Understood.'

'But the others are fair game, right?' said Rocco.

'You know what needs to be done.'

Rocco's thin lips twisted into a crooked smile. Oh yes, he knew what needed to be done.

♦

In the comfort of the airship's cabin, Eckhart lowered her binoculars and nestled back into the padded pilot's seat. She turned her gaze from the view outside to the small side monitor, whose split screen displayed the feeds from her agents' suit cams. She would be able to watch and hear events as they unfolded.

♦

'I feel really bad about leaving you both here,' Kalen said.

Since arriving on the planet, he had been through a lot with Jenna and Tye. He felt as if he was abandoning them to a terrible fate.

'Don't worry about us,' Jenna reassured him. 'We'll be safer than you.'

She might have been right, but Kalen still couldn't help feeling like he was running away. 'Do you want a hand to empty the freezer before I go?' he asked.

'Leave that to me,' Tye replied. 'You go and keep your sister safe.'

Kalen gave his new friend a sharp, appreciative nod, then disappeared through the door to join the others.

'Come on,' Jenna said to Tye. 'I need a hand down here.'

She had already turned off the freezer and was standing in it, unpacking frozen containers. Tye took one from her and placed it on the floor beside the cupboards.

'Not there,' Jenna said.

'Why?'

'If someone comes in, they'll trip over them. Put them up on the bench where they won't be so obvious.'

He restacked them beside the sink, then added the remainder as she passed them out. In no time, the freezer was empty. It was barely large enough to hold them both, but at least now that the chiller was off, it would warm up quickly. In the meantime, their biosuits would protect them from contact with the frigid walls.

'Okay, shove over,' Tye said.

Jenna squatted down and pressed her back up against the side. It was obviously going to be tight, but if short-term discomfort was the price of staying alive, she could tolerate it. And hopefully they wouldn't be in there for long. Tye squeezed in with her.

With the cover still open, they knelt in silence for a few moments. Jenna looked at Tye. Tye looked at Jenna. The idea of hiding had been growing on them since Kalen first suggested it. But now that they were here, sitting in this cold hole, its appeal was fast vanishing.

At last, Tye said, 'This is a stupid idea, Jen.'

'Ridiculous,' she agreed, then climbed back out. 'Come on, we can do better.'

Soon she was flinging open cupboards and drawers, pulling out all manner of kitchen paraphernalia. Knives, forks, and spoons. Bowls and plates. Washing detergent. Soap. A bottle of cleaning fluid. A cutting board. A roll of aluminium foil.

Tye felt quite useless as he watched her rush about. 'If you tell me what you're looking for, maybe I can help.'

'I won't know until I see it. Just something to *Ah-Choo!* Oh-h-h! That freezer's set my cold off again. Not to mention all this running around. *Ah-Choo!*' She sniffed, then plucked a tissue from a wall dispenser and wiped her nose. Screwing up the tissue, she threw it into a bin, which sat on the floor beneath the microwave cabinet.

The microwave!

'Of course,' she cried, looking at it more closely. 'I'm so stupid.' And she raced out of the galley.

Tye followed her through to the egress room. By the time he arrived, she had already pulled one of the biosuit enviro packs off its hook and dumped it on the floor. Hands working quickly, she popped open the back panel, tugged a bunch of wires out of the way, and looked inside. Seeing what she wanted, she pushed one hand in, jerked it back and forth, and then dragged out a canister about twenty centimetres long.

Tye recognised it from his walker classes.

'A fuel canister for the power cell?'

'Nope, two,' she replied, pulling out its twin. Jumping to her feet again, she ran back out the door, calling vaguely over her shoulder, 'Reassemble that, can you? And put it back on the hook.'

Tye had no idea how to reassemble an enviro pack, so he just stuffed the wire bundle back into the cavity and snapped on the cover before rehanging it.

When he returned to the galley, Jenna was struggling to pull the microwave out of its cabinet. He grabbed it off her.

'Thanks,' she said, unplugging its cord. 'Put it on the bench.'

'I wish you'd tell me what you're up to,' he said.

'Making a bomb. *Ah-Choo!*'

'WHAT?'

The microwave crashed onto the benchtop.

'Careful!' she said sharply.

'Sorry, but a bomb?'

'Not a big one. Nothing powerful enough to blow the place to smithereens. I'm just talking about a small bang. Something to knock them off their feet.'

'Ok-a-a-y,' he said warily. 'Um, how does it work?'

'Power cells use hydrogen,' she explained.

No surprise there. Anyone who had completed their walker training knew that most of the biosuits currently in use on Mars were powered by hydrogen power cells.

'And,' she continued, 'hydrogen's explosive *Ah-Choo!*'

'Would you mind not sneezing while you're talking about explosions? It makes me nervous.'

'Sorry. *Ah-Choo!*'

Tye's mind spun in all sorts of nightmarish directions. Power Cells? Hydrogen? Microwaves? Surely this wasn't going to end well! But Jenna was working with such determined fury that he knew better than to cross her.

'So where exactly do you want it?' he asked.

'Somewhere they won't see it straightaway. Maybe over there in the corner?'

He slid the microwave along to the end of the bench. 'Are you really sure about this, Jen? I mean, an explosion in this confined space?'

'Of course I'm not sure about it! But you saw what sort of weapons these brutes have. We'll never outpower them. Maybe we can out-think them.'

When Tye had plugged the microwave into a wall socket and angled it towards the middle of the galley, Jenna removed its turntable dish, placed it in the sink out of the way, laid the two fuel canisters inside, then closed it up.

She stood back to admire her work. 'That should do it.'

'Now all we need is some luck,' Tye said.

'*Ah-Choo!*'

♦

Kalen, Lyle, Annabel, and Cassandra were shoving furniture hard up against the recreation room's two doors. No doubt it was a futile attempt to keep their attackers at bay, but doing something at least made them feel better.

The truth was, none of them had any idea what would happen when the attack started. They weren't armed. They weren't combat-trained. They would be no match whatsoever for the killers headed their way.

'That's it,' Lyle said, sliding a chair into place against the second door and bracing it with a cabinet. 'We can't do anymore.'

'Come over here,' Annabel called, rushing with Cassandra to the conversation pit. They overturned the coffee table and ducked behind it. 'This might give us some cover if they blast the door open.'

It was a sensible, if short-term, precaution. Kalen and Lyle jumped in with them, and they lay down low to wait.

Outside, things had gone very quiet and still. Not the light, peaceful stillness of a summer's evening; rather, the heavy, ominous stillness before a storm.

In Kalen's mind, though, a different storm was already raging. A storm of thoughts.

'I don't get it, Cassandra,' he said.

'Get what?'

'Well, these nut jobs. They want you alive, right?'

'Apparently.'

'Why? I mean, given everything you told us, it doesn't make sense. If you're the only survivor of the program, surely you'd be the one they'd most want out of the way.'

Lyle had to admit the logic of this.

Annabel sighed heavily, as if the weight of the planet had suddenly landed on her shoulders. Glancing at Cassandra, she said, 'You'd expect so. But there's still so much you don't understand, Kalen. There are . . . there are reasons.'

Her unwavering gaze and the firm tone of her voice rang with the hint of some bigger, hidden picture. But a dull thud from inside the egress room turned their attention to more urgent matters.

◆

Rocco and Neale stormed out of the airlock, Strictors at the ready.

'Inside.' Neale knew Eckhart was watching via the camera mounted on his shoulder, but he had promised to keep her verbally updated as well. That way, there would be no misunderstandings. 'Egress room clear.'

They popped the visor seals on their helmets and retracted them. During the flight out to Ma'adim Vallis, they had memorised the layout of the settlement from a plan on the ship's database. Shadows Drift was tiny. Seven interlinked modules— six surrounding a larger central one.

Both knew that in their business, confined spaces could be dangerous, especially the pressurised spaces away from Earth. Their target, Cassandra, was understood to be non-violent, but she and the nurse had been eluding them for a long time. They were obviously intelligent and resourceful. And now that they had enlisted the help of a rover driver and the three kids they encountered in Asheton, things could get messy.

Neale gestured at one of the two hatches. Rocco pushed it open. Beyond, the ring curved away in both directions.

Moving around it anticlockwise, they came upon the entrance to the sleeping quarters on the right and, a little further down on the left, a door leading into the recreation room. They had decided to secure that first. Then, if necessary, they would work through each of the others until they had rounded up all the occupants. It shouldn't take long.

Neale twisted the handle and pushed. The door budged a little but didn't open. Something had been braced up against it.

Rocco stood back and kicked it with the sole of his heavy boot. It gave a little. Neale joined in. Once, twice, three times, they pounded the door. At last, something cracked on the other side and fell to the floor.

The door crashed open. They stormed in.

First impressions were that the room was abandoned. But then the overturned table in the conversation pit caught Neale's eye. Moving a little further in, he saw four people cowering behind it.

'On your feet!' he bawled. 'You better be worth all this trouble.'

As Annabel, Lyle, Kalen, and Cassandra stepped up to the edge of the pit, it occurred to Neale that this seemed too easy. Everybody together in one place? It would have made more sense to separate and make the task of finding them harder. But that was military thinking. These people weren't soldiers. They were probably frightened and irrational.

Rocco had no such doubts as he joined his colleague. His gaze swept the group and came to rest on the woman standing at the end. In her early twenties, tall and fine-boned with striking, green eyes, he knew straightaway who she was.

'You're the one they call Cassandra!' he said accusingly, eyeing her off like some hard-won trophy.

Lyle thought he was leering at her and stepped forward protectively. Rocco swung his weapon at him, his finger on the trigger.

'Yeah, that's right. Be the tough guy. I'm in the mood.'

In spite of the weapon, Lyle refused to be intimidated. 'She's not for the likes of you.'

'Oh, she's special, alright. We'll give her the best of attention.'

'Enough chatter,' Neale said. 'Let's get her over to the ship.'

Eckhart's voice came through on the coms link. 'What about the other two?'

'They're not here,' Neale said.

'Maybe,' Eckhart replied curtly. 'But they're loose ends. Better be sure before we blow the place apart.'

'But—'

'That's an order!'

Neale thought they were wasting time, but he understood the chain of command. Eckhart was in charge. He turned to Lyle. 'Congratulations. You've been elected spokesperson. Where are the other two?'

Lyle had no intention of handing over Jenna and Tye so easily. He decided to play dumb. 'What other two?'

'You must think I came down in the last meteor shower. We know there are two more. Kids. Friends of this Terran. We need to know where they are. NOW!'

Kalen turned to Lyle and said, 'He must mean Jenna and Tye.' He was hoping that if he spooned out some of the truth, these thugs would hopefully swallow some lies along with it.

'Jenna. That's the girl's name,' Neale said to Rocco. 'I never heard the boy's.'

'Jenna and Tye,' Kalen said.

'So where are they?'

Here comes the lie. 'Well, not here, obviously.'

'If you think I'm going to fall for that—'

'No, they never came out with us,' Kalen insisted. *Give them a reason, quick.* 'They wanted to, but Jenna caught a cold in Touchdown. She wasn't well enough to travel. Tye stayed with her.'

There was enough truth here to create some doubt.

'That satisfy you, Boss?' Rocco said into his com.

'I suppose it's plausible,' came the hesitant reply. 'But don't take his word for it.'

'Copy,' Neale replied, adding to his colleague, 'Watch them. I'll go through the place.'

Ah well, it was worth a try.

Neale stepped back through the door by which they had entered. While all the outer modules opened onto the ring, he knew not all were joined to those adjacent.

Being closest to the sleeping quarters, which linked to the galley through the bathroom, he decided to try that first.

There were six bunks affixed to the walls. On two of the lower ones sat some travelling bags, open and half unpacked, with clothes strewn over the covers. Either Cassandra and the nurse had only just arrived, or they were ready for a hurried departure. On his right were two built-in wardrobes. He approached the first, yanked open the door, and shoved the muzzle of his gun inside. Nothing. A check of the second yielded the same result.

There was nowhere else in here to hide, so he stepped through the hatchway into the bathroom. Wash basin and vanity, shower recess, cupboards, mirror, and toilet bowl. Basic but functional. And nowhere to hide.

The last in this group was the galley. He approached the door.

♦

Jenna and Tye had heard someone blundering about next door.

'Get in! Quick!' Jenna whispered. Her voice was taut and sharp. It caught in her throat, tickled it, and gave rise to another sneeze. She clamped one hand over her face and managed to stifle the sound quite effectively.

'This better work,' Tye mumbled as he climbed down into the freezer.

Jenna rushed to the microwave cooker, set it for one minute on high power, then pressed the "On" button.

It was quiet enough; that wasn't a problem. But the timer display was. Bright! Red! Flashing! The beacon atop Olympus Mons would attract less attention. When that goon entered, he would know straightaway that something was afoot.

She had to shade it somehow. Her eyes darted about in a panic. There! A cloth in the sink. She picked it up. It was too thin, so she folded it double, then draped it over the flashing numerals. The light dimmed. Good.

'COME ON, Jen!' hissed Tye from the freezer.

She scrambled in beside him, and he swung the cover over their heads.

Twenty-five seconds had already elapsed.

♦

As the cover closed, the door opened. Neale stepped inside.

The galley was pretty much as expected. Small but cleverly designed for efficiency. Neat, too. Except for those plastic containers stacked on the bench. He guessed they were used to store food. Nothing out of the ordinary there. Not here in the galley. It was late in the morning; they had probably been placed there in readiness for lunch.

Yet, for some reason, they worried him. He looked more closely at the labels stuck to their sides. Vegetable soup. Fillets of fish. Cuts of frozen meat. Bread. Shredded cheese. Margarine. A packet of apple strudel.

All for one meal? That didn't quite ring true, even for the six people their intel told them would be out here.

A knot tightened in his gut.

Now a tiny movement on the side of one of those containers caught his eye. It was glistening. All the containers were glistening, coated in a sheen of frost, which, in the warm room, was melting into beads of moisture. The beads combined to form larger droplets, which trickled slowly down the sides of the containers, glinting in the light from the window, to join a growing pool on the bench.

Until a short time ago, all these containers had been in a freezer. A freezer that had been emptied. Why? And more to the point, where was it? Wait! He remembered from the plan that there was one under the floor. Right beneath his feet.

Then he heard it. A faint humming sound. He tugged the coms earpiece from his left ear to hear more clearly. Better. It emanated from the bench. Yes, from the microwave cooker in the corner. He took a half-step forward, then jarred to a stop.

It was partially covered by a cloth! Why? And why was it angled into the middle of the room, facing directly at him? Who had set it going? What was being heated?

And why now?

Oh God!

Taut reflexes brought up the muzzle of his Strictor. A pulse from the weapon might shut it down before . . .

A blinding flash of light. A pummelling blast. Searing heat. His eardrums heard the explosion just before they were ruptured. But it was the microwave door blowing off its hinges that did the worst damage. One sharp edge struck him in the face.

He was unconscious even before he hit the floor.

♦

The acoustics in the settlement were such that sound didn't travel at all well between the modules. But the explosion was so powerful that Rocco still heard it. He spun about instinctively, momentarily forgetting his head wound. Jagged bolts of pain tore at the staples holding his flesh together. He grimaced, twisted his neck, and hunched his shoulders, trying to relieve the agony.

Lyle saw his chance. He lowered his knees and launched himself across the room. Full Terran strength would have sent him hurtling through the air with sufficient force to flatten even this powerful man. Unfortunately, in spite of weekly sessions in the gym, years of Martian gravity had weakened his muscle tissue.

Rocco saw him coming out of the corner of his eye. His training and reflexes instantly overrode the pain, and his low-G combat kata kicked in. He lowered his stance, side-stepped, dipped one shoulder, and twisted at the hips. Lyle went flying headfirst across the room and struck the wall.

Kalen rushed in to help, but he was no match for the trained soldier. In what looked like one fluid motion, the big man struck Kalen in the chest with the butt of his weapon and sent him tumbling backwards into the conversation pit; then he whipped up his Strictor, aimed at Lyle, and pulled the trigger.

The room lit up with a flash of dazzling blue.

Lyle froze macabrely in the act of getting to his feet. His face turned grey. Air gushed noisily from his lungs. He doubled over, clutching his side.

Annabel screamed. Cassandra watched on wordlessly. Then, together, they raced to where Lyle lay, writhing in excruciating pain on the floor.

Eckhart's voice blared in Rocco's earpiece. 'Neale's down.'

'I'm onto it.'

A quick look around showed that Kalen was too winded to be a threat, and the two women were more concerned about Lyle than being heroic. They probably hadn't seen anybody shot before and would be in shock. Good! That would give him valuable seconds to check on his colleague.

He strode through the door and, a few paces along, swung sharply into the galley. Automatic fans were already spinning hard, sucking out poisonous fumes and replacing them with fresh air. Through the dissipating haze, Rocco could clearly see that the galley was in tatters. The walls were burnt and blackened. Cupboard doors hung loosely off their hinges. Even the cover of a small underfloor freezer had somehow been blown open to expose the empty cavity beneath.

A veteran of numerous skirmishes across the solar system, he wasn't shocked. But he was confused. He saw the remains of the microwave on the bench; obviously, it had exploded. He just couldn't understand how.

Kneeling beside the unmoving body of his colleague, he could see the face was bloodied. A finger pressed to the neck detected a faint pulse.

'Still alive,' he said to Eckhart. 'Just.'

'Copy. Check all the modules. The other two must be in there. They're more dangerous than I realised. Terminate them.'

A crooked smile curled up the side of Rocco's mouth as he pushed his way through to the bathroom and began to retrace his fallen colleague's steps.

♦

Kalen couldn't breathe. No matter how hard he tried to work his diaphragm, his lungs wouldn't inflate. Eyes wide with the effort, he sat up and slumped forward onto the edge of the overturned coffee table in the conversation pit. This took the weight off his shoulders, freeing up his chest muscles to help him inhale.

At last, some air trickled down his windpipe into his lungs and diffused into his bloodstream. The effect was almost immediate. The craving for oxygen lessened a little. Another breath. Yes, better. His chest expanded. It contracted. Expanded again. Mercifully, it regained that glorious, natural life rhythm.

Cassandra! Where was she? He looked across the room and saw her beside Annabel. They were both leaning over Lyle.

Kalen got to his feet. Staggered to them. He was still too winded to speak, but he didn't need to. He could see for himself that Lyle was in a very bad way, teetering on the brink of unconsciousness. If he thought there was any point, he would have offered to help. But Annabel was a trained nurse. There was nothing he could do that she couldn't. He decided to check on Jenna and Tye.

At the door, he peered out in both directions along the ring. There was no sign of that gorilla. He raced noiselessly to the galley. The door was open. What he saw inside left him incredulous. The room was barely recognisable. He couldn't imagine what had caused such devastation.

His eyes were drawn first to the burnt and bloodied fallen soldier, then to the empty freezer beside him. Maybe that other brute had found his friends—no, that didn't bear thinking about.

He finally managed a deep, satisfying breath. Oxygen flooded into his bloodstream. Flowed to his brain. His chest hurt, but his mind cleared a little. If Jenna and Tye had been discovered, he would hear yelling, screaming, the sounds of panic, and feet running. But there was nothing. For the moment, they were still free.

Where could they have gone? He hadn't seen Rocco in the corridor; the soldier must have exited via the bathroom and sleeping quarters. Jenna and Tye had to have fled the other way, anticlockwise along the ring.

Kalen raced outside and along to the next module, the laboratory. He heaved the door open.

The smell of Mars filled his nostrils.

Even now, decades after the last scientists chipped, drilled, cut, and analysed the rock samples plucked from the canyon floor, the sulphurous and faintly chalky odours of the desert still hung in the air.

Boxes lay higgledy-piggledy across the floor. Old pieces of scientific equipment were scattered everywhere. Cabinets were filled with long-forgotten rock samples. Work benches were dirty and littered with beakers and curling glass tubes. Shelves were coated in dust. Obviously, the lab had fallen into disuse years ago.

'Jen! Tye!' he hissed. 'You in here?'

'*Ah-Choo!*'

'Over here,' whispered a voice.

Two familiar heads bobbed up from behind a bench.

Kalen stepped inside and pulled the door shut. 'What the hell happened in the galley?'

Tye jabbed a thumb at Jenna. 'Ask Bonnie Big Bang here.'

Jenna looked pale and very shaken. 'I didn't think it would be that big. Honestly, I didn't.'

'Well, it sure did the job,' Kalen said, his voice mingled with shock and admiration. 'The only problem is, while it's solved one problem, it's created a whole lot more.'

'I didn't think it would be that big,' Jenna said again. 'Honestly, I didn't.'

Kalen looked at her more closely. Her eyes were vacant. She was numb. Shell-shocked. And on closer inspection, Tye didn't look much better. Obviously, the freezer had protected them from the worst of the explosion's heat and flying debris, but its pressure wave must have stunned them. Yet somehow they had survived and made their way into the laboratory.

'It's alright,' Kalen said in his most reassuring voice. 'It's going to be fine.'

'Fine.' Jenna said vaguely. 'I didn't think it would be that big. Honestly, I—'

'Yes, I understand, Jen. Now listen to me. I need you to concentrate.'

'Concentrate.' Her eyes rolled around in opposite directions. 'I didn't think it would be that big.'

'Mm.' *Not good*. He turned to Tye. 'What about you? Are you with me?'

'I think so. More than her, at least.'

'I honestly didn't think it would be that big,' Jenna repeated. Her mind was spinning, looping about itself.

Ignoring her, Kalen said to Tye, 'Okay, listen. They know you're here now, so we need to think fast.' As he said this, his darting eyes locked onto the rear airlock. 'Maybe we can hide in there.'

'Already thought of that,' Tye replied. 'It's the first place he'll look when he gets here.'

He was right, of course.

'Honestly, I didn't *Ah-Choo!*'

Now Kalen noticed Benny, standing silent and unmoving on his charger. 'What about him?'

'Thought of that, too,' Tye said. 'With our luck, he'll pour coffee on the guy and make him even madder.'

Right again. *Damn it!*

There had to be a solution. Obviously, it wasn't going to offer itself up readily, so Kalen would need to go looking. He ran his gaze around the room. Over the benches, at the boxes on the floor, on the shelves. He looked at the window . . . the window? He looked at Benny. He looked back at the window. He looked once more at Benny. Then at Jenna.

A spark flickered in the kindling of his imagination. There was a whiff of smoke. A faint glow. Now a hot flame. In its heat was forged an idea. A dangerous and daring idea. But for it to work, he would need Jenna's expertise.

'Honestly, I didn't think it—'

'Jen, would you forget that, please? Listen to me.' Kalen gestured at Benny. 'Do you know what this is?'

She reached out tentatively and stroked its smooth arm. 'Oh . . . pretty metal man.'

'Pretty metal—!' Tye groaned. 'That explosion must've blown her brain into orbit!'

But Kalen persevered. 'Er, right. A pretty metal man. You've seen lots of them before, haven't you?'

'I think so. Yes. Lots of them.'

'They're called Artificial Companions. ArComs, for short.'

'ArComs.'

'Your dad fixes them.'

'They're called ArComs. My dad fixes them.'

Was she remembering or just repeating what he was saying?

Still, he persisted. 'The sol we met, one of these brought us together. You must remember that!'

Her eyes bounced all over the place. 'I didn't think it would be so big. Honestly, I *Ah-Choo!*—' She stopped abruptly. A neurone in her brain had fired. A synaptic connection formed. She blinked. Focused.

Kalen and Tye saw a faint but familiar light in her eyes. Something was happening. They held their breath.

'I remember,' she said at last. 'A table broke.'

'Yes, it did. An ArCom came, and a table broke. Exactly right.'

She blinked again as another neurone lit up, illuminating the darkness in her mind. 'Outside Mrs Mack's.'

'That's it!' Kalen smiled faintly, daring to hope. 'Come on! Think!'

She recognised his voice. Suddenly, billions of neurones began to fire, sending tiny charges skittering along neural pathways. They zipped and zapped through the mental fog, colliding, ricocheting, creating mini-explosions of thought elsewhere. It was like Guy Fawkes Night inside her skull. She closed her eyes and pressed her hands to her temples. Reasoning started to function. Memories came flooding back. She remembered Asheton. She remembered her father. Jules was his name. He repaired ArComs. She remembered Tye too. And Kalen. He was a Terran, newly arrived on Mars. He was her friend. And he was in trouble. They were all in trouble.

Oh, they were in so much trouble!

Her eyes sprung open, and she rocked her head gently from side to side. 'Ugh,' she groaned. 'Did I miss much?'

'Nope,' Kalen replied. 'You're back just in time. We need your help. Do you remember Mal?'

'Mal? Oh, you mean Malfunction? That idiotic machine that gate-crashed your morning tea outside Mrs Mack's.'

'Exactly.'

'What about him?'

'He was out of control.'

'Obviously.'

'But you did something to him. Made him compliant.'

'Did I?' Another patch of mental fog drifted over her.

'Yes, you did. Think Jen!'

She shook her head. The fog lifted. 'Oh yes, I disabled his autonomy software.'

'Right. Could you do the same to Benny?'

She looked more closely at the ArCom. 'I suppose so. It's an older model, but they're all the same in principle.'

'Right. How long would it take?'

'At the moment? The way my head is? It's hard to say.'

'Try.'

'Probably not long once I get his head off.'

'Okay, start decapitating.'

'But what can he do? He can barely walk straight.'

'For what I've got in mind, he won't need to walk anywhere. Except to the window. And he'll only have to obey one command.'

◆

Eckhart turned away from the monitor impatiently and glanced at her watch. This was all taking far too long. By now, her men should have secured Shadows Drift and begun the walk back to the ship with Cassandra. Instead, Neale was down, and two of the Martian born had somehow gone missing.

She thumped her fist angrily on the chair armrest. How could they lose two kids in such a confined place?

She tried to consider other possibilities. Kalen, the Terran kid, had told them the two Martian born hadn't travelled out here. But he had to be lying. Who else could have taken out Neale?

Maybe they escaped outside in the aftermath of the explosion. She pulled up the plan of Shadows Drift on her monitor. Yes, there was a back entrance. It was probably only intended for emergency use, but in the confusion, they could conceivably have gotten out that way.

The problem was, where could they go? Shadows Drift was one of the more remote places on Mars. She turned on the camera mounted on top of the envelope and panned it slowly around the region. The colour image on the monitor swept from right to left. Nothing. Nothing but the same red dust and grey rocks that covered the entire planet. Only the wind moved.

They still had to be inside!

She flicked the screen back to the feed from Rocco's suit cam. With Neale out of action, it was only a half-screen now.

'What's the story, Rocco?' she asked.

♦

'Standby, Boss.'

He had backtracked through the bathroom and sleeping quarters. The wardrobe doors hung open, showing that Neale had already been through them. But those kids could have found their way back, so he double-checked them and looked under the lower bunks for good measure.

Now he stepped out into the ring. It was empty.

'Rocco?' Eckhart asked again in his earpiece.

'Yeah. I'm going to head around clockwise.'

'Copy.' She glanced at the plan. 'Entry is via the egress room.'

That made sense. It was the first of the second group of interlinked modules. A few paces along, he reached its door and went in. Nothing had changed since they first entered. The same biosuits and accessories were on the same hooks and shelves. The only conceivable place to hide would be inside the biosuits, but they were flaccid and flat. Obviously unoccupied.

He pushed through to the storeroom. It was full of shelves, racks, and boxes of supplies. He made his way carefully up and down the two aisles of shelving, looking left and right for any sign of movement. There was none.

Then came the laboratory. Unless those kids were on the move, keeping just ahead of him, they had to be holed up in here.

Tense, Strictor at the ready, he wrenched the lab door and stormed inside, leaving it open behind him. The place was a mess. And it reeked of Martian rocks! His nose turned up at the terrible stench.

'Anything?' came Eckhart's voice.

Rocco didn't reply. His eyes had homed in on a humanoid figure standing beside the window. An ArCom. His hackles rose. Ever since the one in Asheton had nearly parted the two halves of his skull, he had hated these machines with a vengeance. His first inclination was to blow it away. But no, it was standing too close to the window. While such a shot would have felt good, the consequences of missing it and hitting the window would have been dire. He lowered the weapon and brought his rage under control.

'Rocco?' said Eckhart.

'Boss.'

'Airlock. On your left.'

Obviously, she was watching on via his suit camera. 'Got it. Moving in now.'

He crept along the wall until he could peer inside through the small window.

It was empty.

'Maybe they've done a runner,' he suggested.

'Negative. I did a scan of the area a moment ago. No sign of anyone outside. I suppose they could be hiding among the rocks out the back, but they'd know there was no escape that way.'

'Copy.'

'Rocco?'

'Yep.'

'Change of plan. This is taking too long. Forget them. Get Neale and the girl and bring them back to the ship. You can raze the place once we're airborne.'

Rocco had hoped for a more personal revenge. He wanted to see the faces of those kids in his Strictor sights, the fear in their eyes, as he squeezed the trigger. But he knew if he started disobeying orders, he would be in for a hefty pay cut. And the money was the real reason he had come all the way out here. He had no choice but to obey Eckhart's order.

He shouldered his weapon, turned to the door, and—

'*Ah-Choo!*'

In an instant, the Strictor was in his hands again. He lowered his stance into a defensive posture and flashed his eyes around the room.

'I know someone's in here,' he bellowed. 'Show yourself now.'

Stillness. Silence.

'Last chance, then I start shooting the place up.'

Behind one of the boxes to his left, came a faint movement. Then a head rose tentatively into view.

'That's better,' he said. 'Nice and slow. Come out where I can see you.'

A figure stepped out warily.

Rocco recognised her immediately. 'You're the one they call Jenna.' He said her name like it was a dirty word. 'I should blow you away right now for all the trouble you've caused. Where's the other one?'

Jenna was so scared that she was visibly shaking. Her head was stuffed up, her nose was running, and her ears were blocked.

'Gone,' she said lamely.

'Humph. Well, you can join him.'

He raised his weapon at her and prepared to fire. At that moment, Kalen shot up from behind the bench and moved to Jenna's side. 'I told you she had a cold,' he said.

'It won't be bothering her for much longer,' Rocco snapped menacingly. 'Where's your friend? The other Martian born.'

Kalen and Jenna looked at each other but made no attempt to answer. This enraged Rocco. When he barked commands, he expected an immediate reaction. He aimed the Strictor again, prepared to fire. One pulse should do it—two birds with one stone. Then he could hunt down the remaining one.

Suddenly, he was distracted by a movement at the extreme edge of his sight. Blurred, fast-moving. He jerked his head right to get a clearer view of it. Pain from his wound surged through his head in nauseating spasms. Still, he forced himself to focus. One of the boxes had risen into the air. There was a pair of arms wrapped around it. Beneath were two long, running legs. The missing Martian born!

Tye and the box crashed into him with surprising force. The two went flying across the room. Rocco's feet caught on a leg of a bench. He tripped and went down hard onto his side.

Tye pulled up short, lifted the box above his head, and rammed it down with all his might. Rocco's combat helmet and raised forearm shared the full brunt of the impact, leaving him uninjured. Motivated by anger and the pain, which was now excruciating, he brushed the box aside.

Tye lunged for the weapon, but Rocco had an iron grip on it. The soldier jerked himself up into a sitting position. With a sharp, powerful snatching movement, he broke the young Martian's grip. Tye rolled to one side. Rocco grabbed a loose tab on his biosuit and, with gorilla-like strength, flung him across to the far side of the room.

He leapt to his feet and brought up his Strictor.

Tye groggily got to his feet too, near the open door to the adjacent storeroom.

Kalen and Jenna were standing beside the open entrance into the ring.

Rocco looked at Tye, then the other two. Their time had come. None of them would leave the room alive. Who would be the first? The Terran? Jenna? The other Martian born?

His split second of indecision proved fatal.

'NOW BENNY!' Kalen yelled.

Rocco realised too late that Benny was the ArCom standing near the wall behind him. He swung around just in time to watch it clench the fingers of its right hand into a fist and hammer it through the toughened plastic of the window.

The explosive decompression was immediate and overwhelming. Air roared out through the small window, dragging with it the contents of the module.

Being closest, Benny went first. His tough synthetic body was crunched and bent double as the Herculean vortex sucked him outside to land in pieces among the rocks.

The boxes on the floor went next, bouncing across the ground like cubical tumbleweeds.

Rocco followed. His helmet, which he hadn't had time to seal, smashed against the window's edge as he flew outside and was thrown like a rag doll onto the airless, frozen canyon floor. He was dead before he even had time to cry out. Within a few minutes, his body would be freeze-dried.

Then came everything else: equipment, bottles of chemicals, glassware, loose rocks; even unsecured shelves were ripped from the walls and broken in half as they struck the edge of the window and disappeared outside.

Kalen and Jenna saw none of this. By the time it happened, they were lying out in the ring. Following their prearranged plan, they had bolted through the door as Kalen yelled his instructions to Benny. They made it through just as the ferocious drop in pressure slammed the door shut behind them.

Shaken, they staggered to their feet. Kalen's chest still ached where the Strictor butt had struck his ribs. Jenna panted breathlessly due to her cold. But in spite of it, one selfless thought came to them simultaneously: Tye!

The storeroom was accessed through the next doorway along the ring. They shoved it open and rushed inside. To their great relief, Tye was struggling to his feet just inside the sealed door to the airless laboratory, one arm cradling the other.

'That was amazing, Tye,' Jenna sniffled. 'I didn't know you had that in you.'

He looked away from her and mumbled, 'What else could I do? That looney was going to kill you.'

'Yes, but—'

'I had to—' he began, then stopped abruptly.

'Had to what?' asked Jenna.

'Nothing.'

♦

In the recreation room, Annabel and Cassandra felt the sudden drop in pressure too. Fortunately, once the laboratory doors had slammed shut and the settlement's environment system kicked up a notch to compensate, things settled down quickly.

Kalen raced in with Jenna and Tye.

When Jenna saw what had happened to Lyle, she fell to her knees at his side, her face twisted into a mask of horror. 'He's not—?'

Cassandra looked up at her calmly. 'Dead? No.'

'But it's not good,' Annabel added quietly. 'I don't know what I can do, but Cassie, can you get me the first aid kit from the—?' She stopped abruptly and looked at Jenna. 'I assume we've still got a bathroom.'

'Yes,' Jenna sobbed.

'Okay. Cassie, go in there and bring me the first aid kit.'

'Of course. If it will help.'

Overcome by fear and rage, as well as frustration at Cassandra's unshakeable serenity, Jenna turned on her. 'If it'll help? Of course, it'll help! You said he's not dead!'

Cassandra raised her tranquil eyes. 'I know. I'll get the first aid kit.' And she calmly walked out.

Further infuriated that she was unable to extract any sort of normal empathy from the young woman, Jenna swung around to face Annabel. Her eyes were flooded with tears. Her lips trembled. 'What *is* the matter with her? Doesn't she feel anything at all? She's so . . . so cold.'

Annabel looked at Jenna as one would a naïve child.

'She's not cold, Jenna.'

'Are you kidding? She makes South Cap look like the surface of the sun!'

The nurse fixed her severely with her eyes but, at the last moment, managed to control her tongue. 'There's so much you don't know. Now come on, work with me. We need to turn Lyle onto his side so I can get a better look at this wound.'

By the time Cassandra came back into the room carrying a green case stamped with a white cross, Annabel had ripped away the fabric around Lyle's wound and was assessing it.

'Put it down here,' she said. 'There should be some burn cream in there.'

Cassandra kneeled opposite, placed the kit at her side, and then began searching through its contents.

By now, Jenna had regained a degree of self-control. 'I'm sorry,' she said. 'I didn't mean to blow up at you like that. I just, well, I thought you loved him.'

'Of course I love him.'

'But you don't show it.'

Cassandra ignored this. Instead, she opened a tube she had found in the kit and passed it to Annabel.

Jenna decided to let it pass and turned her attention to Lyle. 'It doesn't look too bad,' she said hopefully as Annabel squeezed some of the white cream onto her fingers and began to massage it into the red, raw wound.

'Maybe not, but those pulse weapons do their worst internally.' She glanced uncomfortably at the young Martian born. 'Make no mistake; this is very serious.'

While they made their patient as comfortable as possible, Kalen and Tye went through to the storeroom to see what was happening out at the airship.

'I'm guessing the other one's still on board,' Tye said, peering out the window.

'Count on it. I just hope there're no others.' Kalen turned to look at his friend. 'Um, by the way, what Jen said about you before? About what you did? She was right. It was well done. Really brave.'

'It's the least I could do,' he shrugged.

'Sorry?'

'Nothing. Don't worry about it. What's the plan now?'

'I don't know, but one thing's for sure: we can't stay here and we can't run away. The rover's our best bet after all.'

'I haven't driven one before.'

'Me either, but I watched Lyle on the way out here. It didn't look too hard. Anyway, if we can't,

Cassandra probably can. Annabel will be too busy with Lyle.'

'Cassandra, eh?'

Kalen heard the doubt in his voice. 'Why do you say it like that?'

'Well, do you really think she can?'

'What are you saying?'

'Look, don't get me wrong . . . I know she's your sister and all, and she seems nice enough, but let's be honest, she's not exactly all there, is she.'

Kalen understood what he meant. And he knew Jenna sensed it too. While his sister was obviously intelligent and articulate, there were moments when she showed a definite disconnection from the real world.

He nodded thoughtfully. 'I'm guessing that's what Lyle meant when he said she was different.'

'Maybe.' Tye turned back to the window. 'So this rover, then. Assuming we can even get out to it, where do we go? We'd never make it to Touchdown.'

'Yeah, forget that! It was a two-hour journey with Lyle. Be nearer three with one of us driving. That ship'd be all over us before we got anywhere near it. No, we need somewhere closer.'

'What about Stewart? It's not that far in a rover. There'll be people there. We should be safe once we're in view of them.'

'Makes sense to me. Stewart it is.'

◆

Eckhart turned off the monitor and stared through the window with a stony expression. An artery in her temple thumped an angry tattoo. She drummed her fingers rapidly on the armrest.

First she had lost contact with Neale, and now Rocco. How could this have gone so wrong? Again!

Somehow, both her men had been outwitted. Dead or alive, they had failed. Which meant she, too, had failed. At least that was how her employers would see it.

But no, there was one more thing she could do. It wasn't a measure Professor Wolf had approved of, but he wasn't here. She was. And she was team leader out in the field. The call fell to her. It would mean the end of everybody in Shadows Drift, including Cassandra, the young woman whose life they had been trying to preserve. That was unfortunate, but such was the nature of their business.

Her fingers stopped drumming. Time to conclude matters.

She dragged the seat harness back over her shoulders, buckled it, and powered up the engines.

♦

'Hey, get a load of this,' Tye called. 'It's lifting off.'

Kalen re-entered the storeroom and looked out at the airship. It was already five metres in the air and climbing.

'Maybe it's leaving,' Tye said hopefully.

'I doubt it. In fact, I'd say things are about to get a whole lot worse.' He raced back into the recreation room, leaving Tye to keep an eye on the airship. 'Listen up, everybody! We need to get out of here. NOW!'

'We can be ready in two minutes if we forget the seal checks,' said Jenna. 'But we'll need to redress Lyle. Don't forget his suit's got a great gaping hole in it.'

'Can't you just patch it?' Kalen asked.

'The hole's too big,' Annabel replied. 'We need to get him into another suit.'

'I'll get one from the egress room,' said Cassandra.

She disappeared, and by the time she returned, the others had already peeled off the old one. They started to push and pry Lyle's limbs into the new suit.

'It looks too big for him,' Kalen said.

'Probably,' Annabel replied, 'but it shouldn't matter. He won't be walking anywhere in his condition.'

'Right.' Kalen called over his shoulder, 'Tye, how're we doing outside? Anything happening?'

'Not yet,' called his voice from the storeroom. 'It's still just floating out there.'

Annabel sat back. 'Okay, suit's ready. Now for the helmet and pack. Help me sit him up.'

Lyle had regained half-consciousness. His face grimaced as every movement sent rivers of pain shooting up and down his body.

'Sorry,' Cassandra said soothingly. 'We're being as gentle as we can.'

Then a violent explosion rocked the module so badly that the cushions on the couch were rearranged and the chronometer on the wall crashed to the floor.

'Talk to us, Tye,' Kalen yelled.

'It's the rover!'

'Bad?'

'The cabin's blown off, and the wheels have all rolled off in different directions.'

Their only means of escape! Destroyed!

'Yep, that's bad!' Kalen stopped briefly, then came to a decision. 'Okay, time to go. Tye!'

Tye appeared breathlessly at the door. 'What?'

'We're moving out. Get your gear on.'

'And Tye?' This was Jenna.

'What?'

'Don't forget one of those packs is missing its fuel cells.'

When Tye rushed off, another thought occurred to Jenna. 'Kalen, you haven't forgotten the lab's been breached, have you?'

He shook his head. 'When we're ready, we'll assemble in the storeroom and depressurise it. We can do that, can't we, Annabel?'

'The outer modules can act independently. There's a control panel inside near the door to the ring.'

'Good. Once that's done, we can make our way into the lab, then out through the airlock.'

♦

Eckhart lowered her weapon and looked down on the pile of tortured metal and glass shards that had been the rover. Good. A direct hit. Its roving scls were over. She rechecked the webbing tether securing her to the interior of the airlock and repositioned herself on the edge of the doorway. Now for the rest of that cursed settlement.

While the airship's autopilot maintained position, she lifted the Strictor once more and panned it across the cluster of modules. Through the sight, she saw a couple of bodies lying on the ground at the edge of her vision. She zoomed in. One was an ArCom. The other was human. In spite of the camouflaged biosuit, she recognised the rippled, muscular physique. Looking at the rips in his suit and the way his limbs and head were twisted, there was no doubt Rocco was dead.

She paused for a moment. Not in sadness but in annoyance at the death of a colleague. Probably two, for she still hadn't heard from Neale. She felt a sudden, urgent need to complete the mission. Yes, she would wipe out this place as a matter of professional pride, in honour of her two fallen comrades.

Taking careful aim, she let go a pulse at the nearest module. It erupted in a blue expulsion of vapour. The walls of the egress room flowered open, macabrely like a bloom in the Terran Spring.

Easy.

This should've been the plan from the start.

Now for the next.

♦

Clay bricks, slabs of render, and chunks of metal rained down upon Annabel, Cassandra, and Jenna as they emerged from the emergency exit. Kalen and Tye followed, with Lyle slumping between them.

The fact that the laboratory was depressurised ended up aiding their escape. The airlock only accommodated four people at a time. If they'd had to use it as designed, they would have needed to exit in two separate shifts, slowing their departure. As it was, they were able to file out unimpeded.

They knew if they ran too far from the settlement, Eckhart would see them from the air. But they had to get a little way clear. Fortunately, a few metres from the rear of the settlement lay a cluster of rocks, a couple the size of small cars. They made a dash for them and ducked out of view.

Lyle was laid gently against one of the larger rocks.

Cassandra knelt at his side, peering at the grey face behind the visor. 'We're safe here for the moment,' she said unconvincingly.

Lyle smiled weakly inside his helmet. 'As long as you're alright.'

An especially large explosion rocked the ground.

Cassandra leaned in closer as another torrent of bricks and clay render thudded into the dust around them. Then something else, small and gold, landed nearby. It flicked about in the dust for a couple of seconds before lying still. It was one of the goldfish from the aquarium.

'Recreation module's gone,' Kalen said. 'That's the end of Shadows Drift.'

He and Jenna peered around the rock to see what was happening now. The airship's nose was coming about. The craft started to power in their direction.

'Probably coming to make sure we're done for,' Jenna guessed. 'A real sadist, that one!'

'We need to make ourselves invisible from overhead,' Kalen said. 'Everyone find a rock and hug it.'

Cassandra repositioned Lyle lengthways along the base of the large boulder, under an overhang, then laid down beside him, protecting his visor with her own helmet. The others all huddled nearby. The grey of their suits was similar to that of the surrounding rocks and provided some camouflage.

The vessel approached them slowly, like a whale cruising across the seabed. When it finally drifted overhead, it came to a complete stop.

'Oh, now what?' Tye muttered.

His voice was agitated, full of dread.

♦

Eckhart unstrapped her harness and leaned forward to peer through the foot-well windows at the ground below.

She doubted anyone could have survived her assault, but she hadn't forgotten the rear exit. It was possible—just possible—that, in the confusion, someone had managed to get out. The walk to Stewart, the nearest settlement, was at least thirty-five kilometres. As far as she knew, no one had ever walked that far on Mars, but these kids had proven themselves determined beyond the ordinary. She couldn't afford to leave anything to chance.

♦

'What's she waiting for?' Tye whined.

'How would I know?' Jenna was curled up motionless at his side. 'Just shut up and make like a rock.'

So he did. For long seconds, he said nothing. Did nothing. Gradually, though, a niggling feeling took root. He shouldn't be lying here like this. Cowering. Beaten.

But the airship, that floating Bringer of Death, remained stubbornly overhead, blotting out the sky. Poised to kill.

The feeling grew and turned into a living thing, pumping in spasms through his body. He began to shake. His mind was clouded by a black fog. Only the feeling mattered now. It was smothering him. He had to get away. To run.

'No Tye!' Jenna screamed.

But he was on his feet. Running. Oh yes, he was running. Running for Jenna and Kalen, for Lyle, Annabel, and Cassandra.

'Tye!' Kalen bellowed desperately. 'Get down!'

But Tye didn't seem to hear. He was sprinting across the canyon floor, away from the settlement, drawing the Bringer of Death behind him. His friends didn't deserve this. It was up to him to put a stop to it.

♦

Rocks didn't run.

Eckhart's mouth twisted into a snarl. So, one of them had made it outside! Maybe he wasn't alone. She scrutinised the ground more closely. What was that? Yes, another one. More. She counted five. There should be six . . . there! The last of them was lying beside that rock, probably injured.

She shook her head in wonder. Extraordinary. They'd all survived. She gritted her teeth. This had to end. NOW!

She set the vessel for auto-hover and pushed herself out of the seat. In no time, she had clipped the harness to her suit and perched herself once again on the edge of the outer door.

She raised her weapon and swept it down to aim at the fleeing figure. It was the Martian born boy. She watched him in her sights, scrambling across the floor of the canyon. Incredibly, it was as if he wanted her to see him.

She squeezed the trigger. A powerful pulse streaked off in his direction.

♦

A dazzling light exploded just beside Tye. A puff of dust erupted, obscuring him momentarily. Chunks of rock flew into the air. The force sent him cartwheeling away from the blast. Luckily, he landed unhurt on his hands and rolled into a sitting position. In spite of being disoriented, he regained his feet and kept going.

The sounds of panicked voices shrieked in his earpieces.

'Stop Tye!'
'Don't Tye!'
'Take cover, Tye!'
He ignored them.
Keep running. Must keep running. I owe them this.

♦

'Where does he think he's going?' cried Jenna.

The question was rhetorical. There was nowhere to go.

Kalen had had enough. He leapt to his feet. Eckhart would notice. He knew that, but it couldn't be helped. Their cover was blown anyway. He had to do something. They needed a way of fighting back.

Not far away, near Benny's mangled remains, he noticed a sprawled figure. Rocco's body. Rocco had been armed! His mind ablur with sudden possibilities, Kalen bounded off towards it.

In a matter of seconds, he had arrived, but the weapon was nowhere to be seen. The explosive decompression must have wrenched it from Rocco's hands and flung it into the distance. There wasn't time to search for it.

For a brief moment, Kalen was disheartened. Then he remembered Neale. He turned and raced into the wreck of the settlement, now no more than a jumble of metal and plastic surrounded by shredded, jagged walls. He came to a stop on what had been the floor of the galley.

He collapsed to his hands and knees and began scrounging about in the debris. There were cupboard doors, now twisted horribly out of shape. And benches, badly splintered. The crumpled microwave door. To his left lay broken containers of food.

But there was no sign of Neale. One of the pulses from the airship must have shifted his body. He looked further afield. There were sparkling shards of glass, maybe from the aquarium; the water it contained had long since boiled off. In a frenzy, Kalen kept hunting. He picked up discarded sheets of panelling, strips of decorative moulding, a broken picture, a chunk of the rock crystal water display, the clock with its face cracked.

At last, he found Neale's body under a flimsy sheet of wall lining, the chest of his biosuit ripped open by a piece of flying metal. If he wasn't dead before Eckhart began her attack, he would have been shortly after.

Then he saw it. Half-buried by the upturned coffee table. Neale's Strictor. He dragged it free. It was blackened and scratched, but it seemed to be intact. A small green light glowed on the stock. Good! It was still powered and active.

He got to his feet. The vessel hadn't moved. It hung in the air off to one side, about thirty metres above the ground. He could see the figure of Eckhart sitting on the edge of the airlock. She was strafing the ground where his friends and sister were crawling desperately, ducking and scrambling for cover.

An overwhelming rage gripped him. He couldn't allow this to happen. They had been through too much to die out here in this barren desert, far from home.

He hefted the muzzle of the weapon into the air and aimed as best he could in his helmet. Before he knew it, a blue pulse had gone rocketing skyward.

It struck the craft's port engine fan. Energy crackled. Sparks scattered into the air. The spinning fan appeared to shimmer. Then its surrounding cowl blew apart. Fan blades were flung like arrows in all directions, some to the ground, others penetrating deep into the body of the vessel.

A hole yawned open in the ship's envelope. It tore upward like a giant zipper. Inside it, Kalen could make out the assembly of vacuum bladders, which held the craft aloft. Several had been breached.

With one of its two engines dead and Martian atmosphere pouring into the vacuum bladders, the craft became heavy and uncontrollable. Bending in half, it veered to the left, listing as it went. Then it lurched sharply downward.

Just before impact, Kalen saw Eckhart dangling below on a short line from the airlock, arms and legs flailing. She thudded to the ground. Moments later, the cabin crashed on top of her. Then that, too, disappeared under the rest of the massive vehicle.

The sounds of breathless panting filled Kalen's helmet. He looked up. People were getting to their feet. Dazed, shocked, and wondering at their miraculous survival.

One figure broke away from the others and headed his way. By its shape and gait, he could tell it was Jenna. She clambered into the ruins and stood by his side.

'Good shot,' she said numbly.

'Not really. I was aiming at the cabin.'

♦

They returned to the boulder, where Annabel and Cassandra were tending to Lyle as best they could.

'How is he?' asked Kalen.

'It's hard to tell in these suits.'

Annabel was sidestepping the question; Kalen knew that. But this wasn't the time or place to press the matter. And even if she knew more than she was saying, there was nothing they could do about it out here.

'Come on, Jen,' he said. 'Let's see where Tye's got to.'

'By now, he's probably halfway to Stewart.'

Back out on the open swathe of land at the back of the settlement, they stopped and looked around.

'Where are you, Tye?' called Kalen.

They knew he hadn't had time to go beyond the range of their suit radios, so they were surprised when he didn't answer. They looked further afield. Several hundred metres away, Jenna saw his lone figure sitting on a rock.

'Tye, are you alright?' she said.

Still, he didn't answer.

Fearing that his suit radio had been damaged, or worse, that he had been struck by a flying rock or one of the spearing fan blades, she and Kalen raced over to check on him. As they drew near, they saw his head hung low, the visor buried in his gauntlets. There was no obvious damage to his suit, but something was certainly troubling him.

Kalen thought he knew what it was. 'We don't blame you for wanting to run,' he said. 'It was bloody scary.'

Tye didn't stir.

'Yeah, come on,' Jenna chimed in. 'I told you before how brave I think you are. Just keep it together a little bit longer.'

Tye jerked his helmet from his gauntlets and got to his feet, looking incredulously from one to the other.

'Brave? Is that really what you think?'

'Of course,' replied Jenna. 'I've known you all my life, but I didn't imagine for a moment you had that in you. You took on a killer. It was incredibly courageous.'

'What you saw wasn't courage—or bravery—or anything like it,' he said.

A cold chill crawled over Jenna. She drew closer until their visors nearly touched. The eyes in the shade of his helmet were darting and evasive. Fearful.

'What are you talking about?'

'Don't you see? All this happened because of me. I told them we were coming out here.'

Jenna's breath caught in her throat. She staggered backwards as if he had struck her a physical blow. It wasn't fear she had seen in his eyes at all. It was guilt.

'YOU WHAT?' Kalen said.

'I didn't mean to, but—'

'Who was it, Tye?' said Annabel. She and Cassandra had overheard the conversation and were walking towards them. 'Who did you tell?'

He sank back onto the rock and lowered his head. 'Nikel.'

'Nikel Pierce? The ninth born? The one who goes with Adam Wolf?'

'There's only one Nikel.'

The women reached them and stopped at Kalen's side.

'Adam's the son of Thaddeus Wolf,' Annabel said, nodding slowly. 'Yes. That makes sense.'

It didn't to Kalen. He was livid.

'What really happened in that holoplex? Wrapped you around her little finger, did she? Made you all sorts of promises, I'll bet.'

'No, of course not. She's not like that. She just asked me to, well, keep in touch.'

'So let me get this straight,' said Kalen. 'While Jenna and I were busting our insides to keep us safe and off their radar, you were talking to her all the time. That's where you disappeared to while we were shopping in Touchdown! You went to contact her! How many other times were there?'

'A few.'

'How many is a few?'

'Three.'

'Three?'

'Maybe four. I don't know. I wasn't counting. Anyway, what's a guy supposed to do when the most beautiful girl in the universe asks him to keep in touch with her? Besides, she wouldn't deliberately do anything to hurt us.' He was sounding increasingly frantic now. 'You know that, Jen. She's been your best friend since—well, forever.'

But Jenna had heard enough. The gullibility and selfishness of one lifelong friend and the apparent treachery of another had robbed her of words. She swung about and stormed back to Lyle with Annabel. Kalen headed into the ruins of the settlement.

Tye suddenly felt very alone. Very small.

'What have I done?' he moaned.

Cassandra sat at his side. She placed a companionable glove on his shoulder but said nothing.

♦

'At least that explains how they found us,' Annabel said.

'Huh!' Jenna grunted. 'If that's supposed to make me feel better, it's not working. How could he be so stupid!'

'Sh,' Annabel said. 'Suit radios, remember? He'll be able to hear us.'

'Good!' Jenna raised her voice a little and locked in Tye's direction. 'I don't keep secrets from my friends.' She recovered her temper and turned back to Annabel. 'Now, where was I? Oh yes, his stupidity. I know he's head over heels in love with Nikel. Most guys are. Or at least with what they think she is. But I didn't imagine for a moment that—'

'His hormones would get the better of him? Welcome to the world of young men. Anyway, he's not the only one at fault, is he? Your friend Nikel has some explaining to do.'

'My ex-friend, you mean.'

'Well, maybe, but don't be too quick to judge. There are always reasons.'

'Mm, I can't wait to hear them!'

Annabel sighed. 'I hope you get the chance.'

Jenna sensed the gravity in her voice, but before she could reply, Lyle stirred. His hand reached up unsteadily to clutch Annabel's suit.

'Be okay,' he gasped weakly. 'You'll be okay. Stay—'

'It's all right, Lyle,' Annabel said, pressing him gently back against the rock. 'If worse comes to worst, we'll take it in turns carrying you to Stewart.'

'No!' He brushed aside her gauntlets and grabbed Jenna's sleeve desperately, twisting the fabric tightly as he drew her in close. 'Be okay . . . stay close . . . airship . . . emergency beacon . . . automatic.'

Then he fell back, exhausted, and passed out.

Jenna was on her feet immediately.

'Kalen!' she cried, forgetting in her excitement that he would have heard them over the radio. 'Lyle says that airship will have an emergency beacon.'

'I hope it survived the crash,' he called back.

♦

It did.

Two and a half hours later, a spec appeared low in the southern sky. It grew slowly in size and resolved into the elongated shape of a large, pale airship.

As it manoeuvred to land, its nose swung into the breeze, and they saw the blue and yellow livery of Phipps Airfreight emblazoned boldly on its side and tail fin.

It alighted shortly after. Bob Asheton jumped out and strode across the desert towards them.

Chapter 20

Kalen and Tye stumbled out of the airlock with Lyle between them.

'Straight through to the restroom,' Bob ordered, pulling off his helmet. 'You know where to go.'

The vessel, while not the *Blue Dawn*, was the same model with an identical layout. They carried the unconscious man in and laid him gently on a bunk.

'What sort of med kit do you carry?' Annabel asked as she and Cassandra removed Lyle's helmet, straightened his limbs on the covers, and worked to loosen the seals, zippers, and straps of his biosuit.

'Only standard issue, I'm afraid. What happened?'

'He took a hit from a pulse weapon,' replied Annabel.

Bob was momentarily taken aback. He knew the seriousness of such a wound. 'Then standard issue won't be much good. What he really needs is a medical centre. Think you can keep him going for a few hours more?'

'We'll do our best.'

'I'm Bob, by the way.'

'I'm Annabel.'

'Yes, I guessed.' He looked at Cassandra. 'And you must be Kalen's sister.'

She acknowledged him without speaking or looking up from Lyle.

'Right, well,' the pilot continued, 'I'll get one of the others to bring in that first aid kit. In the meantime, you can both stay here with him. I'll make lift-off as smooth as I can.'

He, Kalen, and Tye raced through to the observation deck, where Canis was jumping excitedly over Jenna.

'Not now,' he snapped at the dog, dragging it away by its collar. 'Kalen, there's a first aid kit in the galley. Take it through while I get us underway.'

'Sure.'

'And there's an O_2 cylinder on the wall. Better grab that as well.'

'No worries. How long to Touchdown?'

'We're not going to Touchdown,' Bob replied. 'I wouldn't wish the quacks there on any of my ex-wives. He needs a surgeon. That means we make a beeline for Asheton. Now, hurry up with that first-aid stuff. They'll be wanting it.' With a passing glance at Jenna and Tye, he added, 'You two better come with me while I get us underway.'

So, while Kalen disappeared with Canis back through the door, Jenna and Tye followed Bob down into the flight bubble. Jenna settled into the 1st Officer's position, with Tye seated glumly behind her. Bob strapped himself into the pilot's seat. He fitted his earpiece and continued talking as his hands flew expertly over the controls.

'Touchdown Tower, this is SOS-diverted freighter *Red Horizon.*'

'Roger *Red Horizon,*' came the reply on the speaker. 'What's the situation?'

'Worse than I expected. Shadows Drift's completely gone.'

'What do you mean gone?'

'Just what I said. Flattened. Razed. Demolished. Obliterated.'

There was a brief delay, then a sober, 'How?'

'Never mind that now.'

'But who—'

'Shut up and listen, Ian! I've got six survivors on board. Five exhausted but unhurt, one critical.'

'Okay. What do you need?'

'Inform the MSA first, then—'

'Hilbride,' Jenna interrupted.

'Standby.' Bob turned to her. 'Sorry?'

'Ask for Agent Hilbride,' she said. 'He knows Kalen.'

'Okay. Ian, whoever you speak to at the MSA, refer them to an Agent Hilbride. Apparently he knows one of the parties involved.'

'Hilbride. Right. Who does he know?'

'Kid by the name of Kalen Rance. A Terran.'

There was a short pause, presumably while the names were jotted down. 'Okay, got it. Leave it to me.'

'And Ian, before you go—'

'Yeah?'

'You'll need to get a crash team out here too.'

'Who's crashed?'

'Haven't got a clue, but there's an airship gone down. No survivors, I'm afraid.'

'You sure? We're not monitoring any other traffic out that way.'

'You going to argue with me?'

'No, of course not. You didn't get its number, I suppose?'

'That's a negative. It's collapsed on itself.'

'Okay, I'll pass it on.'

'Good. Meantime, I'm hightailing it to Asheton.'

'Understood. I'll call ahead to make sure the right people are standing by when you arrive.'

'Thanks. *Red Horizon* out.' He terminated the call. 'Okay, good to go. Now, let's see if this thing can break some speed records.'

Bob pushed the power levers all the way forward, and the four giant propulsion fans spun up to take-off revs.

'Thanks for coming to get us, by the way,' Jenna said.

'No problems. Everybody flying out here's obligated to respond to an emergency beacon. I just happened to be the only one in the area. Of course, when I saw it was coming from Shadows Drift, I guessed you were in some sort of trouble.'

The *Red Horizon* shuddered, then the ground fell away as they thrust steeply upward and banked onto a westward course.

'That's all I can do here for now.' Bob unstrapped his harness and got out of his seat. 'I might head back and see if I can help. You two stay here if you like.'

'No, I'm coming with you,' Jenna said, unbuckling her own harness.

'Okay. Want to join us, Tye?'

'No, he doesn't!' Jenna said peremptorily.

She wouldn't look at him, nor would he look at her.

Bob had noticed the tension between them the moment they removed their helmets inside the ship. He wasn't sure if it was a reaction to what they'd been through or if they'd had some disagreement. He suspected the latter but thought it best not to intrude.

'Right, well,' he said, 'you're in charge, Tye. We're on autopilot, but if we start falling out of the sky, call me.'

He and Jenna climbed the half-dozen steps to the observation deck. Just as they reached it, Canis came bounding through the door on the back bulkhead. He raced around the floor, bouncing off anything that got in his way. Bob knew that, even though an older dog, Canis was still prone to bouts of puppy-like excitement. But what he was witnessing now wasn't excitement. The creature was frantic, untamed, its eyes mad.

'I've warned you about behaving like a dog in here!' he bawled.

This time, his threats didn't work. The dog slobbered strings of drool everywhere; it barked, it growled, it ducked, and it pounced about like a thing driven wild.

Then Cassandra came in. At once, Canis became docile, as if her very presence had cast some sort of spell over him. Tail wagging and head lowered submissively, he approached her and plopped himself at her feet.

'You've certainly got the knack,' Bob said in wonder. 'That dog needs a psychotherapist. Maybe he's getting claustrophobic. I better take him for a walk when we get into Asheton. Speaking of which, we should be there in—'

'Thank you, Bob,' Cassandra interrupted with that calm, distant air of hers. 'You're very kind, but I just came to let you know there's no need to hurry now. Lyle's dead.'

♦

Lyle's dead.

A quarter of an hour later, those two words were still tumbling around the deck like lumps of ice. Hard, brittle, and too cold to touch.

Lyle's dead. Lyle's dead.

Then slowly, the ice melted; the reality of his passing began to sink in. Everybody gathered in the chairs beside the starboard observation window, looking to each other for support.

'I did everything I could,' Annabel explained as she wiped her red eyes with a handkerchief, 'but without the right equipment . . .'

'Of course,' Cassandra said placidly. 'His injuries were too great. We understand.'

Jenna recoiled. *We understand? I don't. I don't understand it at all.* She looked more closely at that impassive face. How could anyone meet life with such calm, unquestioning acceptance? Surprise, joy, love, fear, outrage, loss, and sorrow. They'd experienced them all in full measure over the past few hours. Yet Cassandra seemed untouched by any of them. Her composure was so complete that it was unsettling.

Jenna started to tremble. Partly the effects of shock, no doubt. But something more too. She needed to get away and seek out the company of someone she knew well. Tye! Where was he? He had disappeared shortly after the terrible news was announced. While the mistake he had made was reprehensible, at least it was behaviour within the realm of her understanding. Unlike Cassandra's.

'I saw him in the galley before,' Annabel said when Jenna asked. 'Looking very sorry for himself too. I was about to go and check on him, but it might be better if you—'

'Yes,' said Jenna, relieved. 'I'll go.'

♦

Tye was sitting hunched over the table when she went in. He'd poured himself some cold water, but it sat untouched on the table with his fingers curled loosely around the base of the cup. He averted his eyes as Jenna slid into the chair opposite.

Long seconds of silence crawled by.

At last, he said, 'Everybody blames me, don't they.'

Jenna chewed her lower lip thoughtfully.

'I can't speak for the others, Tye.'

'What about you, then?'

She leaned forward on her elbows.

'Yes, I blame you.'

He flinched. Hearing the words spoken came like a slap in the face. Equally, though, it was a relief to have them out in the open. With the problem exposed, healing could begin. He looked up at her and braced himself for a serious dressing-down.

'Of course I blame you,' Jenna said again. 'Just as I blame those brutes who blew up the settlement. And the people who ran that illegal program. And Kalen for coming to Mars in the first place. Even myself for getting you involved in this mess. But—'

'You couldn't have known—'

'BUT,' she continued, refusing to be interrupted, 'reckless as you were, I don't believe you meant anybody to get hurt. Neither did Nikel, for that matter. I don't know what she was thinking, passing on our whereabouts like that, but—'

'*If* she did! We don't know for sure.'

'Oh, think with your brain, Tye! Don't you find the timing just a little bit strange? Nikel's never shown any special interest in you, then as soon as Kalen and his dad arrive on Mars, she starts calling you for no reason, inviting you out on a date, asking you to keep in touch.'

'Coincidences happen,' he suggested feebly.

'Of course they do. But not this time. Not given everything we know about Cassandra, and that illegal program, *and* the part Adam's dad played in it. Face it: you've been used.'

'But he mightn't have meant to. You're assuming Adam knows all about this. Maybe he doesn't.'

Jenna leaned back in the chair. 'That's possible,' she conceded, 'but either way, he'll be hearing about it when I get back. I'm going to make sure of that.'

'So long as I'm there too.'

'Why?'

'I want to see his face when you tell him he's not the real Martian firstborn.'

With the chaos of the previous hours, that juicy titbit had escaped Jenna's notice. She flashed Tye a weak smile and said, 'What a delicious thought!'

The tension drained from Tye's body. He took a sip of water.

'I'm glad we're talking again, Jen. I was worried that I'd blown it with you.'

'What?'

'As a friend, I mean.'

'Oh, I see. For a moment there, I thought you were going all soppy on me.'

'Huh, I'll never go soppy on anyone ever again. I promise.'

'Glad to hear it.'

'So what can I do to make it up to you?'

'Coffee and muffins at Mrs Mack's for a month. Your shout.'

'Done.'

'And Kalen too.'

'What?'

'You heard me. Both of us. For a month.'

'He probably eats twice as much as me.'

'Good.'

♦

When they returned to the observation deck, they found Cassandra standing on the port side, staring out the window. The fingers of her right hand were absentmindedly fondling Canis's ears while he sat contentedly at her side. Bob and Annabel had disappeared down to the flight bubble to update Asheton Tower on their changed situation.

Only Kalen hadn't moved. Jenna and Tye sat with him.

'Really sorry, Kalen,' Tye blurted out. 'What can I say? I'm embarrassed. I was a complete idiot. I wasn't thinking straight. It'll never happen again.'

Kalen had been furious with Tye from the moment he learned what he'd been doing behind their backs. But he wasn't one to harbour anger. It was exhausting and, frankly, very hard to maintain. So it was with relief that he was able to let it go.

'In order,' he said, 'nothing; you should be; you were; I can't blame you for that; and . . . what was the other one?'

'It'll never happen again.'

'Right. We won't say any more about it, then.'

They sat still for a time, unspeaking, content just to let the ill-feeling that had arisen between them slowly ebb away.

'So what now for you, Kalen?' Jenna said at last.

'I'm not sure. There'll be lots of questions to answer, I suppose. And a lot more to ask.'

'Of course. But they won't last forever. What then?'

'Too soon to say. I'm only here because my dad brought me. Now that he's gone, I don't know what I'll do.'

'You could always stay,' she suggested tentatively. 'You've got a sister here.'

'She's right!' Tye enthused. 'They can't deport you as an unaccompanied minor if you've got an adult Martian born guardian.'

It was an interesting idea. He glanced over at Cassandra, wondering what she thought. But she wasn't listening. She just continued to stare out the window. At the landscape, maybe? Or the sky? Something else? He couldn't tell.

He felt a tug at his sleeve. It was Jenna.

'Sorry?' he said, for she had been speaking to him.

'I was just wondering if you'd miss your friends back on Earth.'

'Huh, Earth seems like a lifetime ago!'

'Only a few months.'

'Yeah, but—'

'What?'

He sighed. 'It's just that coming out here, doing all this, meeting you; it's made me realise I never had any close friends on Earth.'

'That's just your mood talking,' Tye said. 'You must've had some.'

Kalen went quiet for a moment, remembering what seemed like far-gone days. School. Homework. Those interminable hours on his own. And the running—the incessant, directionless running. It all seemed so distant and empty now, so inconsequential.

'Not really,' he said. 'Maybe it was because of Dad, the way he was, or losing Mum when I was little, or having no other family, but I don't think I completely trusted anybody. Don't get me wrong, I got on with people. But always at arms-length. There was no one I got close to.'

'So you'll stay?'

'Ask the MSA,' he shrugged. 'It'll be up to them.'

'I doubt you'll have any problems there,' came Bob's voice.

He and Annabel stepped up from the bubble and resumed their seats.

'Don't be too sure,' Kalen said. 'I was only in Asheton for a couple of sols, but I must've broken every rule in the book.'

'Bah! The guy I work for has been breaking rules ever since he could crawl,' Bob countered. 'It hasn't done him any harm. Anyway, you had an excuse. You were running from a bunch of mercenaries. This MSA agent friend of yours'll probably want to talk to you about them, but somehow I doubt he'll raise the matter of deportation.'

'Mercenaries!' Jenna said. 'You really think that's what they were?'

'Looking at what they did to Shadows Drift, I don't think there's much doubt about that. Mayhem for hire. Pay the wrong people enough, and they'll do anything.'

'But who would've paid them?'

Bob shook his head slowly. 'I really couldn't say.'

'I could,' said Annabel. 'It was Thaddeus Wolf.'

Bob hadn't been privy to the discussion earlier in Shadow's Drift, so this was news to him.

To his bemused look, Kalen said, 'We'll tell you later. It's a long story.'

'But not the whole story.' Curious faces turned to look at Annabel. She wrung her hands nervously in her lap. 'There are still things you don't know.' She looked across the cabin. 'Cassie, you need to hear this.'

Cassandra pulled herself away from the window and drifted over to sit with them. Canis padded along behind her and stretched out on the floor at her feet.

'I've never told you before,' Annabel said, 'but now that we're coming out of hiding, it's important you know.' She braced herself, then continued, 'That fire in the nursery.'

'The one that killed my birth kin but spared me?'

'Well, that's the thing. It didn't spare you. Not completely.'

'I don't understand.'

'Your mother managed to pull you clear, but not before you were burned. Not as badly as the others, perhaps, but still very seriously.'

'But I haven't got any scars, Anna.'

'No.'

'How can that be?'

'All I know is that about three months after it happened, when your mother and father and Blair—the other man who survived—had left for Earth, Thaddeus came and took you away.'

'To where?'

'He never said. But you were gone for three sols, and when he brought you back, you were . . . better.'

'So he took me to a doctor?'

'Not any kind of doctor I know. Even now, our most advanced nanomedicine can't achieve that degree and quality of tissue regrowth. And certainly not in three sols!'

'Then what did he do to me?' Cassandra asked.

'He wouldn't say. That's the truth. But when he brought you back, you were completely healed.' She hesitated, then added, 'And different, somehow.'

'Different?' Cassandra looked at Annabel for long moments. 'So something *did* happen to make me this way. I've often wondered.' Then, almost as an afterthought, she said, 'I suppose I should thank him.'

'What?' Kalen said.

'Yes. I've seen the way most people live. Worrying about everything, getting angry when things don't go the way they want, feeling abandoned when they lose people they care about. Twisting, turning, up and down, left and right. It doesn't make any sense to me.'

'I thought that was all part of being human,' said Jenna.

'Sadly, it is for most people. They live in an emotional fog. It smothers everything and gets in the way.'

'Of what?'

Cassandra pursed her lips, searching for the right words. 'Our natural goodness,' she said at last. 'The best parts of ourselves come from somewhere far deeper. A tranquil, safe place that never changes.'

'But you loved Lyle,' Jenna protested. 'Love's an emotion.'

'Not *loved* him. Not in the past tense. That's the thing with emotions: they die with life. The sort of love we have doesn't. We're still . . . connected. I still love Lyle. He still loves me.' She hesitated, then looked at her brother. 'Just as our mother and father still love us, Kalen.'

Kalen looked at her bemusedly. 'How could you know that?'

'I—' She broke off and started again. 'Close your eyes.'

'Why?'

'Just close them. There's something you need to see.'

He did, one then the other. For a few seconds, there was only blackness—the shallow, watery blackness of eyelids shutting out the light. Then the blackness intensified, deepened, and drew him in so that he was engulfed by it.

His father materialised there. So did his mother. They floated side by side before him, clear and radiant in the ethereal nothingness.

But they weren't *exactly* as he remembered them. They were his parents, certainly, but they were so much more too. Like precious stones in the rough, kept for years in a dusty box, then brought out and polished to ageless perfection. His father looked serene, happier than Kalen had ever seen him. So did his mother, and her face was clear, unmarred by burns.

They smiled, those two perfect beings, and reached out with gentle hands. On some inexplicable level, Kalen felt their touch. A wave of calm crashed upon him, permeating every tissue in his body. It washed away the guilt, the sorrow, the loss, the regrets, the doubts, and the fear. The great burdens of the past few sols floated free, and he gasped at the release.

Reluctantly, he opened his eyes. The blackness retreated. Faces stared at him. Jenna. Tye. Annabel. Bob. But not Cassandra. She had returned to the windows on the other side of the deck.

He got to his feet, feather-light and unencumbered, and walked over to join her. For a few moments, neither spoke.

'What happened just then,' he said at last, 'what I saw; it came from you, didn't it.'

'Not *from* me, Kalen. But I helped you glimpse it.'

'Glimpse what, exactly?'

'I don't know how to describe it. It's invisible most of the time. But I know it's here. Always. Close by.'

He nodded without really understanding.

His eyes turned to the view outside the window. They were already passing over the rusty redness of Hesperia Planum. Crowded along its distant edges was an array of craters, and further away still, disappearing into the haze, were winding valleys and dramatic uplifts, many still yet to be named.

He had seen it for the first time a few sols ago from the descending shuttle. Then, it looked alien and daunting. But not anymore. His parents had lived down there. It was where they had started a family; where his late mother's life had been irrevocably changed; where he had lost his father; where he had found his sister.

He had ties to this world—unbreakable bonds forged in a time before he was born. They had been there all along, buried deep in the dark, unexplored background of his Terran life. It was only the quest for Cassandra, his strange and wonderful Martian born sister, that had illuminated them.

At that moment, he realised Mars was where he had to be. For most Terrans, it was no more than an obscure red dot in the sky. But for him, it was a place of family, friendship, belonging, purpose. And answers.

'We need to find out what happened to you, Cassandra,' he said quietly. 'We need to know what happened when Thaddeus took you away.'

'Yes,' she said gratefully. 'Yes, we do.'

Kalen sensed a movement behind him. His two new friends slotted comfortably into place at his side.

Cassandra's eyes drifted softly from one to the other. Then she turned back to the window and gazed out at the ancient red land that was her home. And Jenna's. And Tye's.

And now, at last, Kalen's.

AUTHOR BIOGRAPHY

Mark Hazell was launched into the world in 1958, just as the First Space Age was getting underway.

Inspired by the courage, drama, and imagination of those early years and with a love of reading and writing passed on from his father, Mark was by age 12 penning little space adventures for his own entertainment.

He worked in retail sales in his early 20s, then travelled widely and eventually settled down to a long career in the airline industry. In his spare time, he continued to hone his craft, placing short stories in small magazines around Australia. More recently, a lifelong interest in film led him to dabble in screenwriting. One day, he would like to see his work on the big screen.

Mark lives in Melbourne, Australia, where he writes and sometimes plays the piano for anyone brave enough to listen.

www.ingramcontent.com/pod-product-compliance
Lightning Source LLC
Chambersburg PA
CBHW020820180626
46814CB00001B/37